Collision!

Warrior blinked into existence, and the telltale energy discharge blasted away from her. The jump signature was the only evidence of the awesome speeds attained in fold space. Speed that was literally impossible in n-space was converted to energy instantly as the ship arrived. Warrior seemed to flex one last time as she made her presence in the system a solid reality, and proceeded in system, coasting now at her residual and theoretical maximum n-space velocity of 0.83c.

"Translation complete," Janice said and gulped. "Point... point two five seconds elapsed."

Colgan swallowed hard and reached a shaking hand to raise his visor. Before he could, Warrior's computer, finally able to analyse her surroundings again now that she had real data to work with, saw catastrophe looming.

Collision alarms wailed.

Colgan flinched, his eyes widening as his monitors cleared to reveal the danger. "Evasive starboard!" he screamed.

Also available from Impulse Books UK

The Devan Chronicles

The God Decrees
The Power That Binds
The Warrior Within
Dragon Dawn
Destiny's Pawn*

The Merkiaari Wars

Hard Duty
What Price Honour
Operation Oracle
Operation Breakout
Incursion!*
Countermeasures*
No Mercy*

The Shifter Legacies

Way of the Wolf*
Wolf's Revenge
Wolf's Justice*

The Rune Gate Cycle
Rune Gate
Chosen*

* Forthcoming from Impulse Books UK

These and other titles available from Impulse Books UK
http://www.impulsebooks.co.uk

Operation Breakout
by

Mark E. Cooper

Published by Impulse Books UK

Published by Impulse Books UK December 2013
http://www.impulsebooks.co.uk

PUBLISHER'S NOTE
The characters and events in this book are fictitious.
Any similarity to real persons living or dead, business
establishments, events, or locales is entirely coincidental
and not intended by the author.

Books are available at quantity discounts. For more
information please write to Impulse Books UK, 18
Lampits Hill Avenue, Corringham, Essex SS177NY,
United Kingdom.

Cover art: Tom Edwards ---- www.tomedwards.berta.me
Cover design: Dawn Smith www.darkdawncreations.com

A CIP catalogue record for this book
is available from the British Library.

ISBN: 978-1-905380-57-2

Printed and bound in Great Britain
Impulse Books UK

Acknowledgments

Special thanks go to Dave Milne, Michael Russell-Mott, Irene Blackburn, and John Bradley for all their help in making this series better than any one person could alone.

Thanks for everything.

1 ~ Cops and Robbers

"Jump stations report manned and ready," Lieutenant Ricks reported.

"Two minutes to translation, Skipper," the helmsman, Lieutenant Janice Wesley said. Unlike Ricks in the comm shack, she didn't turn to face his station, but gave her report while hunched over her controls. "Drive is hot and in the green."

Captain Colgan nodded. "Thanks, Janice. Go as planned."

Hot and in the green meant the drive was fully charged and ready to perform its magic of wrenching two hundred thousand tons of men and material back into normal space. In other words, in the unlikely event the ship's computer failed to do so automatically, a single button press by Janice would execute another routine jump to a nothing star system in the Border Zone.

Just another day in an endless procession of days, he mused missing the anticipation he used to feel at such times. Nature of the beast he supposed. As a part of the Survey

Corps his jumps back into n-space had held mystery and anticipation for him and the entire crew. Not knowing what they would see and discover had always been exciting. Those days were in the past now. The Corps was in mothballs again; all its ships were docked or parked in safe orbits, their crews reassigned. With the Merkiaari on the move again, and possibly ready for round two with the Alliance, no one expected Survey Corps' reactivation any time soon.

The biggest difference, Colgan decided as they approached the downward translation back to normal space, was not the ship he commanded, so much as his attitude toward his mission. Commanding a relatively new heavy cruiser—she was only five years out of the builders' hands after all—was a promotion despite his rank staying the same. Why then was he feeling as if he had been demoted and shelved far from where the action lay? Was he really so shallow, so needy, that he was suffering from limelight deprivation?

He hoped not. He expected better of himself than that.

Warrior was quite a step up from his previous command of an ageing survey ship converted from a light cruiser. No matter how he had loved his old ship, he hadn't been blind to her faults. She had been slower, less well armed, and less capable in all respects than *Warrior*. Command of this ship was a reward for good work, and it wasn't the only accolade heaped upon him for his discovery of the Shan and his later dealings with them and the Merkiaari. He had been rewarded with a hand-picked crew too—a combination of *Warrior's* existing hands and *Canada's* surviving ship handlers minus her over-sized science department. He even had a couple of medals he was too embarrassed to wear lying around somewhere. No, it wasn't the ship he was dissatisfied with, or his crew, though he did miss some of *Canada's* characters who had transferred to ships better suited to their MOS (Military Occupational Speciality). It was that he missed the sense of adventure, the discovery of new systems and worlds, and hell, he missed Tei'Varyk and Tarjei too. They had become fast friends on the journey to Sol. He missed the sense of wonder he had felt every day the most.

He sighed.

"Thirty seconds," Janice reported.

He slapped his helmet visor closed and tensed against the disorientation to come. Not that it would do any good. It never did.

"Three, two, one, exe—"

ASN Warrior jumped.

Colgan swallowed bile as his stomach rebelled. He knew everything he sensed was only in his head, but his gut knew different. It insisted he was falling. Worse, it knew he was spinning and falling, whirling around and down in a crazy spiral without end. His eyes rolled in his head as the bridge seemed to torque and twist ahead of him. He had seen the like hundreds of times but would never get used to it. Time in the jump seemed extended, though only a fraction of a second ever elapsed in any given translation. Counting silently in his head did no good. It didn't distract him. He seemed to have an infinite amount of time to study his crew. They sat frozen as he did, unaware of his regard.

Twisting...

> *spinning...*

>> *and whirling around and...*

Here!

Warrior blinked into existence, and the telltale energy discharge blasted away from her. The jump signature was the only evidence of the awesome speeds attained in fold space. Speed that was literally impossible in n-space was converted to energy instantly as the ship arrived. *Warrior* seemed to flex one last time as she made her presence in the system a solid reality, and proceeded in system, coasting now at her residual and theoretical maximum n-space velocity of 0.83c.

"Translation complete," Janice said and gulped. "Point...

point two five seconds elapsed."

Colgan swallowed hard and reached a shaking hand to raise his visor. Before he could, *Warrior's* computer, finally able to analyse her surroundings again now that she had real data to work with, saw catastrophe looming.

Collision alarms wailed.

Colgan flinched, his eyes widening as his monitors cleared to reveal the danger. "Evasive starboard!" he screamed.

Janice reacted a fraction of a second before the order was given. She slammed her stick hard over and pulled back, while at the same time goosing power to the anti-grav manoeuvring thrusters in the bow. The ship heaved up and around, still stooping upon the pair of ships in her path but at a shallower angle than before. The bridge crew yelled as *Warrior* sped by the ships, barely missing them.

"Jesus god..." someone gasped.

"Did you see that? Did you see? Did you? Man, we nearly dinged the frigging—"

"Quiet!" Colgan snapped, his fright turning to temper. He removed his helmet and racked it beside his station. What were the odds of translating into a system at the exact time and place as two other ships? Infinitesimal! Statistically improbable... but not statistically impossible. Obviously. "Trim us up, Janice, and someone find our damn referent. Let's be sure we're in the right system, shall we?"

"Aye, sir," Janice said calmly.

"Scanning... referent attained. Helios system confirmed, Skipper," Francis Groves, his XO said from her position at scan. She murmured something to one of a pair of specialists working alongside her. Both of them were new to Groves and Colgan but experienced with *Warrior's* systems. They had inherited the pair along with the ship. Specialist Sheridan nodded as she listened and began working her board. "The... ah anomalies? The ships are at dead stop, Skip. Perhaps an engineering casualty upon emergence and the second ship stopped to give aid."

"Skipper?" Lieutenant Ricks said. "I have a Captain Voyce on the line. He's ah... a little hysterical."

Colgan snorted. "I'm not surprised in the least—"

Francis' eyes snapped up from her instruments. "We have a problem. Two ships but only one IFF—a merchy out of Northcliff called *MV Astron*—and it's squawking 7500."

Colgan stiffened. All ships used transponders to identify them by name and registry, all *legitimate* ships, and were licensed and registered by their home systems to trade. Part of the license agreement was the use of transponders which had the ability to have a four digit code for special circumstances appended to the usual information. 7500 was reserved for jacked ships, or for ships in the process of being jacked.

Colgan turned his station to face the comm shack. "Put Voyce on screen."

Ricks nodded and did that.

Colgan turned back in time to see a very frightened merchy captain appear. He was pale and sweat slicked his hair where it hung messily over his forehead.

"Help us!" Voyce cried. "We can't hold them off much longer!"

"You have raiders aboard right now?"

"Yes, yes! My crew is holding engineering, I have the bridge. Please, we can't hold for long."

"Sound battle stations," Colgan snapped and the alarms wailed throughout the ship. "How many raiders are we talking about? How many aboard?"

"Maybe fifty? I don't know. We killed some, but they have armour and better weapons."

"My marines have more and better, I assure you. Keep your people safe. I'll deal with the rest."

"Hurry," Voyce said and broke the connection.

"Hail the raider ship, Mark. Janice, approach course but keep us in *Astron's* shadow."

"Aye, Skip," Janice said.

"Battle stations manned and ready, Skipper," Ricks said.

Lieutenant Anya Ivanova, *Warrior's* tactical officer, whispered instructions to her tactical team and monitored the enemy as well as the self tests being performed on her weapons. Missile tubes were loaded, the readouts on her board turning green one by one.

The main viewer brightened, but no one appeared. Colgan glanced aside at Ricks but he nodded. The would-be hijackers were being coy. So be it. He didn't need a face to make his demands.

"Raider ship, this is Captain Colgan commanding *ASN Warrior*. Cease and desist your illegal action and prepare to be boarded. Do not attempt to get underway or you'll be fired upon."

Janice guided *Warrior* closer, keeping her speed way down and the ship hidden in the shadow of the huge ship. The raider ship didn't try to run, and that surprised Colgan. Pirates rarely did what they were told even when it was obviously the best course of action. He didn't like their lack of reaction.

"*Warrior*, this is *Jean de Vienne*, Captain Tait speaking. Do not approach or I'll fire upon you and the merchy you so wish to protect. I don't need to tell you what a half dozen missiles fired from this range would do to you both, do I?"

Colgan's face darkened. *Warrior's* shields would probably keep her safe enough, probably, but he would take at least some damage and casualties. *Astron* though would most likely be destroyed utterly. She didn't have shields except for the standard anti-radiation shielding that all ships were equipped with; particle shielding like that couldn't hold against missiles no matter what kind of ship they protected. Military or civilian didn't matter, they were designed to safeguard against solar radiation not nukes and lasers.

"I'm waiting for your response, *Warrior*," Tait said,

sounding smug.

Colgan made a gesture and Ricks muted the contact. "XO, your opinion?"

Francis frowned. "*Jean de Vienne* is a *Banshee* class destroyer, Skipper. If her armament wasn't stripped when she was decommissioned, Tait can do what he says."

"But?"

Francis smiled. "But, he hasn't reacted to our closing on him. Either he doesn't fear us, or he hasn't realised he's inside our energy range now."

Colgan's eyes sparked. A destroyer captain who didn't fear an *Excalibur* class heavy cruiser like *Warrior* would be a fool. "And your vote is?"

"He doesn't know we've closed the range yet, but he will soon. I recommend we engage him with energy weapons immediately. Overwhelm him before he launches."

"Risky," Colgan murmured, but he was leaning that way himself. Lasers and grazers were light speed weapons. Anya would hit Tait the moment she pressed the commit key. She couldn't miss at this range, but neither would Tait and the merchy was vulnerable. "Maybe a decoy swarm set to go high above *Astron* and then dive between them, while we go under and take out his engineering spaces. No power, no bang-bang. Thoughts?"

Francis nodded. "A modification. We go under in stealth mode towing a decoy mimicking our emissions."

Colgan's eyes brightened with interest. "I like that. Anything else?"

"Assault shuttles full of marines take care of the raiders aboard *Astron* while we take out the destroyer. I didn't like how rattled Voyce sounded."

Colgan nodded, neither had he. Voyce had sounded like his crew was hanging on by their fingernails over there, but it was a huge risk to send the marines in before securing the hostile ship. If he got it wrong, his marines would join the merchies in death when the missiles arrived. He would have to ask Major Appleford for volunteers. He grimaced at the thought. Appleford was the sand in *Warrior's* gears, and had been since Colgan took command.

Appleford's file showed him to be a capable marine and his leadership was solid. His men certainly respected him, and they should; his file was replete with commendations for his cool handling of some delicate situations while under fire. He had been in action all over the Alliance and had a reputation for making the right decisions when making the wrong one would cost lives. Some thought him a brash glory hound—he did always seem to land where things were hottest as if seeking them out—and put his successes down to luck not skill, but those who really knew him denied that and wanted to emulate him.

No, his meteoric rise to his current rank of major was deserved in Colgan's opinion; he put no stock in the glory hound business, and felt that he knew the man quite well from his reading. Appleford had no patience for the hero worship that others offered him. How well Colgan knew the frustration of that from his own experience of it after the Shan campaign. Appleford was a lifer, one of the Corps' true heroes, and Colgan would have been pleased to claim him for a friend, but the man had made it abundantly clear that he would not welcome overtures of that sort from him.

He didn't really understand where the enmity came from; he'd found *Warrior's* old hands very welcoming of him and *Canada's* crew. He had made new friends here, but Steve Appleford rebuffed him with no explanation. Well, he couldn't win them all over, he supposed, but he did wonder about it. In the end he had to put the problem down to a clash of personalities and was looking forward to the end of Appleford's current deployment. He was due to rotate out of *Warrior* when they returned from their current mission. That was less than six months from now all being well. He had dealt with the problem the best he could by limiting his contact with the man. He usually used Francis as intermediary, but that wasn't something he could do now. Not when he was putting Appleford and his men's lives on the line.

"Get it set up, XO," Colgan said making his decision and Groves joined Anya at tactical to work. "Live mic, Mark."

Ricks nodded and made an adjustment on his panel.

"Captain Tait," Colgan said. "It appears we have a standoff."

"Do you think so?" Tait said sounding amused. "From where I'm standing, it looks as if I have you where I want you. I'll give you one hour to exit this system, or I'll launch my first broadside into *Astron*. You have one hour. Tait out."

Colgan's eyes hardened and he spun to Ricks. "Get me Major Appleford. I'll take it in my day room. You have the conn, XO."

"Aye, sir. I have the conn," Groves replied moving to take the chair.

Colgan entered his day room heading for the desk and its comp. The tiny cabin was directly off the bridge and Colgan rarely used it. His own cabin was larger and had an office, but this one was better for this. He didn't want to be more than thirty seconds from the bridge while they were at battle stations, and it was private. No sense in making a tense situation public. The crew already knew there was bad blood between him and Appleford, even though both of them strove to be civil in public. They didn't know the cause, hell, Colgan himself didn't know the cause, but they sensed it.

Colgan sat and activated the comp. Appleford appeared on screen. "Major."

"Captain," Appleford said stiffly.

"You've no doubt been monitoring the situation," Colgan said by way of asking without asking. Appleford nodded. That was something. "We have upwards of fifty armed men aboard *Astron* attempting to capture her. Voyce, her captain, tells me that his people hold the bridge and engineering."

"Handy."

Colgan cracked a grin. "Isn't it? They can let us in, or rather you in. After that, all bets are off. I won't bullshit you, Major. Sending your people in now ahead of my attack on *Jean de Vienne* is risky. If they get a jump, they could take *Astron* out and you with it."

"But you don't think they will."

"I'm betting on my ship and crew being better than them and Anya is a damn good tactical officer. Francis has given me some options that I think will more than tip the scales. If it works out, I'll need you again to board the wreck of Tait's ship." His face hardened. "And it will be a wreck when I'm done. Because of the risk, I'm asking for volunteers."

Appleford's face gave nothing away but his voice betrayed anger. "I don't like the situation you've engineered me into, but I like pirates even less. I can't do other than volunteer and we both know it. I'll choose the rest of the volunteers now. We'll be ready to go in thirty."

"Thirty minutes, no longer. Tait gave us an hour and we've already eaten into that."

"Screw Tait."

"Agreed," Colgan said. "But I want to hit him hard at a time of my choosing not his."

Appleford nodded and cut the circuit without courtesy.

Colgan sighed. He really missed *Canada*. His old ship had run like a fine watch, with precision. He hadn't needed to dance around feelings back then. He pushed to his feet and headed back onto the bridge to retake his chair. He wanted Francis back at scan. She was his best.

When the time came, Colgan watched the assault shuttles race toward *Astron* keeping in the shadow of the huge ship. Lieutenant Ivanova nodded that all was in readiness. *Warrior* was in stealth mode, her nanocoat set to black and her electronic emissions dialled way down. Her stealth field was at maximum, keeping any emissions within the bubble of protection it generated, letting nothing escape. It was her equivalent of silent running. That would change the moment she opened fire. No ship could remain stealthed under such circumstances. Her ECM alone would light up the boards of any ship looking for her, and of course weapons fire could be tracked back to a general location.

"The drone?" Colgan asked.

"In position and programmed, sir," Anya said. "I have it mimicking our usual output and following us two thousand metres astern of us. I threw in some random course changes for giggles. Nothing too fancy, but enough to look like real manoeuvring to avoid fire. I figured it would look off if it just went in fat and happy."

"Outstanding," Colgan said. "The decoy swarm?"

"Ready when you give the word, sir."

Colgan nodded, took a last look at the assault shuttles on his number two monitor, and said, "The word is given."

The swarm of decoys punched out of their bays and roared away, heading in a mass over the top of *MV Astron*. Meanwhile, *Warrior* leapt onto a new course diving under the merchant ship towing the hundred ton drone. The decoys deployed between *Astron* and the enemy, spreading out to cover the vulnerable ship, and reaching out with powerful sensors ready to intercept missile fire. They were good tech, designed and redesigned through many iterations to defend against the best the Alliance or the Merkiaari had ever fired at one another. What they couldn't do however, was intercept directed energy weapons. Still, they could and did degrade *Jean de Vienne's* targeting solutions, hashing sensors and generally making *Astron* harder to hit. Come the moment, they would sacrifice themselves against her missiles.

Warrior sped under *Astron* and back up toward the enemy. The moment *Jean de Vienne* appeared in Anya's engagement envelope unobstructed by *Astron*, her preplanned fire mission executed via computer control. Her lasers and grazers spoke, and they had a lot to say. A lot. Anya Ivanova was a tactical officer with some experience under her belt, and she had big ears to boot. She had taken note of her skipper's earlier words regarding *Jean de Vienne* and how taking out her engineering spaces would mean no bang-bang from Tait. That sort of attack guaranteed a lot of casualties and a ship fit only for scuttling after the action. No prize money. Knowing her skipper's thoughts and his attitude regarding raider casualties, she thought it would be a fine thing to make his vague idea into her attack plan. Born on Last Chance (AKA Flotsam) where many raiders were based, gave her intimate knowledge of scum like Tait and his crew. She had no qualms about killing the lot of them.

Warrior's energy mounts swivelled, locked on, and spoke, and went on speaking. In fact, they got quite chatty with *Jean de Vienne's* aft and mid section. Mega joules of energy reached out to rend the ship and were dumped into overworked shields. The shields were mil-spec of course. The *Banshee* class of destroyers were quite respectable ships. Their weapons were older designs, but not greatly different to *Warrior's*. Except in number and output. *Warrior* was an *Excalibur* class heavy cruiser, and only recently superseded by the brand new *Washington* class. A *Banshee* had no business standing toe to toe with any heavy cruiser, and especially not an *Excalibur*. Tait knew that; any captain worth the name would, but to give credit where it was due he had little choice but to try.

Jean de Vienne's shields fluoresced and tried to shrug off the attack. They succeeded surprisingly well in the opening moments of the attack, and gave Tait enough time to manoeuvre. Unfortunately for him, Anya had anticipated everything he could reasonably be expected to do and had taken steps. Tait flushed his tubes, the dozen missiles he had threatened them with leapt toward *Astron* as he powered up, but Anya's decoy swarm was right there waiting. They hashed the missile's targeting sensors and with finicky precision manoeuvred to intercept. A dozen decoys died accomplishing their mission, leaving a like number awaiting their turn should Tait manage another broadside. Colgan didn't expect it. Missiles were expensive ordnance and raiders, no matter how successful, lived their often short lives watching the bottom line. Tait had probably just thrown away upwards of five million credits. Maybe he'd weighed the cost of using his missiles against the cost of his life and ship. Who knew? Regardless, Colgan didn't begrudge the use of his decoys against the missiles; that's what they were for. Besides, any not destroyed could be recovered and reused.

Warrior's energy mounts poured fire into *Jean de Vienne* and her shields were penetrated in multiple strikes. Despite that, the beams were bent and degraded causing Anya's fire to lose effectiveness. The hits were more like glancing blows than knockout punches. It didn't matter. It was part of her job to analyse the effectiveness of her hits and make adjustments. Her tactical team worked with her like a finely tuned instrument to refine targeting solutions, and slowly the glancing blows became slashes, peeling away nanocoat to reveal the armour beneath. Those slashes became hammer blows, and atmosphere belched from the destroyer even as it tried to run.

"Idiot," Colgan muttered as he watched the attack on his number one monitor where it displayed in miniature a view similar to that displayed on Anya's much larger tactical plot piped from CIC.

Tait should have rolled ship and fired his port broadside on the heels of his first, but with *Warrior* the target. That would have forced Anya on the defensive, if only briefly, and may have given Tait a window of opportunity. Trying to run had turned his vulnerable engines toward *Warrior*, limiting his ability to attack at the same time as revealing his ship's main weakness. Colgan nodded to himself as Tait realised his error and tried to correct it with a hard skew turn, wrenching his arse out of the line of fire. It worked, sort of, but only for a few brief seconds. Anya's muttered curse made Colgan smile, but it was a cold smile. Her half dozen clear misses were nothing in the grand scheme. She quickly corrected, and scored more hits. This time the result was more than satisfactory.

"Got him!" Anya crowed as *Jean de Vienne's* emissions spiked wildly. "Look at that bitch flare!"

Colgan nodded as *Warrior's* computer analysed and displayed the new data. "Very nice, Weps, but he's still going for jump."

"Not for long" she muttered.

The flare in emissions faded revealing Tait's ship had been badly damaged. She was streaming debris and atmosphere in her wake from the hits amidships over her fusion room, but the damage to her engines was the real deal breaker for Tait. His propulsion was down by a third. Definite hits on two of his drives then, Colgan mused. The emissions flare was caused by mega joules of energy being dumped into the ship's drives cascading through the engine room into the ship's power grid. Cut-outs and safety systems could limit but never prevent such damage. Enough damage could even force the reactors to shutdown entirely, or in extreme circumstances jettison themselves to save the ship from destruction. Ejection systems and blowout panels were fully automated.

Tait continued his turn and Colgan braced for the inevitable. He was going to attack. He wondered if he was about to receive those hypothetical missiles, but no, Tait attacked with his lasers. Surely if he had them, he would have flushed his tubes at this juncture. Colgan began to doubt Tait had any missiles left to use. Maybe he had shot his entire magazine dry.

Money again.

Anya re-prioritised her targeting and poured fire into the enemy trying to gnaw the hole in *Jean de Vienne's* vitals wider and deeper. She had already holed the ship early in the action, but now she tried to bore into the ship's guts, seeking her fusion room.

"Incoming!" Groves said, but the announcement was unneeded and too late anyway. Lasers were light speed weapons.

"Shields holding!" Anya cried and punched her commit button flat. Without pausing, she set up the next firing pattern in her queue and punched the commit button again, and then again. "He's concentrating fire."

Made sense. *Warrior's* shields and armour were superior. If Tait had any chance he needed to concentrate fire on a small area. His crew's gunnery was exemplary, Colgan thought unhappily. Shields were failing.

"Roll ship, continue action with port-side weapons," Colgan snapped as shield failure warnings screamed.

"Aye, sir," Janice at the helm said and *Warrior* rolled presenting fresh undamaged shields to the enemy.

"No damage reported, Skipper," Ensign Carstens at damage control said. "Shield generators were stressed a little," he added with a grin.

Colgan raised a hand to acknowledge the report. Stressed generators weren't actually something to grin about. Stresses could turn into failures, but he didn't reprimand the man. It was good that his crew felt confident. Colgan had time to wonder if Appleford was feeling as confident, and how the marine's fight was progressing.

Lasers and grazers slashed across the distance between the ships, each pinning the other under lethal beams. Tait's ship was streaming atmosphere, Colgan's seemed invulnerable, but then the first failure aboard *Warrior* occurred and multiple beams stabbed into her bow.

"Report!"

"Magazine three open to space," Carstens said and sighed with relief. "No casualties."

No casualties was just plain good luck. The missile magazines were automated, but often needed crew to debug problems in battle. The attack plan had been to use energy weapons, and so the magazine had not been crewed. Lucky. He didn't like relying upon luck and considered using his nukes or laser head missiles after all, but before the decision could be made Anya succeeded.

"Yes!" Anya howled. "Got him, Skip. That has to be his fusion room. See the spike? Yeah... it's his fusion room, definitely. There go the ejection panels."

Colgan watched the huge hatches blast away from the ship followed closely by the core of Tait's reactor. The ship staggered sideways, a reaction to the ejection mechanism and the core's detonation some thirty seconds or so later. All fire was cut as *Jean de Vienne's* weapons lost power.

"Hold fire," Colgan said. "Keep her under your guns, Weps, but I promised Major Appleford he could visit Tait and explain to him the error of his ways."

Anya chuckled.

Groves grinned. "She's drifting, Skipper. I expect we'll see... yes there see? She's using manoeuvring thrusters to get back under control and trim course. It's all she's got left. She's done."

"Janice, bring us even with the wreck, but do not close with her. Match course and speed to whatever she settles down to."

"Aye, aye," Janice said and started working her panel.

Colgan turned his station to face the comm shack. "Mark, get me an update from Major Appleford, please."

"Aye, sir," Mark Ricks said.

* * *

2 ~ Old Soldiers Bold Soldiers

"He's gone!" Sergeant 'Deacon' Churchill shouted when his captain failed to respond. Appleford was dead and there was no fixing it. He grabbed the armoured arm of Perry's suit and snarled in his face. "*He's fucking goooone!*"

Captain Shawn Perry, 3rd Alliance Marines was in hell. This couldn't be happening. He blinked at Deacon's red face wondering at the rage displayed there. Rage at Appleford's death? No, it was directed at him. He looked away and back down at Appleford's staring eyes, but Deacon wrenched him around and away from the ghastly sight.

"Get a fucking grip and take command!" Deacon hissed over a private channel. "You're in command, sir!"

Command? But he wasn't supposed to... Appleford said... Perry swallowed. He was only a lieutenant last month! He wanted the Major not to be dead so bad he couldn't think, but he had to. The situation was going down the crapper fast. Everything was FUBAR and Appleford wasn't the only marine to die in the ambush they had just walked into. Four good men had been cut down without warning, five including the Major.

It wasn't supposed to happen this way! Marines didn't get their butts kicked by pirates like this, not ever, except maybe on Zelda's ridiculous show. Anger burned in his guts. This wasn't a sensim where the blood was added through computer manipulation. This was real life and death stuff, and it was time to grow a pair and make the killers of his marines, *his marines*, pay! He knew the plan. Appleford had been good that way, keeping his people in the loop. *Astron's* crew still firmly held engineering and the bridge, so nothing had changed... only everything had for one newly minted Captain Perry.

He licked his lips and nodded at Deacon. "I err... sorry," he said and winced. Don't apologise to a ranker, idiot! Be commanding, be confident or at least fake it. "Bring Barnes' fire team forward. Choose someone else to watch the back door."

Deacon's face flooded with relief. "Aye, sir"

Perry watched Deacon head off, and turned his attention to the fight. His men, *his men*, were pinned down just beyond the main corridor leading from their entry point in one of the cargo bays to the central backbone of the ship. Merchies like *Astron* were huge multi-million ton ships, but they were essentially just a collection of hollow boxes linked together and protected by a pressure hull. Crew quarters, engineering spaces, environmental, the bridge, and a thousand other things were packed in between and around the boxes and those fiddly bits all needed pressurised corridors linking them together so that the crew could work comfortably. The boxes, *Astron's* holds, could be pressurised or not depending upon cargo needs.

His marines didn't need an atmosphere to work in; their armoured hard suits were self-sufficient, but the enemy was preventing them from accessing the backbone—the main corridor running the entire length of the ship that linked it all together. No, they didn't need the backbone for its air; they needed it to access the bridge and engineering. Perry couldn't do a thing for *Astron's* crew unless he removed the obstruction and cleared the bottleneck. Unfortunately the hijackers were well aware of his needs, and had taken steps. The men up ahead, though few in number, had barricades and heavy weapons set up. It was one of those H3Bs (Heavy Tri-Barrel Autocannon) that had cut Appleford in half—literally.

Well, he had autocannons too in the form of Sergeant Barnes' fire team. Barnes' heavy weapons squad was the closest thing to artillery support he had on hand. Five men in hard suits equipped with stedimounts, three of them armed with M3Bs (Medium Tri-Barrel Autocannon) which were basically man portable versions of the H3Bs the enemy had set up behind their barricades on tripods. Barnes also had a pair of AARs (Anti Armour Railguns) in his squad's weapon's mix. Appleford had deployed them to protect the men as they dismounted the assault shuttles in the cargo bay, but rather than bring them up afterwards, he had left them as rearguard. There were reasons for that, not least the fear of structural damage to *Astron* should they be used. Perry didn't second guess the decision now, but despite the damage they could do to *Astron* they would do worse to the enemy, and he needed them.

Sergeant Barnes arrived with his men and reported. Perry and the others were sniping at the enemy, trying to keep heads down and limit return fire. There was some cover to be had, and the Marines were making use of it, but they couldn't advance. They needed a heavier barrage than an M18 assault pulser could provide. They were damn good rifles, but they simply couldn't provide the needed weight. Barnes could. That was what his squad was for.

"Welcome to the party," Perry said easing back and around the corner. Once out of the line of fire he climbed to his feet.

Barnes grinned. "Thanks for the invite, LT... ah, Captain."

"We have a situation up ahead. I need it dealt with."

"A pleasure to serve, sir. Just another lovely day in the Corps."

Perry smiled. "The enemy has a blocking force armed with H3Bs," he said and Barnes' smile slipped. Not so happy now eh? "I don't think we have time or room for anything fancy, Sergeant. In line abreast would be best. Just pour fire into them and walk it up the corridor. Before you say it, no I don't give a crap about their casualties or damage to the ship. All I care about is taking *Astron* without more casualties on our side." He glanced at the two halves of Appleford on the deck. "Any more of us dead is unacceptable. Clear?"

"Semper-fi!"

"Oo-rah! Get it done, Sergeant, and don't sweat the ammo."

Barnes organised his squad by placing himself in the central, and arguably the most dangerous, position before ordering his crew to lob sensor balls around the corner. Perry approved of the idea though the few he had used earlier hadn't lasted longer than the time it had taken for the enemy to target them. The golf ball sized sensors had a number of uses in the field. On a battlefield under an open sky, they could be placed at a distance to increase the range of helmet sensors—a very real benefit. Here though, they were only useful in the way they allowed everyone to see the enemy visually without stepping into line of sight. Barnes didn't care about that obviously, because he didn't wait to view the take from the remotes. His squad followed the devices around the corner, and opened up on the barricades while the hijackers were fragging the sensor balls.

Priceless, Perry thought gleefully, determined to remember the trick. The enemy lost a precious few seconds killing the sensors, and Barnes' crew took full advantage.

Three M3B autocannons spun up and hosed the barricade. The distinctive ripping sound of hyper-velocity rounds deafened those nearby as Barnes' and his men marched in lockstep playing their fire over every exposed surface. The two AARs seemed a mere sideshow in comparison, but they actually did more damage per shot than the M3Bs. The difference was hard to determine however. With barrels spinning at 3000rpm and spitting flame, the autocannons' tracer rounds sliced everything in their path like a laser scalpel. The brilliant lines of light connecting marines to their targets were a beautiful sight to Perry and his men. It said progress was finally being made. The AARs thudded repeatedly blowing gaping holes in walls, deck, overhead, and barricades. Where the autocannon rounds seemed to cut surgically through men and material, the rail guns smashed, hammered, and generally bludgeoned through everything in their path. Railgun rounds were solid slugs of destruction. They hit obstacles so hard and fast that they vaporised upon impact, converting their mass and the mass of the target to boiling gas and metallic particles. The flashes of light were bright enough to polarise helmet visors, darkening them to protect vulnerable eyes.

The hijackers couldn't possibly hold. Those that weren't killed immediately fled, or tried to. Barnes didn't check fire. If anything he encouraged his crew to pour it on. He had taken his orders to heart, and besides, marines loved kicking arse. Killing the killers of marines? Bonus! His squad poured fire downrange until one after the other the autocannons fell silent. Out of ammo. The two AARs, one of them in Barnes' own capable hands, continued thudding, mangling the remains of the hijackers and the ship's structure nearby, until even he began to have doubts that Perry would approve, but he would have been wrong there. Railguns had a much lower cyclic rate, which meant they still had ammo to burn, and as long as the barrage continued, any surviving hijackers could not organise to prevent the advance.

"Keep going!" Perry ordered. "Take and hold the junction beyond the barricade."

"You heard him," Barnes growled on the squad circuit. "Simms, Lipton, Grady... disengage your cannons. We'll pick them up on the way back. Use your rifles. Take and hold the junction. Jackson, hug the right wall, I'll take the left. We'll cover them."

"Aye, aye," Barnes' squad chorused.

Perry noted his orders being carried out only peripherally. He had all his men on sensors, but was more interested in splitting his force into two assault teams. He would command the attack upon the bridge, while Lieutenant Barrass and Deacon took care of business in engineering. Barrass was still a little green. Deacon could babysit. He decided to give Barrass one of the AARs too. Jackson. Perry wanted Barnes with him, but would let the sergeant choose who among his squad to send with Jackson.

Perry quickly gave his orders, and they split into two assault teams. Perry led his half of the men along the backbone going forward, while Barrass led his team the opposite way toward engineering. With sensors trawling for any sign of the enemy, and with squads clearing side passages and compartments leading off them, Perry quickly gained ground making up for lost time. Appleford hadn't mentioned any time limits, but Perry knew Captain Colgan would want the fight expedited if only because there was another battle upon the raider ship to attend to. As far as Perry knew, the plan called for *Jean de Vienne's* capture, not its destruction, which meant marines would be needed aboard to secure her.

Resistance finally stiffened and brought the advance to a crashing halt.

Pulser fire crisscrossed the open passage between the two forces. Perry ordered grenades used, and Barnes' hammered away with his AAR, but unlike last time the raiders hunkered down and took their punishment. It wasn't as if they couldn't retreat. They could. They were holding a major junction, and any of three directions would let them escape the fire they were absorbing, at least briefly, but they didn't take any of the choices offered. Perry puzzled over it briefly before calling up a schematic on his HUD. It took no more than a glance to provide an answer. The left and right passages were of no importance, leading to crew berthing areas mainly, but the one behind the raiders led directly to the main elevator shaft connecting this deck with the others. One of the destinations available to that elevator would be the bridge deck and computer centre.

Voyce hadn't sallied, which said to Perry this wasn't the force laying siege to the bridge itself, but it had to be the last blocking force left to stall his marines. Take them out, and the battle was as good as won. He considered and discarded options. He didn't have many. He couldn't flank, he couldn't advance, and he wouldn't retreat. What else was there? Negotiation maybe. The thought didn't appeal. He wondered how things were going in engineering and decided to ask.

"Assault Two, Assault One. Report," Perry said and adding his own fire to that of his men. He didn't hit anything but the raider he had aimed for ducked back out of sight.

"Assault One, Assault Two," Lieutenant Barras responded. "We're at the final hatch now. Hostiles are inside."

That wasn't good. The hijackers could depressurise the ship and turn off the lights. Neither eventuality would hamper the marines too badly. Their suits were self contained. They didn't rely upon the ship's air, and their helmets had the full package. Motion sensors and infrared sensors meant his men could fight in absolute darkness if they had to, but there was another thing the jackers could do that would be a serious problem. They could turn off the gravity. Hell, they could do worse than that. They could scuttle the ship. Boom, everyone dies.

"Are they talking?" Perry said.

"No, sir. I'm about to take them by storm. Orders?"

Orders, right. Barrass was on the spot, Perry shouldn't second guess him, but he really wanted to. He wanted to warn him not to shoot up the ship too badly; he wanted to remind him what could happen if the wrong thing in there was hit. He wanted to say don't fuck up! But he didn't. He couldn't undermine the man's confidence that way. He comforted himself with the knowledge that Barrass had Deacon riding herd on him, and Deacon was an older head with decades of experience. Besides, Perry himself had been an LT like Barrass only last month and they were of an age. They'd both had the same training and knew what was at stake.

"You know what's needed, Paul," Perry said. "And you're on the spot. Report when you have all secured there. Assault One out."

"Understood. Two out."

Perry prayed he'd just done the right thing. There wasn't anything else he could do, and he had his own situation to deal with. He ducked as enemy fire sought him out, slugs ricocheting off the wall by his head followed by plasma. They had him zeroed. More plasma flashed toward him, and he felt the heat even through his suit. Plasma splashed all around him suddenly, burning and scorching his armour. He rolled away, as his armour's nanocoat reacted becoming mirror bright trying to reflect and refract the shots. Light bloomed and flared all around him briefly like a halo as his armour battled to save him. God damn them! He scuttled away and out of the line of fire.

He halted his retreat further back from the front line than he wanted, but even so, he was still vulnerable. They all were. At least the enemy would have to expose themselves for longer to hit him back here.

Someone screamed, and Perry flinched. He lowered the volume of his comm. His men were taking casualties.

He couldn't tell who it had been, but it had been on his command circuit. Not one of Barrass' men then. He tried to see if anyone was down, but most were lying on the deck already to snipe at the enemy.

"Who was hit?" Perry asked over his all units channel. No one replied. "Sound off damn it! Who screamed?"

"It was Lawson, sir," Barnes said. "She's dead."

Damn them! "Copy."

He considered ordering a charge. Archaic, but it might work. It should get them closer at least, but he would take losses out in the open like that. More losses. Another shout, but this one turned into curses until Barnes told Grady to shut it down. Only wounded, Perry realised relaxing a little. He was taking too long to decide what to do! The longer he hesitated, the more casualties he would take. What would Appleford have done at this point?

He called up the schematic on his HUD and tried to find a way to flank, but there wasn't one. This was the only way to their objective. What was left? He considered negotiation again. Trying to talk wasn't what he wanted to do, especially after Lawson, but it might save lives on his side. He sighed. He figured there was nothing to lose by trying.

"Check fire!" Perry ordered and waited a few seconds for his men to comply. He selected a new channel and his voice boomed from external speakers. "This is Captain Perry, Alliance Marine Corps! Lay down your arms and I guarantee safe conduct to my ship and good treatment."

"Fuck you!" someone yelled back.

"You cannot win. We have your ship outgunned and my men are taking engineering from your friends as we speak. Lay down your arms."

This time there was silence. No weapon's fire could be a good sign, but no talking could mean anything. Maybe they were debating the situation or asking for orders. Not likely asking for orders; they weren't soldiers, just pirate scum.

Maybe they were checking on their buddies in engineering.

"How do we know you won't just kill us?"

Perry's eyebrows climbed. That had actually sounded promising. "Because I'm a marine and I say so!"

More silence and then... "We're coming out!"

Perry quickly ordered his men to hold fire but to be ready for any tricks. He watched with his rifle up and aimed as nine space suited figures stepped into the open with hands empty and raised.

"Barnes, get them checked for weapons and squared away under guard.

"Aye, sir."

Perry turned his attention to his objective. The bridge. "Captain Voyce, your situation?"

"Still holding. They're burning through the hatch."

"Right. We've taken care of the final blocking force. I'll be with you in less than two minutes."

"I'm going to hold you to that," Voyce said trying for calm but Perry could hear the terror barely contained. "We lost contact with engineering."

"I know. My men are dealing with that right now. Perry out."

He turned to find Barnes had ordered the raiders to strip. Without their suits they would be less likely to get fractious. The sergeant detailed two squads to hold the prisoners under their guns. More than enough to prevent trouble and more to the point it gave them plenty of men to assault the force attacking the bridge. Thinking about the bridge had Perry advancing to check out the elevator controls. If he'd been them, he would have locked the elevator controls down. He was hoping the raiders hadn't done so. They'd left a blocking force to perform the same task, so there was a good chance the elevator was still operational.

He jabbed a button and the elevator doors opened. His shoulders sagged in relief. He hadn't looked forward to climbing the shaft in a suit with the enemy a single button press away from sending the car down to scrape him and his men off the walls. He would have ordered the attempt and been first up, but he was glad it hadn't come to that.

"Okay, ten men with me into the—" Perry began but Barnes interrupted.

"Recon first, sir. I'm sure you meant me and ten men to recon the situation, didn't you, sir?"

Perry flushed. "Well, of course. I thought that was a given."

Barnes didn't laugh and he had the decency to pretend Perry hadn't nearly made such a basic error. "Very good, sir," he turned away and ordered ten men to join him at the elevator. "You heard the Captain. Standard snoop and scoot. Sensors up!" Barnes ordered and entered the car. "Grady, Lipton, you two run the remotes. The rest of you, guard them and watch the take. Frag any hostiles you see..."

Perry watched the doors slide shut and listened in as Barnes assigned the men their jobs. Everything sounded calm and professional, like a training exercise almost. Just another snoop and scoot, no big deal... and then the doors opened.

"Down!" Barnes yelled making Perry jump. "Get him, get him, get him!"

Perry could hear the sound of the AAR hammering, muffled by the sergeant's helmet. He wanted to ask for a report, he wanted to charge up there, but he didn't even know if his men had exited the elevator. He punched the call button, and jabbed at it again and again. No response.

Someone screamed in agony.

"Okay, buddy, you'll be okay," Lipton said to someone. "They can fix it no sweat. Let me look at it... *let me look!*"

The someone groaned in pain.

Perry had waited long enough. "Barnes, report!"

"A little busy here, Captain. They—" more sounds of firing. "They were bunched up outside the elevator waiting for us. We're getting a handle on it... Grady! Grenades now!"

Perry waited for the explosions before replying. "Do you have control of the elevator? Can I send up the next group?" There was no answer. The sounds of combat intensified. "Barnes?"

"Aye, sir. I'm sending Bell back to you. He's walking wounded. Needs a new hand. I could use some more trigger pullers up here. This is what's known as a target rich environment!"

Sarcasm. Perry sighed in relief. Sarcasm was good. "Right. Send him down. I'll expedite those reinforcements." He had every intention of being one of them himself.

"Copy. He's coming down."

Perry waited impatiently for the doors to open, the moment they did he ushered a corpsman forward to help Private Bell. Perry winced when he saw the remains of Bell's right gauntlet and the red dripping mush pushing through holes where knuckle joints had been. He peered into Bell's helmet and found a white face with glazed eyes looking back at him. His bots had already dosed him for the pain. He was in shock, but as Barnes' said, only walking wounded. He would be fine.

Perry ordered two squads to remain behind guarding the prisoners, and the rest into the elevator to back up Barnes. They had to split into three groups. Elevators aboard ships were never intended to carry squads of marines in hard suits. Perry muscled his way in to join the first group despite some disapproving looks from the men. He needed to see, dammit! How could he make decisions without seeing what was happening? The men didn't care about that. They cared about keeping him out of danger. Bloody babysitters, the lot of them! Well, this baby had a rifle and knew how to use it.

The doors slid aside and revealed the aftermath of battle. Blood splattered walls, burn scars, and crumpled bodies were everywhere he looked, but a quick check revealed none of the dead wore marine hardsuits. The distinctive white nanocoated marine armour would have stood out starkly against so much red. It relieved some of his anxiety, but not all. He could hear the sounds of battle somewhere ahead, pulsers firing in long bursts and the heavy thudding of an AAR. An explosion felt through the deck witnessed grenades still being deployed. The battle was far from over.

Perry waved the men forward and exited the car himself so that he could send it back for another load. The doors slid closed and he advanced behind his marines as they performed the job they knew so well. Perry stepped over mangled bodies lying on blood drenched decks, trying not to slip in the stuff. The damage to the ship wasn't too bad, he thought, noting the scarring and an occasional hole in the deck. Certainly nothing that would prevent Voyce getting underway. That was a relief. It wasn't his priority by any means, but it was a consideration. *Warrior* would have to guard *Astron* for however long it took her to get gone. Anything that extended that time would not be welcomed by Captain Colgan.

The sounds of combat intensified as Perry finally reached the front line. Barnes and his men were firing almost in a frenzy, trying to keep the hijackers from organising. It was working. Perry had no need to make any changes. He opened fire himself, as did the men with him. A minute or so later the reinforcements he'd left behind joined in, and the enemy were overwhelmed. Barnes' AAR fell silent before the end, finally out of ammo but it made no difference to the outcome. Twenty or more men and women lay dead, pirate scum yes, but still people. Perry stared at their remains and swallowed. Just meat now. It made him want to puke, seeing them like this, but he had to maintain composure for the men. He swallowed back the bile, and thanked god no more of his marines lay amidst the carnage. Seeing faces he knew mixed with that... that *abomination* would have been too much. Blood and other nasty things ran down walls and dripped from the overhead where arteries had sprayed or explosions had thrown it. He cleared his throat of the thickness that seemed wedged there.

"Okay, good job. Barnes, see if you can get that hatch open. There's a very frightened merchy captain in there waiting for us. I need to check on engineering."

"Aye, sir."

Perry turned away. He needed not to see that blood for a minute. He had another thought and turned back briefly. "Send half the men back to help move the prisoners to our shuttles."

"Aye, aye," Barnes replied and started detailing off the men.

Perry nodded and stepped away to a cleaner part of the deck. "Assault Two, report status."

"Engineering intact and secure, sir. We found *Astron's* engineers too. They were being held in one of the generator rooms. I think we killed all the hijackers. None surrendered but I have the men running a security sweep in case we missed one."

"Casualties?"

Barrass sighed. "Six wounded and two dead. I should have used the AAR sooner but—"

"Don't second guess yourself now, Paul. There will be time enough for that later during debriefing. I need to contact *Warrior* and find out how things are going out there. Continue your sweep of engineering, and then expand it. Let's check out the other decks, just in case. Send your wounded and dead back to the shuttles. I'll get them to *Warrior* as soon as I can."

"Yes, sir. Assault Two out."

Before Perry could contact the ship, he received an update request through Lieutenant Ricks aboard *Warrior*. He took a deep breath and prepared to explain how he had lost Major Appleford and six good marines.

3 ~ Investigations

The ride to the raider ship gave Colgan time to dwell on all that had happened here in Helios and what he would put in his report. The near calamitous collision upon system entry, Tait's threats and the battle, victory aboard *Astron* tempered with the news of Major Appleford's demise, and then the brief spat upon *Jean de Vienne* when Tait threatened to scuttle his own ship along with Captain Perry's marines rather than surrender his bridge. That had been a bad moment. If Tait hadn't been subdued by his own fearful bridge crew, the outcome would have looked very different right now.

Tait had been one crazy sonofabitch, and Colgan was glad he was dead, but being dead made it very hard to question him about what they'd found in one of his boat bays. There was evidence of blown ships and jacked cargoes in there. Colgan hated to think how many dead crews it all represented, certainly enough to ensure the remnants of Tait's crew would spend many years on a penal station or colony. Hopefully more than that. Murder was punishable by mind-wipe.

Captain Perry's marines had killed almost all of *Jean de*

Vienne's crew aboard *Astron*, though he hadn't known that at the time. A *Banshee* class destroyer in navy hands would have been crewed by three full watches, plus a full complement of marines to handle boarding actions as well as crew the ship's weapons in local control when necessary. In the region of three hundred and fifty men and women customarily crewed such ships. Perry had expected heavy opposition, but when he went aboard to secure it, he found it almost abandoned. Tait had been running only a single watch, and of course they doubled as his boarding party. All told, *Jean de Vienne* had been crewed by less than two hundred individuals. It was little wonder the ship had been so badly handled when more than fifty percent of its crew wasn't even aboard.

The fighting was over, and it was time to deal with the clean up and ramifications of what they'd found. Colgan had decided to see the cargo himself in an effort to estimate its worth and origins, but he already knew his report would light a fire under some of the brass. The Red One Alert had yet to be relaxed, despite no sightings of the Merkiaari. Ships and personnel had been consolidated in key systems in anticipation of an incursion by the Merki that hadn't arisen, and that had put the navy under pressure in other areas. *Warrior's* current anti-piracy patrol wasn't unusual, but the size of its responsibility was. His ship was the only navy asset in a sector normally patrolled by a task force. One ship instead of eight. He couldn't be everywhere he needed to be, so he'd done the only thing he could. He spent most of his time in foldspace, randomly jumping to each of the systems he was responsible for in an effort to keep would-be pirates guessing and wary.

Something had to give, and soon.

If the evidence aboard Tait's ship was at all representative of other sectors in the Alliance, then incidences of piracy was way up. He saw no help for it despite his personal knowledge of the Merki danger. The brass would have to rescind the

Red One and begin patrolling the Border Zone aggressively again. The waste of it all grated on him. The Alliance should be concentrating upon the fight that was coming with the Merkiaari, not diverting resources to combat their own miscreants, but he was a realist. People never changed. War and piracy within the Alliance would always be a problem, history proved that.

The Border Zone grew year on year, expanding outward in unplanned unregulated jumps as corporations and individuals took advantage of untapped resources found in systems far away from Alliance oversight. The core worlds grew in number gradually absorbing the oldest Border Worlds, but the absorption was far slower than the Zone's expansion, and that stretched navy resources to the breaking point. The stability and civilising influence of living within the core was a proven phenomenon. Armed conflict was rare within the core, but the Merki threat meant the military could not simply be based within the Border Zone. The navy and other branches of the military had to protect the greatest concentration of people, and that meant the Border Zone was often left in a totally lawless state.

He was a firm supporter of properly regulated expansion of the Alliance. Growth was important to the Human spirit, and nothing proved it better than the near stagnation the Alliance experienced following the Merki War. The Survey Corps had been the Council's answer to the chaotic unregulated expansion of the Border Zone, and Colgan had been proud to be part of it. The idea had been to survey systems and worlds to target resources on the very best candidates for new colonies. No longer would it be left to chance. Funds would follow to create colonies that from the beginning would emulate the core with industry, law and order, and even navy protection guaranteed from the start. In essence, the Council wanted to create core worlds on the edge of the Border Zone in hopes that such nodes of core world civilisation would spread and have a civilising impact on nearby systems.

"It could have worked," Colgan said to himself and frowned. "It would have worked given enough time."

"Sorry, sir?" Anya said. "You said something?"

"Just thinking aloud."

"About?"

He shrugged. "Survey and how the Council's colony plan would have worked given time."

"Ever visited the Kalmar Union?"

"Ow! That was a sudden turn in the conversation. I think I have whiplash."

Anya grinned. "If you look at Kalmar in the right light, you could be fooled into thinking the Council based its colonisation plan upon the Union."

Colgan frowned. "You sound as if you think that's a bad thing, Anya."

The Kalmar Union was one of a few multi-system political entities within the Alliance. It was the largest such member, and used its power by voting as a block. There were other parties that did similar things, not least the Border Worlds Party whose members were Alliance worlds scattered widely around the periphery of Alliance space. They were sandwiched between the core worlds and the Border Zone and as such weren't truly border worlds but chose to call themselves such. Unlike Kalmar, they weren't united spatially, or economically, or militarily, but they were philosophical and political allies.

"It isn't a bad thing, but it could go wrong."

"Explain."

Anya puffed out her cheeks, obviously wishing she'd kept her mouth shut. "Well, here we are in Helios. It's a nothing system that only has a navy presence because of the gas mine and refuelling station."

"Go on."

"Let's pretend the Council thinks Helios III is a very nice touristy kind of planet that would make a great colony." Anya grinned at his snort. Helios III was a barren rock. The system had no habitable planets. "The Council pumps money into the system, a core world is born. What happens then?"

Colgan frowned. "The idea is that it becomes a stabilising influence... I get it. Like Kalmar stabilised the members of its Union by uniting them under its government, you think your hypothetical Helios would do the same."

"Right, and on the face of it that would seem a good thing, but what happens when my Helios Union decides it doesn't want to be part of the Alliance anymore? What happens when it sets up its own rival Alliance, the Helios Alliance? Perhaps they don't like our taxation policy, or the amount they have to tithe to the navy. You see where I'm going."

"Fragmentation," Colgan murmured uneasily. "But that could have happened at any time in our history, and it hasn't."

"The Alliance is young, Skipper. It was only created to fight the Merkiaari two centuries ago. Human history is thousands of years old and is full of empires that rose and fell. And anyway, what is the Kalmar Union if not a mini Alliance? We don't see it that way because it's benign, which is just another way of saying it's on our side. There's nothing stopping any member world breaking away and setting up shop, except self interest. Give my Helios Alliance enough advantages, and why should it tow Earth's line?"

"It's not Earth's line," Colgan protested automatically.

"But that's how the Border Zoners think, sir. Old Earth, old world thinking. You've heard them. I know you have."

Colgan nodded. People choosing to live way out in the Border Zone were a special breed. They didn't really want civilisation, not the civilisation that the big six and other core worlds represented. They valued their freedom above everything else and that included safety. Given a choice between living on the edge of survival or being fitted with a simcode implant, they would choose the former every time.

"Point taken, but what's the alternative?"

Anya shrugged. "What's wrong with what we have? So okay, expansion is slow, but that's not necessarily a bad thing as long as we do expand. New worlds grow into membership rather than being born into it so to speak. They have to *want* membership and *strive* to achieve it. I think that's better. Slower, but better long term. If the Council wants to help things along, then that's fine, but it shouldn't pour resources into a few systems that in the future could become nodes of unrest or future rivals. The Alliance should spread its efforts by supporting Survey Corps and lending help to the start ups, but it shouldn't build ready made clone-like colonies and just hand them over."

"You've really thought about this."

"Some. I come from Last Chance... Flotsam," she rolled her eyes at the name that had become popular because of Zelda's show. "You can believe me when I say that I know how Border Zoners live and think, Skipper. When I joined the navy and saw other worlds I couldn't believe it. Sheep, I used to think. Worlds full of sheep doing what they were told the way they were told to do it, as long as the credits kept flowing. It's not politically correct, I know—I'm a tactical officer not a politician—but that's how we view Core Worlders. Border Zoners pride themselves on their self sufficiency. They do what they like, think what they like, and don't like being told how to live. They have pride in building something from nothing and surviving on their wits. I think that sort of thing will make stronger colonies and people in the long run."

"You might be right. Not many marines come from the big six, and percentage wise, few come from the older core worlds."

Anya shrugged. "Core worlds have their own militaries. The navy and the marines recruit from anywhere."

That was true. The Border Worlds didn't have the credits to fund proper militaries, and so aspiring recruits turned to the Alliance marines and navy.

Colgan felt the shuttle slow. They were on final approach to *Jean de Vienne*. He'd read Perry's initial report regarding what he'd found, but he was impatient to see it himself. He had to finish this business and jump outsystem. With *Warrior* the only ship in this part of the sector, who knew what catastrophe was looming just waiting for his arrival? Colgan grimaced. He was turning paranoid.

The shuttle made a soft landing in the bay and Anya went to open the hatch. She checked the tell-tales for pressure in the bay and then opened it. The familiar stale air wafted in smelling of old ship, fuel, and hot synthetics. Standard for any ship with time on its clock. Knowing his disregard for polite inanities where ceremony was not only unneeded but got in the way of real work, Anya preceded him out of the shuttle and down the ramp. Colgan followed her down.

Captain Perry met them at the bottom of the ramp. He didn't salute, but Colgan saw his hand twitch and start to rise. He smiled inwardly. Had he cared for ceremony, and had he been arriving on a navy ship and not a captured pirate, Perry would have stiffened to attention and saluted. Here it was not appropriate, but Colgan appreciated the thought. He had wondered whether Perry blamed him for Major Appleford's death, but couldn't ask. By Perry's demeanour, Colgan didn't think so.

"Welcome aboard, Skipper," Perry said and flushed a little.

"Thank you, Captain. I'm going to send Anya off to the bridge while you show me what you've found. I want her to download the logs and any other data we can mine before we blow this wreck to kingdom come."

"Ah… about that. The scuttling charges are all in place as you ordered, sir, but I have concerns about using them."

Colgan's eyebrows rose. "You do?"

"Yes, sir. I can show you why…?"

Colgan nodded and turned to Anya. "You know what I'm hoping for, Anya. Get to it."

"Aye, sir," Anya said and hurried off.

"Okay, show me," he said, wondering what could possibly be good enough to prevent him destroying the ship.

Perry led the way to the boat bay that Tait had been using to store his loot. Upon entering the bay, Colgan noted his crew gathering evidence. Everything was being recorded, and he could have waited to view those recordings on *Warrior*, but he felt better seeing it personally. It would all be reduced to space dust along with the ship soon. Wasteful, but without her fusion plant, *Jean de Vienne* couldn't move independently. He couldn't leave her adrift and a hazard to traffic. Besides, out here in the Border Zone she might well be repaired and sold. A few months down the road he could be facing her guns again under a new name and management. Cynical much? Absolutely. If Perry managed to convince him not to destroy it, he would have to devise something to prevent the ship falling into the wrong hands. He didn't want to. He just wanted to be done with it, off load his prisoners, and get back to work. He couldn't imagine what Perry thought he'd found that might change that. He supposed he was about to find out.

Pallets of cargo were stacked everywhere he looked. Neatly too, and well secured. His crew were recording shipping tags to learn the contents, and if tags were missing they were using pallet loaders to move them out of the stacks so they could be opened. Without looking closely, Colgan couldn't begin to guess what they contained. Packing crates and shipping containers were pretty much generic except maybe when they contained munitions. These didn't. They were all dirty white not the drab green used by Alliance weapons factories.

Perry turned aside and Colgan frowned. They were entering the maintenance hangar, an area off the main bay where shuttles could be dismantled and repaired. There were cargo containers here too. No shuttles. Tait had probably sold them if he'd had them to begin with.

Perry crossed the hangar ducking under a crane's hook that had been left too low, and stopped beside an open shipping container. It was one of the bigger ones, about 3metres square and about half that tall. Perry glanced inside, and then back to Colgan silently.

What the hell was the secret? Colgan marched up to the container feeling a little peeved with Perry. He didn't want to feel that. The marine had performed in exemplary fashion as his report would show, but this silence was annoying. He reached the container and looked inside. He blinked, and looked up at Perry, before looking down again.

"Well... damn." Perry was right; they wouldn't need the scuttling charges.

"That's what I said, sort of, sir. I've sworn Deacon, that's Sergeant Churchill, to silence. His squad too. They found it... him. The thing is, it will leak out eventually, sir. Marines talk. They won't mean to disobey, but..." he shrugged.

"Understood. Is this the only one?" Colgan looked around and noted the other containers were still sealed. They all had cryo units mounted to them, as did the open one. That didn't mean they all contained the same thing, but he had a feeling. "Get Deacon and his men back in here. Let's crack them all and record what we have. The scuttling charges… get someone to remove them all. I don't want any accidents."

"Yes, sir," Perry said and stepped aside to make his calls.

Colgan glared down at the frozen Merkiaari male with loathing. Where did you come from? Why are you dead? Why and how are you here? Question upon question piled up in his thoughts. This find was huge no matter the alien was dead. Where had Tait found it? Wherever it was, it must be within human space; somewhere he would have visited looking to steal or jack something—somewhere in the Border Zone.

Colgan used the comm in his command wand. "Anya?"

"I'm still working on it, sir. Paranoid suckers. They passworded the helm controls!"

"Understood. I'm suddenly extremely interested in this ship's jump log. Extremely. Are we clear?"

Anya was silent for a few moments. "Extremely is understood, sir. I'll make that my priority."

"Good."

Colgan turned to witness a squad of marines enter. They looked worried, and well they should. An incursion had been expected, a Red One Alert was in effect. They were, despite appearances, at war with the Merkiaari. The enemy had failed to show up, until now, but what if they had? What if, out there somewhere, the Merki were cleansing a Border World and the news had simply failed to escape the system? It could easily happen. It had happened during the last war more than once. This find could be the warning the Alliance needed that an incursion was already underway.

"Let's get all of them open," Colgan said to the mustered marines. I want an inventory and vid of everything we have here." The marines moved to obey, using the crane to remove the containers from the stacks. Colgan and Perry watched the progress together. "Are we certain there are no more like this somewhere aboard?"

"Bay Two is being used for its intended purpose. The shuttles are still there minus the two still aboard *Astron*. The cargo pods and containers in Bay One that you saw seem to be full of machine parts, electronics, medicines, and bulk metals. No organics found yet. We're still checking, but these were stored separately and treated differently. The cryo units were a big clue that Tait considered them special."

Colgan nodded. "You realise what this could mean?"

"Yes, sir."

"I'll have the Chief rig a tow. He'll have to beef up our tractors for certain." He frowned at the time that would take, but tractors designed to tow one hundred ton decoys did not have the power to tow eighty thousand tons of broken destroyer. "This is a mess. Even getting this hulk to Helios Station isn't enough. It will have to remain sealed and under guard until someone comes to study it. I'm afraid you'll have to provide the guards, Captain."

"I assumed so, sir. You want me to stay behind with them?"

"Hell no! What if I have another *Jean de Vienne* to capture?"

Perry grinned.

"No, you'll have to assign someone. One of your LTs I suppose. I leave the decision to you. Major Appleford might have assigned you to do it, but no, I need you with me."

"Understood..." Perry hesitated. "About the Major, sir. I don't know if you know. I mean we, the marines were aware..."

"Spit it out."

"I was wondering if you knew Commodore Walder, sir?"

"I met her for the first time when she handed me the keys to *Warrior*. What about her?"

Commodore Walder had been *Warrior's* first skipper and had commanded her for five years until her recent promotion to commodore. Colgan had no idea where Perry was going, or what it had to do with Appleford.

"When the news of her promotion came through, Major Appleford was very upset—"

Colgan's puzzlement turned to temper. "Don't say another word! Not another bloody word!"

Perry fell silent, his face flushed.

Colgan seethed, but he couldn't leave it alone now. "Are you telling me they were involved? That a ship's captain was involved, *romantically*, with a subordinate?"

Perry nodded but quickly added, "Nothing inappropriate occurred, sir, I swear. We would have known. There's no way it could have happened. The Commodore... well, she would never have let it happen, but I believe they had an understanding. The news of her promotion changed things. I think they were planning to retire and get married someday, but she changed her mind. The bad blood between you and the Major wasn't personal, sir. He was a good man and a damn good marine. I wanted you to know that. He wouldn't have liked anyone who replaced the Commodore. It was nothing you did."

Colgan nodded. "I knew he was a good officer. I read his bio when I took command." He'd read all of his crew's records. "Thank you."

Perry looked relieved until one of his men shouted in surprise. He hurried to see what new disaster had befallen. Colgan was right beside him.

"What have we got, Sergeant?" Colgan asked.

Deacon stepped aside by way of answering and revealed the pitiful contents of the container.

"Oh no," he whispered. There were dead soldiers piled up like logs. Frozen and awful. He stared at those uniforms in shock. How could anyone treat the dead like cargo? "God damn Tait!"

"Can we learn where they died from the uniforms?" Perry said, leaning into the cargo pod to see them better.

"Good thought. Sergeant, see if they have any identification, and get the rest of these damn boxes open!"

"Aye, aye."

Colgan stepped away seething, and tried to pace away his anger. The dead Merki he could understand. Macabre yes, but it would have scientific interest and was therefore saleable.

But Human remains treated the same way? Disgusting! It was worse that they'd been soldiers, at least in his eyes. They had died in battle. Their wounds were obvious. They should have been treated with respect and received military funerals and honours. Instead they had been tossed inside refrigerated boxes like so much meat.

"What do you want us to do with them?" Perry said trying to see if any of the corpses were in marine uniform. There was at least one.

He grimaced. "I want to do right by them. I want to give them the honours they deserve, but what I want doesn't matter. This is an unusual situation. Whoever is sent out here will need to see all this for themselves." He sighed and made the decision he knew was necessary, but it grated on him. "Seal the containers and double check the cryo units. It could be six months or longer before anyone opens them again."

"Sir!"

"Now what?" he muttered and went to see what Deacon had found.

This time the sergeant was grinning. "Does first contact with a dead alien trump first contact with a live one?"

Colgan stared into the container, and the alien being inside stared back at him, its huge eyes dull with frost. It was humanoid in shape. One head, two arms, two legs. It had no hair, and its face was very flat with two tiny slits in place of nostrils. The grey tone of its skin could be its natural colour, but also could be a result of death and its frozen state. There was no doubt it had been sentient. It was wearing clothes. He regarded the poor thing sadly, wondering what could have been. His recent discovery of the Shan made this discovery a poignant one. He sighed and looked away at the containers yet to be opened.

"Double and triple check the cryo units when you reseal all this. We can't afford any failures. Not now."

Perry studied the alien. "Nothing like us or the Shan. I've

seen pictures."

"No, nothing like the Shan, or the Merkiaari either," Colgan said looking the alien over again. "Infinite diversity, infinite combinations."

He wanted to go up to the bridge and discover where Tait might have found his cargo, but with one discovery after another right here to be made, he didn't dare leave just yet. Those first shocks had dulled his senses for more, but his anger could and did grow when another container revealed more Human and Merkiaari remains. This time the uniform was instantly recognisable.

"A viper," he said dully. The soldier was wearing the distinctive black battle dress that all vipers, even to this day, wore. "General Burgton will be hot to have him back when he hears about this."

A half hour later they had an inventory of the cargo that included five Merkiaari, both males and females. Three different races of unknown alien. Three! Colgan was still in shock from that discovery. The Merkiaari had been humanity's first experience of aliens, and two hundred years later his discovery of the Shan represented the second. Now within the space of a few years the number had jumped to five known alien races. They didn't know anything other than that they existed, but even that was huge. He wondered if James and Brenda Wilder would be asked to head a team out here, or perhaps Professor Bristow. No matter. He was leaping ahead of himself. Along with the aliens there were a dozen Human cadavers. All had been soldiers. One had been a viper.

He left Perry and his men to reseal the containers and went to join Anya on the bridge. He found her under the helm controls, head and shoulders inside muttering to herself. She was alone. He stood inside the hatch and grinned. She reminded him of Chief Williams when he had lost himself within a maintenance problem. When he sent her up here, he hadn't expected she would need to delve into the ship's guts, but whatever worked he supposed.

"Oh, Skipper, didn't see you there."

"Lieutenant," he nodded and entered the bridge more fully. Unlike *Warrior*, *Jean de Vienne* wasn't accessed directly from an elevator but through a hatch leading to deck one and CIC. "Problems?"

"They thought they were being clever," Anya said and rolled her eyes. "Zelda did it better."

Colgan wandered the bridge, occasionally trying a control or reading a monitor at random. Nothing worked. "Oh she did?"

"Yes, sir. It was in Zelda and the Chaos Engine. Her ship was boarded by a corrupt customs officer who tried to shake her down. Of course our piratical heroine wasn't having any, and told him where to go. When he seized her ship, he couldn't unlock the helm controls or access anything on the bridge."

"Aha, go on."

"Passwords weren't sneaky enough for Zelda. She'd hard wired a cut-out!"

Colgan chuckled. "That's actually pretty good."

Anya grinned. "Tait thought so. When I broke through his passwords and nothing happened, it was pretty obvious what he'd done."

"Are you there now?"

"Nearly. I've traced the circuit. The switch should be..." Anya crossed to the command chair and studied the controls. She depressed one of the many controls, holding it down until a readout changed. The station's monitors lit and filled with data. "This one."

A brief glance told Colgan normal bridge operations had resumed. "Tait probably did it so his crew couldn't stop him scuttling the ship."

"Probably didn't expect one of them to just shoot him in

the back."

"Yeah, lucky for us. Captain Perry was certainly grateful to him. He recommended the man be given a separate cell and extra food at mealtimes. He still wants him mind-wiped after his trial with the rest of course, but good treatment as a reward until then."

Mind-wipe was the standard punishment for murder and other violent crime. Personality death was the closest thing the Alliance permitted within its sphere of influence to the archaic death penalty still observed by some worlds within the Border Zone. It was actually considered worse than death, a fitting punishment then for pirates and raiders who routinely killed those they stole from. They were actually mass murderers, worse by far than any serial killer in scale because of the numbers involved. Merchant ships rarely had crews numbering less than twenty, and many had double or triple that depending upon the class of ship.

"I'm contacting *Warrior*, Anya. Get me those logs would you?"

"Aye, sir, on it."

Colgan seated himself at the comm shack and quickly studied the controls. He didn't often get the opportunity to be hands on, but he remembered his days as ensign when he had stood watches as damage control officer or communications officer. That old training came back to him as he ran his fingers over the controls and punched a key.

"*Warrior*, this is *Jean de Vienne*. Respond please."

"*Jean de Vienne*, this is *Warrior*. Lieutenant Ricks stepped out for a minute, Captain."

"Sheridan?" Colgan asked as she finally leaned within range of the visual pickup and appeared on his screen.

"Aye, Sir."

"Put me through to the Chief would you?"

"Aye sir," Sheridan said again and there was a brief silence. The monitor blinked and the Chief appeared. "Williams."

"Chief, I'm on the bridge of *Jean de Vienne*. We have a change of plans here and I'm going to need your expertise."

"I'm yours, sir. Repairs here are done."

"Good to know. I need you to rig a tow. We have to bring this tub into Helios Station. My guess is you'll need to rig multiple tractors and beef them up somehow."

"No kidding. You realise that hunk of junk weighs like a thousand times more than our tractors are designed to haul?"

"I do, but no choice, Chief. There's some stuff here that will need investigation. I'm going to dock her at Helios and leave her under marine guard."

"Hmmm. *Warrior* is no tug, but if we keep her speed down we should be able to do it."

Colgan winced. He had guessed it would come to this. The bloody trip to Helios was going to take ages. "How far down?"

"A guess for now, but if we use around 20% of standard accel we shouldn't stress anything too badly. It's not the speed, sir. As long as we accelerate slowly we could tow her at flank, well almost," Williams suddenly sounded worried that Colgan would take him at his word and try that. "It's not how fast we can go. It's about how long to slow down. Tractors don't make good inertial dampeners. I think we'll have to do this old school with a proper turnover to slow down."

Colgan nodded at William's worried face on the monitor. "Lieutenant Wesley will enjoy that. It will test her skills. I bet she hasn't had to pull a turnover manoeuvre while towing an eighty thousand ton wreck before."

Williams grinned.

"Okay, Chief. Get your spanners out and do whatever is needed. Let me know when you're ready."

"Aye, sir, but it won't be quick. A couple of days would be my guess."

Colgan nodded and broke the connection. A couple of

days to set things up and probably over a week to cover a distance to Helios that would normally take a fifth the time. Bloody marvellous. He needed to remember this situation wasn't even part of his mission. He had places to be, systems to check, and pirates to harass. He did want to do things right, however, and that meant extensive reports. Detailed reports to ensure all parties realised just how significant *Jean de Vienne* was to the Alliance. Three new alien races. Three! Talk about an embarrassment of riches. When the admiralty read his name attached to the reports they would have apoplexy. His name and that of poor old *Canada* had barely left the headlines, and now this. He was glad he was out of contact from the newsies. They would howl when they heard and couldn't reach him!

He grinned nastily, but then considered the practicalities of the situation. His mission was such that as long as he visited each of the systems he was responsible for, he could write his own schedule. He had in fact been doing that already in an effort to make it seem like his single ship could do the impossible—be everywhere at once. Random jumps at random times to random systems, sometimes back to a previous system in a sort of spin about and look over the shoulder sort of thing, had worked so far. Ask Tait. He snorted. He would continue the strategy.

He owed a speedy response from the admiralty to the men that Perry assigned to stay behind, and the only way he had of affecting that was how quickly he could get the news back to Sol. Drones were slow, there was just no help for that barring the use of jump capable courier ships. Helios didn't have one of course, being a nothing system only here for the convenience of ships like *Warrior* that needed refuelling. He had to use a drone. Setting its drive parameters to the recommended 80% of max would mean a delay of approximately... he quickly did the calculation in his head... seven weeks give or take a day. The recommended setting gave the drone the best chance to reach its destination in what was considered a reasonable time frame. Drive failures increased exponentially the closer to max the drive was pushed. That didn't mean a drone flying at max would always fail, but the probability it would fail would be high.

He could and would jump back to Helios as his mission progressed; just as he would visit the other systems he had responsibility for multiple times over the coming months. He could take Perry's men back aboard during one of his visits. Perhaps if the delay was extended, he could have Perry switch them out so that they weren't left hanging? Yes, he liked that. Still, the communications delay was as always damn annoying. He could buck the odds and set the drone's drive to 100% and pray, not that prayer had ever worked for him before, or he could send multiple drones with different drive settings. Costly that was, despite drones being routinely collected at their destinations and reused after refurbishment. Captains were discouraged from burning through their stock of drones, just as they could catch hell for using up their decoys and missile loads frivolously. They had price tags in the millions. Still, he was due to send a drone soon anyway. If he sent three now, and didn't send his next scheduled drone, he could keep the cost down. He would have to warn the admiralty of his intentions or risk them raising an alarm when he failed to report at the usual time interval. He didn't need the embarrassment of another ship coming out to check on him.

So three drones with drives set at 80, 90, and 100% would be his answer. With luck the fastest drone would not fail. The admiralty would learn of matters here in Helios in about four and a half weeks in that lucky case. A month after that should see a team here ready to investigate... if they had one on hand. How long would it take to scrape one together? He had no idea. He could only help matters by expediting things at his end.

"How are we going with those logs, Anya?"

"I've dumped everything to *Warrior*, sir. Not sure what use we might have for it, but maybe we can figure out where Tait was based. There must be others like him using it for fencing loot and buying stores."

"Good thought." That had actually been one of his earlier reasons for bringing Anya with him to collect the data, but he had other reasons now. "The jump logs are all there?"

"About that. If I'm reading this right, it looks as if Tait got into a little spat with one of our ships a while ago and performed an emergency jump."

"Oh really?"

"Yes. The thing is he caused a mis-jump by activating his drive before it was fully charged."

Colgan winced. He was surprised the ship hadn't been ripped apart. Tait had been a lucky bastard to get away with it. His ship hadn't been destroyed, and he hadn't blown his jump capacitors to flaming flinders either. Amazing.

"Do we know where he came out?"

"Well that's the thing. He dropped into an unexplored system by the looks of it. I wonder what the black boxes and bridge recorders show..." Anya grimaced. "Not likely they're even connected anymore, Skipper. What pirate would want a witness to his crimes like that?"

"Check anyway. Never underestimate the cleverness or stupidity of the enemy, Anya. Still, sensor logs might tell us something."

Anya nodded.

"Tell you what, you stay here and mine every byte of data you can, and dump it all to *Warrior*. I'm heading back there now to start my reports on all of this. Can you catch a ride back with the marines?"

"Sure, Skipper. Grunts can be fun."

Colgan laughed and headed for the boat bay.

* * *

4 ~ Betrayal

Betrayal wasn't a word that Captain Kenneth Stone, 501st Infantry Regiment, considered very often or associated with himself, but he did so now as he studied the woman in his bed. Kate Richmond, late of Bethany's World and former ISS operative for that world, would see it that way. He knew her as he knew himself and from her point of view he had betrayed her the moment he learned the news and kept it from her. No matter he did it for her own good, she would not forgive him. He tried to tell himself it didn't matter as he watched her sleep, but it did. This woman mattered, and that was a problem.

He'd managed to live this long by putting emotion aside whenever it suited him. He could suppress that side when he needed to, the Human side. He was convinced that was a big part of how he and the other veterans had survived so long when their brothers and sisters in the regiment did not. He could switch his humanity off when the need arose. In fact, he'd rarely switched it on during the years following the war. He hadn't seen a need. Most of those years were spent on missions building his intelligence network for the General, and they'd required him to do some questionable things for and to people. His machine persona, the real him, was better for that. He was a hard charging fighting machine, with heavy emphasis on machine. That was his way of coping. He just put it away like a computer filing reports, never letting it touch the dwindling Human side.

He grimaced. Self-pity now? He hated self-pity. It was the most useless emotion of all, and he wouldn't let it take up residence in his head or his database either! At least when he turned off the Human Stone he could be certain of the choices he'd made. No second guessing then. Just rock solid logic from machine Stone. Scenario A happens, respond with Scenario B. Richmond learns of his betrayal and tries to kill him, he kills her and moves on to the next mission. Just add her to the multitude of his victims, and keep on keeping on.

The stab of pain the thought gave him was very real, and he winced. The thought of her dead hurt him deeply. Her dead by his hand... god no, not again. He forced himself not to think about it. The ghosts he carried around with him every day had enough weight to crush him as it was. Thinking along those lines threatened to call them up and drown him in memory.

No!

The scream in his head worked. No memory files opened, and he took a shuddering breath. No, he would not look back at his victims. Instead, he would look ahead and find some way to fix this. He was good at fixing things. It was his best thing... after killing of course. He was like Richmond in that way. Two peas and all that. Both of them were excellent killers. His preferred targets were Merkiaari, and he would never pass up an opportunity to increase his score. Richmond was more egalitarian, not discriminating between Human or alien. Anyone or anything that got in her way was fair game. He could admire that as long as she channelled it to the regiment's benefit, despite the likelihood it would be aimed at him shortly.

He studied her face as she slept the sleep of the righteous. Her heavily scarred face and missing eye did not repulse him. They were just a part of her. Her fierceness was absent in sleep, and the sneer the scars forced upon her lips seemed lessened. She sighed and kicked the covers down a little, revealing one pale breast. His eyes shifted, he couldn't help it, and he zeroed in upon that enticingly puckered nipple. He grinned like a little boy as his targeting reticule locked on and spun pulsing redly centred upon that pink jewel. Pulsing like another part of his anatomy that had stood up and taken notice. He forced himself to look back up at her face, and not see her pale naked perfection riding him as she had last night. His obsidian skin against her ivory... God damn! She was in his head and under his skin. He was fucking doomed.

Her victims, and she had many of them, didn't weigh on her as his did upon him. She was borderline sociopath according to Marion, but he didn't think so. He had known a few in his time. If she'd truly been a psycho of the kind Marion thought, Richmond wouldn't care about her brother as much as she did. Her cock sucking brother. It all came down to that worthless pile of crap. If not for him, he wouldn't be standing here getting ready to betray Richmond.

He was going to fix it, but it depended upon a few things that he still needed to arrange. One of those was getting Richmond out from under foot for a few days. A week would be better, and he might be able to swing even that with Marion on his side. The General would be a problem, but there was a way to get around even him.

I can fix this!

"Richmond," Stone said, deciding that if she caught him ogling her it could only make matters worse. "Wakey wakey, Lieutenant."

Richmond's good eye opened, and that pale blue blazed

with her fierce intelligence. She smiled and stretched her arms above her head, her legs straining making the covers slide all the way off the side of the bed to reveal her naked glory to his hot eyes. She did it on purpose of course, posing there for him, laughing silently at his interest. ISS training or simply a woman's power over men he didn't know or care. He wanted to strip and join her in his bed right now, but the thought of his upcoming betrayal kept him standing there.

"Morning," she purred. "You're up early."

"No, you're up late. It's 0700. You need to get dressed and over to medical. Today's the day."

Richmond propped herself up on her elbows. She was so beautiful. He was sorely tempted to confess all right here and now. He forced himself to turn aside and pick up her battle dress blacks from the chair. When he turned back he had his emotions under control. He had switched them off, and it was machine Stone who regarded her coolly now. He offered the uniform, but she waved it aside.

"Shower first... and god, get me a coffee would you?"

"Coffee yes, but no eats. Medical needs you fasting for their damn drugs."

"Yeah I know. Enhancement take-two is supposedly no different to enhancement take-one," Richmond said heading for the bathroom. "How would they even know, huh? I'm the first to need de-enhancing."

"De-enhancing, right. When they wake you up you'll be fully operational again. No easy system by system start up for you this time round. Straight to the finish line."

"Thank god for small mercies. I can't wait to get back on the horse."

Stone watched that magnificent butt flex as she walked, and forced his brain not to leak out of his ears. He had a mission to perform. He programmed the autochef and moments later brought the mug of coffee into the bathroom. Richmond was standing under the jets, letting the hot water pummel her. He watched her in silence. Her eye was closed, her head tilted up into the spray. Water beaded and rolled down her chest, over her flat belly, and down those muscular thighs.

Stone cleared his throat and offered the cup.

"Thanks," she said and drank. "Damn, I needed that."

Stone nodded and forced himself to about face. He couldn't maintain his composure if he stood there watching her any longer. He went into his living room to wait, and tried to think about the mission. He would need help on this one. Richmond would need backup when she learned what he'd done and no longer trusted him. Fuentez was his first choice, but she'd only been back a few weeks from the Kushiel op and was still working with Liz under The Mountain. As he understood it, she was only present as moral support during Sebastian's installation. It boggled the mind that an A.I needed or wanted moral support, but Sebastian had requested Fuentez be present during the process. She was just an observer. She didn't have an engineering or computer science background, so it shouldn't be a problem for Liz if he shanghaied Fuentez. He hadn't visited the Oracle facility before, but he would have to go there if he wanted her to help with Richmond. That wouldn't be a problem; any viper had access to The Mountain. The regiment's archive was there.

Five minutes went by and Richmond emerged from the bathroom. Stone was reviewing the data he'd been suppressing, and ignored her as she moved around the room locating her clothes. They had been a little, ah... *amorous* from the moment they entered his quarters last night and their clothes had been scattered all along their route to the bedroom. She didn't disturb him as she pulled on her uniform and sat on the couch to lace her boots.

Stone went over the data, rearranged a few things for ease of uploading to the General, and closed the file. He'd massaged the data as far as he was willing to. He wouldn't falsify anything that could come back to bite the regiment on the arse, but he had put more weight on certain aspects while trivialising other parts in an effort to lead the General to the conclusion that he needed him to reach. He didn't know yet how he could rope Fuentez into it, assuming she was willing, but he would come up with something. He always did. Maybe Eric would just order her to go or ask her to volunteer if he asked him. Probably would, but he'd want to know why. Hmmm...

"... you want to come with?" Richmond was saying.

Stone checked his log. He'd missed her asking about his plans for the day. "I have a ton of reports to go through, but I'll deliver you to the tech centre. Wouldn't want you to get lost."

Richmond snorted. "Don't you worry about that. I can't wait to get back in business. It sucks dinoballs walking about in this gravity with only one peeper."

He grinned. It still amused him hearing retro coming out of her mouth. Reminded him of days long gone when he'd run with the Breakers—a gang he'd belonged to during his misspent youth on Forestal. He was born there and the planet still held a few good memories for him, but that was long ago. He owed his military career to the Breakers in a way.

His bashing days had led him into the darker side of Forestal's underbelly first as a courier and later as a cleaner. Cleaning up problems for the gangs, making people disappear, and enforcing for the smaller outfits had led him deeper and deeper into the dirt. He'd been getting a little old for the life when everything changed. Younger competitors were always looking for ways to break in, and he'd had a few near misses, but he finally got caught by the police red handed with a body he couldn't explain and the weapon he'd used in the car with him. Stupid. He would have suffered mind-wipe if not for the war.

The Merkiaari had been a shock everywhere. Individual planetary governments had responded slowly but in general they did do the right things. On Forestal the government increased its ground forces with a forced draft, and the first people recruited were convicts. He hadn't needed force. Mind-wipe or five years in the army? He couldn't sign fast enough. He'd barely been out of boot camp when he was deployed against the Merkiaari and found his calling. Killing murderous aliens intent upon genocide made him feel like a hero. It had made him proud. For someone like him that was a big thing. It pulled him out of the slime to breathe clean air for the first time. He worked with people who had never had to fight and kill others like him just to put food on the table, and he liked them! He risked his life for them, and they did the same for him. Complete strangers became like family.

And then the Merkiaari hit Forestal itself and everything changed again.

Stone shook his head and saw Richmond watching him. "What?"

"Lost in thought?"

"Yeah, thinking about Forestal. Did you know I came from there?"

Richmond shook her head. "I don't think you ever mentioned it."

"It was a long time ago. I don't really think about it anymore. Everything is so different there now. I'm different. Nothing in common I guess. You would probably like what they've done with the place."

"But you don't?"

He shrugged. "It's not for me to say how they want to live, but I remember where the money and fancy tech all came from. They built all that on blood and dirty money, and then lied to themselves about it. The corporations aren't so far removed from the old days as people like to think. They still fight their little cyber wars, and they're not so little mercenary armies still bleed and die for them in the shadows. But on the surface, they're clean and shiny. Hell, the average citizen on Forestal can live his entire life and never see the underbelly. I suppose that's something positive."

Richmond finished fussing with her eye patch. She stood and pulled on her beret. He did likewise and together they left his quarters. Officer country was busier than it had been in years gone by, but they were a little late this morning and had missed the crush. Burgton had been ruthless with his changes to the regiment upon his return from the Shan operation. All of the veteran non-coms had been promoted to officers against their wishes in all cases. Stone was now a captain of all things. He didn't feel like one or want to be one, but when the General wanted something it happened one way or another. It wasn't worth fighting over. It wasn't as if he was expected to run a company, and even if he were, he knew he could do it if he had to. It was more about appearances, Stone figured. With new recruits coming on-line, often with rank in their backgrounds, it was easier teaching and commanding them from positions of authority that they instinctively respected. Stone supposed a new recruit who'd been a captain in his old branch might find orders from a mere sergeant a little hard to swallow.

Anyway, being a captain commanding OSI (Office of Strategic Intelligence) wasn't much different to the way he'd done things before. It was more official looking this way, and he had resources all budgeted to look good should the DOD (Department of defence) pry into the regiment—a distinct possibility now that the 501st was officially on-line again, but his agents and sources throughout the Alliance were still the same people. His staff, like Kate, all had security backgrounds. Every one of them could take care of business in the field when the need arose. Having them as backup freed him up. As he'd said to the General when pitching the need for proper intel weenies of their own, he couldn't be everywhere at once.

What if his luck ran out? Who would take over? He glanced at Richmond marching by his side.

She will.

They entered the tech centre and made their way to medical where Richmond's team of doctors waited. There were five of them; she was a bona-fide viper research project these days. So okay, she needed to be repaired, and the doctors never forgot that her life was in their hands, but the process used would be adapted in the future for other situations. The project was a huge deal to the regiment. For example, upgrades. Software upgrades were relatively simple things, but actual hardware upgrades never happened. The procedure was just too invasive and complicated. Not to mention dangerous. Risk of brain damage had been considered too high until now. If things worked out for Richmond, older vipers like him could have their computer systems replaced bringing them up to date with the newest vipers to come off the assembly line. It wouldn't suddenly turn a MK1 into a MK4, but it would close the gap by a significant amount. Increased processing power wouldn't make him physically Richmond's equal—she was stronger and faster with greater acceleration—but it would let him acquire and service targets as quickly and as accurately as she could. His sensors and ECM would benefit enormously as well.

"Okay," Stone said. "One busted viper delivered as ordered."

Richmond snorted.

"Thanks, Ken. I'll take it from here," Marion said. "You ready for this, Richmond?"

"More than," Richmond said. "Make sure you get the eye colour dead right. I don't want any screw ups."

"Eye colour is the least of your problems."

"Easy for you to say, you won't be the one looking in the mirror at them tomorrow. They better match."

Marion glanced at Stone. "About that. We're going to

take this extra slow to monitor and document things. You're the first to undergo the procedure, and we want to be able to tweak the process on the fly if we have to. We're estimating five days to a week before you're up and around."

"A week! Are you shitting me?"

Stone grinned.

"No," Marion said primly and glared at Stone. "It will be about that length of time. Just an estimate right now."

Stone nodded almost imperceptibly to Marion in thanks.

Richmond scowled and the scars turned her face into a horrifying mask. "Well, damn."

"Don't sweat it," Stone said. "You'll go to sleep and wake up fixed. You won't notice the delay."

Richmond grumbled something under her breath, but nodded and allowed herself to be led away. Marion stayed behind.

"You better be right about this, Ken."

"I am."

"She'll kill us both if it goes wrong."

Stone shrugged. "She has nothing on you. If she kills me, at least you'll know I deserved it."

Marion looked sharply at him. "You're doing it for her."

"That won't matter," Stone said and turned to leave.

"Ken?"

He stopped to listen, but gave her his back. "What?"

"Don't let her kill you. Richmonds come and go, but there's only one you."

Stone chuckled. "That's the nicest thing you've ever said to me." He walked out.

Marion's opinion of Richmond wasn't a surprise. She had never liked her and still considered her borderline psycho. He doubted anything would change that. Marion hated Bethany and anyone coming from there. She had her reasons, but she would never let herself act upon prejudice. Being a shrink allowed her to analyse her own motivations and make allowances. No, they would never be friends, but they didn't need to be enemies either. They were vipers and that made them family. They weren't close family, that's all.

Stone's next stop was the General's office.

He entered the outer office and the General's adjutant, Raph Robshaw, looked up. He glanced at the clock on the wall and then down at his comp with a frown. Stone could read him like a compad. Raph was wondering if he'd screwed up the General's diary somehow.

"No appointment, Raph, so stop stressing. Is he in?"

Raph nodded. "Just got back from Oracle five minutes ago. His next appointment isn't until 0800 so if you want...?"

"Ask for ten minutes would you? It's..." he couldn't say urgent, though it was to him. "Important."

Raph stood and knocked once before entering Burgton's office. He was gone less than a minute before coming out again. "Captain?"

Stone nodded and entered the office. Raph closed the door for him.

General Burgton, CO 501st Infantry Regiment and hero of the Alliance wasn't an imposing figure. He wasn't overly tall at just under two metres, or overly muscular, he wasn't sensim star handsome either. He was average in every way, until he looked at you. Stone had seen men and women stumble when that gaze locked upon them. He had seen them trembling when he was being perfectly nice to them. He just had a presence, and when he focused his attention upon you, you felt it like a blow. When he was being less than polite, watch out! Stone was used to his attention and although he felt Burgton's regard even all these years later, he could ignore the unease it created. Usually. This time was a little different. When Burgton looked up from where he sat behind his desk and those grey eyes focused upon him, Stone felt it. He felt it deep inside. He couldn't do this. He couldn't game his friend.

"I... I... have this thing."

Burgton raised an eyebrow in question.

"Information," he said and felt his face heating like a damn schoolboy. Thank God blushes didn't show on him. "It actually came through the network a few days ago. I should have brought it up before but..." he swallowed. He was fucking it up!

"I understand, Ken," Burgton said kindly.

"You do?" he said in surprise. How? He'd been excruciatingly careful.

"Have a seat."

Stone did as he was bid and tried to relax. He could still do what needed to be done. He hadn't blown it yet. He leaned back, feeling those eyes boring into him, assessing him. He sat forward and clasped his hands between his knees, he was unable to settle and meet Burgton's eyes.

"How is Richmond?"

Stone froze. He did know! Holy shit he was screwed.

"Ken?"

"She's fine. Medical are starting her enhancement today. She's good. Fine."

Burgton pursed his lips. "You've been seeing a lot of her lately."

"Yeah, she's part of my team." Burgton simply watched him squirm, waiting for his confession in silence. "And well... we kind of... we're seeing each other kind of. She and I... we're involved."

Burgton nodded. "I knew that. It was tons of fun watching you both figure it out. I knew you had feelings for her that day in Zuleika. Risking your life with that suicide run of yours to save her was a big clue."

Stone smiled weakly. He felt sick. "I know it's against the regs."

Burgton frowned and waved that away. "If I cared about that, I'd promote her out of your chain of command, Ken. That's the easiest way out for both of you if you want me to apply the regs. Personally, I don't care about them. Bend them, break them, I don't care as long as the job gets done. Let personal feelings get in the way of your duty to me and the regiment, and I assure you I'll care and take appropriate steps."

Stone believed that, and the steps could be serious ones; from ordering him to break the relationship with Richmond, to ordering one or both of them to different planets on opposite sides of the Alliance.

"Understood, sir, it won't be an issue."

"Good. Now, the information you mentioned. What have you got?"

Stone rearranged his thoughts. Burgton didn't know after all. "It's something that came to me through my contacts on Northcliff. One of their ships was jacked out Helios way."

"Helios?"

Stone nodded. "It's one of our systems in the Border Zone. The navy has a gas mining station there for refuelling our patrol ships. Anyway, a heavy cruiser came into the system in time to kick raider butt, Captain Colgan commanding."

"*That* Colgan?"

Stone nodded. "I have the data ready for upload, but it's what Colgan found on the raider ship that's the real news."

"I'll review your data, but give me the highlights."

"The raider ship is known to us. *Jean de Vienne* is a *Banshee* class destroyer that first entered my sights during my op on Thurston. It was delivering arms to the Freedom Movement there. Eric fixed the situation a little later, but *Jean de Vienne* was long gone before that."

"Thurston, yes. I don't recall the ship, but I remember Eric's download of that op. It's where he first met Fuentez and pushed for her recruitment."

Stone nodded. "Right. Anyway, after Colgan's marines made the ship safe they found a lot of cargo aboard. Standard procedure would have them record everything for evidence against the crew and then either confiscate or destroy it. The ship was badly damaged in the battle. Colgan had planned to scuttle, but what they found in addition to the usual types of loot changed things. He rigged a tow and brought the ship into the station."

"Oh really? That seems a lot of work."

"The cargo included cadavers in cryo including bodies of three unknown alien races and... and one of us."

Burgton sat up, his eyes blazing. "Who!"

Stone shook his head. "They don't know. There were Merki bodies and corpses of other Alliance soldiers. None had I.D."

Burgton hissed under his breath. "Who is missing?"

"Again, I don't know. We always have operations running, and we do have people out that way, but none of them are due to report in. It could be any of them... well no, I take that back. The dead viper is male, but that's all we know."

"And we're sure he's dead and not in hibernation?"

"The report says deceased, but I can't verify without going out there."

Burgton nodded and pushed to his feet. Stone watched him pace and knew what he was thinking. The Merkiaari were making their move, but they didn't know exactly where or what the move was. They had to respond, *had to*, but to mobilise the regiment without orders or better data was unacceptable.

"I want to go out there," Stone said quietly. "OSI is working well. It doesn't need me watching over it every minute any more. I can afford to get eyes on scene, and I think this situation needs the best. That's me."

Burgton nodded, not agreeing just acknowledging the words.

Stone licked his lips. "I want to take Richmond and Fuentez with me."

That stopped him. Burgton swung his narrowed eyes onto Stone, perhaps remembering their earlier conversation and re-evaluating. "Explain."

This was it. Lie or come clean? He sighed and chose truth. "Richmond's brother was last seen on *Jean de Vienne*."

"Is he dead?"

"He was taken after he shot his own captain in the back when he threatened to scuttle the ship. He's Colgan's prisoner."

Burgton frowned. "You haven't told her?"

"She would have demanded transport to Helios seconds later if I had, and she needs to be repaired. I held the data back so Marion could fix her first."

"You could ship out without her."

Stone shook his head. "She would never forgive that."

"True, true," Burgton murmured and frowned. "You realise he's going to be mind-wiped?"

Stone nodded.

"Your plan?"

"To make her see what a scumbag he really is, to show her that she needs to cut him loose and move on."

"Why the need for Fuentez?"

"For support. She won't trust me after this. She'll need a friend."

"Fuentez has only been back a month. She's holding Sebastian's hand under The Mountain."

"Can you spare her? Richmond isn't close to many people. I need Fuentez with us."

"Richmond will be fully online by the end of the week?"

"Yes, sir."

Burgton nodded. "That works, just about. Liz told me Oracle will be complete soon. Sebastian is already connected to Oracle's power grid and the cryo plant. As far as I know, all that needs to be done is hook up all his data feeds and seal his matrix into the column. A day maybe two will see it done, Liz says."

"So I can take her?"

"Talk to Eric. If he has no objections you can have her for this. Don't let Richmond's personal situation get in the way, Ken. Merkiaari, dead aliens, a dead viper and all of it inside Alliance space? This could be our first indication of a new incursion. It's bigger than any one of us."

Stone nodded.

* * *

5 ~ Oracle

Stone guided the shuttle into the bay. Hovering and moving slowly, he crossed the busy space toward the parking area following the signals provided by the safety officer. He edged forward concentrating upon the man's light wands, and paused when the officer abruptly crossed them. He lowered power to his anti-grav and the shuttle settled upon her skids. Stone went through his shutdown checklist while the safety officer trotted away to guide another shuttle, this time exiting the bay.

Stone was feeling upbeat and more cheerful than he had this morning. He had the General on side without having to con him into it, and Marion was willing to keep Richmond out from underfoot while he gathered what he needed for the mission. Both missions. The official one didn't need much. A fast ship and one of the regiment's stasis tubes was about all he needed. He had a fallen unit to retrieve. The investigation side of the operation didn't require hardware, or if it did, it would be available on site. Richmond's mission though... if things went the way he thought they might, she would need everything an undercover operative might use on a hostile world. He figured he would just pack for her as if he were performing the mission himself.

The General had given him *Harbinger*, a courier class ship modified with neural interfaces. Harbinger was one of only three ships like it that the regiment used for special occasions. Courier ships were highly automated at the best of times and carried small crews. Twelve was standard spread over three watches, but using *Harbinger's* neural net, it could be handled by three vipers easily. It was the General's preferred ride, his own ship. He used it to visit Earth when drone communication was inadequate or ill advised for one reason or another. It wasn't as if he could just turn up at Sol aboard *Hammer* and not raise questions about a destroyer crewed by non-naval personnel after all, and using a merchy as a passenger ship didn't sit right.

Stone finished his checklist and left the shuttle for the elevators.

He had never visited Oracle before but he had a rough understanding of what to expect, so when the elevator deposited him directly into chaos he was surprised and briefly wondered if he had somehow selected the wrong destination. Couldn't have. There weren't many destinations available from the bay he'd chosen. It was an ancillary bay built for Oracle especially.

He stepped into the centrum but had to step aside as an engineer hurried by pushing a gravcart piled high with equipment. No apology for nearly running him down either. Stone followed the man with narrowed eyes, his targeting reticule locked on and spinning centred on his back. He shook his head as the oblivious techy actually did run some poor fool down and received a chewing out for it. The two yelled at each other adding to the din. Stone didn't think much of their brains.

Oracle's centrum, soon to become Sebastian's home, was

a huge gleaming hollow ball the size of a stadium. There were techs and engineers scattered around doing arcane things with their equipment, busily ignoring each other, and burying themselves in data. The gleaming walls of the centrum were shimmering with the telltale effects that colonisation by nanotech gave any surface when not actively in use. Stone watched in fascination as the techs used areas of the walls as view screens and monitors to display diagrams and test results. He had a passing interest in nano-engineering and other tech. Being the product of some advanced tech himself, it would have seemed strange to him not to take an interest, but the blueprints displayed lost him the moment he tried to understand them. Oh, he could tell it was Oracle's guts he was seeing, but he couldn't fathom much more than that. The techs seemed particularly interested in the matrix column. That made sense. Sebastian needed installation into the column, and there was obviously something impeding that.

Rather than ask around, Stone used his sensors to find Fuentez. A window opened on his HUD filled with green icons representing the techs and engineers, but his attention was all for the single cool blue blip representing the only other viper present—lieutenant Gina Fuentez, Richmond's best bud, and soon to be his co-conspirator. He had decided to let her in on the deal with Richmond. Not everything, but damn near; more than he was comfortable with, truth be known, but unlike the General, she would be with Kate and needed to know. Not that he had conned the General. He hadn't. Burgton now knew what his aims were regarding Richmond and her brother. He just didn't know every detail of how he planned to achieve it. Burgton didn't generally micromanage. He delegated tasks and expected positive results; same here despite the unofficial nature of the mission. Stone appreciated that more than he could say. OSI (Office of Strategic Intelligence) depended on having discretion, but

Burgton had never been shy in granting that.

It still felt odd legitimising his efforts, Stone thought as he headed for Fuentez. OSI (Office of Strategic Intelligence) was the name Burgton had finally settled upon for his new section. He'd based it upon the navy's ONI (Office of Naval Intelligence) It was better than calling his people intel weenies, which they still were, but being called that trivialised their work. They were intelligence agents or operatives—assassins and saboteurs quite often, information gatherers and analysts always, and soldiers no matter the mission. Vipers were always soldiers. They deserved to be treated as such and having a properly named section within the greater regiment felt right and was good for their morale.

According to sensors, Fuentez was near the matrix column but on its far side. Stone couldn't see her, but he headed that way. The column's insulation and shielding had been removed to allow Sebastian's matrix to be installed. He could see the columns guts and Sebastian himself, or his brain he supposed it was. The matrix had been installed but there must have been a setback, because as Stone approached he could see work was underway extracting it from the column.

"...calm down, they'll fix it," Fuentez was saying. "No, they understand that. No I said. I'm not going to... okay, but they'll do that anyway."

"What's the issue now?" Liz said, sounding tired. "Is he still bitching about the buffer memory specs?"

"Not this time," Fuentez said. "Bastian thinks you should connect the neural interface first this time. He says if you do that, he can run a diagnostic on the entire facility himself much quicker than your people, and guide them through the installation. He says it will save time."

Liz frowned. "That actually does make sense. He's already awake and aware. The usual procedure would be to initialise a new A.I's matrix after installation, not before."

"I know. He's thoroughly educated me on the accepted

process that he now wants to throw out the airlock." Fuentez grinned. "I know more than I ever wanted to know about it."

"What's wrong?" Stone said to Liz. He hoped the problem wouldn't mess up his plans for recruiting Fuentez. "I only caught the last part of that."

Liz shook her head. "Nothing serious."

Fuentez sighed. "Bastian says he'll be the judge of that, thank you."

Liz rolled her eyes.

"Ah... Sebastian says?" Stone said.

Fuentez turned her back on Stone and pointed to her butt. Stone blinked, but she wasn't dissing him. She was pointing to a data cable plugged into her primary node that led off toward the matrix column. All vipers had a data node at the base of their spines for hard wire connections. The regiment's simulators could use them, but they were designed originally for uploading and maintaining a viper's software. He'd never seen one used outside of the tech centre before.

Stone made an educated guess. "Sebastian is linked into your internal net?"

"Yep! I'm hearing voices... woo!"

Liz grinned. "Bastian, meet Captain Stone. Stone, say hello to our newest recruit."

Before Stone could answer, Fuentez spoke again but the words weren't hers. "*Ah yes. Stone, Kenneth, Captain 501st Infantry Regiment DGN-896-410-339. Congratulations on your recent promotion, Captain.*"

"Ah... thanks?" Stone turned to Liz. "Is he plugged into our database already?"

"*I am not,*" Sebastian/Fuentez said. "*I am, however, into Gina's files—*" Fuentez scowled. "I've told you about that! Stay out of my personal stuff! *I am not in your personal stuff.* Yes you are. I can feel you rummaging around in there. *It depends upon your definition of personal. I am limiting my rummaging,*

*as you put it, to your professional memories and data. I have
avoided all personal references as I promised."*

Stone listened in amazement. So this is what the General
meant by holding Sebastian's hand? It was like listening to a
mad woman talking to her imaginary friend.

"Tell me," Sebastian/Fuentez said turning his/her
attention back to Stone. *"What was your impression of the
Shan? I find Gina's memories of them fascinating."*

"I liked them."

*"Perhaps you could elaborate? What did you like and dislike
about them? There must be something you do not like?"*

Stone frowned wondering what he was after. "I'm not sure
there was anything to dislike. They're a courageous people it
seemed to me. They fought the Merkiaari twice to a standstill.
The first time they could've had little hope of defeating them,
but they survived and rebuilt their worlds. The second time
they had our help, and worked to exhaustion to keep up and
do their part."

*"Yes, yes, they are fine soldiers I am sure... or warriors in
their own parlance. What of them as a people? How do you see
them fitting into the greater framework of the Alliance?"*

"I'm not sure we're qualified to judge that."

"You may not be," Sebastian/Fuentez said, *"but I am
informed by General Burgton that evaluating the Shan and their
impact upon the Alliance is to become part of my duties. I shall
be devoting a considerable number of my cycles to the Oracle
Project and the Shan. They are a fascinating people. Simply
fascinating."*

Stone nodded. The Shan were that and more. "I came to
see Fuentez about a mission." He turned to Liz. "How long
do you need her?"

"A couple of days. We would've been finished yesterday
but we hit a snag." Sebastian/Fuentes muttered something
derogatory and Liz glared at him/her. "It's not my fault!"

"What isn't?" Stone said.

"I built the column interfaces to designs centuries out of date. No help for that; no one is building A.I tech now. According to my information, all A.I matrix interfaces were the same so that the hardware could be standardised. Capacities and physical dimensions of the matrix itself might vary as tech improved over that time, but the interface couplings were kept standard. I used those designs for the matrix we built and the interfaces in the column."

Sebastian/Fuentez snorted.

Liz glared. "It's not my fault!"

Stone sighed. "What exactly is the problem?"

Liz muttered something under her breath and then shrugged. "He... Sebastian doesn't bloody fit! He's too big."

Fuentez snickered at the unintentional innuendo.

Stone turned to look at the matrix. It did look a bit snug within the column, but it did fit if barely. "He's in. Isn't that good enough?"

"Physically he fits, but the interface couplings are all wrong. We need to switch them out, but there's not enough room to work inside the column with him in there. I have to yank him out again, retrofit the interfaces, and then reinstall him."

"*And this time you will enable the neural interfaces first,*" Sebastian/Fuentes insisted.

Liz waved that away as if a fly were annoying her. "Yes yes. I said that was a good idea. We'll do it."

"Can I have a minute with Fuentez alone now then if you don't need her?"

Fuentez shrugged. "Sure. Have to do it here though. There isn't much slack in the cable."

Stone nodded. "And privacy?"

"*I shall not listen,*" Sebastian/Fuentez said.

Damn that is just so weird. Sebastian had a different intonation to Fuentez, but it was still her voice and body talking to him. He'd be glad when Sebastian was fully installed and he could use his own voice and avatar.

"Can he do that?"

"No," Liz said. "Not really. He hears everything that Gina does, but he can compartmentalise it, which is just as good. Basically, your conversation will be archived and the memory address flagged so that he forgets it's there until asked by one of you to specifically un-flag and recall it. It's simpler if you pretend he's not listening, Ken. It's just as good, I promise."

"Okay, if you say so."

Liz hurried off toward the engineers and those intriguing plans displayed on the centrum's wall. Interface designs maybe? No doubt she had a requisition in or a priority order at one of the nano factories.

"What do you know about Richmond's brother?" Stone began. "Has she confided in you?"

Fuentez nodded. "Some. She's told me some stuff about her time in Bethany's ISS. She used her contacts there to look for him."

Richmond had done a lot more than that. She used her missions to follow up on information received from ISS assets, and used mission funds and time to perform her own investigations. She'd taken extra risks and shortcuts to manufacture opportunities, and had gotten away with it, but unbeknown to her at that time her own commanders had been working against her. They had taken steps to confuse and hide her brother's movements, not just from her, but from everyone. Paul Richmond worked for their masters; Bethany's founding families. Specifically, he had done a lot of work for the Whitbys whom Richmond hated for their part in her father's downfall. Basically, her brother was a merc working for the highest bidder, and that had been Whitby Corp. most recently.

"There's more to it, but that's basically it. She's in enhancement now. It will take about a week. When she comes out she and I have a mission for the General in Helios.

I want you along. The General is okay with it, and Eric has signed off. You up for it?"

"Why are you asking me? You're the captain, Captain," Fuentez said. "I go where the General sends me."

Stone nodded at the expected response. "Good. We have a unit down in Helios but no identification. The mission is to retrieve him and investigate the circumstances of his death. We deal with what we learn, or if we can't, we report that and prepare for a follow-up mission with recon data for whoever is sent. The Merkiaari are involved."

Fuentez stilled, but shook off her surprise a moment later. "And you think three of us can deal with them, why?"

"Because they're dead."

"That works."

Stone snorted. "Yeah, but we don't know why they're dead or who killed them. We don't know how they came to be in the Border Zone, but most important of all, we don't know where their buddies are. This could be the first sign of the new Merki incursion we've been waiting for. The regiment can't mobilise on a whim. The General needs good intel to present to HQ."

"And this relates to Kate's brother how?"

"He was on the bridge of the ship carrying our man and the Merki. He's a prisoner now. They're holding him at Helios."

Fuentez turned grim. "Kate won't like that."

"I know. That brings me to the other part of the mission; the unofficial part. I want you with us to support Richmond where her brother is concerned. She'll need you to keep things under control. She can't go in there gun in hand ready to bust him out of the brig."

"You think she'll listen to me?"

"I hope so, but whether she does or not you'll be there to help her do whatever she decides to do."

Fuentez frowned at him. "You'll be there, right?"

"Of course," Stone said and glanced away at the engineers. "I should get going. The General has given us *Harbinger*. That will cut the journey time by at least a third, but I still don't want to waste any of the time we have. I need to pack a few things for the mission so we'll be ready as soon as Richmond wakes up, and I need to arrange a stand in for me at OSI. Plan to leave in seven days."

"I'll be ready, but what do you really want me to do about Kate? If her brother is one of the bad guys in this, the authorities aren't going to let him go. You can't expect Kate to just shrug and walk away."

"I want her to realise that her brother is a lost cause. That's what I really want. That's obviously not going to happen. The next best thing is for her to talk to him and cut him loose. She has her own life." Fuentez gave him a disbelieving look. "Yeah..." he sighed. "I know, but I can hope. Whatever happens, you're her friend first. I can count on you to do what's right for her."

Fuentez pursed her lips. "You make it sound like you and she aren't together anymore. Did something happen between you?"

"Nothing like that, but I'm her CO. She won't want to confide certain things, and I won't ask. She'll need you before this is done, Fuentez."

She nodded.

"Gotta go," he said and headed back to the elevators. "Tell Sebastian I'll come by for a visit before we leave."

"*I am looking forward to it, Captain,*" Sebastian/Fuentez said.

Stone almost looked back. He shook his head. He was glad it was Fuentez and not him hosting the A.I. He raised an acknowledging hand but did not stop.

* * *

6 ~ Trading Places

Alexander Bohdanko Dyachenko, President of the Alliance, sipped his drink and tried to disappear into the foliage filling this corner of his official residence. Ludmilla, the love of his life and First Lady, had outdone herself with her nature theme. The holographics were top notch and although the President's residence was filled with cutting edge tech, her programmes must be giving the system a real workout. The ballroom had been turned into a frontier world complete with wild animal noises and jungle foliage. The central area gave the impression of a clearing, while the walls were hidden by jungle trees and undergrowth. The ceiling displayed an alien sky complete with bloated moons. He'd asked her what planet it was based upon, but it was a composite of her own design. She enjoyed creating such things.

Neither of them had any illusions regarding their chosen path in life, but had things been different she might have found a place in the media. A photo journalist perhaps. Yes, that would suit her well. He on the other hand had always fancied the quiet life of an author. Not that his little stories ever saw the light of day, but he enjoyed jotting things down. Some of what he wrote might one day find their way to publication as diaries or a biography, but not his fiction. He was far too self-conscious to ever let anyone read them.

He smiled as he watched his wife moving through the room exchanging a few words with their guests. She was a wonder. How she could pretend to enjoy these things he couldn't fathom. If it was pretence. For the life of him he couldn't be sure; she would have made for a great actress. He watched her carrying the day by greeting everyone and making nice-nice to their political allies and enemies alike, and wondered how it was possible to love her more now than the day they had met. He did. He really did.

He should cut this break short and rejoin her, but decided to finish his drink first. Besides, she was better at this than he. If he went back to work now, he might undo her efforts. When he was in this mood it was better to stay apart. She wouldn't thank him for ruining her party by bringing up certain things too soon. He sometimes wished she'd been the one to run for office. He could have spent his time writing a book, or fishing, or... well anyway, doing something else.

If only he could teleport, he mused, he would have used the ability to escape. He could just pop in and out at will. Just a blink and he could be at home in his cluttered office—his real office at home, not the president's office here. Shame the only teleporter in the Alliance was a fictional character on Zelda's show, and even he had limits. Shame about that. Teleportation was a fascinating concept. In his opinion the producers of Zelda and the Spaceways had underutilised it and the character. There were so many plot lines that could be spun from that one idea. Hell, Zelda's companion could have his own show based upon his popularity ratings.

He should be so lucky. Alex scowled at the reminder of his own dismal showing in the latest polls.

Being less popular than a fictional character was

humbling. It put things into perspective in a way. How could anyone, even the President of a star spanning behemoth like the Alliance, take himself seriously when most of its citizens considered Zelda's piratical crew more real and relevant to their lives than the man responsible for their government? He shook his head and sipped his wine.

Strangely, it made things easier for him to think of the Alliance as a single entity rather than one made up of two hundred and thirty four worlds and billions of people, but that was a trap. Yes, he could make decisions and policy to improve things in the Alliance, but he still needed the Council to vote them into existence. Failing to take people and their feelings into consideration was dangerous and indirectly led to these little soirees where he attempted damage control or campaigns to persuade people to his view.

Alex found these functions both tiresome and invaluable. It was damned annoying. If he could dismiss the entire affair as a useless waste of his time, he could have handled the party differently. As it was he had to remain alert and not switch his brain off. He couldn't give himself over to auto piloting his way through this one, muttering platitudes and keeping anything of real import off the menu so to speak. Not this time. If he did, a vote to rescind the Red One Alert would be before the Council after the summer break quicker than he could blink and he would have Admiral Rawlins frothing at the mouth and gunning for him.

The Council was in the middle of its summer recess. It was supposedly a time to rest and reflect upon the previous session's business, but Alex rarely had time to stop schmoozing his rivals. He hadn't been off world in years. Personal trips were out of the question and state visits were hugely complicated. He couldn't afford to be out of contact in fold space for the months most round trips took. Even visiting the big six meant waiting for opportune times like Christmas break, Easter break, or the summer recess and those were core worlds. There was no chance he would ever visit the border worlds while still in office, and the Border Zone itself might as well be as mythical as Zelda's Flotsam. Too far, too dangerous, and just plain impossible for anyone in public office to visit.

A disturbance near the entrance disturbed his pity party and he craned his neck trying to see. He smiled in genuine pleasure when he saw who had arrived, and he quickly put aside his glass to step out of hiding.

"Mister President!"

He ignored the hail as if he hadn't heard it. Ludmilla's little jungle had served its purpose of concealing him, but if he stopped and turned to acknowledge whoever was calling him he would make it all a wasted effort. Besides, he had been waiting for these guests in particular. He hurried to join Ludmilla who was greeting Councillor Tei'Varyk and his mate.

"... live in harmony," Ludmilla was saying. She must have sensed him approaching at her back because she turned to him. "Ah, here he is. Finished hiding?"

Alex grinned. "You were having so much fun; I knew you wouldn't miss me." He bowed to Tei'Varyk and Tarjei. "I'm glad you could make it. May you both live long and in harmony."

Tei'Varyk offered his hand, and Alex placed his palm against it in the Shan form of a handshake. "Honoured to be invited, and may you and yours live in harmony, Mister President."

Tei'Varyk had spoken in flawless English, and even his pronunciation was good despite the inevitable differences physiology forced upon his speech. It was a far cry from their first meeting up on Luna. Alex remembered that meeting vividly. It was his very first with Tei'Varyk and Tarjei, and they had needed to rely upon Captain Colgan as well as the mechanical aid of compad translators. The Shan used coughs and growls to punctuate their own language, and the shape of their mouths affected how they pronounced words. Colgan had become used to Tei'Varyk's form of English during his time living and working with him, and he'd proven invaluable. Alex was used to it now as well and hardly noticed the differences when the Shan spoke before the Council. He could discard his ear-piece and understand Tei'Varyk perfectly well, though most of the other councillors preferred to err on the side of caution and listened to a translator's voice when he spoke.

"Call me Alex, please. This is a party, besides that we're friends I hope."

Tei'Varyk's ears flicked in the gesture Alex had learned to recognise as the affirmative, but the Shan nodded as well. They were all learning various gestures and combinations of them from each other. The Shan delegation didn't often bother to carry their translators outside the Council chamber anymore.

"I understand congratulations are in order, Tarjei," Ludmilla said. "The rumours are true?"

Tarjei flicked her ears but nodded as well. "We are blessed by the harmonies, yes."

"That's wonderful news. When are you due?"

"Due?" Tarjei said uncertainly and looked to Tei'Varyk for help.

"To give birth," Alex said before her mate could answer. "I understand Shan always have multiple births and gestation is much shorter than the Human norm."

"Ah!" Tarjei bobbed a nod. "Yes, that is a truth. Five cubs is the usual number for a first litter, though four is common too. Seven isn't unheard of, but it's rare."

"Seven!" Ludmilla said. "My goodness. That must be a lot of work for the mothers."

"Tiring certainly," Tei'Varyk agreed. "But such a blessing brings its own joy. The harmonies will decide."

"Our doctors could tell you now if you want to know," Alex began but broke off when he saw he had misspoke. The Shan looked horrified by the idea. "I'm sorry. I didn't mean any insult."

"There was no insult," Tei'Varyk said. "My people believe such things must be left to the harmonies. A tradition and perhaps a silly superstition in such modern times as these, but honoured still. Our healers could tell us, or I could ask the harmonies to show me, but the healers wouldn't and I do not ask. It is a temptation I will admit."

Alex chuckled. "Shan abilities do have some downsides then I see."

Tarjei's ears flicked and her jaw dropped in amusement. "He always knows when I'm feeling sad or sick. He often anticipates me when I'm angry, and before I know what is happening he has done something to make me smile."

"How annoying!" Ludmilla said and laughed with Tarjei.

Tei'Varyk exchanged a puzzled look with Alex. He shrugged and shook his head at the Shan. Women were unfathomable no matter their race.

"When will the little ones be born?" Ludmilla was saying. "You know Human pregnancy lasts nine months."

"Nine!" Tarjei gasped. "I had not heard that. My people carry our young between ninety and a hundred cycles... days. So less than half the Human term."

"Three months?" Ludmilla looked down, but Tarjei's robes hid any evidence of her pregnancy.

Both Shan were wearing flowing floor length robes rather than the plain everyday harnesses they had worn the first time Alex met them. He'd learned that the robes were worn by Shan elders, and that it had been decided to extend the custom to the designated Shan Councillor and his mate despite their ages. It wasn't because Tei'Varyk had previously been the Shan ambassador to the Alliance for example. It was a new custom devised for his position as the closest thing the Shan delegation had to an elder on Earth. Tei'Varyk was many things to his people. Councillor to the Alliance, Ambassador for his entire race, Elder for all Shan resident upon Earth, and of course mate to Tarjei.

Alex secretly thought the elders probably wore robes not to enhance their dignity and authority, but rather as a way of hiding their emotions. Shan were very emotive beings. They had many tells related to body language. Their tails especially could gesture in a wide range of motions, each having meanings to those who could read them. Covering themselves in the loose fitting robes must make the elders seem grave and unemotional. A useful illusion that. Alex could wish for something similar when confronted by irritating councillors.

"There are many people here who wish to meet you," Alex said bringing himself back to the present. "We shouldn't monopolise your time, though I wish to. We'll let you mingle for while and meet again later. There's something we need to discuss before you leave."

Tei'Varyk looked intrigued, but he led his mate away to greet the other guests.

"You're going to tell him then?" Ludmilla asked as they watched the Shan join the party-goers.

Alex nodded. "There was never any doubt of that, just the timing. Our people will be there within days if they're not already."

"And Nathan?"

Alex's lips tightened. Nathan Mindel had helped him in the past, but he didn't consider Northcliff's councillor an ally. Far from it. Mindel was the current spokesman for the euphemistically named Border Worlds Party, and as such had been a thorn in Alex's side for nearly his entire term in office. He owed Nathan a favour, and the information should pay the debt, but it went beyond that. Alex wanted Nathan's help again, and he was sure he would be made to pay dearly for it. The Border Worlds Party was the primary instigator behind the proposal to rescind the Red One. Its members wanted the navy back where it belonged, covering their worlds against commerce raiders. Alex totally sympathised with them. They had all become accustomed to having navy protection in, if not every system, at least in systems close by. They wanted that protection back, but the Shan also needed the navy, and arguably had the better claim. Both parties deserved protection.

Alex would love to give it to them, but the Merki threat meant Admiral Rawlins would strenuously resist any move to undo his strategic consolidation, and Fifth Fleet was hard at work helping the Shan rebuild their orbital infrastructure. The only answer was to build more ships; many many more ships, but that would come at huge cost to the economy, and no one wanted that. It was an insoluble situation. More ships, more soldiers, more fuel, more weapons... more more more! The military was voraciously hungry for resources at the best of times, and always had been, but now the precise balance achieved over long years following the last war was tipping toward deficit. The numbers were staggering. Taxes were already higher this year than last, and if the Red One wasn't rescinded soon, taxes would surge. It would happen suddenly, but economists Alex trusted had warned him the signs were already there to see. The corporations were starting to mutter about a slowdown in growth. Nothing major yet, they were simply *"viewing with concern,"* but that wouldn't last.

"I'll show him the data and play it by ear. Is he here yet?"

Ludmilla shook her head. "Not yet."

"But he's coming, you're sure?"

"His chief of staff confirmed the invitation."

Alex frowned. That really didn't mean anything, but

Nathan would probably show his face for politeness sake if for no other reason. That was probably the reason for his late arrival. No doubt he had other plans and would just stop in for an hour using the plans for an excuse. Alex had used that tactic a time or three.

"As long as I get him for a half hour, I don't care when he arrives. Don't let me miss him, my love."

Ludmilla smiled. "I'll bag him for you."

Alex gave her a quick kiss on the cheek and then turned back to business. He had schmoozing to do.

Alex listened politely as Councillor Hartman discussed sending a trade delegation to the Shan with Tei'Varyk, and found himself nodding encouragement as they parlayed the pros and cons of doing so now, while the reconstruction was still underway. He was sure Tei'Varyk had heard many such proposals in his time on Earth. Everyone was curious about the Shan, and ships had already visited the system looking to gain advantage over rivals, but as far as he knew the Shan were being coy about granting any one world favoured trading status. Good for them. Damn good. Better to keep all the vultures at arm's length and let them negotiate themselves to death before picking a few worlds from among the survivors. That's how he would handle it. Turn away no one, but favour a select few. Let them strive to best each other in order to join that special group and earn Shan trade. Don't just give it away. It sounded like Kajetan had given instructions to that effect or something very like it.

Alex approved, though he should remain neutral. As President of the Alliance and Chairman of the Council he was supposed to serve all worlds equally, but it wasn't as easy as that. Some really were more deserving than others... or more needy might be a better way of thinking about it. Everyone deserved peace and prosperity. Some already had it, while others still strove to gain it. Was it right that the core worlds be denied a way to improve upon their already prosperous positions in favour of worlds still in the early stages of their rise? It was hard to say, though from a purely moral standpoint the answer was obvious. The problem with having morals, Alex mused, was that they could tie you in knots.

In the real world the question was mute. There was nothing anyone could do to limit prosperity in favour of the needy. If it could be done it would lead to a race to the lowest common denominator and probably war. If not outright war, certainly secession and fragmentation of the Alliance would ensue. Why would any world agree to lowering or limiting its people's standard of living?

Anyway, everyone equal in poverty wasn't his idea of progress; far better to allow each world the freedom to improve its own situation, while at the same time encouraging the weaker economies and protecting them from predation. The system wasn't perfect, but it did work in most cases.

New worlds joined the Alliance every few decades while new colonies were founded in the Border Zone every year. In the cases where worlds faltered, there were charitable organisations and government policies were in place designed to help with loans and expertise. In the most severe cases, there was always the military option, but the Alliance generally didn't get involved in those unless invited, and even then only in special cases voted upon by the Council. Skirmishes between mercenary companies were far more common, and for the most part dealt surprisingly well with the problem.

Arsenal, the home of the Mercenary Guild, wasn't an Alliance member world but its trade in all things military was heavily regulated by the Council despite that. It had to be. Many of the Guild's best customers were Alliance member worlds, hiring mercenary companies for planetary defence, training, or other similar things. Corporations often used them for security. The Guild was there to keep things within the realms of decency. Decency and war in the same sentence together would seem an oxymoron, but Human history was rife with conflicts that had gotten out of hand. Arsenal imposed the rules of war on all of the mercenary outfits registered with the Guild, and enforced those rules stringently by threat of expulsion or force of arms if necessary. The Council of Regiments, the closest thing to a world government Arsenal had, wanted no trouble with the Alliance.

It was bad for business.

"...medicines and of course the production of IMS compatible nanotech," Hartman was saying. "Thorfinni is one of the largest manufacturers of medical grade nanotech. We're always looking to expand into new markets in that sector, but of course it has become somewhat saturated in the core. The military is one of our best customers. Did you know we manufactured your wrist unit?"

Tei'Varyk raised his sleeve to regard his wrist comp. "This was made on Thorfinni?"

Hartman nodded. "By Intellicorp, one of our founding corporations. They're still headquartered there, in our capital. I caught a glimpse of your unit earlier when you sampled our host's excellent wine."

Alex smiled. Hartman was really good at sucking up when he wanted to—the wine was merely good not excellent—but that wasn't all there was to him. He could switch the charm on and off when the need arose.

"If I do not offend, the rumour is that you and your mate are protected by military grade IMS because of the circumstances of your arrival on Earth the first time."

Tei'Varyk glanced at Alex who shrugged. It wasn't a secret how Doctor Ambrai aboard *Canada* had saved the crew's lives when they fell ill from a cross-species infection. To prevent a repeat he chose to administer the IMS (Integrated Medical System) nanites he had available to the survivors of

Naktlon, and spent most of the trip to Earth monitoring and tuning them for compatibility with Shan physiologies. It had been an inspired but risky piece of work. Ambrai had received some criticism from colleagues for his actions since then. Some considered him to have acted rashly and without thought, but he'd been desperate. Many of the survivors had been near death, including Tarjei, and they'd needed surgery. Administering surgical nanotech to save lives was just one tiny step removed from installing the full IMS suit. A step he'd taken once he'd stabilised his patients.

"The survivors of Naktlon all have the IMS you speak of, that is a truth. May I ask why this interests you?"

Hartmann nodded. "Mainly for the reason I suspect you have guessed. Your people back home haven't been offered the longevity available to all through the application of medical nanotech. The longevity you and your mate now enjoy. I would have heard if such a deal had been struck."

Tarjei whispered something that Alex didn't catch, and Tei'Varyk responded in Shan but using a dialect Alex couldn't understand. He watched the rapid fire discussion and pondered the meaning of Hartman's move. Hartman had an interested smile on his face as if he understood what Tarjei and Tei'Varyk were discussing, but Alex doubted very much that he did.

"No deal has been struck," Tei'Varyk said finally. "Many offers have been made and are under consideration."

Oh well done! Alex wanted to laugh as Hartman's smile slipped. He had to be wondering if he'd missed any of the offers made to the Shan and what they might be.

"I've been asked to offer something to your people. It's perhaps a little radical if compared with the other offers you mention. Will you consider it?"

Tei'Varyk's ears flicked and he nodded, but he was looking at Hartman very oddly and his nostrils were flaring. Alex suddenly wondered if Shan could scent evasiveness or lies. He couldn't believe he hadn't considered that before now. It was easy to forget that Tei'Varyk was special in more than his race. He was Tei, which meant from a Human perspective that he was a very strong empath. That wasn't precisely correct but it served. He'd read everything he could get his hands on regarding the Shan, and he still didn't understand what Tei were. They were empaths, so much was certain, but they were more than that. He had no words for all they could do, but combine those abilities with a Shan's natural senses and you would have something very close to an infallible walking lie detector. Alex tried to go over everything he had ever discussed with Tei'Varyk in his head, and decided he was in the clear. He'd never lied to the Shan.

"This radical offer is made by your government?" Tei'Varyk asked.

Hartman coughed. "Not precisely, no."

Here it comes, Alex thought as Tei'Varyk cocked his head and that busy nose twitched.

"My government is aware of the offer and approves my relaying it to you, but no, it's not a government deal. Thorfinni will benefit indirectly of course. Taxes and the like being what they are. The greater the profit Intellicorp makes, the better my government likes it."

"I see," Tei'Varyk said. "Please continue."

"First of all, this isn't an offer to sell you medical nanotech in bulk or anything like that. It's an offer to invest directly in your economy with a turnkey solution."

"Turnkey?"

"It's what we call a complete solution," Alex explained. "It basically means everything required to solve a problem. Materials, software, training... everything necessary no matter how large or small."

Hartman nodded without rancour at having his sales pitch interrupted. "Precisely. Intellicorp proposes to send ships and engineers to build a nanotech facility on your homeworld. Your elders will decide where to build it and supply the land. Once built, Intellicorp will train a workforce to understand and operate it."

"Why would you do this?"

"That's the radical part. Once complete, the entire facility will be donated to your government at no charge. The idea is that your people can replicate the facility as many times as needed at no cost to the corporation. Your people can then produce as much of Intellicorp's medical nanotech as they will ever need... under license of course."

Ah! Things become clearer. The Shan shoulder all the costs apart from the very first facility, but have to pay a license fee to use it for its designed purpose. Sneaky. The fee was likely to be significant and in perpetuity. Talk about passive income! The profits over time would be huge. Intellicorp would have a lock on Shan trade where medical nanotech was concerned. After all, why would the Shan purchase a competitor's product when they could manufacture their own on planet? No shipping costs either.

It had to be the deal of the millennium. One corporation supplying two habitable planets with medical grade nanotech from the start and with no competitors? Huge! Every single living Shan would need a full IMS suit, and periodically there would be adjustments, boosters, and upgrades to consider. Shan females gave birth to five cubs at a time, and if his reading was right, they might have multiple litters in a lifetime... a lifetime that was about to increase fourfold. The sum profit Intellicorp was about to make was literally incalculable. It would most likely catapult the company to the top spot in its field.

It was an inspired offer and a good deal from the Shan point of view too. Kajetan would accept. There was no doubt in Alex's mind. It might even save her life if the plant could be built quickly, though he doubted that would sway her. Besides, she could've had the IMS treatments that Tei'Varyk had been given already if she'd been so inclined. Fifth Fleet had everything necessary on hand, but Alex suspected she wouldn't accept the treatments until her people could also have them. He hoped she could hold on long enough. He would like to meet the tough old lady he'd read about.

Tei'Varyk was speaking. "... inform them for us?"

"I can do that. It would be my honour to do that for you."

Tei'Varyk bowed. "Then, on behalf of my people, I thank you and accept Intellicorp's gracious offer. It is understood that we reserve the right to reject license terms up to the time ground is broken and work to build the facility begins?"

Alex smiled. He had left himself and his people an out. If negotiations failed or went poorly, the only ones out of pocket would be Intellicorp investors.

"I'll inform them, but I'm sure they've considered that. There are risks inherent in every deal after all."

Tei'Varyk's ears flicked and he nodded.

Councillor Hartman having delivered his offer took his leave. Alex watched him go, knowing he would race back to his embassy with his news. It would've been a big deal no matter the world involved, but Thorfinni was now the first world to nail the Shan down on something, and it was a huge nail. There could be none bigger. None he could think of anyway.

"You've made him very happy," Alex said.

"And he has given long life to millions of my people," Tei'Varyk responded.

"Billions in time," Tarjei said. "This is a huge boon to us."

"I can see that, but nothing is free. You're locking yourselves into exclusivity with Intellicorp."

"Not so," Tei'Varyk said. "The license will be for producing nanotech using Intellicorp's designs. We are grateful and will honour that deal, but there's nothing stopping us from taking what we learn and producing our own designs. It will take orbits... years, perhaps many years but it won't take forever. Besides, there are many uses for nanotech. We can reverse engineer and learn as we did after the first alien war. Merki equipment taught us much. Artificial gravity was one direct result."

Alex nodded. Tei'Varyk impressed him more and more. He had taken a long view regarding Hartman's deal. He was about to suggest they head over to the buffet table for a bite to eat when he spotted Ludmilla escorting Councillor Mindel toward him.

"I have something I would like you both to see," Alex said. "Councillor Mindel will be joining us."

"Of course. We'll be happy to view whatever it is."

Tarjei's ears flicked showing her agreement.

They wouldn't when they saw the content of what he had to show them, but he wouldn't say that. He shook hands with Nathan and introduced the Shan, though of course Nathan knew who they were from the Council chamber. Alex didn't think they had ever met socially however.

"Sorry I'm late. I'm in a rush today, but managed to pry myself loose for an hour."

Alex smiled, but didn't laugh at the obvious falsehood. "You're here now, that's what counts."

"Just for an hour I'm afraid," Nathan grimaced. "More meetings. You know how it goes."

Alex nodded and noticed Tei'Varyk's nose was twitching again. He nearly laughed then, but the thought of a possible Merkiaari incursion in progress in the Border Zone sobered him. Nothing funny about that. He waited while Nathan exchanged Shan handshakes with Tei'Varyk and Tarjei, and listened to the pleasantries as he asked after their well being and Tarjei's pregnancy. He exchanged a look with Ludmilla and she nodded slightly.

"Well," Ludmilla said. "I know Alex has something

important to discuss with you all. Shall we go to his office?"

Tei'Varyk picked up his cue. "A good thought. Let us attend to business so we might enjoy the rest of the evening without interruption."

Fat chance, Alex thought moodily as they left the ballroom and headed for the elevator. He would normally have taken the stairs. His office was on the second floor and exercise was good for someone who spent his working day sitting, but Shan didn't like stairs very much. They could use them, but tended to go down on all fours for comfort. Alex didn't mind, but it occurred to him their robes might encumber the process. So, the elevator.

* * *

7 ~ Consequences

The President's office felt ultra sterile to Alex. He was never comfortable here, and maybe that was the point. The place had no personality at all. It was a symbol of the Alliance Presidency as an institution, not the representation of a particular incumbent. He rarely used it for anything other than news broadcasts or official meetings where people expected a certain level of formality from him, but it was perfect for this discussion. It was a very secure room, and privacy trumped all other considerations right now.

Seating was a problem. He didn't have any of the new Shan seats, but Ludmilla didn't even pause. She went straight away to the sofas and pulled the cushions off. She dropped one on the floor and sat after offering the other to Tarjei. They sat side by side still chatting quietly. Tei'Varyk followed their example using the cushion from one of the armchairs, and to be sociable Alex did so as well leaving Nathan standing there frowning at the group. Unwilling to share the floor, he pulled one of the seats closer and sat, making himself the odd one out. Alex sighed under his breath. The man just couldn't help himself. Ever the outsider.

"Sorry about the seating," Alex began. "I'll mention it to housekeeping. We really should have some of the new ones here of all places."

Tei'Varyk laughed, his jaw dropping and tongue lolling. Alex smiled at the sight. Shan laughter was so contagious!

"We sit this way at home," Tarjei explained. "At home here on Earth and on Harmony. Your perches... *chairs*, feel very strange. I tried a stool once and nearly fell off!"

Alex laughed with Tarjei, imagining it. "But the ones in the council chamber work all right?"

Tei'Varyk nodded. "They were designed for our comfort. Your tables are too high for anything else to work well."

"Good. I can have a couple put in here—"

Nathan interrupted. "I don't have all night. If all you want to talk about is your office decor, I'll leave and let you get on with it."

Alex sighed.

Tei'Varyk bowed slightly to Nathan. "My apologies. Everything Human is of interest to me, even such a simple thing as preferring a chair over sitting upon the floor, but I often forget that to you it must all seem trivial."

Nathan flushed at Tei'Varyk's exquisite courtesy as if at a rebuke. "I was led to believe we were brought up here to learn something of import."

"All right, Nathan, I'll come to the point," Alex said and started from the beginning. "One of our warships, a heavy cruiser named *Warrior*, jumped into a situation in Helios." Nathan would recognise the system, but the Shan would need more. "Helios is a system without habitable worlds, but it's conveniently placed as a navy outpost. They use it as a refuelling point for our patrols out that way. There's a gas mining station there, but nothing else of interest."

"I understand," Tei'Varyk said. "I have studied your... *our* navy. One day, Tarjei and I wish to serve our people in space again."

"I'm sure you'll do well," Ludmilla said with a smile for Tarjei. "Perhaps your people will have survey ships soon. That was one of the things we promised to help you with."

Alex nodded. "It is one goal, but system security comes first my love."

"Always does," Ludmilla said with a sigh. "I wonder if we'll ever consider ourselves secure enough though."

Not with the Merkiaari still breathing, Alex thought grimly. "So, *Warrior* jumps into Helios as part of its anti-piracy patrol and finds two ships in its path. Very unusual. There was nearly a collision as both were at dead stop in the zone... that's the arrival zone."

Tei'Varyk nodded his understanding of the term.

Ships could jump outsystem from anywhere as long as they had their referents correctly locked in to their navigation systems, but they always arrived at the periphery of a given system because of the risk of collision. The navy might chance a micro jump in battle, but they offset the risk with recon data. Basically, they would jump short on purpose to avoid detection, recon the system, and then use that data to plot another jump that avoided collisions and maximised tactical advantage. Admiral Meyers had used exactly that method liberating the Shan.

"*Warrior* avoided disaster but learned that one of the ships was a pirate ship, a destroyer calling itself *Jean de Vienne* out of Kalmar."

"And the other?" Nathan said.

"A merchant vessel, *MV Astron...*" Alex hesitated but there was nothing else for it. "Out of Northcliff."

Nathan stiffened.

Tei'Varyk turned to Nathan. "My sympathies. May the harmonies watch over them."

"Thank you. Did *Warrior* save *Astron*?"

"It did, but the fighting aboard was intense. We lost

a number of marines, and some of the crew were killed defending their ship. I'm sorry, Nathan."

"This was recent I take it? I haven't received any news from home about this."

"Quite recent," Alex confirmed. "Captain Colgan... yes that Colgan." He nodded at Tei'Varyk's start of surprise. "Captain Colgan managed to disable the pirate vessel and board it with his marines. They captured the ship and began the usual investigations. One of those investigations discovered something extraordinary."

Alex went on and explained all he knew about Colgan's discovery and what was being done about it. Tei'Varyk was concerned about the Merkiaari, and didn't care that they'd arrived dead. He rightly assumed they must be active within the Border Zone or they would never have been aboard the pirate vessel. Pirates wouldn't be out exploring, they frequented places where they could raid colonies and stations, or jack ships. It was a foregone conclusion that *Jean de Vienne* had obtained the Merki from one of those places.

"What is Rawlins doing about this?" Nathan said.

"There's nothing he can do," Alex said. "We have a team out there now investigating. There's been no sign of an incursion, and no alert or shout for help. Until that changes all we can do is remain vigilant."

Nathan snorted and shook his head. "When will you admit that our current posture is wrong?"

"It isn't wrong—" Alex began.

"Come on! The danger is in the Border Zone, not the core. Our ships need to be out there actively patrolling and looking for the Merki, not hiding where it's safe!"

"Calm down," Alex admonished. "Yelling at me won't help matters. You know as well as I do that Admiral Rawlins is doing the best he can. We do have patrols and pickets out there. They're the ones who'll give warning. What good would it do for Fleet to race into the Border Zone when we all know the Merki can hit us anywhere they choose?"

Admiral Rawlins' strategic consolidation was designed the way it was because there was no way to anticipate a Merki incursion's target. The properties of fold space drives allowed ships to reach anywhere they want as long as they knew precisely where they were and precisely where they wanted to go. That's all. Two very accurate pieces of astrogation data and enough fuel is all that separated the Merki from any world. Even Earth.

The navy had prepositioned its assets to allow speedy responses to any incursion. It was extremely unlikely that the Merki would target one of those systems, but if they did, they would be annihilated. It was far more likely they would attack a less well defended system, and that's why Admiral Rawlins had argued strenuously for his current deployment. It allowed him to respond to attacks as quickly as possible with a sufficient force to win any battle it was likely to face. In that way he could cover most of the Alliance and keep response times down. But... and Alex was aware it was a big one, it meant the Alliance was forever on the defensive. Their people would die on worlds far away while the navy raced to reach them. There were just too many worlds to cover, and too few ships.

"Bring Fifth Fleet home!" Nathan snapped.

Tei'Varyk jerked, and his ears flattened in dismay.

Alex sighed. He knew it would come up, but he'd hoped for more time. It was an obvious move. They lacked the ships to cover more worlds. The answer? Bring home Fifth Fleet or build more ships. They *were* building ships all the time, but they couldn't build enough and crew them in time to make a significant difference to this event. Besides, Rawlins was right that deploying them in penny packets was worse than not building them in the first place. They needed ships in fleets to oppose incursions of the size they'd encountered last time. Throwing away ships and lives benefited no one.

"We can't do that, Nathan, and well you know it. We have a mutual defence treaty with the Shan."

"They're part of the Alliance now," Nathan protested. "No offence, Tei'Varyk, but your people need to assume the same risks as mine."

Alex winced. This wasn't going to be pretty, he thought, but Tei'Varyk surprised him and spoke calmly.

"When was the last time your world received a Merkiaari cleansing fleet, Councillor Mindel?"

Nathan flushed. "Never, but with the Merki in the Border Zone it could happen any day."

"My homeworld is still recovering from its second cleansing. I think my people are better prepared and suited to evaluate risks than yours are where the Merkiaari are concerned. Fifth Fleet is upholding the pledge the Alliance made to my people by protecting us and helping us with the reconstruction. The treaty is the only reason we are even part of the Alliance. Are you proposing the Alliance should go back on its word?"

Nathan calmed himself and took a deep breath. "No, that would not be honourable, but something must be done."

"Something is," Tei'Varyk said. "Within the year, reconstruction should reach the stage where my people can begin building new ships. Within two years, the first of those ships will be nearing completion. Within five, I believe my people will have replaced all the ships lost to the Merkiaari."

"So soon?" Alex asked.

"I believe so. It may even be sooner, but the lack of trained crews might slow their commissioning."

"What does it matter?" Nathan interjected. "We don't have five years or even one. We need ships now in the Border Zone looking for where those Merki came from."

Alex nodded. "Our investigative team is looking into that. As soon as they have a direction to follow, I assure you the navy will go and ferret the Merki out."

"If all the decisions have already been made, why am I even here?" Nathan protested. "I thought you were looking for input, not validation for decisions already made."

Here we go, Alex thought. "I want you to drop your attempts to rescind the Red One. With the Merkiaari in the Border Zone, you can see how foolish lowering our guard would be."

"And you think I can just wave a magic wand and have the proposal simply disappear? You're dreaming. Northcliff isn't the only world currently at risk from piracy, Mister President. The Border Worlds Party was created because we're all in the same situation. I can't just comm my party's members and say it was all a mistake and that we should now support the Red One Alert!"

"But don't you? Support it I mean," Alex said. "What else can we do now that you know all this?"

Nathan frowned. "I don't know. If I about face like that, I'll be replaced as leader of the party quicker than I can blink."

"The Red One isn't the core issue for your members, Councillor Mindel," Tei'Varyk said. "If I understand it correctly, your position is based upon fear of commerce raiders."

Nathan nodded grudgingly.

"Then rescinding the Red One is just a means to an end. You actually want more anti-piracy patrols, not necessarily an end to the Red One."

"Correct, but the navy refuses to free up the ships we need for that. The only way to get what we need is to go back to a peace time footing."

Tei'Varyk turned to Alex. "I believe you must put it to Admiral Rawlins that either he finds sufficient forces for the patrols that Councillor Mindel needs, or face the very real possibility that the Red One will be rescinded. Councillor Mindel is telling the absolute truth when he says his party will replace him rather than back down on this."

"But..." Alex began, but Tei'Varyk was right. He didn't need an empath's abilities to know that. He'd known it long before this that Nathan was barely hanging on to control of the beast he'd created. The Border Worlds Party was a powerful block in the Alliance Council nowadays, with worlds previously unaligned having joined it since the Shan incursion and the Red One announcement. "Paul is going to think I betrayed him."

"Not at all," Tei'Varyk soothed. "I shall speak with him myself about this. Perhaps something can be done to make him feel better about it. Squadrons of ships might be re-tasked to cover a wider area, but with overlaps so they might quickly recombine into units approaching fleet strength."

"You're talking about a major change in our stance. Splitting one of our fleets into squadrons or task groups is a huge deal for the navy."

"Mister President... Alex," Tei'Varyk said. "You are President, not Admiral Rawlins. It is a good thing that you try to accommodate his plans, but you are when all is said, in charge. Like Kajetan back home, yours is the final word of decision."

Nathan nodded. "He's right. With the Red One in effect we're on a war footing. You have the authority. If you do this, I think my members will be satisfied."

Alex snorted. "And you'll come out of this smelling of roses."

Nathan smile smugly. "That too. Of course I'll have to tell them how I had to talk fast, and how hard it was to convince you. With luck I'll still be leading the party this time next week."

Alex glanced to Ludmilla. She didn't look happy, but she eventually shrugged and nodded. "Very well, I'll do it."

* * *

Part II

8 ~ Planning Ahead

Ping!

Colgan looked up from the report he'd been reading on his comp. "Enter!" The hatch to his ready room slid aside to reveal Lieutenant Ivanova. "What can I do for you, Anya?"

She stepped inside allowing the hatch to close. "Have you got a few minutes to spare, Skip?"

He didn't. He'd been putting off the routine review of reports for too long. A big part of his job was reviewing and signing off on reports about ship operations. In addition to that, he needed to report in to his superiors regarding ship movements in his sector, including anything interesting that might point to raider activity; boring but necessary work, especially when they were due back in Helios tomorrow and needed to launch a drone to Sector HQ. *Warrior's* logs would be appended of course. Thank God he need do nothing regarding them. That side was all automated to prevent tampering. That thought reminded him that Anya had been working upon the data recovered from *Jean de Vienne*. Maybe she had something new on that.

He stood and headed for his little autochef. "Sit.

Coffee?"

"Thanks, Skip. White, two sugars," Anya said and sat. She placed the compad she'd been holding on the desk in front of her.

Colgan programmed the autochef and waited for the coffees to be dispensed. "How's the data search coming?"

"That's what I want to talk to you about. You remember the hassle I had accessing the bridge controls? Tait was one paranoid sonofabitch."

"Zelda fan," Colgan deadpanned and offered Anya her coffee. She took a sip. "How does his paranoia play into your work?"

"He encrypted a crap load of astrogation data. Not all of it, but that made me more suspicious not less. I mean, why encrypt certain data entries in simple navigation logs and not others? I thought there must be a lot of good stuff hidden there."

Colgan nodded and sat behind his desk again. "Go on."

"I concentrated on breaking the encryption. *Warrior* isn't too good with that sort of thing," Anya said ruefully. "She kicked up a fuss something awful; wanted to spit the data out rather than chew if you get my meaning?"

Colgan grinned. Foreign data, especially encrypted data like Anya described, would make *Warrior* think it was corrupted. The navy used encryption protocols that required keys to decrypt those kinds of files. *Warrior* of course had a full set of keys, but they wouldn't match anything from *Jean de Vienne*. In other words, the data packets would fail to match anything she ever expected to receive and would be rejected. There was a serious side to having her do that mostly linked to security and the Hacker Rebellion. Ship computers were designed specifically not to accept data exactly like the stuff Anya had been trying to force feed *Warrior* with.

"Gave her a stomach ache didn't you?"

Anya grinned and nodded. "She bitched and moaned,

but we got it done eventually. Seriously, Skip, I had to compartmentalise the data despite all the counter measures and firewalls built in to *Warrior*. She would have none of it."

"I'm glad to hear her programmers did such a good job. So, what have you found out?"

"A lot," Anya said and scooted the compad toward Colgan. "Names, dates, and locations of the systems Tait hunted in. *Jean de Vienne* was one busy ship. She was jumping all over the zone, Skipper."

Colgan nodded as he scrolled through the list displayed on the compad. Names of systems and the dates of arrival slid by. He paused as more data appeared. Ship names? He nodded as he realised it was a list of ships Tait had pirated.

"What's this last one?"

"That's the real prize," Anya said eagerly. "Tait visited that system multiple times, and there's a pattern."

Colgan frowned. "Pattern?"

"Like I said, this was all encrypted. The rest of the stuff we got from Tait's ship was left unsecured. I think the reason for that is what he did in these systems in particular. I've managed to match a system for each of the ships he jacked, but that one pops up again and again. I can't link it to any missing ships. He only jumps there after a successful attack. What does that say about his reasons?"

Colgan's eyes narrowed. "He was making a rendezvous for offload."

"Exactly, but not with a ship. I'm guessing that system is where Tait got paid, but if he was meeting another ship he would've needed to do it on a set schedule. He didn't. The dates are pretty random. No pattern I could detect there. So what's the alternative?" Anya said and quickly answered her own question. "Pirate base. Either a station or planet that buys the stolen ships and fences the cargoes."

Colgan whistled silently. If Anya was right, they had

a fantastic opportunity to put a major dent in the raider activity in this sector. Without customers and a way to resupply, pirate ships would suddenly find it less attractive to hunt here.

"Do we have anything on the base itself?"

Anya shook her head.

"Nothing in the sensor logs?"

"Nothing. I'm guessing again, but I bet whoever runs the place frowns on ships going in with sensors trawling and weapons hot."

Colgan laughed. In their position he would more than frown. He sobered at the thought of what he would do in their place. A base was an asset for all who made use of it. They would want to keep it safe. It would be well hidden and protected. He would have anti-ship defences on the station itself, or if it was a planetary installation, anti-air lasers and missiles. On top of that, he'd want ships patrolling the system for defence as well as a way to escape if it all fell in the pot. If he jumped *Warrior* into that, he could find himself seriously outnumbered.

He frowned in thought. *Warrior* could take any raider one on one. Even two on one seemed doable. She was a modern heavy cruiser after all. Most raider ships were antiquated older ships that were sold off by their governments to become trader vessels, or they'd been diverted somehow from the breakers. *Warrior* could take them, he was sure of it, but a system containing a pirate base could have dozens of ships visiting in addition to whatever defences it had put together. He couldn't risk his ship against an unknown threat of the magnitude he might be facing.

"We'll need some help on this one," Colgan said and Anya looked relieved. She must have feared her data would convince him to attack alone. "Collate everything you have for the drone. We'll launch it the moment we arrive in Helios. Work up a really good report, Anya. I want command drooling over your presentation. Get some possible scenarios in there," he mused trying to think of everything at once. "Make some assumptions. I want an attack plan based upon a station assault and one on a planetary base. Look up the last few times Fleet hit one of these things and work something up. I know you can't be sure what we'll actually face, but that isn't the point of this. I want Sector to send us reinforcements ready to kick raider butt and take names, not attack independently. This operation is ours. With reinforcements we can recon the system in force and work up a proper attack plan."

Anya nodded. "You want it tempting enough that they'll bite, but risky too, so they'll send decent firepower."

"Exactly. I have no doubt this op will give us a proper workout no matter the ships they send us. I'll need heavy backup." Colgan handed the compad back as Anya stood to leave. "I'll want to review what you come up with before the drone launch."

"Understood, sir. I'll make it tempting, but I don't want them arriving thinking they'll have it easy."

Anya left then and Colgan went to freshen his coffee before turning back to his comp and the reports he still needed to review.

Aboard Warrior, in the Zone, Helios System

Colgan racked his helmet beside his station and turned his attention back to his monitors. So, Helios again. The last time arrival had been a little too exciting for his peace of mind, but this time empty space greeted them. No jacked ships, no raider ships, and no collision alarms.

Good.

"Prepare for drone launch," Colgan ordered.

"Aye sir," Mark said from the comm shack. "Updating the drone now."

Colgan nodded. "Launch when ready, Sector HQ and 80%."

Mark worked his board, adding *Warrior's* log to the drone so that her safe arrival in Helios was reported along with Anya's analysis and the proposed assault on the pirate system. "Update complete. Destination Beaufort. Drive set to 80%. Launching... drone away... drone has entered fold space."

He nodded and turned his attention to Janice. "Helm, new course to Helios Station. I promised Captain Perry he could switch out the marine guard we left here."

"Aye aye, Skipper," Janice said, already working her controls and bringing the ship around. "On course to Helios Station. ETA around midday local at standard in system speed."

He checked the ship's chronometers and noted they'd already been synced with the beacon, part of Mark's job as communication's officer. It was a little after 0900 local time, so they had a few hours flight plus the usual docking shenanigans any ship had to undergo. 0.5 light was standard in system speed—approximately two thirds of *Warrior's* maximum. They didn't need to dash about.

"Very good. There's no need to stress anything."

The bridge settled down to normal daily operations for only a short time before Commander Groves reported unusual activity around the station. Sensors, like communications, had light speed limitations and although Alliance scientists continued to research other methods, nothing had yet been found that could circumvent those limitations in normal space.

"Unusual, Francis? Unusual how?" Colgan said.

Groves brought her sensor data up on the main viewer and overlaid it with her system grid. Colgan's number one monitor mirrored the results. He put Anya's tactical plot piped directly to her from CIC on his number two monitor, but relaxed immediately when he deciphered the IFF ship designations. They were all Fleet.

"A lot of heavy metal docked at the station, sir," Groves said. The cool blue icons of the Fleet ships started blinking on the screen. "Those are all *Excalibur* class heavies same as us." Two other ships started flashing, but alternating from blue to green and back to blue to make them stand out from the heavies. "Destroyers, *Vanguard* class." Another ship blinked counterpoint in dark green. "A courier ship, and lastly the ship on final approach is another courier ship."

"Helios has become a busy little system while we've been away," Colgan said and smiled ruefully. "I wonder what could have—"

"Incoming message, Skipper. Timing suggests it was sent the moment we were detected by the beacons."

He nodded. Someone had been watching for them to arrive. This should prove interesting. "On screen please."

The sensor data was replaced by a woman in uniform. He recognised Commodore Walder and frowned. She should be overseeing operations at Beaufort, not here. The discovery of Merkiaari aboard *Jean de Vienne* might account for the ships dispatched to Helios, but a bunch of corpses no matter their origin didn't rate the sector commander's personal attendance in his opinion.

"Captain Colgan," Walder began her expression hard. "You are ordered to dock your ship at Helios and prepare to meet with me aboard *Audacious* at the earliest opportunity. Depending upon the outcome of that meeting a court of inquiry may be convened to discuss your actions in this system, and the events leading to the deaths of Major Appleford and his marines. Walder out."

Stunned silence at the commodore's abruptness filled the bridge.

Colgan's thoughts flashed to the discussion he'd had with Captain Perry aboard Tait's ship. Commodore Walder had a personal interest in the outcome of any investigation, but pointing that out to her wouldn't be in his best interests.

She was his superior officer and the sector commander. As such, she not only had the right, but also the responsibility to investigate his actions. He could protest. He could insist another officer head the court marshal if it went that far, and he would, but he would much prefer it not come to that. He needed to think.

"Contact *Audacious* and acknowledge the order, Mark. Give them our ETA." He stood woodenly, knowing his face was showing too much but unable to help that. "XO, you have the conn. I'll be in my quarters."

"Jeff..." Groves began but then changed what she was going to say when he didn't stop heading for the elevator. "Aye, sir. I have the conn."

He entered the elevator and turned to face the doors. He didn't see the worry on his crew's faces as the doors slid closed. He was already going over the battle in his mind's eye, and trying to imagine what he could have done differently.

* * *

9 ~ Commodore

The marine guards at the bottom of *Warrior's* ramp snapped to present arms as Colgan's party walked by and onto the docks. Captain Perry eyed them and nodded in apparent approval at what he'd found. Colgan's lips twitched into a smile. Perry was very aware that his marines had some competition here on Helios. All the boarding ramps had marine guards except two. There were a good many fleet ships docked. The unattended ramps led aboard the two courier vessels.

Helios Station was a busy place this week. Vehicles and loaders hurried to and fro moving cargo to resupply the ships with food and other supplies, while other dockworkers monitored the pumps as the station refuelled so many ships at once. No captain would pass on such an opportunity to top off his bunkers. Helios might pump an entire month's production of LH_2 (Liquid Hydrogen) and ^2H (Deuterium) in the next day or so.

LH_2 was critical to spaceflight no matter the ship concerned. It was the main component in the fuel that all n-space drives used. Such drives were based upon the principles found within magneto-plasma rockets, and required great quantities of cryogenically cooled liquid hydrogen to produce plasma for thrust. A ship's fusion reactors produced the other component necessary for the drive to function, namely the electrical power used to create the intense magnetic fields required to both convert the fuel to plasma and direct its thrust. Luckily, DT fusion reactors used deuterium and tritium for fuel in much smaller volumes; they didn't need the same scale of bunkerage as the drives did. *Warrior's* reactors bred their own tritium, and Helios supplied deuterium as its second most important product. Deuterium could be refined from any form of water, which of course Helios had no problem producing. It was a hydrogen gas mine after all. All of which meant that Helios' industry was booming with so many ships docked.

Colgan and his party made their way along the docks taking in the bustle. The slip next to *Warrior* was empty, the telltale above the sealed hatch dark. The next was occupied by one of the courier ships, and the board was lit but no departure time was listed. They past another two empty slips, boards dark again and ramps fully retracted into storage, before reaching a ramp with marine guards. The board above the ramp announced the docked ship as *ASN Trojan*. If Colgan recalled correctly, it was one of a pair of *Vanguard* class destroyers in the system. They walked on by and Colgan grinned at Perry's satisfied smirk.

Perry explained when he noticed Colgan's raised eyebrow. "Slovenly."

That would be the day! No marine was slovenly in Fleet.

The next two ramps also had guards. *ASN Fury*—another *Vanguard* class destroyer—and *ASN Crusader*, an *Excalibur* class heavy cruiser the same as his own *Warrior*. Perry grudgingly acknowledged that the marines were competent.

"I hope you aren't planning on a critique when we go

aboard *Audacious*, Shawn," Groves said.

"No ma'am," Perry said but then grinned. "But word will spread."

"Scuttlebutt does tend to do that," Colgan agreed. "I would really appreciate it waiting to spread until just before departure. This is going to be touchy enough without petty rivalries getting in the way."

Perry nodded. "Do you think the Commodore was serious?"

"She wouldn't have said it if she weren't," Groves said. "Anya here will put her right. Won't you, Anya?"

Lieutenant Ivanova didn't look confident, Colgan noted, but she nodded. "With all the data I'm bringing, it will take her a week just to get up to speed on what really happened out here."

That was assuming she cared about what really happened. He wasn't confident that was the case and he cursed Perry silently for putting that doubt in his head. If he hadn't known of the Commodore's personal attachment to Major Appleford he would have considered this meeting routine, but he did know and his traitorous imagination insisted upon supplying all kinds of disastrous scenarios. That was why he'd armed himself with Anya and Perry, neither of whom had been invited to his meeting with the Commodore. Both had brought the data they needed with them.

In Anya's case, she had *Warrior's* logs, *Jean de Vienne's* logs, and *MV Astron's* logs detailing the battle and the time either side of it. She also had her analysis so recently dispatched via drone to Beaufort with her. Perry had a sampling of the recordings taken from his marine's helmet cams and his personal account of what happened that day. He had witnessed the ambush that killed Appleford and his marines. He had nearly been a victim of it.

The departure board above the next ramp announced their destination. *ASN Audacious*. The guards snapped to attention as they presented themselves, and the formalities were taken care of. It took less than a minute for their escort to arrive, *Audacious'* XO, Commander Healey. Handshakes were exchanged and Healey escorted them into his ship.

"Everything is set up in the briefing room," Healey said.

Colgan nodded, and assumed he meant the Commodore wanted to use the holotank and screens to help her understand the battle. He didn't at all expect what awaited him when the hatch slid aside to reveal her already seated with the senior officers of all the other ships. Francis shot him a worried look, and he tried not to return it, but knew he had failed.

He entered the room and came to attention. He saluted the Commodore as did those with him, but held the salute when she failed to return it, noting the disapproving looks Walder received. Whether she noticed or not, she suddenly stood and returned the salute. He lowered his hand and introduced his officers.

Walder nodded to each of them and gestured to seating. "Give Commander Healey your data. He'll see it uploaded for presentation."

Anya reluctantly handed Healey the case she'd brought, and took a seat on Colgan's left. Groves had the seat on his right. Captain Perry sat next to Anya after passing his case to Healey.

"Before we begin," Colgan said suddenly unable to wait any longer. "I would like to know whether I need counsel."

Walder's eyes flashed. "That remains to be seen."

"No, ma'am. I meant here, today. If I'm not on trial here, why have you convened five senior captains to hear my report?"

There were seven captains present, but two of them were junior grade and wouldn't sit on a panel of judges when the defendant was senior to them. To be absolutely scrupulous, Walder should rule herself out of any hearing, even when she could easily sit as president of the court, because she had links to *Warrior*. She had been her previous captain and known or not, she had a relationship with the now deceased Major Appleford.

Walder leaned back in her seat, as if at her ease, but her words were clipped. "I arranged this gathering for a number of reasons, none of which concern you directly. However, should a court be necessary, I find it convenient to have the components available."

"And so I repeat," Colgan said carefully. "Do I need my advocate for this meeting?"

"No you do not!" Walder snapped.

He surveyed the others at the table and nodded. "Thank you for the clarification, Commodore."

Captain Vardell of *Shannon* leaned forward and braided her fingers on the table. "While Commander Healey arranges the presentation of your data, could you give us a brief overview of what we'll see?"

Colgan looked for permission from Walder, being careful never hurt. She nodded for him to go ahead. "My tactical officer, Lieutenant Ivanova, has brought the logs of the battle from all three ships involved. In addition, her analysis of the data retrieved from *Jean de Vienne*—that was the name the raider ship was using at the time—has identified a possible pirate base—"

Walder sat up straight. "There was nothing about a pirate system in your earlier report."

"The data came to light only recently, Commodore. Anya has been working on decrypting the astrogation logs in her off time. She reported her findings to me while we were in transit to Helios. We have identified a system that may contain a base. I launched a drone to Beaufort with my updated report and logs upon emergence, Commodore."

Captain Narraway of *Audacious* nodded. "We detected the launch."

"In my report I requested reinforcement and permission

to recon the system Anya found, but now..." Colgan waved a hand at the captains. "I'm sure there's enough firepower in system to deal with anything we're likely to find."

The captains looked eager and hungry for action, but when they turned hopefully to the Commodore, they didn't receive the reaction they were hoping for. Walder was glaring. She hadn't been distracted from her goal of lynching him over Appleford's death. Well, no reason she should be. The pirate system could be dealt with by her after the court marshal. Colgan could almost see that decision crystallise in her thoughts as her face smoothed and she nodded.

"If the data supports it, I'm sure we can arrange something. Their demise must wait until after the current matter is dealt with, however." Walder turned to Healey. "Are we ready?"

Commander Healey nodded. "The Lieutenant already did most of the work, ma'am."

Walder's eyes narrowed. "The logs were tampered with?"

Anya hissed at the accusation, but Colgan's quick head shake prevented her denials.

"No ma'am!" Healey said surprised and dismayed. "I didn't mean to suggest... no ma'am. She indexed the files by time and ship name, and tagged them so that they would display correctly and in the correct sequence, that's all. She basically did my job for me."

"I see," Walder said sounding disappointed. "If you're ready? Begin."

Everyone turned their attention to the holotank as it came to life and the lights in the room dimmed. Anya had taken extra care with her presentation. Colgan was impressed with the artistic composition and her care in choosing the most important segments of the logs. She hadn't just dumped the entire log of each ship onto the data crystals, but had edited them together to create an entertaining show that also informed. The raw data was still available of course, but he hoped the show would go a long way toward lowering tensions and directing attention back to the job in hand: dealing with the pirate system and winkling out the location of the Merkiaari.

The holotank began by displaying *Warrior's* bridge recording with sensor and flight data beneath so that everyone could judge the ship's manoeuvres and the orders instigating them. The presentation inevitably began with *Warrior's* almost calamitous emergence at Helios. Anya had to start somewhere, but Colgan didn't care to relive the moment the collision alarms wailed. He was satisfied however with the reactions he witnessed. Even Walder started at the alarm. He furtively watched everyone as they watched the show, trying to gauge their reactions.

"Evasive starboard!"

Janice reacted a fraction of a second before the order was given. She slammed her stick hard over and pulled back, while at the same time goosing power to the anti-grav manoeuvring thrusters in the bow. The ship heaved up and around, still stooping upon the pair of ships in her path but at a shallower angle than before. The bridge crew yelled as *Warrior* sped by the ships barely missing them.

"Jesus god..." one gasped.

"Did you see that? Did you see? Did you? We nearly dinged the frigging—"

"Quiet! Trim us up, Janice, and someone find our damn referent. Let's be sure we're in the right system, shall we?"

"Aye, Sir," Janice said calmly.

"Scanning... referent attained. Helios system confirmed, Skipper," Groves said.

The holotank image changed splitting into two main windows. Whispered comments rose in the room as the watchers digested what was being shown. Colgan watched as Mark received the distress call from *MV Astron*, and informed him. His conversation with Captain Voyce played out, and then the important discussion between himself and Francis regarding a course of action.

"Hold the playback," Walder said and Healey paused the show. "You chose to assault *Astron* with your marines before neutralising the raider ship. Why?"

"As you see, Commodore," Colgan said waving a hand at the holotank. "I discussed the situation with my exec and we decided that a simultaneous attack was the best response."

"You risked the lives of all the marines you deployed. Far safer to take out the raider ship first."

"Safer for *Warrior* and her crew, certainly, but not for the crew of *Astron*, Commodore. You heard how desperate Captain Voyce and his crew were. They were barely hanging on and needed immediate relief."

Walder's lips thinned. "Adding more victims to those aboard *Astron* was not wise. In my view taking such chances with your marine's lives was a dereliction on your part."

There, she had said it outright and revealed her agenda. Colgan was almost relieved to get it out in the open. He took a moment to scan faces. Captain Narraway's expression was a match for Walder's. He was firmly in her court. He didn't know Luke Narraway at all. This was their first meeting. He had no reason to think the man was anything but competent, but without anything more to go on he had to assume Narraway would support Walder's opinions. Narraway was older than her by quite a bit, or he looked it at least. Silver haired and with a cadaverous face, he looked too old to serve, but that must be illusion or else he would have been forced to retire. It seemed likely that he couldn't go higher in the navy or he would have already. Colgan wondered what effect that had on his opinions. He obviously didn't begrudge her success. Maybe his own lack of promotion to flag rank didn't colour his opinions.

If he was any judge, Dave Paice of *Trojan* and Jase Hobson of *Fury* didn't side with the commodore, but then their opinions held less weight. Junior grade captains both, they wouldn't be called to preside over a court. Despite their lack of seniority, their support seemed more aimed toward him than Walder. He was grateful for any support in such a hostile environment, even if it was just sympathy for someone who had seen battle and lost men. If they were here to give opinions on what they saw, then he was pretty sure they were on his side.

The other four captains were a mystery to him as far as their opinions went. He knew two of them slightly, Louise Vardell of *Shannon* and Nick Kennedy of *Resolute*. Both were his age. They hadn't been in the same class at the academy, but they had attended at the same time. They were in the year ahead of him, and had been in destroyers before their promotions. They had seniority by way of time in rank, but his track had been different with less opportunities for promotion. He didn't care. He'd loved his time in the Survey Corps. He had no reason to expect anything but fairness from them.

And finally there was Ben Foden of *Constellation* and Stefan Crane of *Crusader*. Both men were older than him, but younger than Narraway. He didn't know them at all and didn't have anything on their backgrounds. He wished now that he'd looked everyone up in the database, but he hadn't expected them to be present at this meeting. All he knew was that *Crusader* and *Constellation* had been under their command and on station in this sector the longest. As far as he knew they didn't owe Walder any special favours, but they'd been with her longer. They might feel a bond. If not for the Red One, they would all have been part of a single task group with her in direct command probably using *Audacious* as her flag ship. As it was, they had independent commands, but still reported to her as Sector Commander. Her official station was Beaufort with the Red One in effect.

The presentation had already resumed when Colgan turned his attention back to the holotank. The battle had begun. He watched as Tait flushed his tubes at *Astron*, and noted again how well the drones intercepted them. The suicidal robotic machines gleefully threw themselves toward destruction, piling on the accel in an effort to intercept their chosen targets: Tait's missiles. He could almost imagine their computers shouting at each other as they tried to be the first to die.

"Mine! Here I go, weeeee!"

His lips twitched, but he managed to school himself. He didn't need Walder accusing him of not taking things seriously. Half the drones he deployed in that battle were recovered for later reuse, but those expended were well worth the cost. Something on the order of three million credits each, they had saved *Astron*, a ship worth many billions plus the lives saved—an incalculable saving. The navy would no doubt be grateful he had recovered half of his drones, but he would have deployed double the number and been happy to expend them all if it meant keeping *Astron* and his marines safe.

"Hold the playback again, please," Walder said. She had chosen the point in Anya's presentation where the holotank split its output to display *Warrior's* battle together with the assault upon the raiders aboard *Astron*. "Captain Perry, in simple terms can you give me an overview of the mission plan for the assault upon *Astron* as you understood it before it began?"

"Yes ma'am, I can do that."

"Proceed."

Perry swallowed and composed his thoughts. "Major Appleford briefed us before boarding the assault shuttle and during the flight. He included my... *his* noncoms in that. He was good that way."

Walder nodded. "Yes he was."

"The plan was simple on the face of it. The crew aboard *Astron* had control of two key areas, but they were hard pressed. Captain Voyce was holding the bridge, and that meant he controlled the cargo bay doors. He assured us that the raiders hadn't disabled them. As you can imagine, we were hot to get in there and establish a strong point. The Major planned to take control of the cargo bay, and leave a heavy weapons squad behind to hold it."

"And did you succeed?"

Perry nodded. "Yes ma'am. It was no contest at that point. The raiders retreated from the bay. They had to really. As soon as the bay door cranked open, they had to know what was coming." Perry glanced at the holotank. One of the views was from Appleford's helmet cam. "The Major ordered our heavy weapons squad to hold the bay and protect the back door. He wanted the shuttle protected and—"

Captain Vardell interrupted. "You seem to feel that decision needs defending. Didn't you agree with it?"

Perry looked trapped. He shot a look at the Commodore's face and then one at Colgan's. Colgan shrugged at him, trying to reassure and tell him just to be honest. It must have worked, because Perry bucked up and nodded to Vardell.

"It wasn't my place at the time, but no, I didn't agree. I wish I had objected, but I didn't. We followed the plan."

"Why did you feel, at that time, it was the wrong move?"

"I just did... I mean the Major had more experience and was my senior, but I didn't see the point in bringing a heavy weapons team with us only to leave it behind. The shuttle's protection was important, but if threatened, the pilot could simply have powered up and retreated outside to wait. I felt having Sergeant Barnes' squad with us was a better use of their firepower."

"I see," Vardell said. "Thank you."

"Why didn't you bring the matter up with Major Appleford before moving out of the bay?" Walder asked.

Perry looked down, wilting under her glare. "I should have ma'am. Looking back I mean, but the Major specifically ordered me not to take the initiative. I was to follow his orders to the letter."

A rumble of surprise swept around the room. Colgan knew the reasons, and wouldn't question that order now, but the others had to be wondering why Appleford had so little confidence in a captain junior to him.

"I know something of this," Colgan began, dragging attention to him. "Captain Perry was newly promoted shortly before this battle. Major Appleford wanted to ease him into his new post and the responsibilities that go with it. By giving Captain Perry clear and concise orders, Major Appleford took responsibility upon himself alone."

"Convenient," Walder muttered.

He stiffened. "It's on record, Commodore, if you doubt my word. And while we're on the subject of responsibility, Major Appleford and his marines volunteered to assault *Astron* while *Warrior* took care of *Jean de Vienne*. I asked him to volunteer and he did so without hesitation. He was a brave and honourable soldier, and so were... *are* his men. All of his men; and that includes Captain Perry."

Whispers and uncomfortable grimaces were exchanged among the witnesses of the developing feud. He was very aware he was on thin ice, teetering on the edge of insubordination, but it wasn't his fault that Walder chose to air the situation in public. She could have heard his report privately. She outranked everyone here and was responsible for how it would play out. She could clear the room right now if she wanted to, and none could gainsay her.

Walder directed her attention to Perry once more. "Is that correct, Captain? Were you asked to volunteer?"

Say yes, Colgan willed Perry. Say yes for God's sake!

"I was ordered to volunteer, ma'am. We all were."

Walder shot a look of triumph at Colgan. "Ordered?"

Perry grinned. "Its how we do it, ma'am, in the marines I mean. Major Appleford volunteered for the mission and then chose who would volunteer to go with him."

Everyone laughed at that, everyone but the commodore. "Seriously? That's what you want on the record?"

"It's what happens, ma'am. We can't really do it any other way when you think about it. It's not like we ever have solo ops. If we did, we could totally ask for a single volunteer, but for something like this..." he waved a hand at the holotank display, "...we can't have a situation where half a squad goes into battle while the other half stays home. It's just not workable."

Walder didn't look happy but she was a professional and could see the realities of the situation. She nodded. "Fine. Major Appleford chose you and your men for the mission. Let's watch the rest of the presentation. I'll have more questions for you after."

Perry nodded and they all turned to watch.

The holotank came back to life and they watched as Appleford led a squad deeper into the ship while *Warrior* continued her battle. All eyes were now upon the feed from Appleford's helmet cam and those of his men. The display provided a feed from Appleford, Perry, Barrass, and Barnes. All four were labelled with their names and a mission timer. Colgan stole a look at the Commodore's face when the ambush cut Appleford down and the feed from that camera faded to black. She appeared unmoved. The camera had continued to record of course, but the data was of no use from that point on. Perry hadn't bothered to include it.

"He's gone!" Sergeant Churchill snarled at Perry. "He's fucking goooone!" Perry's feed showed he'd been staring at Appleford's bisected body, but the sergeant wrenched him away from the ghastly sight and got in his face. "Get a fucking grip and take command! You're in command sir!"

"I err... sorry," Perry croaked, but then in a much firmer and more authoritative tone, "bring Barnes' fire team forward. Choose someone else to watch the back door."

The relief on Churchill's face was very clear on Perry's feed. "Aye sir."

"That was the point at which you took command?" Walder asked.

"Yes ma'am," Perry said as the battle continued in the background. "As you see, I order Sergeant Barnes to take out the ambushers at the barricade and gain us access to the junction."

"No prisoners?"

"I didn't specify, ma'am. I needed to gain the cross corridor to advance the mission. At this point I'm in no mood to negotiate. Later I was forced to do that, but at this time all I'm thinking about is getting my men into the backbone."

They watched as the heavy weapons team destroyed the opposition, and the marines advanced. The next important moment came when Perry divided his force into two assault elements. Lieutenant Barrass led half the men toward engineering, while Perry led his half to relieve Captain Voyce on the bridge. Barrass made excellent time. His men cleared compartments and corridors very quickly, rarely meeting resistance on the way to engineering. Perry wasn't as lucky. His advance abruptly halted when he confronted a strong and obdurate defence.

Perry spoke up unasked this time. "This was a key moment from my point of view, Commodore. I couldn't advance without taking heavy casualties, and retreat was of course out of the question. I consulted with Lieutenant Barrass and learned the raiders had taken engineering. I needed to move quickly, but according to my information there was no way to flank"

"So you opened negotiations?"

"In a way, ma'am. I asked them to surrender promising safety and good treatment. I told them my men were dealing with their friends harshly in engineering, which they were. Lieutenant Barrass recaptured engineering not long after this, and freed the hostages."

Walder nodded, watching the events play out. "*Warrior* disabled the raider at that point. Did Captain Colgan contact you?"

Perry nodded. "Lieutenant Ricks asked for a sit-rep. By that time we had accessed deck one and encountered the force attacking the bridge. Sergeant Barnes, together with reinforcements commanded by me, overwhelmed the raiders and relieved Captain Voyce."

"I've seen enough. Commander Healey, you can bring the lights back up."

The holotank display froze, and a moment later vanished as the lights brightened. Colgan leaned back and waited for some indication of what was expected of him. Captain Paice of *Trojan* attracted his attention and asked about the Merkiaari found aboard *Jean de Vienne*.

"Do we know how the Merki found their way onto the raider?"

"No, I've heard nothing yet," Colgan said. "As far as I know they're still aboard the raider awaiting dissection. I haven't been in port long enough to get an update. Do you know if the admiralty dispatched a team?"

Paice nodded enthusiastically. "They're working aboard the ship right now. The station doesn't have the facilities they need, and besides, they brought everything with them. It was simpler to let them work with the ah... the *artifacts* right there."

Colgan nodded. It was easier to maintain security too. "You've seen what we found then?"

"The Commodore was kind enough to let us view the remains. Amazing to see so many different aliens in one place and the Merki… big bastards aren't they? I mean I knew that; I still remember the first time I saw a picture of one when I was a kid, but seeing them laid out on a slab like that…" he shuddered.

Colgan's smile was grim. "Live ones are worse."

"I can imagine! All fangs and claws, with that shaggy grey fur of theirs… like a child's nightmare creature come to life. I wish I'd been there with you."

"We could have used you, Dave, no question. It was touch and go there for a while."

"I've read everything I can get my hands on about what went down. If you don't mind talking about it, I'd love to quiz you on the details."

"I don't mind. Everything has been declassified, but I don't think I can add anything that the newsies didn't already get out of me."

He hadn't much liked that part of what happened when *Canada* arrived at Sol shot to hell. The President had asked him to put a spin on the entire matter when the newsies got wind of what happened. He needed public support to prepare for the Merki everyone was sure were coming. For Tei'Varyk and his people's sakes, he had done his best. Since then, the Shan had joined the Alliance. The battle to liberate their worlds and their location had been declassified not long ago. There hadn't really been anything secret about *Canada's* part in the story anyway.

"I wish I could talk to Tei'Varyk. I have recordings of the speech he gave when he accepted his seat on the Council. I would love to hear his side of your battle with the Merkiaari."

Walder knocked on the table with a knuckle, bringing the meeting back to order. "Your exploits are well known, Captain Colgan. I'm afraid your adoring fans are unlikely to be as impressed with your recent performance however."

Captain Paice gasped. "Commodore! I must protest."

"Must you?" she said mockingly. "I suppose you must. A fan should support his heroes after all."

Paice's face reddened. "Despite your obvious wish to discover some fault in Captain Colgan's actions here in Helios, I find nothing to support your bias against him."

"Captain Paice, that's enough!" Narraway snapped angrily. "Apologise!"

"No, it's all right," Walder said. "I'm thick skinned enough to fight my own corner."

"Insubordination to a superior officer should never be overlooked, ma'am," Narraway said, disapproval thick in his voice. "It invites further ill discipline."

"I agree," Colgan said and received a look of betrayal from Paice. "Thanks for the thought, Dave, but I don't need anyone's protection. My decisions, good or bad, stand for themselves, as do the results of them. If I've made mistakes, I expect to be called to account."

"Very noble," Walder sneered. "Men die and you collect your medals, but you're ready to be called to account."

"Yes I am, Commodore. Should I contact my advocate after all?"

Walder's lips thinned as she polled the other's reactions. None but Narraway would look her in the eye. It was obvious that none of the others supported her in this. She looked at Colgan with hatred burning in her eyes. He was fortunate that *Warrior* wasn't her flagship. It would have been torture seeing that look every day knowing he had to take her orders.

He had made a lifetime enemy here and saw no way to fix it. She was his first. Others he knew had made enemies in their rise through the ranks, but he never had. He was as apolitical as a navy officer came. He didn't make enemies, he made friends. He stared into her hostile eyes wishing for a way to pacify her, but couldn't think of anything... well no, wait. Vengeance might go some way toward calming her.

"Commodore, if I don't need to prepare for a court marshal, may I propose we turn our attention to eradicating the scum who attack innocent traders and kill marines in this sector?"

Walder's eyes flashed and her nostrils flared as she inhaled sharply. The rumble of angry agreement swept the room and she nodded.

Colgan relaxed tight shoulders. "My tactical officer, Lieutenant Ivanova, has done a magnificent job with her analysis of the data we captured. With your permission, I would like her to make her presentation before we discuss ways and means."

Walder leaned back in her seat to listen as Anya stood to take Healey's place at the holotank controls.

* * *

10 ~ Stationmaster

The huge wheel of Helios Station hung in the blackness of space, turning majestically as Kate manoeuvred onto the right approach. Eyes closed and linked with *Harbinger* via her neural interface, she *was* the ship. It was like swimming in vacuum. No ship between her and the infinite black, no suit to hinder her movement. She had never felt as free as she did right now. Her legs were the drives, ready to propel her wherever she wanted to go. The nanocoat, her skin bathed in the solar wind. Her eyes were the ship's sensors. She saw everything!

Helios had become a popular destination only recently but already the navy was here in strength with a lot of heavy metal docked nose to station. She would have to be extra careful getting in safely. She could easily imagine what would happen if she miscalculated the angular velocity she needed to match the station's spin. Too fast or slow would have the ship next to her assigned docking slip sweep around and smash her like a bat hitting a baseball. Talk about out of the park! She looked around for obstructions and located another ship approaching from behind—a tanker, heading to the deuterium plant that the station controlled. It was gaining but she was on final and had right of way.

A nanosecond of thought was all it took to cycle through the spectrum and back to visible light. Another burst of pure thought, and her grav detectors reported in. No dangers detected. Another flicker of thought and her anti-grav thrusters in the bow pulsed slowing her. As if she'd raised her hands and pushed against an invisible wall, she felt herself slow, and judged the small rotation she had intentionally introduced into her motion as just about right.

Closer now, very close. She could see her destination with its docking collar, clamps, and umbilicals waiting. She kicked her legs and a brief pulse of thrust edged her toward those docking clamps reaching to embrace her. A push with her hand to one side... another... another... she drifted slowly forward and sideways. The docking collar was dead ahead. She had matched the station's motion. Ten metres, five... one.

Bang! Clang-thump!

"And we're docked," Kate said in satisfaction as the station grapples slammed home. She opened her eyes and turned to the others. "Hey, you think I have a future in the navy?"

Stone grunted noncommittally.

Gina laughed. "Sure, I'll recommend you for retraining. You'll make a good marine."

She growled. "I meant as a ship driver. This is a really sweet ride, you know?"

"Only the best for the General," Gina agreed. "Neural interfaces make everything easy."

"Think so do you?" Stone said. "Ever tried it in combat?"

"Well... no, but—"

"Take my word for it. It's harder."

Gina shrugged.

Kate was sitting at the helm controls on the bridge with the others, but she hadn't needed to use them the entire trip. *Harbinger* was equipped with neural interfaces throughout, meaning she could have flown it from her rack if she'd wanted to. Three of them had handled a class of ship normally crewed by twelve with ease. Gina had monitored environmental and the fusion room, while Stone handled engineering and the drives. Kate had preferred the helm and navigation, but could have performed any or all of the tasks needed to run *Harbinger*.

"I bet I could fly this baby on my own," she said in challenge. "I bet I could."

"Sure you could, as long as you swear off sleep," Stone said. "I wouldn't recommend it though. We're not all machine. We still need some sleep to function."

She shrugged. She'd gone without sleep before.

Stone pushed his couch back and away from his station and stood. "Let's do this and do it right. I had you pack full dress uniforms for a reason." He turned to Kate who hadn't risen. "I need you with me, Richmond. I know you want to see your brother, but when one of us falls everything else comes second."

Kate stood. "Mission first," she agreed reluctantly. She didn't begrudge giving honour where it was due. It was just that she'd been hunting for her brother so long, it was hard waiting even a moment longer. "But I'm seeing him today. I don't care if I have to wake up the entire station. I see him today."

"That's fine."

"We don't know our guy is dead," Gina protested. "I mean the beacon can fail. He could be in hibernation."

"That's rare, but it can happen," Stone agreed. "Depends on the kind of damage. We can hope, but I'm assuming the worst."

Kate agreed. Assuming the worst made all surprises good

ones. She joined her friends as they headed for the hatch.

Kate changed into her dress uniform and met the others at the outer hatch. Stone gave her an approving nod and keyed open the hatch. She noticed the lack of stasis tube and wondered about it briefly, but Stone brought it up as they descended the ramp toward the docks.

"One of us can come back for it," Stone said. "We've been invited to station offices to present our bona-fides."

Gina grimaced and rolled her eyes at Kate.

She scowled. "This isn't one of those greet the heroes type of things is it?"

"Yeah, I think so. Helios isn't strictly a naval station anymore even though it was built by the navy. I guess the civs are excited to see us in the flesh."

"Yeah?"

"Civilian contractors took it over almost thirty years ago and opened it up to traders passing through. Before that, the refuelling facilities were Fleet only and the place lost money hand over fist. Shame there isn't a habitable planet here for a colony. I think it makes a good profit now."

She smirked at his wistful tone. "Thinking about changing your line of work, Stone? Can't see you in trade myself."

"Ha-de-ha. You want to take a wider interest, Richmond. Blowing shit up is great, but building stuff is more important in the long run. Ask the General which he thinks should be the priority in the Alliance."

She had nothing to say to that. It was always easier to tear stuff down rather than build, but destruction was what vipers were designed for and supposed to do. She was good at it.

They stepped off the ramp and onto the docks. Gina took Stone's right side and Kate his left. The arrangement was automatic and they quickly matched stride as they marched along the docks toward a transit hub. Already their uniforms had attracted attention. Pedestrians and dockworkers stopped to gawk. The space black colour of their uniforms would have been enough on their own—navy shipsuits and dress uniforms were white—but the colourful ribbons and medals on chests together with the silver piping down the outside of their trouser legs told everyone something unusual was going on. The combination of black tunics and berets shouted their affiliation to anyone with even a little knowledge of military dress. Wearing full dress uniforms and medals caused surprise to sweep through the crowd as they progressed. She didn't acknowledge them. She kept her eyes cool and straight ahead.

The great wheel design of Helios Station was more than evident as they navigated the crowds. Kate had a good view of the dock as it curved up into the distance. She had seen the like many times, but it still made her think when she saw people and vehicles climbing an incline that never arrived. Walking the docks like this felt like walking on a level plane, yet if she looked back she would find that she had seemingly been walking downhill. She hadn't of course; she was navigating the inside of a giant circle.

Stations were massive constructions. The only things built bigger by man were the shipyards that handled construction of fleet carriers, super dreadnoughts, and the biggest merchant transports. The outer rim they were navigating had a diameter of over 5km, giving Helios the ability to dock and refuel most ships. The system rarely received visitors it couldn't accommodate in one form or another. It maintained its own small auxiliary fleet in the form of tankers and transports able to resupply ships that couldn't dock.

Kate's sensors reached out and pulled in data from her surroundings constantly. They did so automatically, trawling every spectrum and frequency for threat or data she may have set for the current op. In this case, she wanted anything mentioning the dead viper, the battle here in this system, or the prisoners taken and held here, flagged for her attention.

Any information regarding her brother had priority of course, but then it always did. She had set that particular priority the first day after enhancement, her first one, and she'd done so again when her new processor came on-line and she uploaded the backup of her old data. Thank God the damage to her old processor hadn't cascaded into her database. Hymas had run a full backup to storage crystals the day Stone dragged her broken and dying off the battlefield of Zuleika.

Kate kept her eyes moving, studying and cataloguing everything she saw. Her database drank it all in. To an outsider she probably looked like Stone's bodyguard, Gina too, but she knew the others were performing the same sweeps automatically. Stone might be, probably was, already in Helios' security net looking for information. She would be too, but later, and for a different reason. How else could she bust her brother out without getting caught? For now she let her systems access the net, but kept to public areas.

She glanced up, but the overhead gantries and support structures were lost to shadow and distance despite the huge lights suspended there. She cycled through infrared and back but there was nothing to be concerned about. She hadn't expected there would be, but her instincts were always to check. The gantries and whatnot up there made for a good OP for snipers. Most wouldn't think to look up. She wasn't most people. She took note of the massive section seals. They pointed to the station's origins as a naval facility. All stations had them, but blast doors designed as strong as these were intended to withstand more than decompression. Only those resupplying ships with munitions needed such strong safety measures.

She eyed the dock front stores and eateries wondering if she would have time today to investigate them. Plenty of bars with their neon signs advertising cheap prices and entertainment were scattered amongst them. They would cater to all kinds of interesting people. Crews from visiting ships, yes, but more importantly from her standpoint, station personnel. She had an interest in those, especially anyone working for security.

"So, Helios is entirely civilian now?" Kate said noting the marine sentries guarding some of the ramps. "What about security?" Stone shot her a knowing look and her face heated. Damn, he knew her too well. "Marines guarding the dock, see?"

Stone nodded with a small smile upon his lips. "Fleet follows its own procedures as always. Like I said, the station is civilian now; entirely civilian according to my research. They handle their own security. They have a proper system of courts to handle evil doers and drunks." He laughed at something he'd thought of but didn't explain.

"You researched the station?" Gina said in surprise. "Why?"

"Oh no reason," Stone said glancing sideways at Kate again. "You never really know what might come in handy in our line of work."

Gina snorted. "Spooks. You just can't help yourselves can you?"

"Knowledge is power they always say, and I've found that to be true. Besides, Richmond and I aren't spooks or Intel weenies anymore. We're much too dignified and official these days. Call us OSI operatives or agents."

"How about I just call you my friends, or vipers?"

"That works too," Stone agreed. "Don't think opting out of my section gets you entirely off the hook, Fuentez. We all go undercover eventually."

Gina shrugged. "I'll go where the General sends me and do what he tells me to do, but I don't have to volunteer for it."

"I didn't say that, but having the skills as a contingency never hurts."

"Maybe," Gina allowed.

Kate grinned. Gina would make a terrible agent. It wouldn't matter what cover or disguise she used, the moment she opened her mouth everyone within hearing would make her for military. Her personality shouted hard-nosed marine.

Their luck was in when they reached the transit hub. A pod arrived and emptied of passengers just as they reached embarkation. The three quickly boarded and almost immediately were whisked away into the guts of the station. They were the only passengers in the pod. Gina asked about the meeting they were headed for, but Stone didn't know much more than he'd already said. The Stationmaster wanted to see them, and you didn't say no to such personages. Stationmasters might as well sit on God's right hand way out here in the Border Zone. They were the highest authority aboard any civilian station, but in systems like Helios that lacked habitable planets, they governed like kings of old.

The trip through one of the spokes of the station to Station Offices took only a few minutes. Kate spent the time looking at the ships she could see through the tunnel's many windows as they blurred by, but her thoughts were on her brother. How could she get him to safety? Stone knew—he must know, that she wouldn't leave without him. His sharp look when she mentioned station security hinted that he was onto her. Of course he was. He knew her pretty well by now, as she knew him. Would he help? She frowned when she realised that she didn't know him quite well enough to bet her brother's life on it. She thought he would, but he had limits. She would do anything to save her brother, anything at all, but Stone would do nothing that harmed the regiment in any way. Normally she wouldn't either, but her brother was her one exception. She didn't think Stone had an exception where the regiment was concerned. As for Gina, it was telling that she didn't once consider asking her friend for help with this. Gina would give her life to save a friend, but Kate knew beyond doubt not to ask her to break the law.

They debarked from the pod and made their way to the Stationmaster's office. If they hadn't known they'd entered the hallowed halls of station administration, the people they encountered there would have clued them in. They all wore expensive suits, the style she thought of as bureaucrat chic—stiff collared like her dress uniform, but light grey and pinstriped in colour, crisply pressed trousers, and blindingly white shirts. Men and women all wore the same thing just like a military unit, and all wore the neural headsets that let them hold conferences in a virtual environment, but there the similarity ended. These people were a riot of colour and style in personal grooming. Orange hair, pink hair, no hair. Hair in stripes or patterns and not just on heads but also on faces. The General would have apoplexy if he saw this. She guessed that being bureaucrats and civilian at the same time must screw with their brains in some odd manner. They couldn't wear their accustomed clothes while working. The slashed open, colour clashing, near naked—in some cases—styles would be very distracting; so hair colour and style became their way of expressing themselves.

"That's a bit... *much*, don't you think?" Gina said nodding toward someone who was indisputably female, yet wore long thin mustachios. "Ridiculous."

Stone grunted. "Seen worse."

"Ah, you noticed our Genevieve I see," a man said as he quickly approached with a hand out to shake. "She only stuck them on to annoy her sister. It's her birthday. Twins you know."

Stone shook the offered hand. "We have an appointment with Stationmaster Favarro."

"He sent me to fetch you. I'm his personal assistant, Roger Dellani at your service. And you are Captain...?"

"Stone. These are Lieutenants Richmond and Fuentez," Stone said indicating each with a gesture.

"A genuine pleasure to meet you all." Dellani shook each of their hands unselfconsciously, obviously unconcerned with their killer cyborg reputations. Not always a given.

Kate studied and judged him as another bureaucrat, but not a silly one this time...

>_ White male, brown hair and grey eyes, 1.87m tall. 65 years old approx. Unarmed. Threat potential negligible. Addendum: slight limp in right leg, possible sporting injury within the last 24hours. Most popular sport aboard Helios: Gravball.
>_ Searching... no matches found.
>_ Search local database [Y]es/[N]o?
>_ N

Kate dismissed the data from her internal display. She had no interest in the staff up here. Security would be handled at a much lower level. She followed Stone as Dellani led the way to Stationmaster Favarro's office and saw them allowed through the outer office flunkies without delays.

They were met inside by a surprise for Gina. "James!" she squealed and Kate rolled her eyes. "What are you doing here?"

James hugged her and kissed her on both cheeks. "I'm with the team sent to study Jeff's latest find."

Jeff would be Captain Colgan of *Warrior*, Kate assumed. Her mission brief had that detail along with the basics of the battle and the discovery made afterwards. On any normal day she would have been snooping already—simple curiosity would have been enough. She never felt the need to justify herself, but if she had needed to, she had the best justification for breaking into secure data, *like ever!* A bunch of new aliens on a captured raider and no one knows where they came from? Come on! Even a saint would turn hacker given that incentive.

Stationmaster Paulo Favarro beamed happily at the reunion he had engineered. He wasn't what Kate had expected at all. He was old for one thing, like ancient old. She hadn't delved into his background at all, but judging by appearances he had to be well beyond his first century. He obviously didn't care to hide it either. Most would use body mods to suppress the signs, but he hadn't tried. Comfortable in his looks and his age, he had let his hair turn completely silver and his face to wrinkle. It actually made her uncomfortable seeing his senescence openly exposed. No one flaunted their age this way, or very few, but it did draw her attention like a grisly curiosity. Paulo Favarro emanated power. He was The Personage, The Authority way out here. Maybe it wasn't his age that made her uncomfortable after all. Despite her military career guaranteeing there would always been someone judging her actions, she wasn't a fan of authority. Probably something to do with coming from Bethany's World.

Yeah, I have issues. So what, who doesn't?

And another thing. The Stationmaster seemed content to watch the proceedings as if now that he'd set things in motion he wanted to observe the results of his power over them. She didn't like the thought. She would prefer that he come out with what he wanted from them, no matter what it was, so she could blow him off and get on with saving her brother.

James shook Stone's hand and then approached her. "Looking good there, Kate," he said peering into her eyes. "They match."

She grinned and let him hug her briefly. "Yeah. I kind of insisted on that. They're both new from the same batch as my old one. Like 'em?"

"I do. What did you do with the eye patch?"

"It's on the wall above my rack in the barracks. A trophy, sort of."

James nodded. "I have my beamers in my kit. They're not really trophies like you mean. Actually, I'd prefer not to remember some of the stuff I saw, but I can't shake the feeling I might need them again. Stupid I guess, but they make me feel safe."

Kate nodded. Didn't sound stupid at all to her. "Considering why we're out here, bringing them along was a good idea." She wondered if he'd thought about reloads. Shan beamers couldn't use standard power cells. "Who else is with you?"

"Not the whole team. Janice, Bernhard, and Brenda are the real show. I'm just here because Brenda is. We've kept things small this time around."

"Just the four of you?" Stone said, sounding surprised.

Kate agreed. It sounded too low key for the kind of discovery they were here to study. Surely three new alien races rated more?

"Oh no, I meant from our original team. No, we have more. Two teams, sort of, with Janice in charge of both. The other team handles all the lab work as well as the autopsies and dissections. Med techs most of them."

"Autopsies," Stone said in a hard voice and James looked away. "Of the aliens?"

"Well... no. Not just the aliens, no."

Stone's eyes flashed rage, but Kate was the only one to notice. She easily guessed what he was thinking. When a viper went into hibernation, their bots held their cells in stasis allowing repairs to be undertaken, but outwardly they would be dead. Vipers in hibernation didn't breathe or react like a human in a coma would for example; they were more like a machine that had been switched off. With the right nanotech diagnostic tools, a medic could figure it out, but had they even checked?

God I hope so.

"I'm sure they know what they're doing," James said

plaintively. He had seen Stone's reaction now and realised its source. "They know what they're doing, Stone."

"You know that, or you hope that?"

James didn't answer, which was answer enough.

The Stationmaster intervened. He finally rounded his desk and came forward to shake hands. "Well, I'm very pleased to meet you. You're the first vipers I've met in all my many years. I'd begun to wonder if I ever would."

"Is that why we're here, to indulge your curiosity?"

"Richmond," Stone growled in warning.

She shrugged. "Just asking."

Favarro chuckled. "Yes indeed. Of course as Stationmaster I do have certain privileges such as welcoming visitors personally should I choose."

Kate remained wisely silent this time and Favarro laughed at her. Her annoyance edged toward anger, but she stomped it flat and held it down where it squirmed and fumed wanting the release only action could supply. Who said she had no self control? Stone had more than once, but he nodded approval of her restraint this time despite his own impatience with all the grandstanding. They had to have Favarro's goodwill while aboard his station unless they wanted to threaten violence. Out of the question of course, not that violence would get them anywhere had it been an option.

Favarro was still speaking...

"...vulnerable here The Red One alert has stripped my sector of naval protection. The ships currently docked will leave soon and Helios will be left without protection again. We've had a battle right here in system for the first time in thirty years, next time the station itself might be threatened."

"What do you expect me to do about it?" Stone said. "I have no say in how the navy runs its patrols."

"I realise that. I've had representations from my citizens asking me to approach the navy to request a ship be left on permanent station here. We both know that isn't going to happen."

Stone nodded.

"That leaves the other option. It's unlikely a raider would fire upon my station; they want money and goods to sell and that requires them to board and take what they want. If we had marines stationed here—"

"I'm not a marine."

"No, but you have influence, or your general does," Favarro said. "I've already sent drones requesting a battalion of marines be stationed here on a permanent basis. Our biggest customer is the navy after all. I approached Commodore Walder about this only yesterday."

"And she said no," Kate said.

Favarro turned to her. "Not precisely, but it adds up to the same thing. She said she couldn't spare any of the marines she had on hand, but that she would pass my request along. I think her exact words were that she would *pass it up the chain* so to speak."

"Well that's that then," Stone said. "You don't need me. The Commodore will see it's taken care of."

"She was very dismissive of me and the idea, as if I were just an annoyance and Helios only here to serve her." Favarro's eyes glittered with his affronted anger. "I doubt she will pass my request along, but if she does she won't endorse it. She may even sabotage it."

"Why would she do that?" Gina interjected. "Making Helios a marine post doesn't affect her command adversely, it enhances it."

Stone nodded. "It would give her some form of authority in this system where currently she has none."

Favarro raised a hand and let it drop. "I know, I know... I made that point to her myself. Don't get me wrong. I don't want her meddling in my affairs, but the safety of my citizens comes first. I think it may be a matter of principle for her. She just doesn't like it that Helios is a civilian station and thinks we should hire mercenaries."

"She said that?"

"Not in so many words, Captain, but that was my impression."

Kate didn't much like the idea herself. Mercenaries—honourable companies properly registered on Arsenal—had their place, but she didn't think Helios was it. "I'm going to go out on a limb and say you don't agree with her, and that your citizens are horrified by the idea."

Favarro grinned.

"Thought so." She looked the question at Stone and received a shrug in return. "You think a report to General Burgton along with our recommendation might ah... grease the wheels with the navy?"

"General Burgton does have influence with the President. If he were to champion my cause...?"

Champion his cause. *Right!* She didn't quite snort but she wanted to. Stone however was giving the idea serious consideration. Before she could think of a reasonable response, he had taken over the conversation.

"My mission has no bearing on your situation here, but I'll add this to my report."

"Thank—"

Stone interrupted Favarro with a raised hand. "No, don't thank me. All I'm promising is a report to the General. That's all. It will be his decision whether to take your problem to higher authority."

"I understand," Favarro said.

Kate could sense from his apparent satisfaction that he really didn't. He seemed to think the General would automatically side with him once made aware of the situation; that wasn't a given. As far as she could see, the regiment should stay out of it. This was a civilian matter, or at most, a dispute between civilians and the DOD. No matter what Favarro thought, Commodore Walder didn't have the authority to set up new marine bases whenever or wherever she felt like it. At most, she could detach elements under her command for temporary duty, but even then she had to justify her decision to her superiors. A proper post would need budgeting and planning approval from navy department planners, but before that the DOD itself would need to agree there was a need for a marine presence here and get the admiralty on side as well. Kate didn't see that happening. After all, before the Red One alert changed things, the navy had deployed Walder's command to *patrol* the sector rather than set up bases. The admiralty must feel a mobile defence was a preferable and more economical way to protect Helios and the sector.

Well, Favarro could think what he wanted as long as it got them out of his office and back on mission. She was getting increasingly impatient and wanted to see her brother, even if it was with bars between them. Just seeing him alive, in the flesh rather than in her imagination, would go a long way toward settling her down. Before Stone's revelations regarding her brother during her recruitment on Luna, she'd had nothing but her personal belief that he was alive to sustain her. She had always believed he lived, but years of searching had not found him. Now they were on the same station mere hours from a meeting long overdue.

She couldn't wait... but had to. She scowled.

Stone noticed of course and moved to bring the meeting to a close. "I'll send a drone with an update once I've seen our man. If there's nothing else?"

"I can arrange a drone launch for you right now," Favarro said eagerly. "No need to use your own. Helios is more than happy to cover your expenses."

Favarro was pushing, but he would get nowhere with this. Yes, drones were expensive but Snakeholme's location was classified. There was no way Stone would allow anyone access to that data. *Harbinger* was a courier ship and faster than any drone, but it did have limited drone storage. It was one of the modifications the regiment had made so that the General remained in contact while away from home.

"That won't be necessary. Now, if you'll excuse us we need to get on with what brought us here."

"Of course, of course!" Favarro said, hurriedly backing off as he sensed he'd received as much as Stone was willing to give. "It was an honour meeting you all. Please don't hesitate to contact my office if there's anything I can do to help."

Stone nodded and they took their leave.

About damn time!

* * *

11 ~ Fallen

James accompanied them in the transit pod back to the docks, chatting with Gina about their friends and catching up with each other. Kate listened without commenting until he dropped his bombshell.

"You got hitched!" Kate said in surprise. In response he raised a hand to display his wedding band. Very traditional of him and very old fashioned. Few displayed marital status anymore. "Who to?"

Gina snorted. "Oh come on, Kate. Who do you think? Brenda wouldn't let him get away."

James chuckled. "You're right there. I wanted to marry her but would have accepted cohab if that's what she wanted. I didn't get the chance to ask. She proposed the day we landed back on Earth at the spaceport! I said hell yes, and we took another flight straight to New York to meet her parents."

"That must have been..." Kate frowned. "Interesting?"

"Intimidating more like," James said. "Her parents are great, really great, but they were suspicious of my intentions." He laughed as he remembered something about his first meeting with them. "Brenda did warn me with stories about them. I thought she was exaggerating, but no, she really wasn't."

"How so?"

"Elaine, Brenda's mum, is a school teacher. She loves working with kids, and wants more grandchildren. It was major source of contention between them for years. I think Elaine had already written Brenda off as a source of more grandchildren but Brenda's sisters have been... ah, *prolific* let's say in this regard." James grinned. "Elaine was very excited when she met me. I had to promise to supply her with at least two new grandchildren before she would get off the subject. You should have seen Brenda's face when Elaine started giving me tips that she says will guarantee a pregnancy in short order. I thought Brenda would burst a blood vessel when I promised to start practising right away!"

Kate laughed. "What does her dad think?"

"Daniel looked a bit sick, to be honest. He muttered something about emigrating to the Border Zone for some peace, and disappeared into his den."

Gina grinned. "What does he do?"

"He's a doctor working in the local med centre. I think it was his influence that got Brenda started in biology. I don't think either of them thought she would detour into exobiology and make that her career. That's Brenda for you, always doing the unexpected."

"Stowing away that time on your shuttle could have been called doing the unexpected, but I'd call it ballsy," Kate said. "Arguing with the first Shan any Human had ever met for shooting you took guts. How is Tei'Varyk doing by the way? Last I heard he'd accepted his seat on the Council."

James nodded. "He and Tarjei are doing great. He did take his place on the Council, you're right about that. Everything was going well last I heard, and Tarjei was expecting her first cubs. She's due any time now."

"What is it with babies around here," Gina grumped. "Is everyone thinking about getting knocked up?"

"Well I'm not!" Kate said.

"Me either," Gina agreed.

Stone laughed under his breath. "Don't look at me. I don't have the right equipment."

These days none of them had the right equipment. All vipers were sterile, a consequence of the enhancement process. It didn't bother Kate at all. She would have made a terrible mother. Actually, she was pretty sure she'd been born without the maternal instinct gene. Gina wasn't like her though and would have made a great parent. She already mothered her men and treated them like her kids most of the time.

The pod began to decelerate as it approached the transit hub at the docks, and Kate looked to Stone for direction. She wanted to get out of the straight-jacket she was wearing and back into battle dress, but they needed to retrieve their man first.

"Want me to fetch a cryo unit?" Kate asked as they debarked.

Stone shrugged. "If you want. We'll meet you at the ramp."

"Good deal."

Kate hurried away, not jogging but walking with serious purpose directly for the ship. Well before reaching *Harbinger's* ramp, she used her neural interface to unlock the hatch and open it. She went directly to the cargo hold. They had three of the regiment's cryo units aboard locked down and ready for use. She quickly unclamped one from the deck and powered its anti-grav. She ran a diagnostic on it, deftly using the controls to make sure she didn't waste time bringing a bum unit out of storage. The unit's computer reported all in the green, and she manoeuvred it into the elevator.

Stone and the others were waiting at the bottom of the ramp for her when she reached the airlock. She ordered the hatch closed and locked behind her via neural interface, and guided the cryo unit down the ramp ahead of her. Stone led the way along the docks passing the marine sentries guarding the other ships. *Jean de Vienne* was docked just beyond *Audacious*. It also had marine sentries guarding the access ramp, but the unit patches on their uniforms indicated they were *Warrior* crew. James took the lead; they knew him and let him through with barely a glance. They did ask for ID from everyone else despite recognising their uniforms, but they had the grace to look embarrassed about it. Kate felt that was unnecessary. They were doing their jobs and doing them right.

James led the way into the ship. "We've kept all the artifacts aboard for security reasons, but we did move the bodies from the boat bay to medical. There are stasis units there in the morgue and well... the autopsies and dissections can be handled better in there close to the labs. The raiders didn't have much in the way of lab equipment, but the facilities were basically sound. We just brought our stuff in and got to work."

Stone grunted.

"I'm still not receiving a beacon," Kate said. "Maybe it really did fail."

Gina nodded but Stone gave no reaction.

"Brenda and Janice are using a conference room just along here. They would love to see you again—"

"Later," Stone said. "Take us to the morgue."

James nodded.

The morgue as expected was located close to sickbay within the medical department. Medical included the labs where the technicians and doctors James mentioned earlier were working. Their arrival caused a stir. James led them through the gathering crowd, ignoring the whispered questions, and into the morgue where the cadavers were being stored in stasis. He unerringly chose one of the chambers arrayed along the wall opposite the door, and punched one of the controls. The stasis unit slid out of the wall.

James stepped aside, grim faced, obviously expecting a strong reaction. The crowd had followed them to the morgue, but had stopped just inside the room. A hush fell over them as Stone approached the stasis unit. Kate parked her burden and joined Gina to flank Stone. She heard his indrawn breath just as she reached him, and her heart sank. He must recognise the fallen unit. He might even be responsible for sending him out this way.

Stone stared through the transparent cover of the stasis unit at the body within. His face... Kate hadn't expected to find what she saw on his face. It was shock, not sadness or pain. He was shocked immobile by what he'd found and she didn't understand that. She turned her attention to the contents of the stasis unit and knew right away that although the beacon had obviously failed, there would be no resurrection for this man. He'd been killed instantly with a solid shot to the head. She couldn't be certain about the weapon used, but there was very little charring, almost none. It had definitely not been a pulser or other energy weapon in her expert opinion.

There were many possibilities, but an HTR (Heavy Tactical Rifle) like her own preferred Steyr 7.62mm TacSix would produce results just like this. Then again, a Merki gauss cannon could cause similar damage if the blow were glancing. She could see the setup from a sniper's point of view clearly in her mind's eye. He had been targeted from somewhere to his front and below his elevation. One shot and he was done, but it didn't explain how he'd come aboard a raider ship. It also didn't explain the aliens and other Alliance soldiers.

Kate took the time to properly examine the body. The only injury she could detect was to his head, but there was massive trauma. The right side of his head was missing from just above his cheekbone extending up at an angle to the back of his head, leaving the remains of the left hemisphere of his brain exposed. Lucky for them in a way, because his processor might still be intact—viper processors were located deep within the brain on the left side. If it proved to be intact, downloading his logs would be a snap. If not, the data would be harder to recover but not impossible back on Snakeholme. The doctors would need to physically access his memory crystals—they couldn't be removed safely outside of an operating theatre, located as they were in the chest cavity protected by plasteel armour directly behind the breastbone. She knew the process. Hymas had backed up her data in a similar way, not removing them in her case, but using a hard wired connection to the crystal's interface while under local anaesthetic to backup their contents.

Kate frowned at the classic Y incision left behind by the doctor performing the autopsy. What had he been looking for when the cause of death was obvious?

"Stone?" Gina said gently. "You knew him?"

"Yeah," Stone croaked. "I knew him... a long time ago. This isn't possible."

Kate glanced at Gina who shrugged. "What isn't?"

Stone took a deep bracing breath and straightened. "Where's his uniform?"

"I'll get it for you," James said and hurried away.

"What's the deal, Stone?"

"There's something screwy here," Stone said, keeping his voice down. "He's one of the units listed MIA from round 2 at Forestal—the second Merki incursion of that system. He was my CO back then, Captain Degas 3rd Battalion Charlie Company 501st Infantry. He... Tony was lost in one of the many dustups we had back then, and we couldn't recover him. The Merki hit us hard with reinforcements from orbit and overran the ground he was defending." Stone sighed and looked back at his dead friend. "When we finally kicked their butts off the planet and started the cleanup, a few units were unrecovered. We assumed their bodies were destroyed by arty or the air-strikes we called in. The General was one of Tony's LTs back then and was promoted to fill his slot. This was a few months before his Garnet op. You know the one I'm talking about?" Kate and Gina nodded. "They were best friends, a bit like you two. Recruited together, fought together... fuck, he's going to need to hear about this right away. I'll have to send that drone sooner rather than later."

Kate hesitated. "You think you should?"

Stone's eyes narrowed. "Why not?"

"Just wondering what there is to say about it. We have nothing but his name to tell the General. How did this guy get here and why? We don't know. Who are the other soldiers with him? We don't know. How did the aliens get—"

"I get the picture," Stone said with a frown. "Maybe you're right. Okay, I'll give it a few days. We need more information, you're right about that. Tony being here means at the very least that the Merki captured him, or recovered his body. That's unprecedented. Merki kill, that's all they've ever done. They don't take prisoners—ever."

Kate nodded. That was well known. No quarter was asked or given by either side.

James came back into the room with a folded viper uniform in hand. He wasn't alone. The man with him was wearing scrubs, obviously one of the doctors James mentioned earlier as part of the team. James handed the uniform to Gina and introduced his companion.

"Captain Stone, Lieutenant Fuentez, Lieutenant Richmond, meet Doctor Harvey Borthwick."

"You can't take this specimen!" Borthwick said, glaring at them.

Kate felt her hackles rising and missed the signs. Gina didn't, lucky for Borthwick. Stone had hardly moved when Gina slapped a restraining hand on Stone's chest hard enough to rock him back on his heels. The surprise on his face was enough to make him hesitate and regain control of his temper.

Meanwhile, Gina had taken firm control of the situation.

"You will be releasing Captain Degas into our care, Doctor," Gina said coldly but calmly. "In addition, you will turn over to us all recordings, notes, and relevant materials used during his autopsy including blood and tissue samples. I shouldn't have to remind you that viper construction and technology is classified ultra secret, and is covered by the Alliance's Military Secrets Act, a document you are required to comply with or face incarceration. I suggest you read section 56, sub-section 5a paragraph 18 of the AMSA. I believe it's titled 'Military Applications of Cybernetics and Nanotechnology'."

Borthwick spluttered.

Gina handed the uniform to Stone. "Kate, if you'll help Stone dress the Captain, I'll go with James and Doctor Borthwick to collect any samples they may have. James?"

James looked at Borthwick and then back to Gina. "Ah... I guess... follow me?"

Kate grinned at Borthwick who hesitated to follow as James showed Gina the way to the labs. He finally realised the inevitable and hurried to catch up with them and the crowd at the door dispersed.

"That was unforgivable," Stone muttered. "I nearly—"

"Don't beat yourself up. I nearly ripped his head off myself, and I'm faster than you. If anyone had killed him, it would have been me."

Stone snorted. He looked at the battle dress blacks he held and shook them out. The collar and right shoulder of the uniform was stiff with dried blood and less savoury things. He sighed and turned to the stasis chamber.

"Open this thing up and let's get going. I want him safely aboard *Harbinger* ASAP. We have some information to gather and a drone to launch. I've got to wonder how many of our lost units were actually taken by the Merkiaari."

"Yeah, I was thinking about that," Kate said as she

worked the controls to shut down the stasis field and open the chamber. "I heard that the Merki we took home were freaks—"

"Genetically engineered."

"Like I said, freaks."

Stone rolled his eyes. "We've always known that Merki troopers were engineered. The new model troopers we fought for the Shan were no different in that. They're just new and improved."

"That's my point. The Merkiaari we fought were more intelligent but just as big and strong as the ones you fought before. Right?" Stone nodded. "Well then, they didn't use anything they learned from captured vipers against the Shan... maybe our tactics, but certainly not our cybernetics or nanotech."

Stone frowned. "You're right. I wonder why not."

She leaned into the chamber and lifted the body out. Stone quickly dressed it allowing her to transfer it to the cryo unit they'd brought with them.

"You want me to head back to the ship?"

Stone hesitated.

"You could hang here and view the other bodies. We need to start figuring out how the hell they ended up here in the Border Zone."

"No, we'll head back together. I know you want to see your brother, Richmond, but let's do this right. I promise to let you go the moment we get back aboard *Harbinger*."

Kate's lips thinned in annoyance but she stopped the protest she wanted to voice. Stone wasn't going to change his mind. There was no point whining about it. While they waited for Gina to return, they busied themselves poking into things. Kate started it after closing and storing the now empty stasis chamber. She opened the one next in line.

"Take a look at this ugly bugger!"

Stone came over for a look. "He... it? It might be a real

good looker to others of its kind," he said doubtfully. "I wonder what they call themselves."

"Greys," she said sagely. "Zelda's fan club has known about them for ages. They built the Chaos Engine."

Stone sighed. "This is serious stuff, Richmond."

"I am being serious." She grinned. "Didn't I read about aliens visiting Earth way back?"

"Myths and legends. Those stories started before Mars was even colonised. Nothing was ever proved as far as I know."

"As far back as that? I didn't realise."

"Yeah. We only had the homeworld back then, over populated and running out of resources. Mars was a fluke. The terraforming project was a desperate attempt to solve some serious issues. It nearly didn't happen at all. The cost was staggering, but luckily we had some visionaries who pushed on despite the do-gooders insisting the money would be better spent on increasing welfare budgets. It worked out and we gained another world full of resources at a critical time in history. If not for Mars, we wouldn't be here today."

"By us you mean vipers?"

"I suppose so, but I meant Humans in general. We would have wiped ourselves out. When someone else has what you need to survive, war is the result. Think about all the little wars and revolutions you've ever heard or read about happening in the Alliance, and then imagine all of them happening on one planet. That was Earth before colonisation began."

Kate whistled silently. Stone was right; they were lucky it had worked at all. No one bothered with terraforming any more—the process was too expensive and too long term an investment. The invention of foldspace drive meant there were plenty of habitable planets for colonisation within easy reach with more discovered every year.

Stone stored the alien and moved to open another chamber. He grunted when a Merkiaari trooper was revealed.

A big one. Female then, Kate thought looking her over. The monster was unclothed but without getting more touchy-feely than she felt comfortable with, she decided its prodigious size was enough to mark it as female. The shaggy grey fur hid details of her anatomy, but she took particular interest in the creature's chest and the wound that had probably killed her. The burnt fur and cauterised hole on the left side was classic pulser damage. Stone closed the chamber.

Together they had time to investigate the entire contents of the morgue taking particular interest in all the different types of alien. No two were the same race except for the Merki. Each type was distinctly different in colour, size, and shape. One had a human-like face—two eyes, two ears, one nose and mouth—the other two didn't resemble Humans or Shan at all. The Grey had a horribly flat face without a nose. Kate made a point of scanning everything with her sensors so that she had as complete a record as she could devise without using proper medical scanners. She did notice something significant. None of the new aliens, unlike the Humans and Merki, had died by violence. There were no obvious wounds at all, and she wondered why they were dead. She did notice some scarring around throats, but upon closer inspection decided they hadn't died of strangulation. She didn't know what had caused the pale band of scarring, but it didn't seem likely as a cause of death.

Gina finally arrived and she was *pissed!*

"What's up?" Kate asked her friend, taking the sample cases and stowing them in the cryo unit's storage compartment beneath the control panel. "They give you trouble?"

Gina growled something under her breath. "James is keeping Borthwick away from me. Lucky for him."

"Oh yeah?"

"The fu... the good doctor tried to hide some of the blood samples. I don't know what he thought he would learn, or what good it would do him, but I got them all in the end.

Sorry I took so long. I had to go through the video record of the autopsy to make sure I didn't miss anything before I deleted it."

Kate remembered her thought regarding Degas' logs. "They didn't extract his memory module did they?"

Gina's eyes hardened. "No. I checked for that specifically."

"You did?" Kate said. Gina's forethought impressed her especially as she'd only just thought of it herself.

"It was my thought that Borthwick or his team would go straight for the prize, but they didn't. Maybe they thought the data would be encrypted, which it is, but still... I expected them to at least try."

"Good thinking," Stone said approvingly. "And you protested you wouldn't make a good agent."

"I would make a terrible agent," Gina protested. "I just put myself in a nosey civs place and figured out what I would want to extract from a dead viper."

"Exactly what a good agent would do when gathering intel."

Gina scowled.

Kate grinned at Stone. "Okay, so they took blood and tissue samples but we got them back. You took all the recordings?"

Gina nodded. "And deleted the backups off the system."

"Good. Are we done here?"

Stone nodded. "We're done for now. I'll want to come back, but probably not until tomorrow. I think I'll spend the rest of the day poking into things on the net."

"I'll come back with you, but then I'll visit with James and Brenda," Gina said thoughtfully. "I'll try to pump them for information. Borthwick is a dead loss now. He'll order his team not to talk to us."

"Good," Stone said. "Let's get out of here."

Kate activated the cryo unit's anti-grav and they retraced

their route out of the ship and back to the docks.

The marine sentries snapped to attention and presented arms as a sign of respect as the cryo unit floated down the ramp towards them. Beyond them a crowd again began to gather to watch. They had obviously learned about the viper presence on the station from their earlier sojourn to station offices. The crowd remained quiet and respectful as the cryo unit reached the dockside. Stone chose the forward position ahead of the unit and set the funereal pace, Kate had the controls behind the unit. That left Gina to march in slow step with them on the right of the unit.

They marched along the docks, eyes front and ignoring the crowds. The marines guarding *Audacious* snapped to attention as they neared, and a group of officers just then leaving the ship came to attention at the bottom of the ramp. They saluted and held them as the funeral party marched by. Kate recognised Captain Colgan of *Warrior*. He was famous within the Alliance for his discovery of the Shan, but more recently his face had been prominent on the recent news broadcasts about the Merkiaari threat and the Red One Alert.

Finally they reached *Harbinger* and navigated the ramp into the ship. As soon as the hatch sealed and locked behind them, they relaxed and Kate took the cryo unit down to the hold while the others changed. She hurriedly locked the unit down in its niche and connected it to ship's power for the trip home, before hurrying to her cabin to change. Stone had promised to let her go see her brother, and she was holding him to that. As she stripped to her skivvies, she used viper comm to contact him.

"Don't even think about trying to stop me leaving the ship, Stone."

"I wouldn't dream of it," Stone replied.

"Because you promised and... I can go?" Kate said pausing with only one leg in her battle dress. "Really?"

"I promised didn't I? Look Richmond, I know what family means to you. I know you've been waiting for this for years. I won't stand in your way, but remember that everything you do reflects on the regiment and the General. Everything."

She bit her lip. "I'll be careful."

"Careful hell, just be sure no one can connect you to the bodies! Stone out."

Kate chuckled.

She quickly finished dressing and then put away her dress uniform. She shouldn't need it again this trip. She hesitated over taking her pistol with her. There was no rule or law against military personal carrying weapons even on civilian stations, but it was certain she would be asked to disarm before they would let her see Paul. She decided to leave it behind. She settled her beret on her head aligning the viper badge precisely over her left eye and flattened it down properly on the right. One last look in the mirror and she was out the door striding quickly along barren corridors heading for the airlock.

Gina was waiting for her. "Good luck."

"Thanks," Kate said and the hatch whooshed open. "Later."

"Later."

She stepped out and the hatch locked behind her.

* * *

12 ~ Prodigal Son

Kate entered security as if entering enemy territory with all her systems trawling for emissions. Her HUD (Head Up Display) had windows open detailing various data points such as whether or not there were active motion sensors—there were and lots of them. Her sensors had detected gun ports in the overhead. They were closed but they weren't exactly invisible to the naked eye and had probably been designed that way as a deterrent against wrong thinking. Her sensors compared their targeting emissions with the properties of known weapon systems and labelled them as the ever reliable Petreus Systems XMH-4S 4mm mini-autocannon. The name was a little misleading in her opinion. No cannon worthy of the name fired a mere 4mm projectile, but Petreus didn't agree and with their autocannon firing 6000 rounds a minute with ammo storage to match, few cared to dispute them. They were compact, deadly, and reliable; what more could you want from a discreet sentry gun?

Kate presented herself to the security checkpoint guard and asked to see her brother. That's when things started to go wrong. The guard frowned at her request and consulted her comp. Kate waited, looking and scanning her surroundings. Her targeting reticule danced over her internal display briefly locking on to targets and storing locations. If she had been armed, she could have totally taken this place apart in five seconds flat. Servicing targets already zeroed in like the sentry guns and the few live guards was literally child's play to any viper. It was a good thing doing so was off the menu.

"Lieutenant?"

Kate focused upon the woman. "Yes?"

"I think there's been some sort of screw up. Did your CO send you down?"

"No. This is personal. He's my brother."

"Ah, then I think you need to talk with my supervisor. Are you armed?"

"No. Why do I need to see your supervisor?"

The woman stood. "I'll escort you to him, Lieutenant. He'll explain. Sorry about this, but I need to scan you."

What the hell? Kate stepped forward allowing the woman to wave her wand over her body and wasn't surprised when it beeped, but it wasn't picking up a weapon. It was confused by her cybernetics, which did have a detectable low level power emission. She could have used her ECM (Electronic Counter Measures) to cloak herself, or spoof the woman's scanner, or both, but she was in uniform and not attempting to hide.

The guard frowned at her scanner's readout.

Kate sighed. "Cybernetics," she said. By way of an extra hint she turned her shoulder toward the woman to reveal her unit designation.

"Oh! Is that what I'm seeing?"

This one was a little dense it seemed. Kate was wearing her uniform and beret with the viper patch staring the woman in the face, and she hadn't put it together.

"That's so magalicious! Really freaking frosty. I've always wondered..."

Kate blinked at the street speak. Maybe she was just young and inexperienced, not particularly stupid. She revised her estimate of the guard's age downward toward the *barely out of pigtails*' range.

"Go on, ask."

"Well it's kind of personal?"

"Ask or don't. I want to see my brother. Preferably today."

The woman winced. "I think maybe I should just take you to my boss."

"Fine, lead the way."

She followed the guard and waited as she used her wand and codes to enter the secured area. Her sensors continued cataloguing everything and located a lot of cameras and motion sensors throughout the entire area. The station used to belong to the navy. She would bet quite a few credits that this area had been the brig even back then and hadn't changed much in the time since the civvies took it over. She couldn't see a stealthy way of busting Paul out of here. She could do it fast and dirty no sweat, but if she did that she would be running for the rest of her life. She hadn't needed Stone's warning, not really.

She followed her escort into an office and was introduced to Supervisor Tom Croft. They shook hands and Croft waved his underling out. Kate declined the seat offered, impatient to get this over and see her brother.

"I'm sorry you came all this way for nothing, Lieutenant. I can't understand how it happened. I wrote the report myself and saw it dispatched via drone a month ago. This is so embarrassing."

Kate felt bad news looming. "Embarrassing?"

"That you came here to Helios instead of Northcliff."

"Wait. Are you saying my brother isn't here?"

Croft nodded glumly. "All of the prisoners were sent to Northcliff for trial. The ship they tried to hijack was a

Northcliff registered merchant you understand. We loaded them aboard a ship heading out that way and glad to be rid of them. Sorry about your brother, Lieutenant, but it didn't sit right with us having them lying around down here breathing our air and eating our food for free. We did send our own personnel along as escort. They'll reach Northcliff safe and sound, don't you worry."

Worry? This was a fucking disaster! Her eyes narrowed, or was it? She had already decided that busting Paul out of here stealthily was unworkable, and doing it any other way would mean looking over her shoulder for Stone or one of the others for the rest of her life. Was there a way to avoid that? That was the ten quadrillion credit question right there. The prisoners were gone, on their way to trial at Northcliff. That was fact and unchangeable. She needed to go to Plan B... she didn't *have* a Plan B! One thing was certain, she was in the wrong damn system and she needed to change that fast.

"How long for them to reach Northcliff, do you know?"

Croft made a quick calculation on his comp and grunted. "They're about two thirds the way there... call it another ten days or so before they translate back to n-space. Add another day to reach the station, and maybe one more to get the prisoners logged in and down world. So, two weeks at the earliest, maybe more depending on whether the captain wants to save on fuel. You know how traders can be; they're always watching the bottom line."

"Two weeks then," she said, pacing the office, her thoughts racing. *Harbinger* could do it in less if she pushed her. Courier ships were the fastest jump capable ships in space. "Two weeks to get there, and then pre-trial hearings to hear the pleas..."

Croft was frowning now. "You do realise your brother is guilty? I'm sorry, but there's no doubt what the verdict will be. You do understand that you can't help him?"

She would see about that, but she couldn't tell Croft she

was going to break her brother out and help him disappear or die trying along with anyone who got in her way! She made herself nod and forced herself to show grief on her face when all she really felt was impatience. She wanted to be on Northcliff waiting for her brother's ship to dock, not playing catch up here.

"I realise that, but he's my only family. I want to be there for him. I can at least pay for a good attorney. Maybe I can get mind-wipe off the table at least."

Croft regarded her doubtfully.

Yeah, it was bullshit. They both knew mind-wipe was mandated for this. No prosecutor worthy of the name would bargain with anyone caught in the act of a hijacking. There were few things considered worse out in the Border Zone where every colony, station, and ship lived in fear of piracy and the mass murders associated with such crimes.

She had a thought. "You wouldn't have vid of the prisoners would you?"

Croft nodded. "This place is under constant surveillance. Want to see him?"

She nodded. It was a long shot, but she only had Stone's assurance that her brother had even been held here. She doubted he could be wrong about something so important, but she could hope... Croft turned his screen towards her and that was that. He was older and he hadn't shaved, but it was him. Paul Richmond, sitting in a cell alive and not particularly well wearing a hideous orange jumpsuit that made his pasty complexion all to evident. He hadn't been eating well, she thought. Dark circles under his eyes and worry lines had aged him. He looked up towards the camera and she caught her breath as eyes identical to those she saw in the mirror every morning glared at her. She ignored the obscene gesture he made and studied those eyes. Pale blue and cold as a glacier, just like hers. She had to save him.

She straightened. "Thanks."

Croft nodded and turned the display back around. "Anything else I can do, Lieutenant?"

"No. I appreciate you meeting me and letting me see..." she waved a hand at the comp. "You know."

"Happy to help."

Kate took her leave and made her way back to the transit pod. She had absolutely no interest in anything Helios related anymore. Her focus had shifted completely to Northcliff. She needed to research the planet, its judicial system, and its penal system among other things. How quickly would pre-trial hearings take place? Within days of the prisoners' arrival on Northcliff would be problematic—even she couldn't plan a breakout that quickly. There were limits even for viper ingenuity. On the other end of the scale, months wouldn't work for her either. Stone would be all over her arse if she waited that long. Weeks then. It had to be within a few weeks or never. She couldn't see herself successfully evading Stone while rescuing her brother if it took longer than that. He was too good.

She realised as the transit pod whisked her away and into the first tunnel that her mind was made up. She wouldn't ask Stone for help. Gina was out also, but that decision had already been made when she first considered it shortly after their arrival. The decision made, she had to plan a way to evade Stone long enough to jack *Harbinger* out from under him. She grimaced at the thought of betraying her friends. Friends, but for how long? She was considering going rogue... no not considering. Her mind was made up and she was a rogue already, a rogue planning her escape. Her friends would put her down for the good of the regiment the moment they understood that.

For the good of the regiment, she mused, was something bandied around in the 501st as cover for when things went badly wrong. On Snakeholme that often meant a viper being euthanized. Sanctioned murder was the reality but that sounded so barbaric didn't it? It was accepted by all as unavoidable—the Gospel according to Burgton. The thing of it was, she bloody agreed with him! In Stone's place, she would put her down the moment he learned what she was planning.

She shivered. He would do it too. She knew he would do it, probably agonising all the while even as he pulled the trigger to add her to the legion of ghosts he carried with him. He had a line he wouldn't cross—for the good of the regiment was a diamond hard armoured line he would not cross. Her line was her brother. She would sacrifice anything and anyone for Paul.

So, she had to finesse the bloody ship out from under Stone and Gina, and keep far enough ahead of them to free her brother. After that, it didn't matter what they did to her. She didn't want to die, but risking her life was something she was practised at. It would catch up with her one day. What better way to die than saving the life of her only family?

"Can't think of a thing."

Kate kept away from Stone the rest of that day. She spent her time in her cabin researching Northcliff trying to throttle her impatience to get moving. Stone had indicated earlier that he planned upon visiting *Jean de Vienne* again tomorrow. That was when she would make her move. She didn't want to confront him or Gina. She wanted to slip away without fuss.

Gina was still visiting with James when Stone contacted her via viper comm. Kate considered not answering for a nanosecond or three, but that would only make him come down from the bridge and visit in person. She had to put her research on hold and pick up.

She sighed.

"Yeah?"

"Are you okay?" Stone said. "Want me to come by?"

Actually, a certain kind of comforting would be good right about now, but that was a slippery slope. If she had sex with him now she would be tempted to reconsider her decision not to ask for his help. Too risky. He did squirrelly things to her thoughts when they were together.

"No."

"No you're not okay, or no you don't want me dropping by?"

Kate grimaced, he was pushing. "No to both." The silence stretched. "You still there, Stone?"

"I'm here."

She had to know. It had been in the back of her mind, festering, gnawing at her confidence in him. Croft said that he'd sent a drone with a report about the prisoners being shipped to Northcliff. How was it that Stone hadn't known that? He knew about the battle, he knew her brother was a prisoner, how could he not know where they were being held? She was about to ask him and blow the situation out of the water when he spoke again.

"Richmond... Kate I'm sorry."

She stiffened. "About?"

"Not telling you about your brother before your enhancement. You needed repair so I withheld the data. I knew if I told you about him being here that you would be hot to reach him and wouldn't wait."

"How long did you delay me?" she said coldly. "You were fucking me and all the time you knew my brother was rotting in a cell?"

"No! Shit, Richmond, you know me better than that!"

"I thought I did."

Stone growled angrily. "You were in enhancement for a week. I knew a few days before that. I swear to you, I withheld the data so that when you came out here with me you would be fully operational and able to do something for him. Something better left unsaid."

She wanted to believe, and she could if she chose. She could simply choose to accept his explanation. Leaving Snakeholme nine days or so earlier wouldn't have made any difference as far as getting to Helios in time to see Paul. He'd been shipped out weeks before. Her enhancement did give her a chance to rescue him, a much better chance than if she'd remained offline. He was right about that. Stone seemed to think Paul was still here. He seemed not to know what had happened. Appearances could be deceiving however. He was good, certainly good enough to be playing her. The thought stabbed, but she'd played others in her time and done worse. She knew how to play the game.

She swung her legs off her rack and calmly buckled on her holstered pistol. She drew the weapon in a servo enhanced blur, tightened the thigh strap and settled the belt on her hips before trying again. Better.

"Okay," she said putting warmth that she didn't feel into the word. Her face stiff, she stared at herself coldly in the mirror. "I believe you. Thanks for telling me." Her voice was dead now. "Richmond out."

* * *

13 ~ Rogue

Kate reclined on her rack and stared unblinking at the overhead of her cabin. With her hands folded behind her head, anyone entering would guess her to be relaxing or daydreaming. Nothing could be further from the truth. Her internal display was awash in data—she had dozens of searches running. Lists of data cycled constantly in windows competing for attention with other windows containing pictures of people and places associated with Northcliff. Everything she did now had only one purpose; furthering her personal and self-imposed mission.

> >_ TASK COMPLETE. [S]AVE [D]ISPLAY [P]RINT [U]PLOAD?

Kate frowned in annoyance when all the windows she had been using minimised and parked themselves at the bottom of her display. What the frig? She was tempted to just save and dismiss this annoyance, but it would bug her if she didn't at least find out what the data was.

Save and display.

A new window opened listing vid and text files in a menu format for viewing. She chose some at random and watched the prisoners in their cells. Her brother was one of them of course. The vid that Croft showed her was on a secure network, which meant her earlier search commands had finally progressed out of the station's public Infonet. She had forgotten to terminate those searches. Her processor was still pursuing the Helios mission in addition to her personal one. She hesitated, but let it continue working its way through its priority list. She didn't need the extra cycles for anything.

Kate dismissed the window and went back to work.

Northcliff was an interesting place and she found herself wondering why she had never visited it before. Not that she had travelled to more than a tithe of known colonies, but Northcliff seemed a particularly apt place for her to have been sent while working for Bethany's ISS. Espionage had been a large part of her job at one time, with various parties using her and those like her to stab a competitor in the back... sometimes literally. She was assassin trained after all and no one had ever sent her anywhere to make nice-nice. It made her sick thinking about all the times she knew, *she knew*, that her superiors were on the take and were sending her on unsanctioned operations.

The Ten, especially Whitby, must love Northcliff. It was ripe for exploitation. It had no significant naval presence except for a small picket force, and although it was an Alliance member, it was also right on the edge of colonised space. All of which meant that a ruthless company like Whitby Corp. could pretty much do as it liked with very little regulation to hold it back. Northcliff was out there hanging on the edge of nothingness at the extreme edge of the Human sector. It was as close to being a real Border World as it was possible to be without actually giving up Alliance membership. Apart from the Shan way *way* beyond any current dream of Alliance expansion, there was nothing but the Merkiaari. Little wonder then that Northcliff clutched at the straws offered by corporations like Whitby Corp. Climbing into bed with them was a way for Northcliff's government to gain at least some influence within the core.

The idea seemed to be that with so much invested in their world, the corporations would pull strings on Northcliff's behalf if for no other reason than self interest. It was a horrible way to purchase a little safety, but understandable she supposed. The thing of it was, Northcliff had never—and would never—gain what it hoped from the arrangement. Whitby Corp. was too big to fail just because one of the worlds it had interests in collapsed. As important as Northcliff was to its people, it was just another piddling little Border World to corporations that could buy and sell such worlds at will.

Northcliff had aspirations no doubt. It had patterned itself upon successful colonies such as Thorfinni, Forestal, and even Garnet—though Garnet was an exceptionally hostile world in comparison to the others. All three had grown into the powers they were today through their industrial might. Industrial powerhouses they might be now, but back in their early years they had been convulsed by mini wars as corporations struggled and fought each other to dominate their chosen planets. That was pretty much over with on those colonies these days. The corporations now chose to battle it out on the stock markets, and rarely in the military arena anymore. Flare ups did still happen, but in the main back-stabbing was reduced to hostile takeovers or outbidding rivals in multi-billion credit deals, not military operations or black ops fought with mercenary armies... mostly. Northcliff was still at the beginning of its journey. In evolutionary terms, they were like the first critters just learning to crawl out of the sea and onto dry land. They had a very long way to go yet.

The irony of course was that Northcliff was the closest Alliance world to the Shan. It was already becoming an important waypoint for ships wanting to visit them. Anyone wanting to make the huge jump had to stop at Northcliff for fuel and provisions. Any ship returning also had to stop to off-load cargo and refuel before proceeding on. There had been no way to foresee the discovery of the Shan, but had there been a way, Kate had no doubt Northcliff's government would never have sucked-up to the likes of Whitby Corp. by deregulating its banks and implementing so many corporate friendly laws. She wondered if, over the next couple of years, the government might try to undo the damage. It would take very brave officials to try because accidents happened to people like that. She should know, she had often been tasked with creating them.

"Richmond," Stone said via viper comm.

"Here. What's up?"

"I'm on my way out. Want to come?"

Kate's heart sped up and she swung her legs off her rack. She was armed and fully dressed already, and had been waiting for him to make a move. She was more than ready to get going, just not in the same direction as Stone.

"Richmond?"

"Is Gina back?" she said casually, but praying her friend stayed clear.

"Not yet."

"I'll wait here for her. I still have data searches running. Rain check?"

"If you want, but you don't have to stay aboard to monitor your run. We have net access anywhere on the station."

Kate checked her sensors. Stone's blue icon was at the outer hatch waiting for her to join him. She closed her eyes briefly, feeling her loyalty to him and the regiment pulling her, but her love for her brother was stronger. It might tear her in half, but she knew which would win. She should widen her scan beyond the ship. Knowing her luck, Gina would just now be coming up the ramp and she would only succeed in exchanging one problem for another. She held off on that for now.

"Yeah I know, but this way I can lay around and still call it work."

Stone laughed and she joined him for effect. She squeezed her eyes shut, hating herself for playing him, but knowing she had no choice. When he figured it out, he would be in a rage and she would be dead meat. Keeping one step ahead of him was a priority now.

"Okay, make the most of it, Richmond. Tomorrow I want a report on everything you've found out. I better be impressed."

"I'll polish it until it gleams. Promise."

She watched his icon on sensors as Stone left the ship. The moment he did, she left her cabin heading quickly for the bridge. She reached out to the ship via neural interface as she stepped into the elevator and prepared for departure. She was about to find out how hard a ship designed for a crew of twelve was to fly solo. On her way up she contacted Station Central and filed her flight plan insisting on a priority routing to bypass the outbound queue. The request was acknowledged and she was told to wait while they shuffled the roster. No doubt someone at Central was cussing her out for screwing the schedule to hell and gone, but her request wasn't actually that unusual. Courier ships traditionally had priority because of their role in the Alliance. They were absolutely crucial to the free and fast movement of information from system to system, and that was critical to the economy.

She entered the bridge and chose her seat at the helm. She could do any or all of this from her cabin if she wanted, and once in foldspace she probably would monitor things from there, but for the n-space leg of the journey she wanted to be on the bridge. She took her seat and strapped in before closing her eyes. She found it easier with her eyes closed. Stone said... anyway, she just did. She put thoughts of her friends away and locked the door on anything that reminded her of them.

She brought up *Harbinger's* navigation systems and sensors. At the same time she ran diagnostics on the drives and fusion room. She had the capacity, but already she felt her processor being stretched. She had never seen it use this many cycles. It was at 80% capacity and an automatic resources warning suddenly tripped. She ignored the warning flashing on her internal display. Reaching out through her neural interface to disengage external power caused a brief spike up to 82% and back.

"What are you doing, Kate?"

She jumped, and spun her chair to look toward the elevator, but no one was there. Her heart slowed when she realised Gina had used viper comm and was coming up the ramp toward the ship. She quickly changed the codes to the outer hatch, encrypted them, and turned back to the helm.

"Hey, Gina. What's up?"

She accessed one of the dock's security cams and watched Gina trying to override the hatch controls. Kate triggered the stand clear warning on the docks. The board above Gina changed announcing *Harbinger's* imminent departure. The ramp disengaged and began automatically retracting. Gina was forced to scamper back down the ramp as the pressure doors rumbled into place sealing off the slip.

"Dammit! You crazy cow! What the fuck was that?"

Kate winced. Gina rarely cursed. "Sorry about that. I've got somewhere I need to be."

The umbilicals disengaged and retracted leaving the station grapples the only connection to the station and the last impediment to leaving. They weren't under her control.

She queried Central, and was rewarded with her departure time and position in the outbound queue. She checked her time-line and put a countdown up on her internal display. She didn't have long to wait. She rushed through her last few checks. Everything was ready. She watched the countdown intently.

Clang!

The grapples released the ship and Kate, eyes still closed and linked with the helm, pushed hard against the station with her hands. *Harbinger* reacted like the thoroughbred she was, and sprinted in reverse away from the danger of collision. God she was a good ship. Her anti-grav thrusters were powerful and precise. She was an absolute dream to fly. Kate flipped herself over and engaged her mains. It felt like going from a slow walk to a jog and then a sprint as she poured on the power. *Harbinger's* main n-space drive was, like her foldspace drive, way overpowered for her mass. All courier ships were designed that way to minimise flight times. The only ships faster in n-space were navy fighters. Nothing was faster than a courier in foldspace.

"Kate! Where the hell are you going!?"

She cycled through the bridge stations checking that all was well. She made an adjustment to her fusion room, increasing output in preparation for the jump. She didn't charge the drive yet. There was no hurry. Navigation... she adjusted her outbound course to match her flight plan and eased into her assigned lane. She was gaining on the ships ahead, but they would jump out or she would before any reasonable proximity alert would trip. Environmental! She had forgotten to switch to internal atmosphere! Throughout the ship, ducts opened and began recycling the air and water now that the ship wasn't using station resources.

"Richmond," Stone growled ominously and Kate stiffened. "Turn the ship around."

She swallowed, but didn't answer.

"Let's talk about this. Whatever the problem is, we can deal with it. Together we can deal with anything this screwed up universe can think up."

If only she believed that.

"Richmond, answer me!" She cringed at the anger in his voice. She initiated charging the foldspace drive and began calculating her jump. "Turn that fucking thing around now! That's an order!"

"Do it, Kate!" Gina said. "Please don't do this to yourself, to us. *Please!*"

She accessed viper comm and responded to both of them on her squad wide channel. "I'm sorry. He's my brother. I have to do this."

"Rogue, Richmond. Think dammit. You're going rogue!"

"I've been thinking about nothing else since I found out! I. Am. Not. Stupid!"

"Then stop acting like it!" Stone stormed. "I can't let you go! I can't!"

"I know," she whispered. "Gina?"

"What?"

"Don't come after me. Please don't let them send you against me. I... I can't let them stop me. I'll do whatever I have to do. I don't want to hurt you. Don't come."

"I follow *my* orders," Gina said in a hard voice. "I'll do what I'm ordered to do. Please turn around. We can fix this. I swear on my life I'll help you get your brother. *I swear it!*"

Tears leaked from her tightly closed eyes. The jump drive was charged and in the green. She input her destination and the comp calculated her jump point. She saw it appear on her system plot and she locked it in. The countdown began. She opened her eyes and flipped open the safety cover on the manual override. This one thing she would not handle via neural interface. If the comp failed to make the jump, she certainly wouldn't trust it to follow her processor's command to do so.

"I can't put this on you, Gina," Kate said. "I'll be doing some things that... let's just say, I don't think you're ready for some of the things Stone and I have done in the past. I'm sorry. It's for the best."

Ten seconds to jump.

"Richmond, final warning. Turn that bitchin' thing around!"

"No."

Five seconds.

"Listen up, bitch girl," Stone said, his voice deadly calm and cold. His retro origins were showing. "I ain't funnin' wit' yer no more. Turn yer carriage aroun' or when I catch up wit' yer, I gonna put a cap in yer fuckin' head!"

"Goodbye."

"Richmond! I'll—"

Foldspace enclosed her and cut her off from the last friends she had in the universe. She was rogue. The entire regiment, given the chance, would put her down for it. Stone would; even Gina would now, and Gina would have been the last person in her opinion to judge someone. It was done. She was on her way and on her own.

Kate wiped her face on her sleeve, angry at the sentimental bullshit that had made her cry when not even her father's death had managed to do that. She made herself think ahead to the mission, and not back to Helios where Stone was no doubt raging about her and promising retribution. He would come. She didn't doubt he would come. She didn't know how he would manage it, but she had to watch for him on Northcliff. She would keep her sensors on permanent over watch for viper emissions.

Stone would have accessed her flight plan by now, and in his position, she would be checking ship departures looking for the next outbound trip to Northcliff. There would be at least some freighters going her way, probably with the Shan as final destination, but she had a huge advantage in speed. It would take her ten days or so to reach Northcliff, while anyone else would take at least a month. She frowned... unless he bummed a ride from the navy? No, she couldn't see that happening. A ship like *Warrior* or *Audacious* wouldn't provide taxi service, not even for a viper. Even if they did, they would still take something on the order of three weeks to get there.

No matter how she cut it, she should have at the very least ten days to do something before Stone could possibly get there, and probably a lot longer. Still, that didn't give her the luxury of hanging about. She accessed the helm and pushed her foldspace drive's output up to 90% of capacity. Even she wasn't brave enough to run it at max for the entire trip. She might push it a little more for the second half of the trip if things went well and she settled into running *Harbinger* solo without serious issues.

She settled back and began cycling through the ship's systems, making decisions and adjustments. She tried to ignore how alone she felt.

* * *

Helios Station, Helios, Border Zone

"Goodbye."

"Richmond!" Stone roared. "I'll—" *Harbinger* vanished from station sensors, and he withdrew his tap from the net.

"She's gone," Fuentez said in a hushed voice. "She's gone."

She sounded shocked, Stone wasn't shocked. Pissed off, yes. Angry, absolutely. But shocked? No, not at all. He had planned and schemed to allow Richmond to perform her little personal project, even taking the ship was covered, but she wasn't meant to go alone! That's why Fuentez was here.

Well, it looked as if Marion was wrong. Richmond hadn't killed him, she had done worse. She had sidelined him as if he meant nothing to her. She had made him irrelevant! She was supposed to have killed him or marooned him here and stolen the ship with her best friend, not this!

"We have to fix this," Fuentez said.

"Not we," Stone replied. "Me."

"But—"

"Shut it!" he snarled. "You were supposed to go with her! I told you why I wanted you here. I told you about her brother. Why are you still here and not with her?"

Fuentez looked confused and hurt. Stone sighed and tried to think.

"I don't understand any of this," Fuentez said finally. "You said she needed help with her brother. Where's she going then?"

"Northcliff according to her flight plan."

"Northcliff!"

He nodded. "She might have left that to throw us off. I'll need to be sure of her destination before I go after her."

"But what are you going to do to her?"

He gave her a pitying look. "What ever I have to do. Follow me."

Fuentez had to jog to reach his side. "Where are we going?"

"Security. I want to know what Richmond learned that set her off. Her brother obviously isn't where I thought he was. If he were here, Richmond would be figuring out a way to bust him out of the slam not gallivanting off like Zelda!"

"You think he's on Northcliff?"

"If her flight plan isn't false, she must think he is."

"We can't kill her."

He stopped and turned toward her, aware his face was cold. "Maybe you can't."

"But this isn't a whig-out, she isn't really a rogue! She's

just... she's AWOL. That doesn't rate a death sentence, Stone."

"She's a danger. Anything she does that is traced back to the regiment will hurt us all. I can't allow that."

He turned away and Fuentez followed in silence.

* * *

14 ~ A Deadly Gift

Day 5

Kate was going stir crazy. Her plan to monitor ship's operations from her rack had lasted only three days before she started to get the feeling she was missing things. She hadn't dared to sleep, her paranoia wouldn't let her. She had access to all parts of the ship and all its systems via neural interface, but it wasn't enough to settle her misgivings. The only thing that worked was inspecting the ship in person.

"Bloody ridiculous," she muttered to herself as she stalked angrily through the ship's empty corridors towards engineering. She was angry at herself for giving in to fears that made no logical sense.

Ridiculous.

It really was. On the trip to Helios with Gina and Stone, none of them had felt the need to visit any area other than the bridge, their cabins, or the refectory. Neural inspections and diagnostics had sufficed for all systems just fine on the trip out, and they'd handled running the ship by taking turns to sleep. Maybe she was just tired, but she couldn't shake the feeling that she needed to visit each section at least twice a day.

"You're just tired. You're imagining things."

Maybe... probably.

It didn't matter if the reason was real; it felt real even if the source was merely her imagination. Besides, she couldn't sleep. If she put herself into maintenance mode, her processor would enforce her downtime for however many hours she chose, but what if the ship needed her? Oh sure, she could set some kind of an alert to wake her, but she couldn't set alerts for every contingency. She hardly knew herself what could go wrong; she wasn't really navy after all. She knew how to push the right buttons to make it go, but she really didn't know how it all worked. And besides, she wasn't happy with being awoken after the shit had hit the fan; she wanted to prevent it from hitting the fan in the first place. So she stayed awake and prowled the empty ship. What else was she going to do with her time? Her research into Northcliff was complete and she couldn't do anything more until she translated back to n-space.

She entered main engineering and paused to listen. Nah, it sounded the same as last time—no warnings, beeping sounds or flashing lights greeted her. Still, while she was here she might as well run a diagnostic directly off the boards responsible for the actual systems they controlled. She turned to her right and headed for the main engineering control boards ignoring the two story bulk of the foldspace initiator coil that ran horizontally along her path. She had to pass between the initiator on her right and the drive assembly itself on her left. The huge machines dwarfed her. The almost subliminal howling coming from the drive as it worked its incomprehensible magic to propel her through foldspace set her teeth on edge. She laid a palm on the drive and felt the vibration, listened to the low frequency keening howl of stressed machinery just within the audible range of Human hearing; she didn't need to change parameters to hear it. It was clearly audible. Real, not imagination. She was pushing the ship hard, but it felt the same as the last time she was here. *Harbinger* could take it.

"Tough bitch, aren't you baby," she whispered stroking the metal. She closed her eyes listening as the drive crooned its song to her. "Just like me. We don't need anyone to do our jobs, do we?"

Hell no.

She moved on and came to the engineering station that she wanted. She could have used her neural interface even here, but that would have negated her reason for visiting. She ran her hands briefly over the panel, stroking the shiny surface. Why did engineers always make their toys so wonderfully touchable? So tactile. Had a soldier designed it, it would've had a completely different feel. Engineers liked shiny. They got off on clean, smooth, ultra efficient designs—it was like a religion to them. If something broke, they couldn't be trusted to simply fix it; they had to redesign the bloody thing!

She smiled and ran a diagnostic on the drive.

She was no engineer, but she did appreciate efficiency. In her line of work it was a life saver. Vipers were efficient at everything they did, and she had been that way even before enhancement. So it didn't take her long to decide her paranoia was just that. Everything was fine. Good. Nothing to worry about... she ran the diagnostic a second time growling under her breath. Stupid. She wasn't like this usually. She was never unsure of herself when in her element. On an op or on the battlefield doubt never entered her head. Often wrong but never in doubt Stone would say. She smirked imagining him saying just that, but then scowled. That bloody man was in her head way too much. She had to cut him out of her thoughts and feelings before she reached Northcliff, because the next time they met was sure to be bloody.

She patted the so touchable interface and headed out.

Day 7

She had broken her record, but she wasn't happy about it. 180 hours without sleep. She'd needed to order IMS to begin administering periodic stimulants. It was a way of gaining a boost without resorting to melee mode, which would be pointless in this situation and not something to attempt for days on end in any case. A chemical boost was nothing in comparison, but she needed it. Her enhancements meant her body didn't need the help, but her mind most definitely did. Strong coffee just wasn't cutting it anymore. As long as she ate regular meals and took her supplements, her systems would keep running optimally. Her processor regulated everything, keeping her in tip top shape and fighting trim, but her attention span and ability to think straight had begun to degrade. Hence the IMS sanctioned stimulants circulating through her blood right now.

She was in her cabin again, attempting to keep her mind occupied with make work. She couldn't add anything to Operation Breakout—her code name for the op she intended to use to save her brother—so she was going through the stuff she had originally been sent to Helios to investigate. Not that she could do anything with it, but it kept her busy and not stressing about things she couldn't do anything about. The ship was running itself, and despite her misgivings about it, she hadn't needed to intervene in anything even once. She would keep up her inspections, but just for something to do and to put her mind at ease rather than any real need to make adjustments.

She closed the file she'd had open on her internal display, frowning at what she had read. She wondered if the others had noticed that all the Humans, and the Merkiaari too for that matter, but all of them had died of wounds incurred in battle. The new aliens had not. Why then were they dead and found together? In what battle could so many different people—and she called the Merki people only reluctantly—

be involved and the Alliance unaware of it?

The current fear according to the reports was that a new incursion was underway in the Border Zone somewhere, but that didn't make sense to her. Not even a little bit. What was she missing that had so convinced everyone else? Oh, she understood the fear. Of course she did. Bethany's World, her homeworld, had suffered an incursion that inflicted terrible losses to her people and damage to her world. The psychological effect of that incursion was still being felt by her people even to this day. No, she did understand but that didn't make the facts as she saw them add up to a new incursion. Were they really saying that three new alien races were living on a planet or planets in the Border Zone and no one knew? She didn't believe it, she just didn't.

Another important point she couldn't ignore was the origins of the dead soldiers. They had each worn different uniforms. That was key to her doubts. When was the last time so many different forces had been deployed together? The Shan incursion came to mind, but outside of that? She couldn't think of a single instance in recent years. When the Alliance had a problem these days, the Council sent the navy and marines to sort it out, and then if garrisons were deemed necessary, the army went in to keep the peace. They didn't send forces culled from its member worlds, if for no other reason than simple efficiency. They all had different command structures. That was one reason why the Alliance navy, marines, and army existed in the first place.

No, there was something off about the entire thing.

She opened another file and watched one of the autopsies being carried out. She didn't pay too much attention and quickly skipped through it not really expecting to learn anything new. The cause of death for all but the new aliens was obvious, so she skipped ahead until she reached one of those examinations. She was very interested to watch the doctors remove the alien's clothing, because it was obvious to her right away that they weren't wearing uniforms. The aliens were civs, she was sure of it. Uniforms tended to have things in common like insignia. Even the Merki used graphics on their uniforms, so it wasn't just a Human tradition. The new alien's clothing was devoid of anything like that. She supposed they might not use insignia. The Shan didn't after all, but then they didn't use clothes either! She had to go with gut instinct here, and her instinct was telling her these new aliens weren't military. All three were different races, but all three wore a collar of similar design. That was interesting. Very. Perhaps the collars were their form of displaying a Shan's clan or caste?

Hmmm...

"Cause of death was...?" she murmured and frowned as she found the information. "General system failure? What the hell does that mean?"

It meant the aliens had stopped breathing, that's all it meant. A more useless diagnosis was hard to imagine. Basically, the doctors could find no single cause of death. No wounds, no sign of disease, nothing on the toxicological screening to suggest a cause; they were dead just because. She scowled and skipped ahead to the end where someone, one of the techs this time, was examining one of the collars. Kate paused the image. The collar wasn't a piece of clothing or an insignia of any kind. It was a device of some kind. Playing the vid again, she watched as the tech took it apart trying to understand its use and construction. Might it be some kind of comm? Wrapping around the neck it might operate like a throat microphone. Not according to the final report though. It had no recognisable transmitter embedded within it, but it did have a receiver. Very odd.

She closed the file and opened another.

This one made her pause. It was vid from *Jean de Vienne's* bridge recorders—raw footage from the ship's black box. It had been abridged for the purposes of the investigation and showed the time leading to the capture of the bridge. Paul was on the bridge sitting at Scan, but his attention was all for his captain who was threatening to scuttle the ship. She knew that hadn't happened, but how it didn't happen surprised her. Paul stood and simply shot the captain in the back before he could make good on the threat. Nice. It was something she would have done, but it surprised her that Paul had taken the responsibility and initiative. He had changed a lot. She had expected changes, but not in the direction he had taken.

She reran the vid again and again, watching her brother gun his captain down in cold blood trying to make the new reality jibe with her memories of her kid brother following her around. She couldn't do it. This man was a stranger to her. He was still her brother, but she didn't know him at all. The boy she had known was very far from the man he'd become, but then she'd changed too. She wasn't looking forward to explaining to him just how much she had in fact changed. He couldn't be called a proper Bethanite anymore, not from the evidence before her, but had he changed enough to understand her choices? No proper Bethanite would. Vipers were anathema. They were soulless machines, cyborg freaks that had betrayed Bethany's children into death. She knew the real story, and the tales taught were very far from the truth, but Paul hadn't seen everything she had seen. When he learned that she was one of those cyborgs now it could turn ugly. It didn't matter. He was her brother and always would be. She would save him despite himself if that was needed.

She sighed morosely and closed the file. The next one was a vid of the bridge again. The captain was dead and the marines had disarmed everyone ready to take them into custody. She watched as the crew were searched and led away. She frowned as Paul's turn came and paused the playback. There was something in his hand... she reversed the vid and played it again. The marine approached and Paul coughed. He raised the hand to cover his mouth briefly and lowered it again when the marine reacted predictably by aiming his rifle at him. She paused the vid. Paul's hand was empty. She reversed the vid and played it again in an effort to see what he had transferred to his mouth.

"Son of a..."

It was a data crystal. What the hell was so important that he'd risked getting shot over? She would have to ask him, because he swallowed it as she watched. The marine didn't catch the move, and after a quick search Paul was led away to his confinement. Whatever the data was, it must have been important to him, but she couldn't see how it could affect what she had to do. She put it out of her mind.

Day 9

"Surprised?" Stone said with the grin Kate knew so well.

She nodded and stopped the playback. Surprised didn't really cover it. She was a single day out of Northcliff. Tomorrow her plan to save her brother would meet reality. With that in mind she had decided to get ready by doing something she'd been putting off the entire trip. Salvaging Stone's gear. She knew he wouldn't have left Snakeholme without bringing a few goodies. Like her beloved HTR that she had brought as a contingency despite knowing the mission didn't require it, he would have brought something interesting with him. Considering his background, whatever Stone had decided to bring would most likely prove extremely useful at gathering intel. He was the go to guy for data after all, just as she was the go to girl for shooting people in the face.

She smirked, but the expression didn't last long. She glanced around Stone's meticulously tidy cabin and back down to the compad he'd left out for her to find. She didn't play his message, but knelt before the battered looking trunk. It was a civilian design used by millions of travellers throughout the Alliance. They were equipped with anti-grav and very popular with tourists in the Border Zone. Old and worn, aluminium sides dented and scratched, exactly the right type for her destination... it would blend in splendidly. She flipped open the catches and lifted the lid.

Clothes. She lifted them out, her eyebrows rising when she realised they were women's clothes not a man's. She shook some of them out and smirked. Yeah, it was as she'd thought. Stone had chosen blindingly upbeat touristy colours. Always good camouflage in the Border Zone because the natives would beat feet to avoid anyone they suspected were tourists in need. He had her sizes right of course, but he'd also supplied clothes for Gina. Kate was a giant compared to her friend who wasn't much taller than Stone even in her regulation boots. Kate had always been very leggy even as a kid. She went through the various outfits but found nothing suitable for a man. He had obviously not expected to be with her.

She frowned.

The trunk contained more than clothes. There were sample cases containing... cosmetics? She stared at all the different varieties, but there were only one or two she recognised. Goop Original was one of her favourites for styling her hair for example, but she hadn't heard of most of the other brands. No way in hell they were legit. They were stored in small amounts the way a salesperson would store samples he was trying to peddle. A good cover and one she might well consider using on the station tomorrow. They were some of Stone's specials she was sure. Gina would probably call them spook supplies. Kate grinned, imagining her friend's face if she'd seen this.

She didn't know what it was all for yet. No doubt there would be a list on the compad. None of it appeared overtly dangerous, which was good because she had to get it down world through customs. So there would be no weapons here. She would have to source those on Northcliff. Of course she could be wrong. Knowing Stone, she might combine two or more of the cosmetics to make explosives. That wouldn't surprise her in the least, she had used that trick herself a time or two.

Kate pushed to her feet and backed up to sit on Stone's rack. She held the compad between her knees and played his message.

"Surprised?" Stone said with that shit-eating grin of his. "If you're in my cabin reading this, then I guess Marion was right and I'm dead. She said you would kill me one day." He shrugged. "Whatever you did or didn't do, know that I don't blame you. I knew what you were from the moment we first met, and I knew what I was getting into. I know what your brother means to you... I remember what having one was like, so don't sweat it."

"Smug bastard," Kate muttered. "You think you know me, yet you thought I'd kill you and run?"

Then again, if pushed to it she might well have done just that. He would have needed to push her hard for that to have happened. *Very hard.* Maybe if he tried to physically restrain her from leaving? Yeah, that would have done it. She would have beaten the crap out of him if he'd tried, but to kill him... Well, it hadn't come to that had it? With luck, it never would. She needed to get in, grab her brother, and get the hell out before Stone could catch up with them.

"...don't forget Fuentez isn't you. Make allowances and use her properly. Don't put her in the position of killing innocents. She won't do it, Kate. She isn't like us. You'll need to set it up in a way that leaves her in the clear. We both understand some things need to be done despite collateral damage, but she'll stress over it and fuck it up. She won't run with you. She'll get herself killed one day, trying to save everyone but herself... anyway, that's a problem for Eric to deal with if he can.

"I've put together a few things for you and Fuentez. I think you'll find them useful. The I.Ds are clean, so you can use them or not. It's up to you, but they'll withstand scrutiny. The passwords for the wands are on this compad. You can draw up to fifty thousand from each, and yes the money is untraceable. The regiment has funds stashed in all major banks for this sort of deal. You won't have any problems." Stone looked away for a moment toward the cabin's hatch. "I've got to go. You're coming over soon for a little one on one," he grinned like a naughty little boy. "Good luck… and Kate? Run far and fast. The General will send someone after you unless you turn yourself in. We both know that ain't happening. Stone out."

Kate pursed her lips and played the entire thing again.

"…that ain't happening. Stone out."

"Richmond clear," she whispered and turned the compad off.

* * *

Part III

15 ~ Bad News

The foldspace drone translated back to n-space within a few kilometres of its intended destination. The accuracy could be deemed miraculous, but it didn't care after its initial assessment of the system satisfied its programming. All it cared about was determining that it was in the right place and safe from collision. It decided that it was. It scanned its surroundings a second time, looking for Merkiaari ships and emissions, but found nothing matching the profiles in its database. It decided self-immolation was not required, and deactivated the nuclear device built into its core. Finally, with something approaching electronic satisfaction at a job well done, it performed its primary task of transmitting its data to one of the ships docked at station, and then signalled its readiness for pickup to Helios Port Control. With nothing else to do, it activated its beacon and went to sleep.

Aboard ASN Audacious, docked at Helios Station

"Damn it to hell!" Commodore Walder snarled.

Colgan shifted uncomfortably and glanced at the other captains sitting around the conference table. No one was happy with the news, but they were being circumspect and not showing it. The same couldn't be said for the Commodore, unfortunately. She wore her emotions on her sleeve as the old saying went. He didn't know her well, but he had a feeling this was out of the ordinary for her. He couldn't imagine anyone reaching her rank with so little control over her emotions. It had to be the loss of Major Appleford that had so unbalanced her. The others were being very proper and pretending not to notice.

"Well," Walder sighed, and glanced around at her captains. She grimaced at their blank expressions and waved a hand. "Sorry. The political landscape has shifted, ladies and gentlemen, and we have to pick up the pieces. I find myself out of position, off my station, at a crucial time. To put it bluntly, I'm AWOL."

"Surely not that, Commodore," Colgan protested. "Beaufort is Sector HQ that's true, but your command encompasses the entire sector not just that one system."

She nodded. "True, but I need to be in Beaufort planning and overseeing all the changes these new orders mandate. The drone brought them from there, meaning they've been delayed by an extra month to reach me."

Colgan nodded. There was no arguing that, but her staff at Beaufort wouldn't be sitting idle. Her XO was there and would surely be working hard on contingency plans for her approval.

Captain Foden of *Constellation* leaned forward and laced his fingers together on the table. "Where does this news leave us regarding the mission we have planned?"

"Up shit creek," Captain Vardell of *Shannon* muttered and blushed when the commodore frowned at her. "Sorry."

"Up shit creek," Walder mused. "Nice phrasing, Louise, but I don't think our situation is quite that bad. I've had some time to think about what our redeployment should look like, and I don't need to be at Beaufort to get started. In fact, I'll need to begin right here if I'm going to make up for lost time. I can't affect anything while in foldspace after all."

Everyone nodded or muttered their agreement. It was a law of physics that ships were out of contact while in foldspace. A month to reach Beaufort meant she had to give orders now before leaving the system if she wanted to preposition her assets so they would be where she needed them to be in a month's time. Colgan wondered what that meant for *Warrior* and him. The drone had changed everything. Thankfully the Red One Alert was still in effect, but their new orders to redeploy forces into larger groups meant Walder would have more ships at her command very soon. She might even have the proper number to patrol her sector properly again—meaning aggressively—and if so, she could use some of the ships she had here to take out the pirate base before she had to comply with the new orders and deploy them in other areas. That would be a good move in Colgan's opinion. It would really put a dent in the sector's raider activity and make everyone's life easier; a definite win for Walder and everyone under her command.

The commodore activated the holotank and everyone turned their attention to its output. It was displaying the Beaufort Sector and included the ships currently assigned to its protection. Colonies were tagged with their names and spatial coordinates in green, as well as other assets such as Helios, which had no habitable planets. Helios III was a barren rock, but it was important because of the station and the gas mining facilities it maintained. The system stood out on the display; it was cluttered with eight blue ship icons— six *Excalibur* class heavy cruisers and two *Vanguard* class destroyers. The rest of the sector was barren of protection, and that looked so wrong. It made Colgan uncomfortable just looking at it. It was this sort of inequity of protection that had made the Border Worlds Party successful in their recent bid to overturn the navy's war preparations.

"I'll add the ships that I'm expecting to be deployed to our sector," Walder said and manipulated the controls to add two squadrons of heavies and a single destroyer squadron. "Be advised that this is speculative based upon previous correspondence I've had with other sector commanders. As you can imagine, we often discuss what-ifs."

"You really think we'll... *you'll* be assigned two squadrons of heavies, ma'am?" Louise said doubtfully.

"Yes and no. I expect I'll have to share them with the Arcadian Sector. You've seen the new orders. We aren't going back to our previous peacetime posture, but to a modified version of it. We're being expected to patrol our area with multiple groups of ships each having two or three units each. The idea is to aggressively patrol our sectors but to choreograph our movements with overlaps so that we can combine all our ships into squadrons approaching fleet strength without undue delays."

Colgan nodded along with the others. It would take a hellacious amount of planning to accomplish, but assuming they were careful to jump in and out of each system in line with their time tables, it should work. Information and orders could flow between the groups and between the units in them very quickly. Foldspace and the use of drones had always been a huge limitation to information flow. This way, every ship should receive the rally order within an acceptable time frame, allowing them to combine into a force sufficient to confront a threat. In the current climate, presumably that would be the Merkiaari.

"Now then, I've done some basic planning, but I want your input to refine it," Walder went on and suddenly the ship icons began their dance in the holotank.

Colgan slid his compad close and activated it to take notes, his eyes never leaving the tank. He was fascinated by the complexity, and yes, brilliance of her vision. Basic she called it. Basic it most certainly was not. What he was seeing must have kept her up all night working. Perhaps her outburst was the result of a lack of sleep as well as emotional stress.

"Commodore?" Captain Vardell said. "You have *Warrior* and my own *Shannon* out of position at this point." The display froze and the two ships blinked.

Colgan frowned, not seeing it at first. Vardell advanced the simulation slowly and revealed what she had seen. Colgan stiffened, but did not confront the commodore. It would do him no good. He could guess at her reasons without needing to humiliate himself, but he felt sorry that Vardell was being tarred with his brush. She didn't deserve being cut out of the action this way. Certainly her crew would resent it even if she did not. He was surprised the commodore hadn't tried to include Dave Paice of *Trojan* on her shit list, but perhaps her plan required both of her destroyers. In fact, he would wager it did. Captain Vardell had done nothing to deserve this, where Dave had thrown his support behind the actions that had resulted in Major Appleford's death. Colgan was sure Walder would have cut *Warrior* and *Trojan* out of her sector entirely if she could; she could not, but this would do as well.

Walder smiled. "Sorry, Louise, I know how this looks but it's not what you think." Vardell tried to hide the doubt on her face, but failed. "No really." She caught Colgan's eye. "Anything to add?"

Colgan shook his head.

"I'll explain then," she went on and took control of the tank again. "If Louise hadn't stopped the simulation you would have seen the following evolution."

Colgan turned his attention back to the display and watched as *Warrior* and *Shannon* were cut from the elegant dance of ships and appeared in Northcliff. He leaned forward and studied what the other ships were doing. They recombined, jumped into the pirate system and hammered it. It was all speculative of course, based upon Anya's data and plan, which in turn had been based upon old battles in similar circumstances. Meanwhile, *Shannon* and *Warrior* proceeded on after briefly pausing at Northcliff to... Tigris? Why Tigris he wondered. The ships within the pirate system scattered again as if hit with a hammer, and the dance resumed, but *Shannon* and *Warrior* did not rejoin it. Rather, they seemed to orbit it, barely a part of the show, and jumping in and out of random systems.

"Do you see it?" Walder asked, and she was talking to Colgan and Louise exclusively. "No?"

Vardell shook her head, and Colgan said, "No Commodore, I do not."

"We all know why this is happening... the new orders I mean. The Border Worlds Party pressured the Council and served them with an ultimatum. *Warrior* and *Shannon* are my response."

"Showing the flag?" Colgan asked and Walder nodded. "You believe this is the best use of limited resources?" By his tone he made it abundantly clear that if she did, he did not.

She grimaced. "Best use? Not at all, but important and necessary at this time. There's bad blood between us, we all know it, but I swear this decision has no bearing. This is politically necessary. I've tried to cover all contingencies here. Your ships will show the flag in my sector's hot potatoes— Northcliff, Tigris, and here at Helios—but you'll still be available at need and able to rally to us if we all stick to the time-line."

"Here too?" Captain Vardell said in surprise.

Walder nodded. "The Stationmaster has been calling for a ship or two to picket this system for years without success, but recently he managed to attract the right kind of attention, or the wrong kind from our point of view. He petitioned to have Helios made into a marine outpost, and someone listened. I have no orders to facilitate that at this time, but I'm told they're coming. In the meantime, I'm to keep him quiet. I think the note said and I quote, *"shut him up for god sakes!"* end quote."

Colgan snorted. "I see. Why *Shannon* and not *Trojan* or *Fury?*"

Vardell looked hopeful.

The commodore dashed the hope. "I think I'll need them in the pirate system to scout ahead, and two *Excaliburs* are more impressive than one for showing the flag. I'll have four heavy cruisers and two destroyers with me. I'm confident we can take on a few raiders with that weight of metal."

The others mumbled their agreement. Colgan had to agree with them. He doubted they would meet anything out there that they couldn't handle. Anya's data seemed to indicate that pretty well based upon other pirate systems the navy had cleared.

The simulation resumed and everyone settled down to work. They refined the time-line together and generated the tables they would all need to keep coordinated. Hours of work modifying plans, revising contingencies, and working up attack or defensive plans based upon every possible scenario they could conceive of saw them done, and the meeting breaking up. Colgan left *Audacious* walking with Captain Vardell; she was senior and he would have to defer to her while *Shannon* and *Warrior* travelled in company.

"Well, she certainly knows how to stick it to those she has a grudge against," Vardell said and grinned at him.

"I'm sorry you've been caught up in it," Colgan said as they walked along the dock.

"Don't be. If she hadn't picked me she would have picked one of the others. She's right about the politics, unfortunately."

Colgan nodded.

"We'll need to get our execs together, and it wouldn't hurt to have our comm officers in on the meeting."

Colgan nodded again. "I'll send them over to *Shannon* as soon as I get back aboard. The timing of this is going to be a stone bitch."

"You've got that right. We have to coordinate our jumps and speed very closely. Going a little too fast or too slow in foldspace will scatter us all to hell and gone. Our tables won't mean a thing then."

Very true. They had to trust that every ship's drive was accurately calibrated and well maintained so that the same settings used in different ships actually translated to the same real world velocity. Considering the awesome speeds attained in foldspace, even tiny errors would become unworkable very quickly indeed.

They parted ways at *Warrior's* ramp, and Colgan made his way back aboard. He went straight away to the bridge and told his XO and Lieutenant Ricks to head over to *Shannon* for a conference. They called their replacements up to the bridge to take their stations and left soon after that. Colgan took the conn himself, and went over his new orders in his head. Showing the flag was essentially a nothing assignment, but it didn't *have* to be a mere gesture. Two *Excalibur* class heavy cruisers translating into a system together should never be considered a mere anything. They could do a lot more than make political hay for their masters, and Colgan was determined to make that point to Captain Vardell when he had matters settled in his own mind. He would not allow himself or his ship to be turned into a political pawn to pacify politicians, when doing so sacrificed his duties as a naval officer. There should be a way to do both; he was determined to find it.

* * *

16 ~ Round 2

There was no calling him back now, Valjoth thought with heavy satisfaction. He really should not gloat, but it was hard not to. He had thought these thoughts far too many times during this very *very* long journey in the otherness of foldspace, and though essentially true, it had been just as true the moment the ship left Kiar. There was no communication possible until they translated back to n-space. Higher energy states, such as the ever so useful foldspace, didn't play nice with any type of known communications technology. The vermin makers and builders of such things swore there should be a way around the limitation, and they had orders to make it so, but nothing they had tried yet had worked.

Valjoth was in two minds about it.

A way to communicate in foldspace would change everything about how he performed as First Claw of the Host. Everything. From planning to execution, everything would change in fundamental ways. It would make certain things easier, but it would also be a way for the Hegemon to micromanage him and the Hegemony in general. There wouldn't be a need for him to be a part of this cleansing force for example. With foldspace communications a reality, he might be forced to stay in Kiar and give his orders from there. He hated the thought. Never to experience battle again, to lose any opportunity to rend the vermin with his own claws; he'd rather be dead. Theories regarding higher energy states where such communications might become a reality were only that so far. Despite some of the advantages he might glean from the discovery of another type of foldspace without the current limitations, he hoped it never happened.

Theories were all well and good, but he preferred realities; especially where they intersected with his own area of expertise—battle and exterminating vermin. Innovations did affect how he planned for those things, so he did have to keep a claw in the pot, so to speak, but he didn't really understand the makers or their fiendish love for innovation. Take for example the last time he had reviewed the research into foldspace. What was the point of it? They already knew how to enter it, navigate it, go faster or slower... what more was there and who cared? Who but a maker cared why foldspace worked the way it did? Sometimes he wondered if they really did care, or whether they were just ensuring their own perceived usefulness to the Hegemon. It was hard for him to think like a maker, and distasteful he admitted, but he made the effort now and then; how else could he be sure he understood what they were trying to do? Anyway, he had to keep himself aware of them and their work in case they really did invent something useful.

And how had his thoughts become entangled by builders and makers when the ship was about to translate to n-space? His first battle of a brand new war was about to begin. He needed to concentrate upon that. He wondered how the other cleansings were progressing. No way to know. He had to trust those he'd chosen to command them. He really hated that part; the trusting. Now there was a good reason for the plus side of the foldspace comms column if ever he'd heard one! He could micromanage his commanders even as the Hegemon did the same to him! Perhaps they felt the same as he when they sent him out to do their bidding? That was a thought.

"Status!" he barked.

"Unchanged, my lord," Usk said. "It will be unchanged the next time you ask too."

Valjoth shot a look at the shield bearer, but it bounced off. He wouldn't be much of a shield if he couldn't withstand his patron's moods. Finally he grinned, accepting the implied rebuke, but it was for form's sake only. They both knew he didn't mean it.

"Very well, Usk, I shall ask again only after translation to make the liar of you."

Usk looked worried suddenly.

Valjoth laughed, gnashing his fangs at his oldest companion. Those around the command centre also laughed, and Usk growled as if angered, but everyone knew him too well. Blood Drinker's command team had been together all their lives. They were from the same batch and vat as well. Born together and trained; they were like one being—a perfect team. Valjoth had insisted upon the best for his ship, and he had the power as First Claw to make it stick. They knew him and his moods; they knew the difference between playful anger and the real raging-on-the-killing-edge kind.

He turned his thoughts back to the war. "Zillah's cleansing should be well begun."

"If he held to your timing," Usk agreed.

"He better," Valjoth snarled, and this time all knew his temper was real. "Each fleet's First Claw has the same instructions. I picked all of them because they seemed able to follow orders."

"Any can do that, lord, but these orders are... twisty?"

"Different you mean."

"No, I really did mean twisty," Usk said and gnashed fangs. "No one has ever fought like this before. The tests you put them through seem to show they understand the reasons for them, but I have my doubts."

"I know you do."

"Yes, but I was here when you came up with the plan, and even so I have doubts. They only know what you've told them you want. They didn't witness how your ideas grew and don't have the benefit of knowing why you think this new way of fighting will work."

Valjoth thought about that for a moment, and didn't like his conclusion. "You're saying I did not explain the plan as well as I should? You should have pointed that out when I could have done something about!"

"If I thought that, I would have, my lord. It's part of my duty as shield bearer to give council. You explained things better than any could have or any commander deserves. They exist to obey you after all."

Valjoth nodded, but blind obedience wasn't what he wanted. He would take it over disobedience of course, but he wanted his fleet commanders to think for themselves and see why his orders would work, and not just obey them out of their training or fear of him. What he really wanted, he admitted to himself, was to be in five places at once so that he could lead each battle himself! He hated trusting them to do the right thing, when he wasn't sure they knew what he thought the right thing was! They weren't fools, but they weren't him, and everyone knew he was... odd. Different then. He was different and he thought differently.

They knew what he wanted them to do, or they said they did, but their instincts would fight against some of his notions. He had known that would happen at the time, and he'd tried to frame his instructions in such a way as to appeal to their own sense of rightness. It had been fiendishly hard not to simply roar his orders into their faces and stomp about, but that would have defeated his purpose.

He ultimately wanted to turn his fleet commanders into a team like the one he had here on *Blood Drinker*, one that understood him and his views on things, but unlike those here they all came from different batches and vats. They weren't all the same; they all had different strengths and experiences. How did the vermin-spawned Humans cope? They squeezed out their pups individually the same way as the full bloods did. No batches or vats for the Humans. How did they train their young troopers?

It didn't matter how the Humans did what they did, only how he responded. He wanted to match and eventually best them, but they were so different from his people that his methods would be different; *had to be* different, and the Hegemon were a factor he could not ignore. They still hadn't seen the need to increase production of the new troops beyond the meagre and inadequate three batches in ten. Hegemon oversight meant his battle plans had to satisfy so many criteria. They had to have a good chance of victory and be achievable with the meagre resources the Hegemon allowed him to use, but they also had to be understandable by those carrying them out while being different enough to surprise the enemy. Those differences had caused mayhem among the Hegemon and his own commanders, but they were so necessary.

Everything depended upon him being able to surprise the Humans, but traditionally that was something they excelled at doing to his people not the other way around! His people had their strengths, but quick thinking and adapting to circumstances had never been one of them... until now; until him and those like him. They were so few, those oddities who could think in strange ways—strange to other Merkiaari. How many had he lost to challenges and mishap? No way to know, but he suspected the handful he had saved were a mere tithe of those quickened. Their temperaments were such that very few survived training and the daily challenge of living among batch mates bigger and stronger than they. Invariably they were the runts of the batch, and like him they had to live on their wits until maturity lent them skills enough to avoid challenges or win them through cleverness. He had promoted those he had found, nurtured them within the Host to become some of his best ground commanders, but there were too few of them. None were seasoned enough to become First Claw to any of his current cleansing fleets, certainly they would not be respected in that role and that was death to any Merkiaari because challenges had to be answered.

He had high hopes for the oddities, as some in the Hegemon insisted upon calling them. If they survived the coming battles with the Humans, they might move up and help him build the Host stronger and make it quicker to respond to surprises. That would defang the Humans and make much of what made them so dangerous irrelevant.

"Approaching translation in ten, nine, eight,..."

Finally!

Rarely had he spent so long in foldspace. He had visited every one of the thousand suns that comprised the Hegemony, but even then the trip back from the farthest Merkiaari outpost had been broken up into manageable chunks. This journey though was a different matter, and that brought fuel to mind—

"Translation!"

He roared as the universe tried to squeeze him out of existence, or he tried to. It always happened, and the others were experiencing the same distress. Did the Humans feel this... this *utter* confusion? He hoped they did because if not it was yet one more thing to fear about them. He struggled to move, but as always his body wasn't his own. This loss of control was intolerable for any Merkiaari. That was one of the reasons that ground troops spent the journeys between worlds and battles asleep in hibernation chambers. Allowing his troops to experience this would win the war for the Humans before it began. They would come out of foldspace raging. Before he knew it, half his force would be dead at the claws of the other half.

Blood Drinker blinked into existence and the energy discharge blasted away from her. Other ships arrived all around her, and the light show was extreme. Shields fluoresced as each ship encountered its neighbour's foldspace wake and shunted it aside. Generators howled deep within ships armoured and protected against such titanic forces, but they were designed to handle worse if not this precise situation. Valjoth had thrown away doctrine yet again and forced his ships to translate back to n-space in tight formations. They arrived very close to each other; too close according to the ship's proximity alerts. Alarms sounded on every ship, and computers screamed about imminent collision, but they were wrong about that. Every ship in every cleansing fleet deployed in this new war had practised this manoeuvre among many others. The entire fleet was awash in coruscating energy, but it caused no damage.

"Status!" Valjoth said, making good on his earlier threat. What good was any threat if not followed through, even one as harmless as this?

Usk turned his harried face toward his lord, he was still receiving reports, but he answered in order of priority as he should. "All ships report successful translation, my lord." He slowed his words to gain time and hear more on his headset. "No collisions reported. The formation is... within predicted values."

"Yes, yes," Valjoth said impatiently. "The enemy?"

"As predicted also. There is a small force of guardships orbiting the fourth planet, but it wouldn't threaten even a single force of our own guardships. *Blood Drinker* alone could destroy them all with ease."

"Good!" He was very pleased with that particular news. He had reports from the recon drones he'd ordered sent to all of his targets, but this was the first that he was able to confirm. "The colony?"

Here Usk hedged. "It appears very small. Not really a colony but more like an outpost or watch station. I cannot be certain, my lord, from this range."

Understandable again, as the recon drones had been unable to venture into the inner system without being detected. Valjoth had absolutely forbidden that. He had to maintain surprise for a while longer, and then he wanted the exact opposite. He could hardly wait to see the reaction. He wanted his presence to shatter the Human's calm complacency, but only at a time of his choosing. That had been another thing his commanders found hard to grasp. Sneaking about was distasteful to them, but they understood the advantage of doing so, but then to throw away that advantage? They just didn't understand what it would do to the Humans; he had studied them and did know.

In some ways they were very like the other vermin his people had fought and subjugated, especially the Shintarn and Parcae, but in others they were very different. They seemed to defy logic on purpose. They were warlike yet were also builders like the cursed Kiar had been, and professed to love peace—patently absurd; their own actions belied it. They were also makers, like the Shintarn and Parcae, poking into things and making them reveal their secrets, yet they truly excelled at fighting; very Merkiaari-like that was. They were incomprehensible to his people because they didn't fit a known pattern. They were Merkiaari-like in their love of battle, yet not like as well—they had wars among their own kind! Inconceivably wasteful though it was, Valjoth could see how it made them better fighters. Real battle was always a better teacher than mere training, and they did always seem to be killing each other. Perhaps they had their little wars amongst themselves for entertainment; he could see the attraction, but even he would shy away from such a waste of troops. Proposing a similar system of Merki on Merki real battle training would have him put down as mentally defective, and rightly so. Challenge between individuals was one thing, but setting his ground troops against one another en masse? He shuddered at the thought of what it would do to discipline.

Perhaps it was simply the Human's bad luck that their worlds were so isolated from other vermin worlds. The sectors of the spiral arm that they called their own were devoid of any but their own people. The opposite situation held true for the Hegemony, and well it did. The vermin-cursed Kiar would never have envisioned a need for enforcers if they had felt secure. His people might never have been created, Valjoth mused, if not for Kiar paranoia. The same would have resulted if Kiar and Human had switched location within the galaxy. Perhaps the Humans would then have ruled their own Hegemony, and the Merkiaari would never have existed. Could it be simple happenstance that they had evolved to fight their own kind simply because there were no alternative enemies in their sectors?

He realised Usk was awaiting orders. "Call the fleet to order, Usk!"

"Yes, my lord, but your ah... *new method* of arrival means that it's already in battle order."

"Exactly!" Valjoth said with heavy satisfaction. "Now you begin to see method in my madness, eh?"

"Yes, my lord, your madness has proven useful time and again."

"Was that a joke, Usk? How very... *me-like* you suddenly seem."

"The Hegemon forfend!" Usk said with genuine-sounding distress. "I did not mean... that is to say..."

"Enough!" Valjoth roared. "My shield bearer should

know when I jest and when I do not. You are, as always, the best of warriors and companions. Fear not. I have not infected you with my madness."

Yet.

Usk straightened at the praise. "Your orders, my lord?"

Valjoth studied the holographic display at the centre of the command deck while his highly trained and matched command staff went quietly and efficiently about their duties. His formation was indeed battle ready, but he had far more ships than he needed to cleanse this system. He could detach some of the guardships and a single troopship to deal with Usk's not-colony and the Human ships loitering there. Despite his rather exciting entry into their system, they didn't know that their deaths had come upon them. They had ships, but none were patrolling. Human technology was on par with Merkiaari tech, yet unlike every single Hegemony system, this one didn't have a single defensive satellite or station; not one! It really was a very poor way to run a system. Although he was the beneficiary of their incompetence, he found himself disapproving on general principles.

"I suppose I cannot justify taking *Blood Drinker* into battle so soon," he said sourly.

"Definitely not," Usk counselled, and realised that his lord wanted to engage in some slaughter personally, but could not be seen to suggest it himself. "We could go down to the surface?"

Valjoth brightened. "Excellent notion, Usk! That is just what we shall do. Choose one of the troopships and assign a guardship squadron as escort."

"A full squadron?"

"I know it's far too many for this little fight, but I want everyone to keep thinking as a unit. They must fight and manoeuvre together the way our interceptor pilots do."

"Forgive me, lord, but interceptors are tiny things. You cannot think to make the fleet so agile."

"No, but I want us thinking about how they fight and why they fight the way they do."

"It's because of the way the Humans—" Usk's jaw snapped shut.

"Yes? You were saying about the Humans?"

"You cannot turn us into them, my lord."

"Kiar rot my fangs and may they fall out if I should try!" Valjoth said, shocked that anyone should accuse him of that, and doubly so that it should be Usk. "*We are Merkiaari!*" He roared, and this time everyone on the command deck turned to watch. He rarely became truly angry, but often put on a show of it, but this was real and they knew it. "We are fighting Humans who, like it or not, defeated us once before. I do what I do not to become them, but to destroy them! One of their strengths is that they fight as a unit. What have I been telling you and any who would listen?"

"To train and fight together, but we have always done that, my lord."

"*No!*" he barked. "Think, Usk, think! Our troops fought on the same battlefield; that is not the same thing! Our new troops have learned what our interceptor pilots and the Humans have always known—how to support one another in battle. Do not our guardships protect the troopships? Does *Blood Drinker* not protect all?" Valjoth didn't wait for an answer. "Our ships will fight in formation, not just arrive and depart battle in them! They will, or I will know why not! Now give the order."

"Yes, my lord," Usk said in a chastened tone.

Valjoth ignored the injured tone and glared around at the observers. They all suddenly found things to do. He turned his attention back to the holographic system display, and fumed. If Usk didn't understand him after all this time, what chance did his commanders have? It didn't matter, he supposed, as long as they obeyed. No, it did matter, and he castigated himself for wavering in his own certainty for even a moment. He couldn't be everywhere and watching that they remembered his new way of doing things. He had to teach them why it worked, not simple obedience.

Traditional doctrine had always worked before, that was the rub. Before the Humans they would have attacked en masse to overwhelm the vermin. Each ship would find a target and destroy it, and then repeat as long as necessary, but the Humans had shown that a numerically inferior force could best a superior one if the right tactics were employed. It worked in space as well as on the ground. They had a nasty habit of retreating and luring an enemy into a bad position to annihilate it, but they also protected each other even to the ultimate sacrifice of their own lives. He had studied battles where Human ships had used themselves as shields to protect other ships, until both were destroyed or the attacker was. Sometimes the Humans lost, but they took a heavy toll before they did. He wanted that kind of spirit instilled in the Host. They already did it in a limited way, so it wasn't exactly anathema to his people. Guardships were named thus for their primary role of protecting troopships after all. Surely the next tiny evolution of that principle wasn't beyond his people or his ability to teach?

He glared at the display and the system it detailed. The Human's vermin-spawned navy was not present. That was excellent news to him, but ordinarily it would have been considered a bad thing. Doctrine again. The reasons were many, but in this instance he celebrated because he didn't want to fight a protracted battle. Not yet. The journey had been long; fuel was his priority right now, or should be. He realised he hadn't even thought to ask about it! One of his greatest hurdles had been persuading his commanders that arriving in a hostile system low on fuel was a good idea when it was patent insanity! It really was and he knew it, but it was his kind of insanity, which meant it wasn't insane at all, just twisty thinking.

Why was he doing it this way? The Hegemon had certainly wanted to know, and despite heated discussions with them, they had allowed him to try this. The distances were so vast that doctrine would have forced him to attack a system that he did not consider a good strategic target simply because it had always been considered wrong to risk battle with less than 50% fuel aboard. 50%! As if any ship commander worthy of the name would even consider retreating, let alone running all the way back to his starting point; the idea was ludicrous. It would never happen, and that was part of what he was fighting in his efforts to reform doctrine.

He believed retreat was an important tactic. It was not cowardice or running away from battle when used to reposition forces to better advantage. If there was one thing the Humans had taught him from his research of them, it was that retreat was useful; that and fighting in proper formations. There were many other things besides, but those two were the most important. Unfortunately, it was also the hardest for Merkiaari minds to grasp.

He watched one of his troopships manoeuvre into the centre of a guardship formation. It slotted itself into the gap left for it, just like one of the simulations he had insisted they practise. It lightened his mood, seeing how well it was performed. Such a simple thing, but it showed how well they had learned to manoeuvre among so many ships in close proximity. Their first practise runs had been worse than just embarrassing, he remembered. They hadn't needed to scrap the ships, but they had needed extensive repairs.

The troopship and escort set course for the fourth planet and battle. He wished he could join them.

"Fuel," Valjoth prompted, forcing his attention back to the rest of his fleet and away from envy. They and not he would fire the first shots of his new war. They and not he would kill Humans, the first Merkiaari to do so in centuries. "Where do we stand, Usk?"

"Reports are still coming in, my lord, but I estimate we have 18% remaining. That is an average. *Blood Drinker* is down to 6%."

Valjoth's eyes widened and he fought to control his expression. That was... a little disturbing. He had calculated that *Blood Drinker* would arrive with a surplus of twice that amount, and his ship was the most powerful unit in the fleet, meaning it was the most massive and fuel inefficient. 6% surplus was nothing. They could have run dry entirely and lost the ship in foldspace.

"Well," he said finally. "We can update our estimates with hard and reliable numbers now."

Usk wasn't fooled. He gnashed his fangs in amusement. "Yes, my lord. I think we can do that for certain. Any future planning should take them into account. Yes?"

"Yes," he said grumpily, but then he brightened. "Well we are here and the war is begun. What do you think of it so far?"

"It's boring," Usk said sourly.

"Boring? *We can't have a boring war, Usk!* What would the Hegemon say? Let us bring the rest of the fleet to order and get started. Set course for the gas giants. I want this system cleansed and this fleet back in foldspace on schedule. I put great weight on that. I have to prove it can be done. I don't want anyone using my tardiness as an excuse not to follow the plan."

"No one would dare, my lord!"

"Maybe so, but we both know they would be thinking it even if never uttered aloud."

The fleet having arrived in formation—in extremely close formation if Valjoth was truthful—quickly set course for the closest of the two gas giants the system had and the torturous task of refuelling so many ships without the benefit of proper gas mines. The current formation had nothing to do with the refuelling, but it did have the effect of making the course change quick and efficient. The formation was for practice and for getting his ship handlers used to such things. His future tactics relied upon them knowing what they could do with their ships; knowing instinctively and not simply assuming they knew because doctrine said so. Doctrine, some of it at least, had lost the last war for them. It wouldn't lose this one; it wouldn't win it either—he would.

* * *

17 ~ Cleansing

Riding a gravsled again was glorious. How he had missed this! It had been far too long since he had taken the gunner's position in combat, and he took full advantage of the opportunity now. Usk was enjoying himself at the controls, while Zeng Kylar watched for threat beside him. The arrangement was most improper; Usk was his shield bearer not her, but Valjoth didn't care in the least! It felt so good to leave his concerns behind on *Blood Drinker* and just be himself for a while. Combat was in his blood; Merkiaari had literally been designed for this, and they all revelled in it. He took aim and potted another Human trying to run, and laughed as it fell.

"Did you see that?" he yelled to Kylar in glee over the sounds of combat. "I took its leg right off with one shot!"

"It's still alive. Did you mean to miss?" Kylar responded taking aim with her cannon. "I'll fix it. I won't tell anyone, don't worry." She fired and turned the Human into a red smear on the road.

He spluttered. "Miss! Did you hear that, Usk? She

accused me of missing! I *don't* miss!"

"It's true," Usk yelled back to her. "He never misses, but he does like taunting his prey. He plays with his food too!"

Valjoth growled indignantly. It had taken skill to hit such a small target at this range, he'd hit exactly what he aimed for, but he was having too much fun to justify himself or reprimand his companions. Besides, they were all enjoying the outing. Usk had recruited Kylar to help protect him so that he could fly the sled without fear that some Human would take his lord's fangs as a trophy. He grinned at the very idea. The Hegemon would be very put out if they had to find a replacement First Claw for the Host. He would be too.

He pointed to the right. "*That way!*"

Usk fed more power to the sled's anti-grav and they accelerated along the street. Valjoth opened up on the buildings with concentrated plasma in three round bursts. The buildings were shattered and debris soared high into the air. Fires roared and buildings slumped, collapsing into the street. Glorious! Usk swerved suddenly as a Human vehicle made a run for it.

"Yes! After him, Usk!"

Kylar took aim and fired on full auto! The huge cannon she carried boomed over and over, but she was a formidable female. She took its recoil as the cost of doing business and was unfazed. She snarled as Usk's manoeuvres caused her to miss entirely. He had to swerve to avoid obstructions and burning vehicles.

Valjoth laughed. "Ha! You missed, don't tell me you meant to do that! And you accused me of missing! Oh, ha ha ha!"

She gave him an evil look and hefted her weapon thoughtfully.

"Now, now, none of that! I'm your lord, remember?"

She growled, spun taking aim, and blew the fleeing vehicle completely into the air. It somersaulted and crashed back to the road skidding along on its side. She fired again, and it blew up, a fireball rising high above marking its grave.

"Nice shot!" Usk yelled, slewing the sled to avoid hitting the wreck.

It really was. She'd hardly paused to aim. "Find us something else to kill, Usk!"

"Yes, my lord," Usk said turning his attention to his scanner. He must have located something, because he spun the sled expertly around and accelerated down another street. "There's something this way. Our troops are after it already."

Valjoth grunted and reloaded. Knowing his troops they would have slaughtered everything before he could get there. They wouldn't leave any for him, even if he ordered them to. By this time they would be raging and doing what troops did to vermin. They were programmed in the vats for their role as all Merkiaari were, and then highly trained on top of that after reaching maturity. They would not wait for anything, and quite right too. He hadn't specified which troops to send here. It was simply random chance that all the troops were of the old type. Not that it mattered; this cleansing was hardly taxing. As Usk had thought, this wasn't a colony; it was some kind of outpost, and a small one at that. The city they were playing in was the only one on the entire planet! It was a waste of a perfectly good planet in his opinion. It could support billions of Merkiaari and the climate was perfectly pleasant. Humans would find it comfortable he was sure. Why then such a poor attempt to colonise it?

"There, lord!" Usk yelled, pointing ahead.

Kylar raised her weapon. "Target!" She fired, and something exploded.

Valjoth used her shot for ranging. "Locked! Firing!" he yelled and happily blasted away.

Bub-bub-bub! Bub-bub-bub-bub-bub-bub-bub-bub!

It was a small craft; a lander or a shuttle. He blasted away at it, while his troops assaulted the defenders, of which there were many. Explosions and plasma bursts filled the air, and the fight had become quite significant compared with others of this cleansing. Admittedly that wasn't saying much; opposition was poor and poorly led, but still. Any action was welcome. He had to go back to *Blood Drinker* before the end of the day.

He blazed away at the shuttle as Usk brought the sled to a halt in line with another one, but he kept his spacing. No sled pilot wanted to park close to another, not after his first battle and witnessing what happened when they lost containment to enemy fire. Its gunner was taking on a Human nest, and the two were duelling with plasma and mass driver inspired slugs. Valjoth briefly considered helping out, but preferred to disable the shuttle's engines.

He kept his fire concentrated upon the drive section of the tiny ship, determined that it would not lift, but he didn't seem to be making much progress. Like their vermin-spawned navy, Human shuttles were incredibly tough for their size. A Merkiaari ship of this sort would have succumbed already, but then the builders didn't make anything like them. Biology was one reason. Merkiaari were physically much bigger than Humans and needed shuttles ten times bigger, but the most important reason was that to maintain parity with Human tech, the builders had needed to design everything bigger and bulkier. That had led to some great things; things like the stupendous *Blood Drinker*, the most powerful assault class ship yet added to the Host. She was truly a power to be reckoned with, as was the entire Host of course. What rankled was that *Blood Drinker* and other ships weren't built the way they were out of choice. It was necessity.

One day, the builders would match the Humans ship for ship without needing mass to make up the difference, and then the galaxy would see something! But for now he could glory in things the way they were, and he did. He couldn't help thinking that size mattered, because in any Merkiaari's world it did! Bigger was better, and to date, it always had been. The Humans though were a warning that things would and must change, and those changes were already starting to happen. The new troops, this new cleansing using new doctrine that he was compiling, new ships using new formations and tactics; all old ideas to Humans maybe, but new to Merkiaari minds willing to try them out and make them their own.

The Humans would rue the day they chose not to cleanse the Merkiaari at the close of the last war, but not for long. He was going to ensure that when his replacement took command of the Host, hopefully in the far distant future, that lucky Merkiaari would not inherit the Human threat that he'd been left to deal with. He was going to cleanse them out of existence, and his name would be known forever afterwards as the one who had safeguarded the Hegemony from the greatest threat it had ever faced.

Finally his fire achieved something, and the shuttle erupted with flame. "Look at her burn!" he yelled. "They aren't going anywhere in that thing!"

Kylar took no notice, she was busy blasting away at the Humans and having a good time. Valjoth turned his weapon onto the defenders and joined her. What the Humans thought they were doing protecting a shuttle with nowhere for it to go he couldn't imagine. Their ships in orbit were dead; there was nothing but a debris field in a slowly degrading orbit left up there now. He didn't really care, but it was curious. They had nothing to do now but die, and he was happy to help them with that.

Finally he ran out of targets and the troops dispersed looking for more prey. Valjoth dismounted the sled with Usk and Kylar hovering protectively nearby as if he couldn't defend himself. Really, it was embarrassing the way they coddled him sometimes. Like vermin protecting their young.

He wandered amongst the Human corpses noting the

numbers and calculating how many of his own dead lay with them. Three or four to one in his favour he would judge. Not great but not too bad either. Troops of the old type were inferior in combat against Humans when compared with what modern batches were capable of, but four Humans in exchange for every one of his troops sent to the recycle vats was about right. If he remembered his statistics from the closing stages of the last war, and he did because everyone knew he was an absolute fiend for recalling such things, then the Humans had not improved themselves significantly. Admittedly it was hard to judge based upon a simple skirmish like this, but he was satisfied with four to one. He wouldn't see ten to one or better without deploying his modern troopers.

"Let us see what was so important to them, Usk!" he boomed happily. He was never quite as content as he was when wading through vermin blood. "You never know, there might be something interesting in there."

Usk regarded the still burning wreck doubtfully.

"I'm not going in there," Kylar announced backing up and eyeing the tiny hatch and dirty smoke coming from it. "I'll keep watch from out here."

"You're just worried about singeing your fur," Usk muttered as he entered the shuttle ahead of his lord to check for danger.

Valjoth ignored them and edged into the small craft. Kylar would never have fit, the tiny hatch barely had room for him to enter and he was much smaller than any female. Kylar was a giant among her kind. The craft was Human sized of course, and although his blasting had opened up the hull at the rear, the breach wasn't a good entry point. It was still burning back there for one thing, and the ragged holes were sharp edged and too small even for him.

He looked around and found the power was still on, so the place was well lit. The smoke wasn't too bad further in. It was the ventilation effect of an open hatch that made it seem thick billowing out of there. Usk was ahead of him checking for vermin, and while he did that Valjoth poked into things.

He didn't expect to find anything particularly revealing. The entire system had been a bit of a disappointment for his first battle against Humans. Not that he was complaining about the lack of a proper welcome. It was imperative that his ships refuel and move on without word of their presence getting out to the Humans in general. The system was simply a convenient refuelling waypoint to his true target, but still, it would have been more memorable had there been something challenging to fight.

He opened a compartment and rummaged around inside it, but there was nothing interesting... Human foodstuffs, and what he thought might be a medical scanning device of some kind. No weapons. He ripped the door off the compartment just because he could, and followed Usk toward the pilot's cabin. He was just being sour because he had to go back aboard *Blood Drinker* soon. It had been a long trip in foldspace and he wasn't looking forward to more of the same. That was all. He had these black moods from time to time, but luckily they rarely lasted. He always found something to occupy his thoughts to stave them off. Usk would say it was a lack of exercise, and a good fight usually did free him of dark thoughts, but then so did a tactical problem he posed himself. Idleness of thought, not of the physical, was the one thing that was guaranteed to bring the mood on.

"Lord!" Usk called and returned with a struggling Human in his grasp.

Valjoth beamed at his shield bearer. "Well done, Usk!" he bellowed. "That's a nice one. Any more up there?" Usk gave the struggling vermin to him and came up with a second Human. "One each! Excellent."

Usk grinned. "Kylar will have to find her own."

Valjoth laughed and examined his vermin. Male he

thought it was. Humans didn't vary in size as much as his people did, but he recalled fur on the face like this one had, was one important way of telling the difference. The cunning beasts sometimes shaved though, so Usk's prey might be either gender. It did have bumps on the front that could be mammary glands for feeding its young. Many vermin females had two of them instead of six proper teats, but they performed the same function. He frowned at Usk's Human; the Parcae didn't have them. Those bug-eyed little nuisances all looked alike to him no matter their gender. He examined his Human more closely. Yes, he believed his was indeed male. A male and female hiding together... a breeding pair perhaps? Hmmm...

"Is there anywhere for young to hide up there?"

Usk nodded and handed his Human to Valjoth to check the cockpit.

Both Humans were screaming and struggling. He quite liked the noises they made, but he didn't want them to injure themselves. He lifted the female by her neck with one hand and roared full in her face. It... she fainted quite nicely and the male started crying. Water leaking like that was common among vermin. Merkiaari eyes had proper inner eyelids to hold moisture in. They rarely cried. Gas or other toxins could bring it on, and tears served to flush them out, but not much else could cause it; fear produced rage not tears.

Usk came back empty handed. "Just those two, my lord."

"That's unfortunate," Valjoth said feeling amusement at Usk's suddenly downcast demeanour. "I'll give the male to Kylar. It's bigger."

Usk nodded grimly. Giving her the lesser of the two might be insulting, not that Kylar was that touchy really. For a female, she was the pinnacle of calm thoughtfulness, but better not to take chances.

They made their way back outside to Kylar who

brightened the moment she saw the vermin. He gave her the male, and watched as she ripped it in half. Very satisfying it looked too. He glanced at the female in his grasp and sighed before giving it to his oldest companion.

"You're too generous, my lord," Usk said in delight.

Valjoth gnashed fangs. "Yes I know, but if I can't make my shield bearer happy, I wouldn't be much of a companion would I?"

Usk woke his Human and popped her head off with one squeeze of her neck! Oh, that was excellent of him. A very economical kill to be sure. Tidy too. Kylar was covered in vermin blood still steaming in the cool air, but Usk was free of gore. That wouldn't normally be a concern but they had to spend time together in the sled yet.

Thinking of the sled, they headed back and climbed aboard.

"Find us something to do, Usk."

Usk nodded but said, "We have to leave soon."

"Even more reason to hurry then!"

Usk spun the sled expertly, allowing it to skid sideways until he had it aimed at the street he wanted, and then went to maximum power. He didn't feed the power in gently; he slammed the throttles to the stops and roared along the street. Kylar shouted in glee, and Valjoth gnashed his fangs in laughter at her antics. She was blasting holes into the buildings as they sped along for no reason and having a fine time doing it.

Valjoth turned his attention to Usk's scanner and thought he knew where they were going. His shield bearer had obviously decided there wasn't time to hunt their own prey, but there might be time to join a hunt already underway. The scanner revealed a pack hard at work, its force of grav sleds spread out and herding the vermin—if vermin there were—toward destruction. It was pack doctrine in action, and it usually worked well within urban environments like this. Somewhere ahead of the stampede, his troops would be ready and waiting to cleanse the Humans from this bad excuse for a colony. It would be done, and done quickly. There weren't enough of the vermin left to require even one more day on this world.

Usk raced through the city determined to reach the final battle before it was over, and he did, but it was a close run thing. Most of the Humans were already dead when he powered down the sled and dismounted to shadow his lord.

Valjoth wasn't disappointed, well not too disappointed. There were still a few stragglers to take care of, and Kylar even caught one for him without needing to be asked when it made a break for it! That was remarkably decent of her considering where they were. The blood and screams were having a predictable effect upon her; she was agitated and close to raging.

"Go on, have fun," he said giving her his permission to leave him. "Usk will stay."

She didn't need telling twice. She screamed her battle cry and ran off.

Valjoth shook his head and glanced at Usk. "She's young."

"Not that young," Usk said watching enviously as the closest pack to them butchered the remaining vermin and began checking the heaps of carrion for fakers.

"Now, now, we had our time on the battlefield. You can't begrudge her these years."

"I don't," Usk said. "*Really!*"

Valjoth just stared at him.

"*Really!*"

Valjoth didn't believe him, but let it go. Besides, if he was honest with himself he still yearned to do as Kylar was doing, but maturity and his... ah, little *differences* allowed him to control such urges. It didn't mean that he didn't have them though. He had heard the whispers; the rumours about him and how he was unnatural in the way he controlled the rage. Unnatural? Maybe it was, but it was useful in someone with his responsibilities. Besides, weren't the gene splicers cultivating his ability in the new batches? He knew they were, and it was just one of the things that made those troops so useful.

He wandered amidst the heaps of the dead. He had hardly lost any troops here. The stampede had worked as doctrine intended, and the grav sleds had reaped a heavy toll upon the vermin. This wasn't a battlefield really; there had been no battle. It had been a slaughter. Something made him stop his wandering and back up a couple of steps. He reached down suddenly and pulled a Human out of the heap.

"What do we have here?" he said, showing Usk.

"A young one, my lord. Alive?"

Indeed it was, but not faking death or unconsciousness; it had a head injury and was covered in gore. He studied the creature, holding it up by one arm to see it better. A male, he decided, and a small one. He didn't know how to judge age in Humans, but it wasn't adult in size. The fur on its head was pale in colour as was its skin, but the paleness was not natural or healthy for it. Valjoth looked away to find Kylar had returned and together with Usk was waiting to see what he planned to do with his Human.

"I'm saving it for later," he abruptly decided. "Have we a collar?"

Usk shook his head but Kylar thought there might be one in the sled. She went to look. While she did that, he carefully tried to wake the creature. It groaned and its eyelids flickered as it stirred. He shook it, and the eyes snapped open. It cried out at the sight of him, but he was pleased when it stopped after only a brief struggle to be free. It glared at him. So! A fierce one then. He grinned back at it.

"Humans don't make good pets, my lord," Usk said doubtfully as Kylar returned with an obedience collar. "They never last long."

True. Humans were a little like Merkiaari in that they preferred death to captivity, but this was a young one. Perhaps he could train it to survive. It would give him something to do on the journey. There was little else for him to do in foldspace; all his planning was long since complete. He snapped the collar around its neck and waited for the device to adjust its size before letting the creature stand on its own feet. It bolted immediately as expected. Kylar handed him the controller and he used it.

The creature staggered and fell tugging for all it was worth upon the collar.

He had chosen strangulation over direct pain stimuli for its first lesson. Time would tell, but pain could be endured up to a point, suffocation couldn't. Besides, he didn't know its pain threshold yet and didn't want to kill it or make it mindless accidentally. He collected the Human and allowed it to breathe again. When it opened its eyes he showed it the controller so it knew where its pain had come from, and then strangled it again. This time it just watched him until it fainted. Excellent! It was an intelligent specimen; he had hoped it would be. It had learned that running was pointless already. He felt quite optimistic that he might train it to at least survive for a short while.

"Can I ask why you even want a Human for a pet?" Kylar said. "Wasn't the entire point to cleanse them entirely?"

Valjoth watched it coming around again. "It's just an experiment. We know they won't be controlled, not like the Parcae or the Shintarn let's say, who do whatever it takes to survive today so they might rebel again tomorrow with better hope of success. I simply wonder if Humans can be that pragmatic. I don't think they can; they're too much like us."

Kylar drew back, obviously affronted by the thought of being likened to any vermin, even one worthy of giving Merkiaari a true challenge as Humans had done in the past.

"I admire that about the vermin; their pragmatism I mean."

Usk rolled his eyes and shook his head at Kylar, trying to make her drop the subject, but she ignored him. She tended to do that, and it drove Usk to distraction, which of course was why she did it. Valjoth enjoyed them both and their rivalry; they were immensely entertaining to him.

"I did wonder about that," Kylar admitted. "Why we didn't cleanse them completely last time I mean."

"Oh that has nothing to do with why I didn't erase them. No, the Parcae—and the Shintarn for that matter—are much too useful to force into extinction. The Hegemon would have my head if I deprived us of useful species that way. No, they just needed the usual reminder of their situation. It will hold them for another half century or so."

The usual for the Parcae was decimation not annihilation. Other vermin needed lesser or greater object lessons depending upon species, but putting down four in ten always worked. They even chose by lots which of their people would die when their battle was lost. They never needed to be forced to hand them over either. He suspected they chose amongst themselves before they even began their rebellions and considered it an honour to serve their people in that way. They would think it very unfair if he killed five in ten instead of the usual four. Not traditional at all they would probably say, as if rebellion were just a game. Maybe to them it was.

Vermin madness.

* * *

Davy glared up from where he lay as the Merki talked amongst themselves. His hand stole up to the collar around his neck. He couldn't stop himself from pulling at it, even knowing it wouldn't come off. His eyes slid from the Merki in charge to the giant he was talking to; it was head and shoulders taller.

He remembered what that meant from school. It, the giant, was a she. A female death trooper. The worst of the worst.

He had to get away, but how? Everyone was dead except for him. Even if they let him go, how long could he survive here alone? How long would he want to? He wanted to scream for help, but his teachers and friends were all dead. They were all around him, piled high where they'd fought and died without hope. He felt numb. Was that grief? He couldn't believe everyone he had ever known was dead. He was the last Human; he might never see another, *like ever!*

His parents... he wanted to scream and never stop, but in his head he heard his dad telling him to be calm and think it through. Think it through, Davy, he would say. I know you can do it... but his dad had been talking about a math problem, not this!

Think it through, think it through, think it...

* * *

18 ~ Arrival

Bang! Clang-thump!

Kate sighed tiredly. Docked finally. She stood and headed for her cabin to change clothes when all she really wanted to do was enter maintenance mode for some much needed downtime, but she could sleep in a hotel when she got down world as easily as here. Besides, she wanted to get settled on Northcliff before her brother's ship arrived, not be scrambling for a base of operations when that event happened, which it would any day now. She had already tapped into the Infonet for news, and into the station's net for its ship list. Her processor would raise an alert the moment her brother's ship translated into the system.

In her cabin she stripped and took a shower to wake herself up a bit, before redressing in one of the outfits Stone had supplied. As she pulled on the stylish purple trousers with the see through net panels down the sides, she folded herself away gradually allowing her Cherry Jackson persona to take over. Cherry was a real person to her—one of her alter egos who had a surprising number of uses. Everyone loved her. When Cherry looked at you her eyes said, *'let's be friends'* and you found yourself smiling. Whether she was a teenager away from home for the first time, a silly tourist sowing her wild oats while travelling the Alliance, or a young salesperson on a business trip, Cherry Jackson got the job done. It was uncanny how easily Kate found it to become someone so opposite to her real nature. Handy though. One of Stone's I.Ds was for Cherry because he knew she was a favourite cover story of hers.

Thinking about I.D, she ordered her processor to reset her simcode implant in case immigration checked. Northcliff was an Alliance member world despite its edge of the Border Zone location. No doubt its assimilation into core world civilisation was well under way and using simcode readers was part of that. All vipers had re-programmable simcode implants, but it wasn't a new convenience for her. Bethany's ISS had replaced her original implant as part of her spinal cord when it recruited her years ago. What *was* new was her ability to re-program it on the fly. Her processor had a lot of identities to choose from. Very useful they were too, especially when simcode implants were meant to be tamper proof and were therefore automatically accepted wherever they were used within the Alliance.

In her experience nothing was really tamper proof. The degree of security just depended on how much time, money, and effort one was willing to spend to compromise it. In the simcode implant's favour, it took government level resources to cheat the system... or General Burgton level of time and determination. Come to think of it, both things applied where vipers were concerned. The regiment did have its own planet and fledgling navy after all.

Kate chose a hideous shirt to go with her purple trousers. It was lime green with lemon stripes and was designed to be worn untucked. She admired the results in the mirror, but shook her head unsatisfied. Her military haircut needed disguising, but because it was shaved tight to her skull on the sides she would need something extra to pull off the look she was going for. She grabbed her Goop and got to work styling it into spikes to distract the eye. Ten minutes later she used the setting agent on it and admired the result.

"You look gorgeous, Cherry," she said and frowned. "You look *gorgeous*, Cherry!" She said again, adjusting her tone of voice lower. Sultry worked better. Cherry wasn't a dippy tourist this time around. She was a thirty-something young business woman on her way up in the world. Well on her way to better things, but not quite there yet. "Hi, my name is... *Hi!* I'm Cherry, Cherry Jackson? I'm here to see... I have an appointment to see..." she nodded.

She hadn't lost her touch.

Makeup was last. She chose the lemon stripes of her shirt and matched it for eyes and lips. She dialled in the codes and waited a second for the nannies in the eye shadow and lipstick to adjust before finishing her disguise. Last of all she did her nails. Lemon again. She would have preferred black or maybe a very dark purple, but Cherry the up and coming business woman preferred bright and cheerful, not dark and mysterious. She could already feel the colours settling into her psyche as she studied the woman in the mirror. She pouted and smiled, practising her moods. The cheerfully outrageous colours and clothing were making a difference. Cherry was feeling more real, more in control of their body.

She shuddered. On ops like this it was spooky being Kate Richmond. Sometimes she worried that there might be something not quite right with her head, and at other times she knew beyond question she was a psycho. It didn't matter really. She hid it well and could function like a normal person when she had to, but letting her alter egos like Cherry out to play now and then was good for her. Better they come out like this than in an uncontrolled way. She knew that Hymas had been watching her for instability. Not so much now that she had undergone a second enhancement without a whig-out, but she did still keep a watch. Hymas had tried to have her scrapped early on in the recruiting process. She had wheedled that out of Stone one night when she asked about Hymas' vendetta against Bethanites. There was history there. She didn't know everything, but she would one day. Kate respected Hymas because she knew the woman was right to be wary around her despite every other doctor's contrary view. She really was a dangerous psycho... just not all the time. The only ones who needed to worry were her enemies, and the General chose who those were these days.

She frowned.

She had never liked authority, and resented those with power over her, but she needed the discipline of her military career to keep her head straight. She was a weapon in need of targets, and the regiment provided her with those. That was one of the reasons why she disliked being an officer. It was better someone else decided who needed to die. OSI (Office of Strategic Intelligence) had been the perfect solution. She could have been happy there performing missions and planning ops for the others, while letting Stone and the General aim her in the right direction. It had been great— just enough direction to satisfy her needs without too much oversight to make her resent it.

She sighed. Well, that life was over now. It hadn't worked out, that was all. It wasn't the first setback she'd had in her life and it wouldn't be the last. She didn't know what the future would bring, a quick death probably, but she wouldn't go quietly. Until then, she would live her time to the full, and she already had some idea of what to do after rescuing Paul. If she only had limited time, she wanted to use it wisely. Bringing down a ruling family of Bethany—the Whitby family—would make a fine epitaph. Anyway, that was for later.

It was time to go, but before leaving the ship she needed one last disguise. She rummaged in Stone's trunk and located the medical kit. Inside amongst the bandages and nano injector cartridges she found a box of surgical gloves. To outsiders they would be just another part of a standard med kit, but these gloves weren't standard. Each cellophane packet contained a single glove designed to disguise a viper's right hand. It was a fingerless glove only covering the hand and each finger to the first knuckle. It would be useless for medical purposes. She tore open the sterile packet with her teeth and pulled the glove on, working her fingers and smoothing it over her palm with her other hand. Her weapon's bus was completely covered. The glove slowly shrank as it reacted to the heat of her body, wrinkles smoothed out as it tightened, until it had blended with her hand. It would take a close inspection for anyone to realise the glove was even there.

Customs and immigration, as expected, was busy as hell. That was both good and bad in her opinion. Bad, in that it slowed her down and she was impatient, but also good because she was just one of hundreds of people eager to get down world. The customs people were only interested in shoving as many bodies through its procedures as it could before another ship docked and the flood of passengers started over again.

Kate checked that her ECM (Electronic Counter Measures) was ready to spoof the scanners and shuffled to the front of the line. Stone's battered trunk faithfully followed her movement, humming quietly on its anti-grav. She ran a sensor sweep looking for anyone taking notice of her, but detected nothing outside of the usual security precautions. No unusual movement caught her eye, no one watching her or suddenly turning away when she turned to look. She had a window open giving her the feed from dockside security cams, but again everything seemed normal. She had a nearby cam zoom in to study her own face. She forced the annoyance out of her expression and replaced it with Cherry's *'let's be friends'* look before dismissing the window.

"Next!"

She shuffled forward.

"Name, homeworld, destination, reason for visiting?" the bored customs official said by rote and without catching Kate's eyes.

Realising her *'let's be friends'* expression was wasted on this man she let it drop. "Cherry Jackson, Beaufort, your lovely capital city, and business."

He nodded. "Arms up at your sides for the scan. Anything to declare?"

"Nothing," she said and raised her arms for him to wave his scanner over her. A security alert blinked onto her internal display and kept flashing as he speedily worked the wand expertly over her body. Another indicator lit. Her ECM was countering and sending back a false reading. Both alerts disappeared when he moved on to her trunk.

"Did you pack this yourself, anything perishable inside, anything unsafe or volatile?"

"I packed it, nothing perishable, nothing volatile, but I'd appreciate some care. It has all my samples."

"Samples... pharmaceuticals?" His eyes narrowed.

"Oh no, nothing like that!" she said, trying to sound scandalised. It didn't sound quite right though, more like she was horrified by the very idea. Good enough. "I'm visiting your world with the latest cosmetics to come out of the core. They're guaranteed to knock years off your appearance. Why, they're better than body mods and a fraction of the cost!"

"Uh-huh," he said. "Open it."

"But!"

"Open. It." His voice was harder now. "You can do it here with me or in a cell a couple of hours from now."

She grumbled as expected but unlocked the trunk.

He ran his scanner over the contents, adjusted settings,

and did it again. "Okay, you're clear. Next!"

She locked her trunk before proceeding through the checkpoint towards a shuttle. The faithful trunk followed two paces behind with Stone's bomb making and snooping supplies safely inside. She sneered at the so-called security measures, but kept it off her face. This kind of thing was why people like her were needed in the first place. There were always home grown trouble makers, but the problem was made massively worse by off world backers. Security at the interface between worlds—the stations—was so important, yet it was ridiculously lax. People like her had to come in and clean up messes that were allowed to happen due to weak security, yet if asked, people out here in the Border Worlds would protest any proposal to tighten it up. They didn't really want core world rules and regs, but they secretly wanted the affluent lifestyle found there. Those that wanted neither simply emigrated further out where the cycle had yet to start. Northcliff was an Alliance member but it was still at an early stage in its journey from true Border World to Core World. It was definitely on the path, but not there yet by a long way.

Kate delivered her trunk to the cargo master of her shuttle, and then boarded to find a seat. The shuttle was nearly full when she buckled in, and just minutes later they were on their way. She closed her eyes trying not to let the other passengers annoy her with their inane chatter and squirming around. The shuttle was a small one and the passengers were packed in shoulder to shoulder as usual. They were built for fast economical movement of people, not for luxury.

Her seat jolted, and then again, making her tense and grit her teeth. The guy behind her was messing around with the vid screen in her seat back. That would normally be fine, but his ham-fisted incompetence at finding what he was looking for was being transmitted through her seat as he punched buttons as if pounding nails. She opened her eyes and glared at the shuttle's overhead as he pounded away at the menu buttons. The steward floated expertly along the aisle pulling himself hand over hand in the micro-gravity using the seat backs and stopped to help. He murmured a warning about damaging the equipment before moving on.

Kate closed her eyes again. Her nemesis seemed to have found something to satisfy him, but thirty seconds later he was at it again. Thump... thump... *thump-thump!* In a fit of temper she sent a concentrated electromagnetic burst into his vid unit using her ECM. It was meant for spoofing security cams or sensors when a viper didn't care about damaging a system, but it worked on any sensitive electronics. It fried the unit, and the passenger shouted as a wisp of smoke rose from the burned out circuits, curling into the air above her seat before being sucked away into the shuttle's ventilation. She smiled grimly, and closed her eyes as the steward came back to take his name and seat number. He would be charged for the damage.

The shuttle landed at the Kastoria Spaceport an hour and thirty minutes later. She would have preferred a faster trip, but Northcliff was a popular destination nowadays, since the new trade route to the Shan had opened, and air traffic over the capital was heavy. They'd had to circle. The spaceport was located in a valley sandwiched between two mountain ranges. If she bothered to look it up, she was sure the valley was the result of glaciation in the distant past. From the air it looked sparsely forested with the spaceport an ugly scar in the middle. Roads and maglev rails led to and from it like a demented spider's web, supplying the port with workers, passengers, and cargo.

Kastoria City itself was built upon the slopes of the foothills and mountains. She supposed the mountains were pretty enough compared to the deserts, but she couldn't work up much enthusiasm as she collected her trunk and headed for the exit from the transit lounge. They weren't very impressive examples. They weren't grand ranges with massively tall peaks like those on Snakeholme, and the trees looked stunted and scraggly unlike the lush forests back home... she frowned. Home was Snakeholme, or it had been until this. Where was home now? Certainly not Bethany, not anymore.

Bethany was like Alizon in its lushness and beauty. Both planets were renowned for it. Grand waterfalls and canyons, mountains and forests were numerous. The climate was mild never severe, and the gravity was below that of Earth, especially Alizon. Both worlds could be called paradises with economies heavily vested in tourism. If you had the money, wanted ease and beauty without the dirty reality of other worlds in which Humans lived and strove for better lives, then immigrating to either one would do. Bethany especially, if you didn't care who ran the government, or how. Not something she would recommend anyone do, and she was born there. No, she preferred Snakeholme, where it took effort to thrive, and where the world reminded you of it every day.

Kate stepped outside and was rocked back on her heels by the heat and glare. Compared to the air-conditioned interior, the heat outside felt unbearable. Sweat beaded upon her brow; she was in danger of having a catastrophic deodorant failure and she had barely been outside a minute yet. She looked around for a direction to follow, and saw a sign through the shimmering air pointing to the maglev station. All routes it said. Her eyes automatically metered light levels, but she put on a pair of sunglasses because everyone else did, and turned to follow the crowd along the baking plascrete.

Northcliff was different in a lot of ways. The sun was a white dwarf and its light was harsh. Gravity wasn't particularly low at 0.97g, but much of the planet was arid. Temperatures were high in most areas, probably one reason the mountains were chosen for the city. At least at higher climes the population could expect a little relief from the heat with mountain breezes. Really, with the terrain of the entire planet to choose from, what other reason could there be for the colonists to cut terraces here and build their capital on them?

Kastoria City wasn't the only important city on Northcliff. There were plenty of others spread over its three huge continents. The planet had a large percentage of land compared to sea. Over 60% of the surface area was land with large deserts. That hadn't deterred the corporations building there of course. In fact, it attracted them more strongly. Many industries found the resources in the deserts useful, and vast solar and wind farms made power inexhaustible and totally free after the initial investment had been paid down. Nanotech factories consumed materials like silicon at a prodigious rate, which is plentiful in deserts of course, and other resources could be found from mining at extreme depths. Not a hardship with modern mining machines.

All of the desert cities were built around huge factories and were governed by the corporations that had built and owned them. Their citizens lived and worked within the city environs, rarely if ever leaving to visit other places. Kate was glad she didn't need to visit them, not because they were distasteful places to live or anything like that—they were ultra modern cities with every convenience and pleasure anyone could want. Keeping their workers pacified and under control was important to the management, and the carrot was always better than the stick for doing that. No, it was because the cities were tightly controlled and security would be tight. It had to be. Cyber theft and industrial espionage was rampant between competitors, and although such clandestine wars in the core had cooled, that wasn't true at all out in the Border Zone. Corporations had teeth out here. Their mercenary armies were serious military assets the equal of some government forces in the core.

Kate followed the crowds toward the maglev station, ignoring the hopeful cab drivers. Her trunk wouldn't fit in a cab, but that wasn't her reason for choosing the train. The trunk could have been locked down on the car's roof if she wanted. No, she just didn't want to be on her own again so soon. Ten days in foldspace going stir crazy... ten frigging days of boredom was enough. She wanted to mingle a little and relax, breathe the air of a new world, and try to blend with its people to get her head in the right space. All too soon she would be working to free her brother and then running for her life.

She rode the maglev into the city and then accessed the Infonet again to find a hotel. She chose one called The Crowne because it was near the station, not because of its service. She was sure that would be fine but its location was more important because the station was more than just a maglev terminus; it was a transport hub with a connection to Kastoria's extensive subway system. Multiple routes out of an area was one of the things she looked for when on an op like this. The taxi rank and hire cars were of less interest—she wouldn't get far outside the city before running out of roads to use—but she noted it for completeness. Any of the cars would be easy to jack from the owners if push came to shove. The Crowne had another thing going for it; it was big enough that it had a bank and a few stores on the premises. She wouldn't find what she most needed there, namely weapons, but she should be able to buy a good portable comp and some more clothes. Stone's selection had been useful but minimal.

She entered the hotel bypassing registration and headed for the bank. The android teller smiled blankly and waited for her to make a request. It was a female design as most droids used in banks were, and very stupid. That was what she wanted. There would be human bank employees around, but she didn't want them remembering her or the transaction she was about to make. She withdrew both wands that Stone had supplied and inserted the first one into the desk.

"Thank you, Ms. Murillo," the droid said. "How might I help you today?"

"I'll be making a withdrawal," Kate said.

"Please enter your password."

Kate quickly entered the password on the account, but watched her sensors close. Now was the time for anyone overly interested in her to make a move. Nothing showed up, but she went the extra mile.

Computer: initiate full spectrum security scan. Range out to 200 metres.

>_ SENSORS: FULL SPECTRUM SWEEP IN PROGRESS.

"Thank you, ma'am. How much would you like to withdraw today?"

"All of it. Large denomination platinum wafers."

The droid blinked twice as it tried to process her request. It smiled. "Please choose a number between zero and your available balance and state it clearly in standard English. How much would you like to withdraw today?"

Kate growled under her breath. "Fifty. Thousand. Credits."

"Thank you. How would you like... *fifty... thousand... credits...* dispensed?"

>_ SENSORS: THREATS DETECTED.

Kate froze, but then she sighed as the so-called threats were listed. Her sensors had simply picked up the emissions from bank security, not true surveillance gear. It was all standard and passive stuff, not weaponised. She dismissed the alert and concentrated on what she was doing. God she needed sleep, her brain was turning to mush.

"Like I said. Give me hard currency. Fifty platinum wafers."

The desk spat out a pile of platinum. "Thank you, Ms. Murillo. Have a nice day."

She swept the money off the desk and pocketed the little stack along with the wand. She shoved the other wand into the slot.

"Thank you, Ms. Jackson," the droid said. "How might I help you today?"

"I'll be making a withdrawal," Kate said again, without the sigh building in her chest. She really needed her downtime, like yesterday.

"Please enter your password."

Kate quickly entered the password on the account and went through the entire procedure again. She stashed the second fifty thousand in her other pocket.

"Thank you Ms. Jackson. Have a nice day."

Kate ignored the dumb machine and hurried to the hotel's registration desk where she paid for a suite for two weeks in advance. The concierge was dismayed when she paid him with cash, but hard currency was still legal and he had to take it. She used her Cherry Jackson identity for the registration.

Once in her room, she set the do not disturb order on her door, and ran a security sweep of the entire suite for form's sake. It came up clean as expected. She took a shower, but fell into bed naked and with moisture still beading on her skin. She was that exhausted, she couldn't think straight.

Computer: initiate maintenance mode. Reactivate combat mode in 24 hours.

ACKNOWLEDGED. MAINTENANCE MODE IN 3... 2... 1...

Lights out.

* * *

19 ~ Desert Planet

Although the wadi was many more klicks from her target than Kate was really happy with, it was the best choice she had for a stealthy landing site. She hovered above it on antigrav staring down at the ground through the cockpit's side window, and carefully manoeuvred the shuttle to clear the escarpment to her right and the fallen rocks littering the ground. The wadi was an unusual feature of the Konuhara Desert, which was a vast area of rolling sand dunes that continued for thousands of klicks in every direction. She had trained in desert conditions before, but she had never seen one like this. The deserts she'd experienced had been arid rocky wastelands, not rolling dunes of yellow sand. Ironic, because most would think of sand when picturing a desert, but few were really like that. Well this one was, and it was a vicious one too. According to her instruments, it was 60°c outside and that was in the shade of the escarpment.

She managed to set down without crashing, always a plus, especially when her deposit was riding upon her ability to return the shuttle undamaged. As soon as the skids were on solid ground, she powered down and collected her pack. She was armed with the minimum she was comfortable with, a pulser in a shoulder rig. She chose not to bring anything else in case she found herself under scrutiny. It was unlikely, but not impossible that someone would come out to check on her. She had a story ready for that eventuality, and a weapon for personal protection was something everyone was expected to carry outside of civilised areas. Civilised in the Border Zone meant within sight of a city or settlement, but on some planets the term could be debated within city hall itself!

Kate opened the hatch. "Woof!" she gasped as the heat rushed in and slapped her in the face. Hard. "Damn me, this is gonna suck."

Sweat burst instantly upon her face as she jumped down and locked the hatch behind her. She pulled up her hood and secured it over her face before she lost too much moisture. She had brought water with her, but she couldn't afford to let dehydration get a hold on her. She pulled on her backpack, took a GPS reading, and with a map open in a window on her display headed for her objective.

This was her third day on Northcliff. She was much poorer in the pocket but far wiser than when she'd arrived. The money wasn't a concern. It had been well spent on a few very necessary items like the brand new comp and comm dish in her backpack. For the bargain price of an extra thousand, it had come preloaded with a suite of applications designed for the cyber enthusiast, or for the would-be terrorist depending upon your viewpoint. She had spent considerable time finding the right kind of dealers—shady—to approach with her queries, and the costly answers received were a large part of how much wiser she was with regard to Northcliff. The place was a bloody powder keg! She wouldn't have known by the evidence of her eyes, but under the surface Northcliff was seething as the corporations fought to control an emerging power in the Alliance.

It was the Shan causing it of course. Not that it was their fault exactly, but they were the reason for Northcliff's rise to prominence so fast. In fact, it was the speed of that rise which was more directly responsible than the aliens themselves. The influx of off world business and money had caused a boom, but as with any boom in industry a less savoury side of economics had raised its head. Corruption. The news was full of the latest scandal of big money interests buying their way through rules and regulations, greasing the wheels so to speak, to get their way. Nothing new about that, but it was the sheer scale of it here that made it notable.

While arming herself with knowledge, she hadn't neglected the essentials. She had found plenty of places in the less reputable areas of the capital able to supply her with weapons and ammo, but it was her new bodysuit that impressed the most. She had wanted a sneaksuit like the ones she had used on her ISS operations, but this one was better. It was a new design based upon the skinsuits that marines used for piloting their mechs. Powered armour was climate controlled, but in the field the marines couldn't just climb out to do their business. They were often locked into their mechs for days at a time, and that created a need for truly reactive skinsuits to make life bearable. She was wearing hers right now, and despite the heat she was comfortable. The nannies built into the reactive cloth scavenged sweat and other wastes, even dead skin cells, and recycled it all to heat or cool the suit. Her movement provided the power in the form of kinetic energy. It was a very elegant solution to the conditions on Northcliff, and most natives wore something like it beneath their street clothes.

Hers was mil-spec and a little bit more special of course. It came with a full face hood with eye protection as sneaksuits invariably did, and the manufacturer hadn't skimped on the usual things like IR masking, and reactive armour either. It was flame and penetration resistant. If shot she was sure to be unhappy about it—it couldn't replace real armour after all—but she would have a few extra moments to react. She was more than happy with her purchase despite the cost, and wouldn't be going back to her old sneaksuit design from now on. Maybe she should invest in Yamaichi Opticom, because if this was an example of their future products, they were going to hit it big.

So, the desert.

She wasn't here for her announced reasons. When hiring the little single seater shuttle, she had needed to fill out reams of paperwork and waivers on top of leaving a hefty deposit. That deposit had taken care of nearly her entire remaining budget, but as long as she didn't ding the shuttle she would recover it all. So far so good with that. She'd managed to fly around and land a number of times without problems. Her stated reason for needing a shuttle was sightseeing, so she'd made a point of visiting various notable landmarks. She'd bought a good camera to back up that story, and she'd used it extensively to take shots of boring vistas all over the place, but although the subterfuge was probably unnecessary, the camera would be useful now that she was close to her real target.

Konuhara Penitentiary.

It was the only prison on the entire planet, and would be where her brother was delivered to when his ship arrived. Located in the middle of the largest desert thousands of klicks from anywhere, it was escape proof, and that wasn't something she ever said lightly. It didn't mean it wasn't breachable from outside. Obviously she could get in. Any viper could get in and out... *probably* out, but could she get out with a civilian along without risking his life? Hmmm... that she wasn't so certain of, and she had to be absolutely certain of success. She was okay with collateral damage. She certainly expected some on this op, but this was her brother's life on the line and she had no intention of making him a statistic.

Konuhara was certainly escape proof from an inmate's perspective. She doubted anyone would even consider trying to leave. Outside the walls they had a thousand klick walk without water or hope of shade in 60° heat to reach the nearest settlement, and all the while trying to evade recapture from well equipped guards searching for them from the air. Without outside aid, escape was impossible and the no fly zone ensured any such aid could not reach the walls by air. So much she knew from publicly available sources, but she was out here to scope the place for herself and determine whether those sources had it right.

Her sneaksuit regulated her temperature. She was actually pretty comfortable as she ran through the desert heat, but that didn't make things easy. The sand wasn't firm underfoot and travel was taxing even for her enhanced body. She didn't think she would have been able to make the journey before becoming a viper and that was a serious problem right there. She hadn't reached the prison yet, and already she doubted her brother's ability to make it out on foot even with her help. She would check the place out, but the further she went, the more she realised this wasn't going to work. She needed another plan.

Finally after hours of slogging over dunes, she climbed a rise that revealed the prison. She lay prone in the sand to study it. The heat and blinding light made the place ripple and shimmer like a mirage, but this dump wasn't a mirage. It was a place of misery, containing the worst scum Northcliff had to offer. She was no bleeding heart, but she'd rather be dead than held there. Then again, she'd rather be dead than mind-wiped too, so there you go.

Everything in life was relative depending upon how you looked at it.

She switched to X3 to study the walls and defences. Solid plascrete walls twenty metres tall without gates ringed the cell blocks. There were towers of course, and her sensors were tracking targeting emissions from the sentry guns. She watched a shuttle arrive and land within the compound. It had been tracked all the way in by missile batteries located in bunkers outside the walls and upon the roofs of the cell blocks. These guys were serious. The no man's land around the prison was mined and too wide to leap across even by a viper, and the defences didn't end there. She watched hunter killer android guards patrolling the mine field and the walls. The mines weren't motion activated then; they must be set to detect bio forms. Basically, anything with a heartbeat would be taken out. That was why the prison used droids outside the walls. Clever.

Kate pulled her camera from her backpack and recorded everything, but with a sinking feeling in her gut she already knew attacking this place would be a lost cause. She frowned as the shuttle lifted and flew away having delivered its cargo of prisoners. She snapped away at it, getting some good shots, and wondering if she might get in that way. If she could get aboard one of those shuttles, and if she could get the codes to make the defences stand down for her, and if she could find her brother quickly in a prison containing thousands of prisoners, and if she could get him back to the shuttle, and if...

She shook her head at her fantasy. Who was she kidding? It wasn't going to happen. She might get in that way, but as soon as she tried to get Paul into the shuttle alarms would sound. It would be targeted and blown out of the sky even if it had time to lift. Somehow she doubted it would. She didn't have an answer to that problem. Anything she did here was a huge risk and Paul was so vulnerable, so Human. Maybe she could bundle him into armour or something, but even if she had the time, armour didn't make anyone completely safe.

She opened her pack, pulled out one of her bottles, and briefly raised her hood to take a good long drink of water.

She needed to think what to do. She eyed her comp and the dish she'd brought. In conjunction with some of Stone's nano spies, she had planned to use her comp to snoop on the prison's computer network. Some of his gifts were purely for data gathering, others were designed to attack in various ways. She hadn't come to breach the prison today, so she hadn't brought the weaponised versions, but she did have the ability to properly scope out the place. Did she still want to?

She frowned down at the walls and made a decision. It was an easy one to make. She was here and might as well gather all the Intel she could. No point in wasting the trip. She had originally thought to learn the frequencies used by the prison and listen in to any chatter. With luck, she might have picked up more serious intelligence like pass codes, safe routes through the mines, guard schedules and more.

She delved into the pack again and pulled out an aerosol. It looked like any other beauty product, one of many available in any number of well known stores, but this one didn't contain moisturiser. She twisted the bottom and pulled. A metallic cylinder slid into her hand. To the naked eye it looked empty, but it wasn't. A microscope would have revealed thousands of nanobots awaiting activation, each programmed by a master spy named Stone. Activating them was easily accomplished using TacNet. She had a dedicated channel for things like this or for monitoring the feed from remote sensors. She had never used TacNet this way outside of the classroom, but vipers never forgot anything once learnt. They literally couldn't forget anything. Nothing at all. She gave the bugs their target and away they went. She discarded the empty cylinder upon the sand.

She plugged in the dish to the comp and aimed it at the prison before calling up one of the handy apps she'd paid through the nose for. The system was completely passive. It sucked in data and gave nothing back, which was essential. She couldn't afford to be detected by anyone, especially not droids that had no other purpose than killing stuff in the shortest possible time. She watched the comp's screen as it trawled for emissions. It would pick up more than the data directed her way from the nannies busily vacuuming data. The system was sensitive enough to collect any unshielded signal no matter the type or frequency. When it found something, it briefly analysed and recorded the data unless it fell outside of the parameters set to validate the signals received. In others words, it stored the good stuff and dumped the bad before moving on and performing another cycle. It was a way of sampling everything and allowed her to quickly narrow down her search for useful Intel.

Kate watched its progress and gave the computer a nudge in a different direction here and there. For example, the droid's guard frequency was very active but of no use to her. She instructed the comp to ignore that one from now on. The droids communicated with each other all the time to keep their spacing, to alert each other when targets were sighted or eliminated, or to call in backup. None of it interested her. Another tweak of parameters eliminated the prison's general housekeeping channel. That one monitored lighting and the like. Things like climate control and water recycling were computer controlled and monitored in any building. Again, unless she wanted to back up the toilets and flood the place, none of it was any use to her. Dump it.

She watched and waited, allowing the comp to compile its data until she was sure she had everything of interest. She sent her spies their suicide command and packed her gear. She had a long run back to the shuttle. She wanted to reclaim her deposit and get back to the hotel before dark. With a prison break impractical, she needed to think of other ways to get Paul away from Northcliff. She needed to research the justice system and figure out whether she might spirit him away during his processing.

She shouldered her pack and headed back.

CROWNE HOTEL, KASTORIA CITY, NORTHCLIFF

Her brother was here. His ship had arrived during the night while she slept, but the alert she'd set woke her as soon as it docked at the station and the ship-list updated. He was here. They were on the same planet together for the first time in years. She didn't know what to feel. Excitement, apprehension, fear? All three, she decided. She was excited to see him again, and glad he had made it this far in one piece. She was apprehensive because she knew what needed to be done, but not how to do it, and feared she might fail. She also feared their first meeting. Would he still know her? Would he blame her for their father's passing, and his own less than stellar life since then? Would he hate her, be disgusted with her? Would he understand the choices she'd made?

She was going to drive herself crazy thinking about it.

Paul was in Konuhara Penitentiary right this minute awaiting trial. She hated that, but there was nothing she could do about it. She had analysed every byte of data she had vacuumed out of the place, and knew a prison break was out of the question. That knowledge at least opened up other possibilities. She could discard the prison and concentrate upon other avenues. There weren't many, but what there were had advantages over a frontal assault on a maximum security prison. She could think of five possibilities, and each had their own difficulties associated with them, but none sucked as hard as a prison assault. Freeing Paul while he was in transit between the prison and spaceport, or between the spaceport and the courts were both good possibilities; especially the second. Paul would be transferred to an armoured car at the port. She should be able to ambush it relatively easily despite the escort it was sure to have. Attacking the court itself was another, but less satisfactory, option. After sentencing, there would be a last opportunity to get to him en route to the medical centre where mind-wipes were conducted—there was little doubt what the sentence would be. His guilt and that of the other prisoners wasn't in question. Justice in the Border Zone was swift. The trial would be little more than a tick box exercise and chance for the media to witness the law being upheld.

The final option was an intercept within the medical centre itself. That one was the easiest option because it was a public place with no security. She could just walk in, disguise herself as one of the techs and almost literally walk out with him after taking out his escort. The risk was that if it didn't work for any reason at all, if she were delayed for example, Paul would cease to exist. His body would be walking around with someone else living in it. That was a horror she was determined to prevent. No, she didn't like operations without a fall-back position. She was leaning toward intervening in the journey from the court to the medical centre.

That decided, she needed to scout the route. She could do that later but for right now she needed more hardware. Specifically, she needed something to stop an armoured car without killing everyone inside. She needed artillery, and she needed it yesterday. She didn't have the contacts, but she did have a pocket full of platinum and a starting point. Felix, the squirrelly little arms dealer she'd bought her pistol from might have something or know someone who did.

She left the hotel and took a taxi to Felix's store. It was a legitimate business that sold legal weapons for personal protection, but it was his under the counter stuff that was the main attraction. The computer and nifty applications came from under that counter. It was like magic that thing. If she asked for a tank, she would be only mildly surprised if he reached under there and pulled one out. She snorted at the image that popped into her head, and her driver cocked his head at her.

"Nothing, just thought of something funny."

He nodded.

The taxi dropped her outside the store and drove away.

Kate checked her sensors and ran a security sweep, but it came up negative. She was half expecting Stone to pop out of the shadows and say boo, any time now. Realistically he should still be en route if he was coming at all, but she had no intention of being caught napping. She looked around one last time and opened the door into the store.

"Oh no, no, no! No refunds!"

Kate smirked. "Relax, Felix, I'm looking to buy not bust your balls." She didn't care what his real name was, but she highly doubted it was Felix. "I need something special."

His eyes narrowed. He approached slowly, just like the nervous squirrel he reminded her of. Looking beyond her and outside for a moment for anyone snooping, he locked the door before regarding her with calculation. "How special?"

"AAR kind of special."

He hissed between his teeth. "Illegal on Northcliff. Mil-spec stuff needs special permits. Do I look like a merc company to you?"

"You look like a man in need of money to me," Kate said. He also looked like an unscrupulous little weasel, but she wouldn't hurt his feelings by saying so. "I have a pocket full of platinum with your name on it."

She could almost see the credit signs flash into his beady eyes, but then he shook his head. Her heart sank. She didn't have time to shop around.

"I don't know why you need an AAR," he said and raised his hands in a warding gesture. "And I don't want to, but I have something else that packs the same kind of punch. Cyclic rate is low though and magazine cap is tiny, but stopping power is off the charts. Still interested?"

"Penetration?"

"Armour piercing, it will go through 75mm ballistic plate no sweat. It's a 20mm cannon... sort of."

She frowned. "A 20mm autocannon?"

"Not an autocannon, more like an overpowered HTR."

That was intriguing. "Show me?"

Felix beckoned Kate to follow him and led her into the back. He had a machine shop back there for making one off items for customers, but he swept through without stopping and went down a set of stairs into a basement area. It was a firing range for testing his products. There was a single plascrete lane with a target at the end and not much else. He unlocked a cabinet and stepped back.

"I call it a bastard gun, because I made it out of this and that. It's unique. Fires these," he said offering her a huge projectile.

She took it from him. It was as long as her hand from wrist to fingertip. She looked at him in disbelief, and he had the decency to look embarrassed. It was a god-damned bullet! A sure as shit chemical propelled bullet almost big enough to be mistaken for a mini-rocket.

"You built a smoke pole... *why?!*"

He blushed and mumbled something. "I just wanted to see what I could do with one. You know, just to see how far I could push things? Look, if you don't want it that's fine. You can find your damn AAR elsewhere, and good luck!"

"Whoa now, no need to get testy." She weighed the bullet in her hand and inspected the tip. "Armour piercing?"

"Of course." He sounded insulted she'd needed to ask.

She tossed the bullet back to him and approached the cabinet. She stared at the monstrosity he had built and fell in love on sight. It stood on its stock at the back of the cabinet gleaming in understated brushed black finish. It was as long as she was tall with a muzzle brake as big as her fist. A recoil compensator like that was a warning of serious power. A bi-pod had already been mounted. It was an absolute beast of a gun. She doubted Felix had thought it through and designed it to be a crew served weapon, but it must be too heavy for an unenhanced person to tote easily.

"Come to mama," Kate whispered reaching for it, and

Felix smiled with pride. Credit signs were back in his eyes. She scowled at him as she cradled the weapon. "How much?"

"Well, like I said its unique. Priceless."

"How. Much. Felix?"

"Twenty."

She gasped in outrage.

"That's about what you'd have to pay for that AAR you ain't going to find!" He was getting bullish now. "You're in a hurry; I can smell it on you. You'll pay."

She gritted her teeth. She could just kill him and take the damn thing, but she knew she wouldn't. "You can smell that, huh?"

He nodded seriously.

"Can you smell how I'm going to kill you if you don't throw in a decent optic and fifty rounds of ammo?"

"*Fifty!*" he screeched. "The magazine only takes five rounds! This isn't an autocannon. I told you that. One round per pull of the trigger is all you get. I'll throw in two mags fully loaded, no optic."

Ten rounds should be more than enough, but for twenty thousand he deserved to bleed a little. "Nuh-uh, fifty rounds and the optic. I could have squeezed you for a laser targeting system, Felix, be thankful we're friends so I won't, but no money until after a test firing, and you supply the ammo for that."

Felix's eyes bulged.

"Breathe, Felix."

He gasped, sucking in air greedily. "Twenty rounds and the optic... a decent quality holographic model, but not top of the line. I won't budge on that."

Kate pursed her lips. With her abilities she didn't need top of the line. After the first round down range she would adjust to the weapon and be pin point accurate from then on. "Twenty rounds, the optic, and you still supply the test fire ammo."

Felix growled, but he licked his lips, and Kate knew she had him. "Platinum in my hand, no credit."

Credit, as if! "I have the platinum in my pocket right now. The test?"

He bowed to her like a gentleman and swept a hand toward the firing lane.

She regarded it doubtfully. "If this works as advertised, your lane isn't near long enough."

"It works. I have battleship armour built in to that wall. Nothing here will breach it, not even that."

"If you say so," Kate said doubtfully. "If it blows out your wall, I'm not paying for the damages."

"It won't. I've fired it before."

"Yeah?"

"One round. It was enough to prove the concept works."

Hmmm. One round didn't work for her. No way to be sure it wouldn't jam on subsequent shots. "I'll need to put at least a full mag through it. Just to be sure." He shrugged unconcerned, and that made her feel a little better. "Okay," she said and grinned in anticipation. "Let's do this."

* * *

20 ~ Bang Means Stop

Kate watched her brother's trial on the net. She had a window open on her display so that she could see the coverage while staying in position snugged behind her weapon. She had chosen a rooftop OP along the route the armoured car would take from the courts to the med centre. She had scouted the entire route after leaving Felix yesterday, and there were plenty of good spots to choose from, but this one worked well from the point of view of a quick withdrawal.

She watched as one by one the prisoners were sentenced. Paul's lawyer stood with him, but didn't say much that was in any way helpful or new. He tried to apply mitigation again to reduce the sentence. Paul had killed the crazy pirate captain and saved many lives, he said. A lot of good marines owed their lives to him blah blah blah, and he would like to throw himself upon the mercy of the court pretty please? The judge glared, said no, and the next prisoner was up. None of it surprised Kate or anyone else. The court would go through the motions with each of the prisoners and then sentence the lot to mind-wipe, nice neat and completely legal. The

Border Zone would be down one entire crew of raiders, and Northcliff would gain a nice new batch of docile citizens ready to work.

Everyone's a winner.

Kate scowled, except for the poor saps who were about to get their brains turned to mush. Well screw that. She wasn't letting it happen to her brother. Not while she had breath in her body. She stroked The Beast's trigger guard, anticipating what it would do to the enemy vehicles. The armoured car and escort was the enemy now. She had nothing personal against the city's law enforcement, but they were in her way. That wasn't a good place for the KSD (Kastoria Security Department) to be. She would save her brother, and they would leave Northcliff safely. There would be no trusting to luck, nothing left to chance. Anything she needed to do to make it happen she would do. This was just another op. Like all of her previous ops, she would succeed.

"Luck is not a factor," she whispered her personal mantra. It never was with proper mission planning in place.

As expected, the armoured car containing today's batch of prisoners entered the street in convoy escorted by Kastoria and prison security. There were four cars in the escort; two in front and two behind. Prison guards rode in two of the four, and those were the most dangerous. Each one had two Human guards inside, but each had a hunter killer android from the prison battalion riding shotgun. The androids provided the firepower while the Humans gave the things their orders. She was familiar with the model used.

Hunter killers weren't particularly stupid examples of droid design like say a sentry droid, and that was a problem. If the guards gave the correct commands, she would have a real battle on her hands even if she took out their Human masters first. Tell an HK to prevent any escapes for example, and it might well kill all the prisoners reasoning that they couldn't then escape. Very logical, clever almost, and job done. On the other hand, tell it to kill any attackers, the damn thing would chase her off world and across the known universe to fulfil its programming. So a lot depended upon how good the Human guards were in a crisis. If they panicked and said the wrong thing from her point of view, they could make life difficult.

The two Kastoria security cruisers escorting the convoy were nothing to worry about; they were traffic units at best. She still needed to neutralise them of course. If they did nothing to oppose her, they could still go vertical and follow her withdrawal by air. That was something she couldn't allow. She anticipated the officers driving those two units had orders to clear traffic and enable a speedy journey to the medical centre, not to actually defend the convoy—that's what the droids were for. If they had any sense they would call for backup and stay in their vehicles when the attack came. She was pretty sure it was SOP on Northcliff as it was on most civilised worlds. Shootouts between the white hats and the black hats like in the early days of colonisation were long gone from here.

BOOM! Clack-ching!

The Beast's recoil was massive, but she had practised in Felix's basement. In the end she'd run two full mags through the thing despite his bitching about costs and production time for the rounds. Her viper targeting and reflexes were fully dialled in. Somewhere in her database there was a listing for her new toy, probably entitled Weird 20mm Frankengun or something like that, containing its specs and the parameters she needed to fire it accurately. Whatever the case, the spent brass was still spinning through the air when she sent a second round downrange to join the first through the armoured car's engine bay and turbine casing.

BOOM! Clack-ching!

The armoured car shuddered to a halt as its turbine self-destructed, its titanium fan blades splintering and screaming outward at high velocity. The engine casing had been compromised by her shots, but she had no fear that the prisoners would be hurt. Most of the shrapnel would still be caught by the casing as designed, but the engine bay itself was armoured and would catch the rest.

She turned her attention to the escort. All four cars had stopped, but only the droids had emerged. SOP was standing her in good stead. She targeted the closest droid. She could have taken its head off, but androids didn't generally keep their brains in their heads. Heads were just for sensing and looking good to Humans. Hunter killers had their processors in their chest cavities encased in heavy armour proof against most commonly available weapons. Nothing man or droid portable was strong enough to prevent penetration by mil-spec artillery like hers however. Nothing short of battleship armour was stopping her today.

BOOM! Clack-ching!

Droid down.

BOOM! Clack-ching!

Droid down.

Both androids were cut in half, their torsos blasted open and internals obliterated. They were inert junk now. No threat, but she was far from done today. She wanted the guards too scared to exit their vehicles and force her to kill them. She used her final round to kill the first cruiser's turbine stone dead before replacing her magazine with a fresh one and giving the same treatment to the other escort vehicles.

She leapt to her feet and withdrew from the roof as soon as the escort was out of commission. She had minutes at most to secure Paul and disappear. It was a shame, but she had to leave The Beast behind. It didn't matter; it had served its purpose. Felix had really come through with his Frankenstein's monster. Overpowered smoke pole or HTR... it didn't matter what he called it, that thing was fun and effective.

Once on the street, she pulled her sneaksuit's hood up and over her head and face before sprinting to the armoured car. She was monitoring law enforcement channels, and backup had been called as she knew it would be. She had a window open on her display to monitor the time-line, another with sensor data told her the guards were staying put in their vehicles, and a third would be put to good use in a moment. She pulled a tub of face cream out of her pocket, discarded the lid and slapped it down—open end flush against the lock controls of the armoured car. She held it there as data flashed into the once empty window. The nannies in the cream had gone to work. It took just a few seconds.

WORKING...
17...
17390...
17390SJI37...
17390SJI3790AWQ278... DONE.

Kate let the tub fall to the ground and punched the code into the keypad. The door unlocked and she heaved it open to slam against the sides of the car. She jumped up and into the dim interior. Her sneaksuit adjusted to the new light level quickly, and she could make out the terrified faces of the prisoners staring back at her, trying to shield their eyes against the glare of the sun. Their wrists were shackled with cuffs linked by chain to their ankles. She would have little trouble snapping those chains, but time was pressing. She would just snatch her brother and carry him to safety.

She searched faces but didn't see him. "Paul! Paul Richmond!"

No one stirred. They just stared at her, hopeless resignation in their eyes.

"Where is Paul Richmond?" she snarled at the first prisoner sitting to her right. She grabbed and dragged him to his feet. "Where?"

He gasped and shook his head.

"Where is he?" she said to another man, this time thrusting her pulser in his face.

"Who?"

"Paul Richmond. He was in court with you. He killed your captain. Where is he?"

Fear flashed onto his face and he pointed deeper into the interior. Kate snarled and looked again. A man tentatively raised a hand and she grabbed him. An alert popped up onto her display. The guards were getting brave. They had exited their cars, probably with heroic thoughts of taking her while she was in here. Without turning to look, she fired half a dozen shots out the open door. The red icons on her sensors stopped advancing.

"I'm Richmond," the scared man said.

She slapped his face twice for wasting her time. "You're not him. Where is he?"

He cowered back, trying to protect himself. "I'm Paul Richmond... please don't hit me again. I'm him. I'm Paul."

She growled and looked to his nearest neighbour and pointed her pulser at his chest. "Where is Richmond?"

He shrugged.

"You want to die? Tell me where he is!"

He smiled mockingly and she shot him dead. She moved to the next prisoner. "Paul Richmond, where?" He pointed to the impostor and glared a challenge at her. She shot him in the face and moved on. "Your turn."

"Take me with you, and I'll show you... *please!*"

Disgusted she turned away. He didn't want to be mind-wiped and would say anything. She turned back to the impostor. He was the only one who might know something. She blasted the anchor pin on the floor to release his chains, and snatched him up. He weighed nothing to her enhanced muscles. She put him over her shoulder ignoring his cries to be left alone, and leapt out onto the street. Pulser fire, badly aimed, peppered the side of the armoured car behind her. She ducked and returned fire, before turning to sprint away with her unwanted booty screaming bloody murder as he bounced on her shoulder. She hadn't tried to kill the guards. They would heal from the wounds, probably.

Sensors reported security cruisers converging on the convoy, but she had a plan for this. She ran at Human normal speed, assuming she was being observed. Indeed, she was being pursued now as the random shots sent her way revealed. She zigzagged more for form's sake than any real fear. If hit, she would survive though if her passenger were to be hit it would seriously upset her. He was her only lead to finding her brother.

"Drop me! I have to go back. You don't understand, I made a deal!"

"No."

"Drop me you crazy bitch! You don't know who you're dealing with! They'll kill us!"

"Shut it, or I'll leave you here without a head."

That shut him down, but she wouldn't make good on the threat, at least not until after she had squeezed him dry. A deal he said. What deal and with whom? She would find out.

She checked her time-line, but she was on schedule. Security would be circling the convoy overhead about now, and headquarters would be ordering checkpoints and barricades set up in the surrounding streets. They wanted her trapped within their lines, but they didn't know what she was or what she was capable of doing to evade them. An unenhanced Human would find it hard to breach their lines. One encumbered by a felon who didn't in fact want to escape would have zero chance. They were well trained and had practised scenarios where the OPFOR (Opposing Force) pretended to be terrorist cells. She had read reports on the last games as part of her research for Operation Breakout, so she knew what their first response had been, and what their future moves *should* be if they followed their SOP, which so far they had to the letter.

She had her street map open on her display and the first waypoint was coming up. She ducked into the street out of her pursuer's line of sight and accelerated to max. Keeping an eye on sensors, she managed to avoid being seen by zigzagging her way across the map heading generally west until she reached the depot. There were other ways out of the zone, but this one appealed to her on a number of levels. It was fully automated for one thing. No one to see her arrive or depart. Another was the timing. If the convoy had been even ten minutes later, she would have used an alternate escape route. And lastly the use of a recycling depot harked back to the origins of her self-imposed mission to find her brother. It was at a similar site that she had lost him in the first place. It felt right that they emerge together from this one.

She scowled beneath her concealing hood. They wouldn't emerge together, because she had failed to save him. *Again!*

She entered the depot and headed for the trucks. The noise inside was incredible. The building-sized machines towered high above her, crushing and shredding the contents of their hoppers so that their nano disassemblers could get to work. She didn't know much about nano-engineering, only the basic stuff taught at school, but she knew the molecules stripped from the trash by the nano-d would be combined in other machines here by nano-a to create cubes of raw materials for later use in the factories. She ran between towering walls of such material. The blocks produced were piled high all along here ready for shipment. There was a dizzying array of colours and types, each made of various metals, glass, even the basic fibre and minerals used within the autochefs found in every home in the city for food.

"Are we there yet?"

Kate growled. "Shut. Up."

"Come on, I'm going to be sick."

"Then puke, don't bother me."

The entire depot was automated including the recyclers and the trucks that delivered the trash. The timing of her attack upon the convoy was important because the trucks were due to leave the depot precisely on the hour and...

"Shit!"

The bay doors were opening. She needed to find the right truck before they all started leaving on their programmed routes. Each truck had a number. Each number was linked to a zone within the city and she needed truck 16 to reach her third waypoint. She finally found it after a long and frustrating search almost too late. It was next to leave. She opened the inspection hatch, dumped her burden inside, and scrambled in to join him before locking the hatch behind her. The aroma of rotting garbage was... interesting. Okay, it was sickening, but she had more important things to do than puking. Her guest was doing enough of that for both of them.

Before doing anything about him, she made certain to disable the truck's compactor by jamming its sensor with a scrap of trash she found lying on the floor. The trucks were very basic machines and didn't have much autonomy. They simply used GPS to find their destinations and stopped where they were programmed to stop to make collections. She had no fear her tampering would throw up a fault that might prevent the truck from leaving the depot. It wouldn't try to use the compactor until it was something like half full. Until then, it would go about its business.

Just then the truck jolted into motion, proving her right.

She kept a window open on her display to track her progress through the city, and turned her attention to her prisoner. It was dark inside the truck, but she didn't raise her sneaksuit's hood. She wanted to stay anonymous in case she decided to let him live, unlikely as that seemed right now. Her anger was still simmering just below the surface. The lenses protecting her eyes had turned clear, but it was still too dark. She wanted to evaluate his answers by watching his eyes and face, so she switched to low light amplification mode. Colours bled away to monochrome and her surroundings brightened enough to make out details.

"Who are you?"

She ignored his question. "Let's not pretend I'm going to answer any of your questions. Instead, let's pretend things can remain civilised between us. You really don't want to experience the alternative. Believe me."

"What do you want?"

"Who are you?"

He couldn't see her face. It was too dark and besides that she was still wearing her hood. He did try though. He stared into the darkness at the shadow she had become to him, and attempted to lie. That was just too much. Her frustration exploded out of her, and she was across the space in one leap so fast he didn't have time to flinch. She lifted and slammed him bodily against the side of the truck.

"*You're not him!*" she screamed, and hammered him into the side of the truck. "You." *Slam.* "Don't." *Slam.* "Want." *Slam.* "To lie." *Slam.* "*To me!*" she shrieked the words into his face.

He gibbered in terror, saying something about his family and money, and doing a deal. It was all jumbled and confused; too confused for her to make sense of. She forced herself to show calm, but she wasn't calm. She was so far from calm, he should be dead already. Lucky for him, she needed what was in his head.

"*Start...*" she took a calming breath and made her voice pleasant. It was really hard to do. "Start from the beginning. Name."

He swallowed his panic back. "Danny Cole. I'm—"

She raised a hand and he flinched, but she hadn't meant to strike him, just to silence him. "How do you know Paul Richmond?"

"I don't, but I knew his lawyer." He bit his lip. "Is that okay?" he added fearfully.

"His lawyer's name is?"

"Malcolm Redding? He did some work for my company before... before it went under. He knew I needed money."

"Hmmm. Go on."

"I own... *owned* a construction company. I was doing really well, but I expanded too fast and overextended. My loans came due and I couldn't pay. A client of mine defaulted on a big job, and I had to eat the loss. I lost everything. I have a wife, kids... I need the money for them! You have to let me go back and do this! You have to! Please, it's all for them. If I don't go through with it, they'll take the money back!"

She was starting to get a picture of what had happened, but it didn't add up. Where would Redding get the kind of money he would have needed to bribe a man to take Paul's place, and why bother? Certainly Paul would have paid any amount to avoid mind-wipe, but he wouldn't have had that kind of money... would he?

"How much?"

"Five million."

"*Five?!*" she gasped, that wasn't the number she had been thinking. Five was... a lot. She didn't believe for one minute that Paul had that kind of money.

He nodded. "Three to cover my debts, and two for my wife. She needs it to keep the house, and then there are the kids to think about."

The poor sap. He was basically getting a lobotomy in Paul's place so that his wife and kids could continue living the life they had become accustomed to. That kind of money would provide a life of luxury out here in the Border Zone.

He could have simply declared bankruptcy and started again. Maybe sold the house he was so concerned about his wife keeping, and downsize his life. Get a job. Something! Anything but leave his kids fatherless this way. Mind-wiped he would be a different person. All former ties cut, a new identity and life provided to him far away from here. He would just disappear.

Not her business.

"Redding came to you with an offer. Five mil to take Paul Richmond's place? And you said yes?"

He nodded.

"Do you know where Richmond is now?"

"No. Redding must have bribed the guards. The fix was in and we switched places before leaving the courts. I never spoke to him or anything. Redding made us switch clothes, the guards put the chains on me, and that was it. I guess Redding will get him off world or something."

Kate grunted. There wasn't much doubt of that, but she would have to check out Redding to be sure. No one set up something like this, spent so much money without expecting a return. Paul would be in hock forever for a favour of this magnitude.

"You're not going to kill me are you?"

She pondered that. Was she going to kill him? She could right now. His body would find its way into the recycler eventually, so no need to even put herself out hiding him. He didn't know anything that would help her, but then he didn't know anything that would hurt her either. He was basically nothing to her; a nonentity.

"If I say no, what will you do?"

He swallowed. "Give myself up."

"And?"

"And... and I won't tell them anything about you. I don't *know* anything!"

Very true. "Good. In case you have a change of heart,

remember this: If you talk I'll kill your wife, your kids, and your fucking pets before I'm done. I'll track your body down in its new life and tell it what I did before setting it on fire. Do you believe me?"

His eyes were wide and his face very white. "Yes," he whispered.

"Very good! You're a perceptive man. Sit there until I tell you."

His legs collapsed.

* * *

KASTORIA CITY, NORTHCLIFF, BORDER ZONE

The man had walked by the shop twice before stopping to peer through the display window. The sun's harsh light reflected back from the light grey plascrete sidewalk, and the shiny glass of the windows, but he didn't seem bothered by it. His sunglasses had reacted as their nanocoat was programmed to do, darkening the lenses to a black that matched his obsidian skin.

He touched the surface of the window and rubbed his fingers together at the tingling that caused. The glass was armoured against plasma and its surface had been nanocoated. Hutchinson & Gilbert Protection Specialists sold weapons and preferred people not steal them. The shop was open, but he didn't enter right away, instead he peered inside looking for the owner. Felix Hutchinson. He located the little man after a moment and moved for the door stepping quickly inside.

"Help you?"

The man nodded. "Felix Hutchinson?"

"That's me. Do I know—"

The bullet punched Felix in the forehead killing him instantly, but the assassin never left things that mattered to chance. He stepped closer, looming over the body and put another two rounds into its chest obliterating the heart. The suppressed slug thrower was nearly silent, and the targeting very precise—tightly grouped and machine-like. The man had bought his weapon from Felix's biggest rival the previous day. He stared down at the body, assessing the scene.

He pursed his lips briefly before putting away his gun and retrieving a different weapon from his coat. This one was a snub nosed pulser designed for close in work. He stepped over the corpse and aimed the weapon at the armoured door set beneath the counter. He triggered a long continuous burst, careful to burn the lock enough to make it appear he had failed to get through. This death was a random robbery attempt, not an assassination.

Before leaving, he emptied the register of platinum and completely destroyed the security system. Locating and corrupting the data backups was child's play to him, but he didn't rush the process. Felix had kept copies of his files on the net. There would be no record of this visit or that of a tall woman carrying a long and heavy looking bundle the day before.

The assassin left the shop, not looking back.

* * *

21 ~ Intervention

Kate returned to her hotel distracted by the news coverage on the net. The recapture of the fugitive, Paul Richmond, was big news right now and she was watching for any mention of the impostor Danny Cole. There was nothing, and that was good, but she would watch until his mind-wipe was confirmed. KSD, the entire department, were being hailed as heroes. No mention had been made so far of how easily they had lost their prisoner in the first instance, or the way said prisoner had turned himself in. All of that was glossed over in the city's haste to reassure its citizens that everything was under control. A story was concocted to cover the recapture and life went on.

She locked her door after pressing the do not disturb button. She needed a shower in the worst way. Her street clothes had the faint but lingering aroma of garbage. Her hair too. Charming. She would throw away the clothes, but not her sneaksuit. She would have to hope that airing it out would help. It was much too useful to discard, and replacing it would impact her dwindling funds too hard. She begrudged every credit now. She hadn't anticipated a need for more money at this stage. She had expected to be aboard *Harbinger* with her brother on their way to jump, not contemplating yet another search and possible rescue attempt.

She crossed the room already working zippers and buttons, heading for the bedroom's on suite bathroom. Another headline flashed into the open window on her display, and she paused to analyse it, but it quickly became apparent there was nothing new. Citizens were advised that zone 5 was still off limits blah blah, and that ground traffic was being diverted over or around the affected area blah blah.

"Yeah, yeah... old news," she murmured and stepped into her bedroom.

Snick!

Kate froze, and looked down at the tripwire. "Well... fuck."

"Don't. Move," Stone said in his quiet and most dangerous voice.

Her attention flicked to her traitorous sensors. Nothing. He wasn't behind her as far as they were concerned. The room was empty. Neat trick. She would have to learn that one if she lived. She'd been monitoring her sensors for viper emissions especially since her arrival at Northcliff; all for nothing if Stone could spoof her systems so easily.

"Reach for the pulser. Two fingers only. Do it slow."

"You said not to move," she said dryly.

Stone didn't laugh. "Do not test me. You're one step from being the latest ghost in my database." He pressed the muzzle of his weapon hard against the back of her head. "Rogue, Richmond. I don't need to do anything but put you down. Be grateful I'm even talking."

There was that. Standing orders for rogue units was immediate disposal often with extreme prejudice—the only way to take a viper down quickly. Scrapped for the good of the regiment was policy, not just words. He wouldn't even need to justify the action. All he needed to say was: she went rogue.

She delved into her pocket, and with thumb and finger she withdrew the pulser he was interested in. She held it out to the side, dangling for him to take. He did so, but was taking no chances. Absolutely none. He kept his own weapon painfully hard against her skull, and reached carefully to take the pulser from her. She didn't try anything. He would pull the trigger. She knew he would, and there was the tripwire as well. She didn't know what it was connected to, but she had armed whatever it was when she stepped on it. She must have because it hadn't done anything, like blow her legs off. Yet.

"Back towards me," Stone ordered already backing away himself. "Slowly."

"The tripwire?"

"Sonic disruptor, set to paralyse not kill if you're wondering. I've just disabled it. Step back, now."

She did as he said, but tried to keep him talking. "I'm surprised sonics work against us."

"When I build something it works, even against one of us. Most wouldn't. Our processors automatically analyse and filter anything harmful if given the time. It depends how clever you are with cloaking."

"Inside knowledge must help."

"I couldn't do much without it," Stone agreed. "Keep backing."

Kate took another step, trying to come up with a plan. Stone was a MK1 viper. An original like Burgton. She was the latest and greatest off the line, making her faster and stronger, but even so she didn't like the odds. She might beat him and survive the fight, but would she be in any condition to continue her mission?

"...and subliminals are even worse, they can be a real bitch to filter out. They wouldn't be subliminal if they weren't. Stop there."

She stopped. "You were saying about subliminals?"

Her eyes darted around looking for a way to get the drop on him. Her sensors were still blithely informing her that she was alone. He must be using ECM somehow. It was all she could think of. She had to guess exactly where he was from the sound of his voice. She conjured imagery in her mind and a window opened upon her display showing a still shot of the room. He was—*should be*—behind the couch with the windows at his back near one of the building's support columns holding up the floor above. In his place, she would have her back hard against it to prevent surprises, like getting thrown through the window by a rogue viper unit.

"Keeping me talking is a good tactic, Richmond, but it won't help you. I know all your moves. I helped write the book you were trained with."

She snorted. "You think a lot of yourself, don't you? I arrived on Snakeholme already well trained, Stone. You recruited me, dammit. You should know that."

"I do know, that's part of why we're still talking." A set of restraints landed at Kate's feet. "Put those on, and we can keep talking. Don't put them on, and you're done. Choose."

Choose. Just like that she had to choose captivity and transport home, or risk a fight and possible death? She had her brother to find! It wasn't as easy as he made it sound. Choose, like she ever really had a choice where her brother was concerned. Her father's death had wiped away any she'd had. She had tried to bring up Paul properly. Prepare him, as their father had prepared her, for life on Bethany, which had some particular challenges not found on other worlds. Society there wasn't so much repressive as it was particular in its details. There's a right way and a wrong way to behave in every situation. Smile with this degree for first meetings, smile with that degree for friends. Even insulting someone with a cultivated sneer was covered. She had taught him when it was permissible to shake hands, when not to, and when insult became outright challenge actionable in court. All of it was bullshit to someone like her, someone who had travelled the Alliance and seen how people were meant to live, but absolutely essential for any proper Bethanite wanting to live on Bethany's World. Bethanites were very proper in superficial things like manner and dress, yet The Ten ruled like despots smiling with the proper degree of sincerity at all times of course.

"Kate," Stone said very quietly. "Put them on... please."

He called her Kate. He only ever used her first name when the conversation switched from business to personal. It meant something. It meant he wasn't as unaffected by her decision as he wanted to appear. She took a breath and bent to retrieve the restraints from the floor. They were heavy duty plasteel manacles. He must have had them made special. She wouldn't be able to break them. She hesitated for another long moment and then slipped them on.

"You can turn around," Stone said when the manacles clicked shut. He sounded relieved. "Sit."

Anger at his order flared and heated her face. She wasn't his dog! But when she turned and saw his face the anger fled. He looked haggard. Tired and worried, but very obviously relieved that he hadn't yet had to put her down. She read all that in the instant she saw his face. She knew him that well. It gave her hope that things would turn out, or it did until she sat on the couch and he asked another question.

"How the hell did you manage to screw this up, Richmond? I provided you a ship and an opportunity for your little side project. I even supplied backup in the form of Fuentez."

"Is she here?"

Stone shook his head. "She's on Helios doing the job... where we should be. She's covering our butts while I fix this. I saw the trial, and I see you here without your brother. What happened?"

She told him. All of it. From the moment she arrived on Northcliff, to stepping on his tripwire. He listened without interruption. He had his V2 pistol in hand but down by his side. When she'd finished her story, he stashed the weapon out of sight under the light jacket he was wearing and finally took a seat. He perched on the edge of it, leaning toward her, but it was a good start. Sure he could leap into action in milliseconds; so could she, but she took his posture as a good sign.

"My sensors tell me you're not here, Stone."

He smirked.

"Oh, get over yourself!" she growled.

"I've lived a long life, Kate. I've picked up a few things in that time. Actually, Fuentez taught me this one... or part of it. She picked it up on Kushiel."

"Gina did?"

"She had to shut down all her data ports when Sebastian tried to hack her systems. That had the effect of making her disappear as far as our IFF and other emissions are concerned. She turned into a black hole from Eric's perspective. It gave him a bit of a turn apparently. Combining her trick with some of my gear set up to copy your output, and then bounce it back to you..." he shrugged. "I'm suddenly a ghost."

"Cool." Her suite must be swarming with nannies broadcasting to spoof her sensors. "I hope you know how to counter your countermeasures." He sent her a look that said of course he did, and she shrugged. "It would be a bit of a bastard if the Merki figured it out. Just saying."

He smiled briefly.

"I'm glad Gina isn't here."

"There's more to your friend than her Marine Corps background, Kate. I wasn't kidding when I told her she should pick up some of our OSI training."

Kate shook her head. "You had it right in the message

you left me. She won't ever be easy with collateral damage, Stone. She wouldn't be able to do what we do, not without agonising over it."

Stone regarded her oddly, almost with pity. "What makes you think I don't agonise?"

Her jaw dropped.

He shrugged. "It's not about whether or not it bothers us to do what we do; it's about whether or not we can do the job regardless. Anyway, that's all beside the point. You fucked up. You went in to get your brother and came away empty-handed. It's time for your post mission analysis, Richmond. Lay it out for me. What went wrong? How does it leave you exposed? Can the situation be retrieved? How?"

She frowned. "You sound like you're thinking of helping?"

"Let's just say that I haven't decided not to help. It depends on what I hear out of you over the next few minutes. Make it good."

Feeling hopeful, she thought hard about what had gone wrong and how to fix it. The biggest thing was not knowing her brother had a powerful friend at his back. If she'd known of his deal with his lawyer and whoever was backing him, she could have stayed back and let Danny Cole be mind-wiped as he wanted. She explained that to Stone.

He nodded. "So lack of Intel screwed the plan. Lucky I'm here then."

She growled at the insult to her abilities. "There was no indication, none."

"There's always something, Richmond. Always. Is there anything to link you to the fiasco... excuse me, escape attempt?"

"Nothing."

"You're right about that, because I took care of it for you."

"Of?"

"Felix Haliwell."

She frowned. "You killed Felix?"

"You killed him. The moment you decided it was a good idea to buy a non-standard weapon from him he had to die. It can and will be traced back to him, Richmond. You left it at the scene didn't you?"

She nodded.

"I cleaned up your back trail for you. Felix and those you spoke with to find him are no longer a factor. You made it necessary. You could have used a standard weapon and security would have learnt nothing from it. Haliwell's death is on you."

"Okay."

"Okay? That's all you have to say to me?"

"What do you want me to say? Am I supposed to cry over that weasel? I needed an AAR and I needed it the next damn day! This is my brother's life we're talking about. If you think I give a crap about some little gun runner that fleeced me when he knew I was desperate, you can think again. I needed that damn gun, and it worked great. One thing I'll say about Felix, he was a very good gunsmith."

Stone nodded. "Fair enough. I'm not going to bust your balls over him. All I care about is keeping your name and that of the regiment clear of any involvement."

"Okay then. As far as I know, there's nothing linking me or the regiment to any of this. Is that clear enough for you?"

Stone nodded. "The next step. Can we still retrieve the situation? Do you know where your brother is?"

"No... no I don't, but I have a lead. Malcolm Redding."

"The lawyer?"

"He paid Danny Cole to take Paul's place. I want to squeeze him and find out where Paul is."

"There's another way, and a better."

She raised an eyebrow. She didn't know of one.

"Follow the money, Richmond. It's basic stuff. You didn't

think of it?"

She raised her manacled hands and wiggled her fingers at him. "I have a lot on my mind."

He looked at her for a long assessing moment and made a decision. "Fine. We get your brother and then we leave. This is the last time, Richmond. Whether he comes with us or goes his own way, after this he's on his own."

She didn't respond.

"I need an answer."

He hadn't asked a question. She shrugged. "I hear you."

"Not good enough. I've never given a rogue a second chance, yet here I am doing it with you. I guarantee that I won't be giving you a third. This thing with your brother ends here, or I end you. Is that clear enough?"

She nodded.

"I need to hear it, Kate."

"I understand."

"You understand and agree to the terms? You had better mean it, Kate. Save us all some time and be honest. *Can* you let him go?"

Could she? Not without seeing him safe first, she was certain of that. She hadn't seen him in person since before he went missing all those years ago. Her entire life since then had been overshadowed by what had happened and her effort to fix it. But what if? What if she did get him out of the situation he was in? Did she expect him to come home with her, live on Snakeholme? What would he do there? He wouldn't fit in at all, and probably would refuse to go in the first place. She couldn't force him, and what else was there? Let him go his own way. Stone saw it clearer than she ever could.

"I agree, but I have to talk to him. I have to make it right between us, Stone. I don't want to be like this forever."

"This?"

"Wondering where he is, how he is, whether he blames

me for things. We live a long time. You have anyway. Would you want to be left wondering for centuries?"

Stone's eyes went distant for a long moment before focusing upon her again. "No, it sucks. I'll help you get to him, and I'll help him leave if that's what he wants, but in the end you come back with me no matter what he decides. I won't let you go again, Kate. I won't let you go rogue."

"Understood."

He nodded, stood, and stepped forward to remove the manacles.

Kate rubbed her wrists free of the phantom weight, and Stone stepped away. "Thanks."

"Go take a shower, you stink."

"Thanks," she said again but wryly this time. "That's just what a woman yearns to hear after a long day." It was a good idea. She wanted to be clean and wearing fresh clothes. She headed for the shower smiling. "Want to wash my back?"

"No," he said coldly and Kate's smile fled.

She made herself keep walking as if it didn't matter to her, but it did. She had done worse than risk her life when she abandoned her friends on Helios. She had broken something precious. Stone's trust.

* * *

Stone watched her disappear into the bedroom and forced himself not to follow. He turned away to stare out of the windows and over the city. When Richmond spoke of her brother and not wanting to spend her life wondering about him, he had understood perfectly. He knew his brother had died long ago, but that made things worse not better. He'd never had the opportunity to make things right between them and regretted that. His situation wasn't the same as Richmond's. His brother hadn't gone missing, they had just drifted apart. Long before the Merki War they had become strangers to each other, but centuries later he still thought of him. In his head, he saw two boys playing in the yard and always would. For as long as his heart beat and his processor cycled through its endless code, his brother would play with him in that yard.

His attention briefly flicked to his sensors, but when he realised he was checking that Richmond hadn't tried to skip out again, a brief burst of annoyance flashed a snarl onto his face. This was getting bloody ridiculous! She was really getting under his skin. Getting? He snorted at the thought. There was no getting. She was firmly inside his armour already and digging her out would hurt too much. He was so screwed.

He decided that what he needed was the distraction of work, but first he might as well clean the room of his gear. He was sure Richmond would appreciate it. Using TacNet, he sent the suicide command to his nanotech henchmen so that her systems would come back on-line. The tiny machines throughout the suite acknowledged the order and self-terminated, falling to the carpets as microscopic dust. He moved to the bedroom door and retrieved the sonic disruptor and trip wire. He grinned remembering the look on Richmond's face when she'd seen it. He laughed under his breath. It was even funnier because she hadn't been one to fall for the trick during her training on Snakeholme. She had impressed him by steering her squad-mates clear of all his traps that day, and the tripwires were a special synthetic very hard to detect. Well, it just went to show luck played a part despite Richmond's personal disbelief in it.

He took his seat on the couch in the main room and accessed the net with a coded thought to his processor. He wanted to know everything there was to know about one Malcolm Redding, and his law firm. Did he have family, friends? Was he in financial difficulties? If he had suddenly received a legacy, inherited money or property for example, where had it come from and when? The timing of something like that would be telling.

He ran a second search on Danny Cole.

Richmond seemed to feel the man was a fool to take Redding's deal, and dismissed his story as a dead end because of that prejudiced view. Stone didn't share it however. He understood Cole very well. A man willing to sacrifice himself to something worse than death for those he loved would have made for a good viper candidate. Had Cole been military and sent to Luna with Richmond's intake, Stone was almost sure that he would've paid special attention to the man as he had with Richmond. The point was he wanted to know more about Cole's business and financial collapse. There was something there; what he didn't know, but something about it rubbed him wrong. He wanted to know more.

While the searches ran, he used the suite's autochef. He hadn't eaten yet and was hungry. He programmed coffee and sipped it while the autochef prepared the meal. His taste buds were very determined that he eat a plate of steak and eggs before too much longer.

The food was pretty good for autochef fare, he thought as he chewed. Meat was meat, and eggs just eggs, but he remembered some real stinkers he'd been forced to eat in the past. Technology was always improving, and autochefs were no different in that. New ingredients from worlds discovered over the years meant the manufacturers were always pushing the envelope of what was possible. Delays in software and hardware updates meant he could order a meal here, and then order the same one on Alizon, and have it taste subtly different unless he specified what he wanted very carefully. It made him feel old.

He snorted. He *was* old *and* getting senile if a plate of food could make him start evaluating things.

Stone finished his meal and took another cup of coffee back to the couch. He checked his sensors, but Richmond was there, still in the shower. What the hell was taking her so long? Water baby. He smirked at the thought. She always dove into a shower or pool at the least provocation. She would live in one if there had been a way to do that. Data started coming in on Malcolm Redding and he reluctantly turned away from thoughts of a naked and wet Richmond in the shower.

He burrowed into the data.

* * *

Kate stared blindly into the spray from the shower head, and watched Stone move around on her sensors. They had come back online without warning sometime ago. He must have deactivated his spook squad. Those sneaky little nano-pests of his had really thrown her off kilter. She would have to secure some for her own use on future ops, assuming he let her out of his sight after this. She sighed. Things could be a lot worse, but she had a feeling that rebuilding trust between them would take time and effort on her part. As for their personal situation, she wasn't sure it was salvageable, but trust had to come first. It would be the foundation for anything that followed.

She turned off the shower and quickly dried herself on huge fluffy towels the hotel provided its guests. It was quicker than using the warm air dryer in the shower, and she was hungry. Watching Stone moving around and realising he had hit up her autochef for a meal made her want to do the same. She left the bathroom and padded naked around the bedroom, diving into drawers for fresh under things and then the wardrobe for one of the hideously loud touristy outfits she had bought to augment those Stone had supplied. She wouldn't wear her sneaksuit again so soon. She had hung it on the door, hoping the subtle but noticeable aroma of garbage would fade before she needed it again.

When she entered the main room again, fully dressed and ready to eat, she found Stone already back at work. It was a snub that he hadn't waited for her to return before eating. His way of saying he was still pissed, and not yet ready to forgive her. He was sitting on the couch working on the net. He was staring into the distance at nothing, or seemed to be, but in reality his eyes were focused on streams of data. She had come to recognise a viper hard at work with internal business. The eyes seemed unfocused but weren't. They seemed not to move, but did in small ways, and if she watched very carefully she could see his pupils react to what he was seeing. An unenhanced Human would see a man lost in thought, but she knew and wondered what he was doing. He wouldn't tell her until he was ready and she wasn't going to ask. She'd be damned if she would beg for data.

She headed for the autochef.

She took her time cycling through the menu unsure of her appetite. She should probably choose something filling and sensible and boring, but she was feeling a bit down. The breakfast menu was tempting, but it was late afternoon already; it seemed a little too decadent of her to choose buttermilk pancakes with strawberries, blueberries, and maple syrup. She glanced at Stone. Fuck it. She wanted happy food.

She chose the breakfast with a plate of bacon on the side just because she could, and coffee. Coffee of course wasn't in question. When the autochef dinged, she took the tray of food over to the couch and dropped heavily onto it in an effort to make Stone take notice. He ignored her. He knew she was there of course, but he was 'too busy' to even glance at her.

Fine!

She tucked into her food and when his hand sneaked toward her tray to snatch a piece of bacon, she smacked the back of it. He turned to regard her in surprise, but it was her turn to ignore him. She chewed her food staring straight ahead as he had been. She went through the bacon and then the pancakes. The fruit made her groan in pleasure, and Stone snorted obviously thinking she was taunting him. She wasn't... well not much. The food was really good. She relented by leaving one strawberry for him, just to show him some mercy and prove she could have left him nothing, but was choosing to share. He took the strawberry, bit into it, and smiled.

Mission accomplished! A smiling Stone was a Stone on the path to forgiving her. Forgiveness would lead to trust, and trust would lead to sex, and sex would lead... it would lead to regaining what she had lost. His friendship.

"I know where your brother is," Stone said dropping his bombshell. "You're not going to like it."

Kate's jaw dropped.

* * *

22 ~ Old Acquaintances

Kate muttered another curse. "Fucking Whitby. Can you believe it, Stone? Of all the people I never expected to meet again this side of hell, Captain Dickhead Whitby the *turd!* What are the odds?"

Stone coughed to smother his laugh. "Richard Whitby *the third* isn't in the Rangers anymore, Richmond. Seems like he's moved up in the family business. Can't say I blame him. He put in his expected five year stint, as every well to do son of Bethany must, but he was never going anywhere in the military. He's not cut out for it."

"Big surprise," she sneered. "He's nothing like Ian."

Stone nodded. "Hiller has the moves, no question, but he had more motivation than most."

That was true. Ian Hiller hated the Whitbys as much as she did and with more reason. He'd had closer dealings with them than she had. She hated all of The Ten, but it had actually been the Baxters who had destroyed her father not the Whitbys. That wasn't the case with Hiller. His entire family was made destitute by Gerald Whitby, the current head of the family and holder of the Whitby seat in Bethany's government. The Whitbys had propped Ian up as a figurehead to control the Hiller vote, humiliating him every day until he'd become desperate to escape Bethany. His induction as a viper into the regiment had been his salvation.

Kate's beef was with all of The Ten because they were all insufferable shits and ran her world with no regard for its people, but Whitby in particular because the family was at the top of the food chain currently, and ruled Bethany's Council with ruthless efficiency, and she admitted reluctantly, political skill. She hated politics. It killed more people with words than a soldier ever had in battle, but those wielding the words didn't care as long as their lily-white hands stayed clean. Despite being an assassin for them on occasion, and knowing at the time how they were using her to bring their rivals grief, her hands were cleaner than theirs were by far.

"Fucking Whitby," she spat. "What is he thinking? How could Paul link himself to them, Stone? Why the hell choose Whitby Corp?!"

"Shut it down, Richmond," Stone said under his breath. "You keep on bitching about Stonefield's management, and I have a feeling security is going to take notice. He nodded toward a huddle of people glancing at them and whispering. "The nice citizens are wondering if they need to call the psyches. Smile." He nodded politely to the bar's patrons and smiled. They turned away.

She shut up, and drank her beer, but resentment was simmering just below the surface. Three days in Stonefield and they still hadn't found a way through to her brother. They knew where he was. She had seen him on the street surrounded by a security detail. Who did they think he was, the bloody President? It was annoying as hell and worrying too. Why did he rate such extreme security measures?

Stonefield was owned and operated by Whitby Corp. and was one of the many new mega-city/factories in the deserts of

Northcliff that had sprung up since the discovery of the Shan. Everyone living here ultimately worked for Whitby Corp. or one of its affiliates. It might seem otherwise, but scratch the surface and she would quickly discover a real estate company owned by Whitby Corp. owned the bar that sold the beer she was drinking. The nano-smelters, mines, nano-assembly lines, the shipping companies, employee housing, the malls, the bars, breweries, agridomes... everything owned, rented, or operated by Whitby Corp. and its affiliates. Stonefield's rival cities were owned and operated the same way by rival corporations. Paul could have chosen any of them, but he hadn't. He'd chosen this one.

Why?!

Kate growled in frustration and Stone gave her a warning look. "What are we waiting for?"

"I told you, I have to study the situation."

"I hate this. We know where they're keeping him. We could get him out easy enough."

"Richmond, I'll say this one more time. The regiment can't be connected to this. Cannot and will not. If, as you say, we bust him out and escape, we have to do it through normal, explainable, means. We can't leave them questioning how it was done. It only takes one person speculating a little too freely for this to blow up in our faces. It explodes, and I guarantee you won't like facing the General when we get home. Your brother will be the least of your worries then."

She grimaced. She could imagine. "Yeah, yeah." She took a sip of her beer ignoring the absurd alert that flashed a toxicity warning on her display. So alcohol was a poison, who cared? That was the whole point in drinking it! "Why do you think Paul and Dickhead are so chummy?"

"Working on it."

"That's what you said last time, Stone."

"And I'll say it next time too unless you leave me alone *to work on it!*"

She smirked.

Kate glanced around the bar slowly taking inventory of the patrons and staff. None seemed overly interested in them after the whispering group left the bar. She was sure they'd only been interested because they were strangers. There was nothing else to differentiate them from the locals, not even their clothes. Stone had mentioned needing to buy some that better blended with the locals when they first arrived in Stonefield, and they'd made it their first order of business. Their tourist colours had stood out too much. Most of the bar's patrons wore company colours—blue one-piece coveralls over their skinsuits, declaring their allegiance to Whitby Corp. Different colours and badges spoke of the varied divisions within the greater corporation, or of affiliated companies under contract to Whitby. The time of day meant very few people were wearing their civilian clothes. It was just after midday, and most here would be returning to work after their noon break.

Stone had chosen the bar because it was close to Dickhead's hotel. Stone had sent his spies into the building using the comings and goings of hotel staff to infiltrate the penthouse where Dickhead was staying. It was in that suite of rooms that Paul and his new best friend were doing interesting things—things that Stone was trying to wheedle out, things that must be extremely important to Whitby Corp. Seeing as profit was God to any corporation, Paul must know something worth a lot of credits. Why else spend five million to save him?

Stone muttered a low curse, but Kate couldn't make out what the problem was. He was muttering constantly under his breath, as if giving orders audibly to his minions. He wasn't of course; he was using TacNet to control and monitor them, He was totally lost to his battle in the unreal world of the net. He trusted her to keep them safe in the real one.

She kept her head and eyes moving slowly and constantly,

searching for odd patterns of movement. Her sensors were watching the surrounding streets. Stonefield seemed like an open enough city, but that was illusion. Every street, every building, every park and open space was under constant security surveillance. All corporate cities were like that. They were under near constant cyber attack by competitors. It was their countermeasures that were giving Stone fits. His nano-spies had to navigate through a blizzard of invisible sentries in any building he found of interest, and those sentries were designed to specifically detect exactly what he was attempting. Security was tight. It always was in these pseudo cities. They weren't really cities at all, but mega factories, and like the huge machines they were, each part of the city had a purpose. The mines supplied raw materials, the nano-smelters refined it, the factory complexes used what the smelters produced, the ports transported the products, but the rest of the city supplied the workforce and supported all their needs. That was just as important to the operation. All of it was ultimately owned and protected by the corporation that built it; they took that protection very seriously indeed.

While Stone fought his electronic battle, using his minions to thrust and parry his way into the hotel to vacuum data, Kate kept watch and prepared to battle other threats. Security didn't just consist of Whitby Corp. personnel; it had divisions supplied by mercenary companies. While Whitby employees—no better than low paid drones—acted as civil police and first responders, the mercenaries took the place of a true military. The day she couldn't outmanoeuvre a corporate owned police service was the day she'd eat her beret, but mercenaries were a different bowl of sushi altogether. They varied widely in competence, but in general, they were a match for the smaller militaries of worlds outside the core. Veteran soldiers often gravitated from the Alliance army or marines into those kinds of outfits come retirement.

She was vigilant.

Another round of drinks later, and Stone surfaced to find Kate with empty glasses in front of her and an impatient expression on her face. She watched him drink his own brew, before demanding some answers. He took his time, thinking about his answer before giving it to her.

"We have a problem, and by we I mean the Alliance."

Kate blinked. How could her brother do anything to threaten the Alliance? "Huh?" she said intelligently. "I mean... what do you mean?"

"Richard Whitby and your brother are partners. They have some kind of deal worth a lot of money. I couldn't get all the details, but they're talking billions, Richmond. That five million you told me about?"

She nodded.

"I heard them laughing about it. They called Danny Cole a fool for giving up his life for chump change. Since when has five million ever been chump change? The lawyer took ten percent commission over and above the five mil, but Whitby considered their overhead nothing to worry about."

She shrugged. "He's rich."

"I know that, but... you had to be there, I guess. This deal is something huge. It was the way they talked about it. They're expecting to hit it big. Think about what big means to someone like Whitby, Richmond."

She whistled silently. "And you don't know any of the details?"

"I didn't say that. I said I don't know *all* the details."

She frowned. "So far I haven't heard anything that worries me let alone the Alliance. How does any of it help me get my brother back?"

"I'm coming to that. I couldn't do more without tipping them off, but I did get a few hints. It's all linked to our mission on Helios. Those dead aliens did come from somewhere out here in the Border Zone."

"Well, we already guessed that."

"True. They didn't say it outright, but I got the impression that its location is your brother's contribution to the expedition they're putting together."

"Expedition?"

Stone nodded.

"And we don't know the destination?"

"No, but your brother does. We need that data."

Her thoughts flashed to the data crystal she remembered Paul swallowing back on the bridge of *Jean de Vienne*. He must have copied a portion of the jump log and erased the original. She had to admire his quick thinking. Without that data, he wouldn't have had anything to trade for his freedom. He was five million up and counting.

"Well, we planned to grab him anyway."

Stone nodded but he looked grim. "That was the plan, but we can't leave without that data no matter his decision. He can come with us or he can stay here, but that data comes with us no matter what it takes."

"We need to get it back to Helios and Commodore Walder ASAP."

"We do," Stone agreed. "I'm glad you see that."

"Of course I see it. It's obvious. The navy needs to scout the system and estimate the threat before anyone can go in and clear the Merki out."

"Right. We need a new plan. If I can't sniff out the jump coordinates, we'll need to get them out of your brother." Stone looked her in the eye, grimly. "Whatever it takes, Kate. He will cough up that data."

She stiffened at the implied threat. She'd die before she let him or anyone hurt Paul, but he knew that. She nodded slowly, not to agree with him, but to acknowledge his threat. If it came to it, she would get the data out of Paul herself, but without force. Besides, Stone was scary good at this sort of thing. He'd get the data without needing threats of violence. She was counting on it.

"What's the plan?" she said as they left the bar.

"We need to get into the penthouse. I can't access what I need from out here in time."

"In time?"

"They're outfitting a ship. We have less than a week before they leave the system."

"Oookay," she said, realising the urgency now. If it wasn't one thing, it was another. "I vote we cap a couple of the hotel staff and go in posing as them."

He gave her a look.

"What?"

"I just realised Marion was right about something."

"What?" she said again, and this time it sounded like a whine.

"Nothing important," he muttered. "It's a decent plan as your plans go."

"Hey!" she protested.

"But there's no need to kill anyone at this stage." He noted her scowl. "Maybe later."

She snorted. He was offering her a bone to placate her. She wasn't a complete psycho! She frowned. Had Hymas said something to him? She shook her head. It didn't matter.

"So, where are we going?" she said.

"If we're going in as staff we need a simcode reader."

She nodded. They would have to read the simcode data of some of the staff, and then they could program their own implants to match. Security in places like Dickhead's hotel, high-end hotels catering to corporate execs and their own owners, would rely way more upon simcode implants than visual I.D. There might not be any staff working there with matching builds, she mused. They would have to check on that. It would be better to choose people they could be mistaken for, at least from a distance.

"Any idea where to get one?" she asked.

Simcode readers weren't readily available. They couldn't

just buy one. Security services and government agencies would have them, and places that needed really good and expensive security measures, but no one else would need one.

"They don't grow on trees," Stone said. She nodded, not that trees grew in the desert. "I could build one given time, but I think we'll just do it the easy way and steal one."

"Oh good!" Some action at last.

He smiled.

STONEFIELD, DOUNA WASTES, NORTHCLIFF

They chose one of the distribution centres for their larceny. Unlike the ports, which operated 24/7, the distribution centres were a daytime operation. Two shifts of employees worked to package Stonefield's products and transport them to the ports where they were boosted into orbit. At night, the depots were shut down and handed over to the crews responsible for maintenance and replenishment of the packaging lines. The crews were small, making the site seem deserted. In comparison to the day, it *was* deserted, but that didn't mean security was lax. It wasn't and for good reason. Finished products were literally stacked unattended awaiting crating and shipping, making all the distribution centres an attractive target for theft by employees and outsiders alike. Simcode protocols were definitely in effect here, making it one of Stone's prime targets for securing what they needed.

Night was definitely best for burglary, Kate mused, as she studied her entry point. Traditional, and kind of fun when she didn't have orders to slaughter some poor soul for getting on the wrong side of someone important. Stone was monitoring the area and her objective from a distance. That was nice too. He would know if anyone sounded an alert or made a call for backup, and should be able to run interference. She could get used to having a partner on these things.

She hunkered down into cover and contacted Stone via viper comm. "In position."

"Acknowledged. Patrol approaching from your nine o'clock—airborne."

She glanced up and edged further back into the deep shadows between one of the sprawling warehouses and the loading dock. She was wearing her sneaksuit with its hood up and mask in place, and had left her street clothes with Stone, but she didn't want to take chances. The suit's IR masking capabilities were excellent, and in the cool night air of the desert, she should be like a hole in the air.

Nothing to detect here, move along, move along.

The warehouse at her back would contain the crates and other things used to package and ship stuff through foldspace. Most merchant ships transported cargo in holds pumped down to vacuum. It saved on environmental costs. Cargo needed protection against the cold and harsh conditions found in holds with minimal particle shielding.

Her sensors told her that the loading dock was unguarded by droid or human guards, but it was a sensitive area, and patrols were numerous. She waited and the patrol cruiser entered her area of responsibility at last. She was monitoring her sensors close in, while Stone kept watch further out. The system was working out really great. It allowed her to concentrate on sensing emissions close by and countering them with ECM. She had dedicated a lot of her processor's cycles to that task and tagged it as a priority.

She watched the cruiser's searchlight sweep the area in front of the loading bays counting under her breath.

Thirty-two, thirty-three...

"Going in now," she said when the patrol moved off. She sprinted toward the loading dock.

"Three minutes."

She had three minutes until the next patrol arrived. "Copy."

Her ECM alert flickered as it intercepted and neutralised security cams at the dock. She could have fried the system, but that would have set off the alarms. ECM was able to spoof the cameras and other security measures in a gentle way when necessary. A flicker on security monitors as she raced by, and then back to normal with none the wiser. The unseen threat of the security nanos were more dangerous to her, but again ECM should handle it... *if* her systems proved to be the more advanced. They should be, but there was never a guarantee. Corporations like Whitby Corp. researched and manufactured such things after all.

Her ECM alert flickered on and off repeatedly as she sped through the building. She used the blueprints she had up on her display to navigate her way from the business end of the facility and into admin areas. Employees wouldn't enter the building through the loading bays. They would enter at the other end—the facade that fronted the transpo hub. That would be where they had to pass through security to clock on shift.

She moved out of industrial areas and into the administration spaces. She walked stealthily by offices used for monitoring inventory levels and shipping schedules, noting the signs pointing toward Human Resources. The map on her display confirmed her location. She chose the correct turns heading toward her objective without pause or error, her ECM indicator was on solid now. She imagined the security nanos swarming around her; they must be trying to attack constantly, only to have her ECM thwart them at every turn. There was no evidence of the battle, but she must be winning. Stone would have alerted her if an alarm had sounded.

Keeping her steps silent as she navigated the corridors, she slowed to a crouching wary walk and stopped before an office door. This was the risky part. The door was locked of course, as were all the doors, but this one led into the security department itself. It might be manned... she checked, but her sensors said no. The outer office was empty. Good deal. She had a stunner as well as a pulser on her belt, and had been prepared to take out anyone inside, but it would be better to slip in and out stealthily. Sensors reported the monitoring station further in was manned, but that was to be expected. With luck, she wouldn't need to go in there.

She reached to her hip and the decoder clipped to her belt that Stone had given her. He loved his gadgets. She could have used some of the face cream nanos for this infiltration, but he insisted she use one of his other toys. She grinned remembering the look he gave her when she told him how well the cream had worked on the armoured car. He agreed they would have worked here too, but the cream was a fast and dirty method. What was it he said? Oh yeah, not very refined. Quick and dirty wasn't good enough this time, and she had to agree. There were alarms and advanced security to by-pass. The armoured car's lock was nothing in comparison.

She applied Stone's decoder and it easily diddled the lock. She had to admit Stone knew his stuff. She'd used other decoders in her time but this one seemed smoother and faster than the high-end electronics supplied by ISS for her missions way back when. Now though, she was packing more and better tech, but most of it internally. It was forever part of her. Electronic locks like this were actually simple, technologically speaking, but that was by design. Neural tech was banned, and linking locks to the net opened them up to tampering. This kind of lock needed to be opened by the user in person.

She shook off her preoccupation and eased the door open. She was greeted by silence, not screaming sirens. Stone stayed off the comm. Goody.

She crossed the outer office quickly and applied the decoder to another door. The room in which she stood was more like a lobby area than an office, or perhaps they called it a reception? Whatever. The locked doors led to various rooms used for interviews, monitoring the facility, managing personnel, etc. The one she entered was a locker room. She raced between metal lockers to the door at the far end, and applied the decoder one last time. Before opening the door, she used her sensors to locate the security cams inside. There were two, one in each opposite corner covering the door. There was no way to enter without being seen. When she spoofed those cams, she would have very little time before someone noticed. She had to be in and out fast enough to release the cams without notice or setting off alarms.

Computer: light amplification mode.

The room brightened a little, enough to see without using the flashlight on her hip, and she gave the command to her ECM. She opened the door, and stepped into the armoury. Her attention flicked to the cameras in the corners, but the ready light on each no longer glowed. Her ECM had disabled them. She had less than a minute. Ignoring the weapon racks decorating the walls containing rows of gleaming pulse rifles, she dived toward the steel cabinets that ringed the room. Her fist hammered into a door and it buckled away from its frame. She jammed her fingers into the gap and ripped it open. She glared inside the cabinet and discovered spare body armour. Her fist flicked out at another door, and it folded inward. The door came off in her grasp to reveal handheld scanners and simcode readers. She snatched what she needed and dashed out of the armoury. She gave the order to release the cams as she crossed the threshold, slapping the door closed at the same time.

And waited... and waited... and... and nothing! No alarms sounded and no contact from Stone giving dire warnings. She grinned fiercely. All she had to do now was retrace her route out of the building, and meet Stone at the perimeter fence.

Damn, she was good.

"Got it," she reported via viper comm.

"Good. Hurry it up, we don't have all night."

She scowled. The nerve of him! "On my way, ETA five minutes."

"Copy."

Bloody man! No well done, Kate. No, way to go, Kate. No, I was worried and I'm glad you're okay, Kate! She growled under her breath, but she didn't hang about. She made her way out of the building, waited for a patrol to fly over, and hurried to make her rendezvous with Stone. Behind her, she left the distribution centre unaware anything untoward had happened.

* * *

23 ~ Resolution

Kate finished taping the unconscious pair's hands and feet, absently pocketed the tape, and stepped back to study them where they lay on the floor. She wasn't happy with what she saw.

"Yours is a bit tall, don't you think?"

Stone shrugged.

"You don't think someone will notice that you shrank almost half a meter in a day when they see you?"

"Maybe, maybe not, but there's nothing I can do about it. Yours is close enough."

She nodded. The woman did have the right build and hair colour—completely the wrong style of course, and very unflattering on her, but overall Kate was pleased with hers. It was Stone's that worried her. The two men looked nothing alike. Stone was obsidian skinned, wide shouldered, and barrel-chested. He was completely bald and barely 1.7meters tall for God's sake! He looked nothing like the hotel employee who was easily a half meter taller with long hair in tight braids... well he had the right skin tone she supposed, but that was all. In fact, he was the only black skinned man on the night shift at the hotel. All the others were female, or pure Anglo with tanned skin, or had a mixed Anglo and Asian heritage. That was why they grabbed this guy in the first place.

"Maybe I should go in alone."

"No," Stone said decisively, and stopped her from replying with a raised hand. "I said no. I'm not letting you and your brother out of my sight. Besides, I'm the better e-man."

He was, but she was no slouch in the cyber warfare department. All vipers were trained for it, and she had been good before that, but Stone was Stone. He'd been their instructor.

"E-geek you mean," she muttered.

"Sticks 'n' stones... scan their simcodes and let's get this show on the road."

Kate rolled the hostages onto their bellies and used the simcode reader to scan the implants in their spines. She stored the woman's data in her database for future use. She was turning into a bit of a collector of simcodes; she had a nice selection already from her ISS days. Now she had a new one. She sent Stone an upload request via TacNet.

>_ CONNECTION REQUEST ACKNOWLEDGED.
>_ CONNECTION ACHIEVED... STONE, KENNETH,
CAPTAIN 501ST INFANTRY REGIMENT, SERIAL NUMBER
DGN-896-410-339.
>_ UPLOADING DATA PACKET...
>_ UPLOAD COMPLETE.

Satisfied, she broke the connection and rolled the two unconscious lemmings onto their backs again. Stone came forward with a couple of med-patches in hand. He applied one to each of their guests, choosing the back of one hand. The patches adhered to the skin and began the timed release of a drug that would keep them comfortably asleep for twenty-four hours.

Kate checked her appearance in the mirror one last time. The hotel uniforms they'd purchased didn't do much for her from a stylistic viewpoint, she decided. The dark tightly fitted trousers, white shirt, and dark waistcoat were a traditional style that many hotels used. The prancing unicorn motif on her left breast stood out starkly in white. Stone's uniform was a match for hers. He joined her before the mirror for a moment, his eyes flicking over their reflection critically, and nodded. They looked the part, and their simcode implants would now transmit the correct data when interrogated by hotel security, but they didn't look like those they were pretending to be; Stone especially. From a distance, she would pass, but he wouldn't. He wasn't concerned, or so he said. She didn't know why.

She checked the time. It was dark outside and her shift at the hotel would start soon. She glanced back at the lemmings, but they were sleeping like babies. She looked the question at Stone and he nodded before heading for the door. It was show time. She followed him outside and together they turned to follow the sidewalk toward the station. The apartment they had just left wasn't far from the hotel by public transpo. It would take mere minutes by maglev, and they arrived at the station just as a train arrived. They chose the first carriage they came to and took seats. The maglev train accelerated out of the station barely a minute later.

Two stops went by, and they stood silently together in preparation to debark. The train's carriage had remained empty. They were the only two passengers, though other carriages seemed to have commuters in them. The train slammed into the braking zone at break-neck speed and decelerated into the station. It always surprised her how quick maglev propulsion could slow a train weighing thousands of tons. They left the train and made their way out of the station.

The staff entrance at the back of the hotel had simcode protocols and required they pass through one at a time. Stone went first, and Kate followed him a few seconds later. Their arrival and entry went off without a hitch. Stone's earlier recon of the hotel meant both of them had detailed specs of its interior, and with a blueprint of the layout open on their HUDs, they made their way through staff areas unerringly. Sensors indicated the place was a hive of activity. Thousands of people staffed hotels of this size, but at night many less were needed; hopefully that meant they could navigate the place without anyone being suspicious. No one knew all the faces working here.

Stone led the way into the industrial-sized kitchens. Without slowing, he snatched up a tray of food readied for someone's late night meal. At his action, Kate abruptly wheeled to the left and grabbed a trolley to push. Neither needed to consult the other; they knew each other's moves. It was a simple wheeled trolley with a dull metal finish, and had a few covered plates on it.

Stone led the way toward an elevator. It was one of three used by housekeeping and room service. Security on the elevator recognised their simcodes and opened the doors for them. Stone stepped inside, and held the door for her. As soon as she had the trolley inside, he let the doors close and discarded his tray on top of the trolley. Food spilt off the edges of pristine white plates, but he took no notice as he pulled out one of his toys from a pocket. He applied the device to the elevator controls and used it to by-pass the code needed to operate it. His override made the elevator take them directly up to the penthouse without stops on the way, and ignoring anyone calling for it.

Kate pulled her pocket pulser free and checked it. She didn't plan to kill anyone today, but it was possible she would need to threaten violence. She set it to minimum and engaged the safety. She glanced at Stone, but he was watching the indicator lights above the door. Neither of them spoke. She turned her attention to the doors and her sensors swept outward as they neared the penthouse level; they found plenty of returns. Security cams and other security measures quickly painted themselves onto her display, but she wasn't concerned. Their simcodes had already been accepted; there was no reason to expect they wouldn't be on the penthouse level as well. The security cams would only be a problem if a human operator took the unlikely step of checking to see if their codes matched the images in the employee database. It wasn't something she felt was likely.

The doors slid aside and she pushed her trolley out of the elevator and into a short corridor. There were two doors at this level leading to the two huge penthouse suits. Stone indicated the one on the right furthest from the elevators, and she stopped before it. Sensors indicated there were guards on the inside. She hadn't expected that, but she took it in stride. She pressed the call button and waited. She pressed it again and waited. No answer. The guards were right there by the door, but the lazy bastards weren't answering! She glared at Stone; he shrugged. She leaned on the cursed button.

"What the hell!" a voice said from the intercom.

"Room service," she said brightly.

Stone snickered.

"We didn't order anything. Get gone."

Stone frowned, and raised an eyebrow at her. He conjured up a sonic grenade and offered it to her. Where the hell had he been hiding that? She took it from him, armed it, but kept the trigger depressed in her fist. She pressed the call button again.

She thought for a moment and smirked. "I have to deliver this, sir. Even if you no longer want it, you have to sign for it."

"Like hell! If you don't flit, I'm going to come out there

and show you why you should have! *Now fuck off!*"

How rude! She leaned on the button and got ready to move.

The door began to open, but before it opened all the way, she dropped the grenade through the opening and yanked the door shut. The grenade went off barely a second later. Her processor reacted by filtering out the sonic disruption, dulling her hearing in the correct ranges. She twisted the door handle, broke the latch, and pushed inside the penthouse. Two bodies greeted her; Stone stepped over them and pulled them out of the way. She wheeled the trolley inside and closed the door.

She checked her sensors but the two guards were the only people in residence. Her heart sank. "Paul isn't here."

Stone hurried away, heading for the sitting room. "Never mind that. We need the jump coordinates. Maybe I can strip the comp they're using."

She felt torn. She was here for her brother, not some stupid bit of data. He was her priority. She glared at the guards. Maybe they knew where he was, or when he was coming back? She sighed. They would be unconscious for a while, and she hadn't brought anything to wake them. She secured their hands and feet with tape and searched them for anything useful. Both were armed. She took the weapons, unloaded them, and tossed them into the far corner. She stripped their wristcomps and brought them to Stone where he already stood hunched over a computer. He had attached some of his own electronics to it, and was typing like mad when she joined him. He glanced at the wristcomps without pausing, grunted something unintelligible, and turned his attention back to his work.

"Anything?" she asked.

"I only just got started. If it's here, I'll find it."

"Can I help?"

Stone sighed. "Go check the rest of this place out. Bring

me any comps you find."

She nodded and moved out. He was just getting her out of the way, but she had nothing better to do than monitoring the security net and her sensors. She might as well check the place out. She knew no one else was in the suite, so she didn't clear each room as she would have upon entering hostile territory. She searched each room thoroughly, but there was nothing that Stone would find interesting. The only electronics she found belonged to the rooms, built into the furnishings. The penthouse came fully loaded; even the bedrooms had mini-autochefs. She considered programming a coffee into one of them. Why the hell not? She programmed a latte and waited for it.

Her sensors reported the entry into the suite before the coffee was ready. She cursed. She had been looking forward to trying it. She headed back to the main living area and heard raised voices. She recognised them immediately, and her heart leapt. It was Paul. The other was Dickhead Whitby.

"Stop there!" Whitby ordered. "Move a millimetre and I'll shoot to kill."

"Richmond," Stone growled over viper comm. "A little help here."

"Coming," she said brightly.

Her sensors reported two targets, both armed, confronting Stone. Stone was where she'd left him at the comp station. She couldn't tell which target was Paul, and didn't want to risk him, but she came into the room ready for action with her pulser in hand. She was in combat mode, pretty much her default condition, but that was fast enough for any target less than another viper or multiple Merkiaari. Snapshot—part of a viper's TRS—took in the room at a single glance, and targeted both hostiles. A coded thought made Whitby the priority. He had a powerful pulser in his hand pointed at Stone's face, while Paul backed him up with a more concealable and reasonable looking pulser from a distance.

She shot Whitby between the shoulder blades without slowing.

He cried out and fell toward Stone, but he wasn't dead. It was a risk not simply killing him, and truthfully, she would have preferred to do that, but she'd left her weapon on minimum for Stone. She had things to prove to him. One of those things was that she could still be professional and keep the needs of the mission in the forefront of her thoughts. He might need to question Whitby, so she hadn't killed him. Simple. Unfortunately, that left Paul. She wouldn't shoot him, but he didn't know that. Most would have spun toward her and returned fire immediately, but he surprised her. He took the opportunity to kill Stone. It was something she might have done in his place. He had already been facing the right way with a weapon raised and Stone in his sights. Paul fired, and started turning toward her, already sure that he had dealt with the threat.

Stone went down, and Kate roared in anger. It wasn't a scream or a shriek. It was a roar. Nothing like that had ever left her throat before, but it did now. Her targeting reticule swept instantly to Paul and she fired in a single heartbeat. Without a thought, she gunned her brother down. She cried out a second time, but this time in shock. He fell bonelessly in a heap, his weapon skating across the tile away from him. She stared down at him, unable to believe what she'd done. Thank God, she had set her weapon on minimum. She could easily have killed him. She could have killed her own brother!

She took a deep breath, and went to check on Stone. His steady blue icon on her sensors told the tale of a wounded, pissed off, but essentially intact viper. As she approached he stood unaided and went back to work on the computer. His waistcoat had a new hole in it over his left side. Blood was flowing sluggishly, but it wasn't gushing. His ribs must have taken the impact and his sneaksuit had absorbed enough of the blast to prevent a serious plasma burn.

"Ouch," she said, inspecting the burnt material of his waistcoat. "Does it hurt?"

The shot hadn't been stopped by his sneaksuit after all; she had thought the small amount of blood meant it had, but it hadn't. It wasn't bleeding heavily because the blast had cauterised the wound.

"Does it hurt she says," Stone muttered. "Damn fool question. *Of course it bloody hurts!* Secure them both, or are you planning to let them have another try?"

"Don't get pissy," she grumbled, trying not to let him see her relief. "If your bots are handling the problem, just say that."

"My bots are handling the problem," he deadpanned. "Now secure the prisoners if you please. Whitby is stirring."

She spun and her pulser was rock steady in her fist aimed at Dickehead's face. Her targeting reticule was locked on and spinning. It pulsed redly almost demanding she open fire. She hated him, and she hated what he stood for, but she didn't shoot. She put up her gun and retrieved the tape from her pocket a second time. She bound his hands and feet, ignoring his groans. The minimum power hit he'd taken was wearing off. Such a low powered shot was more like a stunner blast than a killing blow from a pulser.

She left Whitby groaning where he lay, and went to check on Paul. He was still out. She hated to do it, but he was safer secured. She taped his hands and feet, but picked him up and put him in one of the armchairs to make him more comfortable. His head slumped forward. She took his face in her hands and studied it, letting herself absorb his reality. He was here before her and alive. Finally, they were together again. Her only family... she glanced at Stone. Say rather, Paul was her only blood family. He was really here. The changes in him were even more obvious than she'd seen on the video at Helios. The baby fat she remembered from before he disappeared was gone, replaced by hollow cheeks, sharply defined cheekbones, and strong square jaw. He had always been a looker, but now his dark stubble made him look dangerous. He *was* dangerous. His captain, and Stone for that matter, proved that. She wished he would open his eyes; she wanted to see them. She wanted to see recognition in them when he saw her, but he would be out for a few more minutes if Whitby were anything to go by.

She rejoined Stone.

"Anything?"

Stone nodded. "Encrypted, but its here."

"Can't we just take the unit?"

"No. If I could've done that, we'd be on a shuttle already." He gave her a disgusted look. He handed her the med-patches. "For the guards. Leave Whitby. I might have questions."

She nodded.

The two guards were still unconscious. Sonic grenades were effective ordnance, a lot more effective than a pulser set on minimum. She slapped one of the patches on each of the guards, making sure to get them on bare skin and smoothed out to ensure they received the maximum dosage of the sedative.

"So the data is off-site?" she asked upon her return.

Stone nodded. "And it's only accessible on registered comps like this one. Taking it with us won't do shit."

That was true and annoying. Registered comps were a pain, because they allowed access to data on secure networks, but didn't store any of that data internally. They had minimal caching and protocols that ensured the data was erased milliseconds after viewing. Registered comps were the bane of an e-geek's existence because it meant they couldn't steal data remotely; they had to infiltrate the comp's location and access it directly. They didn't like that. Unlike Stone, most e-geeks were armchair warriors, and worked their magic from tricked out command centres in bombproof basements.

"You'll never crack our encryption," Whitby said, glaring at Stone.

Kate wondered if he would remember her, but there was no recognition in his eyes as he transferred his glare to her when she snorted.

"Nothing is crack-proof," she said, and believed it. Given enough time, anything could be cracked. The trick here was doing it before morning and shift change at the hotel.

"Who sent you? Intellicorp, Wellington and Biggs, someone else?"

"Wouldn't you like to know?"

"Kate," Stone said by way of warning.

She didn't need the warning. She knew not to involve the regiment. "This is a purely private enterprise, Mister Whitby, but keep speculating if you think it will help."

"I don't believe you."

"That it will help? I think you're probably right about that."

Whitby glared, and she grinned. He turned his attention back to Stone. "I'll cut you in if you stop this now."

Stone nodded. He did something with the comp and said, "Go on, I'm listening."

"I'll cut you in for a cool two percent after expenses."

"Hmmm. I don't consider that very tempting. Try again by all means."

Kate shook her head. "Expenses could eat up all our profit."

Whitby glared. "*Fine!* I'll cover the costs."

"Two percent of net then?"

Whitby nodded.

She tried to look insulted. "Do we look stupid? We're worth more than that. How much is your boy there getting?" she waved vaguely at Paul.

Whitby grimaced. "Five."

"Five! He gets five and you want us to accept just two?"

Whitby licked his lips. "If... if he weren't around you could share the five between you."

She nearly shot him on the spot. Stone's growled warning made her stop her instinctive move for the pulser in her pocket, but her rage-filled glare was enough to scare Whitby into silence. She forced herself to disengage her target lock, and her reticule faded from where it spun between his eyes. She turned away and went to check on Paul, but he was still unconscious. With nothing to do, she prowled the suit and took the opportunity to try that latte. It was as good as she'd hoped it would be.

When she returned she found Whitby out for the count with a med-patch on his neck and Stone still messing with the comp. She turned to Paul and stumbled to a halt. His glacier blue eyes were open and glaring at her. She didn't need to guess whether he recognised her. It was obvious he did and he wasn't happy to see her. She swallowed back her first words, and tried to see it from his point of view. Here he was, doing some business, probably the deal of a lifetime, and his sister arrives to mess it up. She would be pissed too.

"Hey, long time no see, baby brother," she said. "You're looking... different. Good, but different."

His glare faded a little. "Ten years is a long time."

He sounded exactly as she remembered. If she closed her eyes, she could fool herself into believing nothing had changed, but a lot more than time separated them now. Did he know what she was? If he did, how would he feel about it?

"Closer to twelve."

"What are you doing here?"

She hooked a thumb toward Stone. "Obvious isn't it?"

His eyes flicked to the comp and back to her. "That data is my ticket, Kate. Don't screw me over, please."

"It was your ticket, now it's ours," Stone said joining Kate to stare down at Paul. "Your sister has been searching for you for more than ten years, but you don't care about that, do you?"

"Stone don't," she said.

Paul glared but kept silent.

"No, Kate, it needs to be said. He knew you were looking for him. Didn't you?"

"I knew."

"You knew?" she said feeling her stomach sink. "Why didn't you contact me?"

"Because he didn't care; it's been all about him and what he wants the entire time. He never gave a second thought about going off the grid and leaving you wondering."

"Shut up," she said, but Stone was on a roll.

"He never cared about you or your father. You remember the data I gave you on Luna? I looked into his disappearance when I researched you. That thing he pulled that killed his friends and started your crusade?"

She nodded numbly.

"It smelled. It was a setup from the very beginning. He's a user, he—"

"*Shut up!*" she screamed at him.

"Ask him," Stone said and finally shut his mouth.

She turned back to Paul. "Tell him he's wrong. Tell him it wasn't like that. Tell him!"

"It wasn't like that," he said, not meeting her eyes, and she groaned. He was lying; she knew he was. "It wasn't!"

"Tell me how it was then. Tell me how you didn't know I was searching for you. Tell me how you didn't know I was doing The Ten's dirty work for favours so I could find you."

He looked away.

"Bastard," she hissed between her teeth.

He glared. "Don't pretend you wouldn't have done the same in my place. I know what you've done, you soulless freak! You're not really my sister! You're just a computer in her body!"

Stone snorted. "Bethanite propaganda never changes. Only the gullible believe it. Most of Bethany's population qualify unfortunately."

Stone's words gave her time to rally from the shock. "You don't believe in that crap, Paul. You were never one to follow the populist line."

"I didn't before, but I do now. You think I don't know what you've been doing all these years? I kept up. You're a fucking assassin, nothing more than a murderer for hire. You look down at me, *well fuck you!* I've never killed anyone for money."

It hurt. It hurt deep down, but she didn't show it. He was just lashing out. She told herself he didn't mean it. He was just frustrated at losing his sweet deal. He had to realise his expedition wasn't going to happen now. If he were stupid enough to continue with it, he would arrive to find the navy already there.

"Oh really?" Stone drawled. "How many died at Helios? You weren't crew on that raider I suppose. Just visiting the bridge the day you killed your captain were you? I don't think so. How many ships did you jack, how many murdered crews are in your past? We've seen the inventory of the cargo found aboard. Don't try to tell me you're innocent. You haven't been that since you led your friends to their deaths. Oh, and why did you do that I wonder? For cover. You had to disappear, so you made it look like you died with them, just so you could climb into bed with Whitby Corp. Paid well, didn't they? I bet you didn't give a second thought to your sister. She never entered your head as somebody worth thinking about, did she?"

"My sister is dead."

"I'm not dead," she said, still reeling from the loathing she heard in his voice. She'd known it might happen. Considering how vipers were viewed on Bethany, it had seemed likely he would detest her, but somehow she had fooled herself into thinking it wouldn't happen. Stupid to have hoped their reunion would be a good one. "I'm here to make sure you don't get that way. You're coming with us."

"Fuck you, I'm going nowhere with cyborgs."

"You're assuming I'm giving you a choice," she said coldly.

"Kate," Stone said and moved away. "A word?"

She left Paul glaring hatefully and joined Stone at the computer. He made an adjustment, grunted something under his breath, and input more commands in a blur of fingers that flashed windows onto the screen full of code.

Stone kept his attention on the comp and kept his voice low. "We can't take him out of here unwilling; it would attract too much attention. Assuming you avoid that, how will you get him up to the station? I said I would help him leave if he wanted to do that. He doesn't."

"I'm not leaving him here. He might hate me, but he's still my brother. He goes with us."

"How?"

"Ummm," she looked around the room for inspiration and her eyes fell upon the trolley. She smiled. "Got any more of those patches?"

He tossed the pack to her, and she caught it. "How long to get what we need out of that thing?"

Stone leaned over the comp. "Could be minutes or hours. There's no way to be certain, but whatever happens we have to be out of here by morning."

"Agreed."

She went back to Paul and sat opposite. "I promised Dad I would look after you, but that wasn't why I did it. You'll always be my brother no matter what you think of me, and I'll go on loving you no matter what you've done." He sneered making her want to smack him, but no, she was calm calm calm now. "I'm going to take you with me. Before you start bitching, you should think about it. Whitby will drop you the moment he wakes; he won't protect you now that there's nothing in it for him. Your expedition is scrubbed. If you doubt that, you better be prepared for a naval task force to be waiting when you leave foldspace."

"Don't be a fool! This deal is worth billions. I'll talk to Whitby and cut you in."

"I would sooner bed down with a snake than deal with a Whitby. I don't know how you can ignore what they are."

"They are power."

"Powerful liars. They use our people how they please, and destroy their lives on a whim. The Baxters ruined our family, and Gerald Whitby holds their leash. How can you stand to be near them knowing what they did?"

"Dad was a fool—"

Her palm landed upon his cheek before she knew what she was doing. He was lucky she hadn't put any real force into it. "Don't you dare. He loved you. Bitch at me all you want; hate me even, but don't you dare blame him for anything. He loved you. He did everything for us."

He raised his bound hands and rubbed at his cheek. The shape of her palm was emblazoned there. "He always loved you best."

"That's a lie!"

"He did. When you joined up, he was all about how proud he was of what you were doing. Showing pictures of you in your uniform to everyone who stopped by, but would he listen to me when the Baxters made their offer? No. He never listened to me. It was all Kate this and Kate that. I told him what would happen if he didn't go along, but he wouldn't listen to me. He treated me like a damn stranger, not someone who had an interest in the family business."

She shook her head sadly. How could he be so blind? "The Baxters killed him. They didn't shoot him, but they might as well have when they ruined us. He gave up when they took his pride from him; that's the truth, and for you to ignore that and work for them in any way disgusts me."

"And you disgust me. I meant what I said earlier. My sister is dead. I won't go with you."

"Oh you'll go."

"No."

"Yes," she said and held up the med-patches. "When you wake, you'll be far from here."

"You can't keep me a prisoner forever."

"I don't plan to. I'll get you off Northcliff and then we'll talk about your next step. The money you need for a new face won't be coming now." He started and narrowed his eyes at her. "Don't look so surprised. It was an easy guess to make. You can't walk around as you are for long despite Danny Cole taking your place. Someone who knows your face will recognise you, and then where will you be? You need a new face and then there's your simcode. It will give you away on any Alliance world."

"Whitby is going to fix that," he said coldly.

"Really," she drawled. "You really think they'll follow through now that their billion credit deal is a bust?"

His lips thinned but he kept silent.

She sighed. "I'll get you away from here. As long as you stick to border worlds you'll be fine."

"You've ruined everything," he snarled. "Whitby was paying me five percent."

"I heard."

"Fifty million credits, shot; at least that much. It could have been a lot more!"

She smiled. "What's out there that's worth that much?"

He clammed up and refused to answer.

She shrugged. "We'll know soon enough. Now take your medicine baby brother," she said and opened one of the sealed packets she held. "It's time to go night-night."

"Stay away from—"

She tagged him on one cheek with the med-patch before he could move.

"You... bitch..." he slurred and his head slumped to one side.

"Sleep well," she said and patted his knee. He was already out and didn't see the misery on her face. She rejoined Stone.

He looked beyond her to Paul and then captured her eyes with his as she approached. "Your plan?"

"We'll take him down in the trolley's storage compartment. He should fit."

Stone sighed. "I didn't mean that. Where will you take him?"

She shrugged. "Any border world will do. The closest is Tigris. There's nothing much there to worry him."

"*Harbinger* can get him there in less than two weeks, but what then?"

"I'll give him some cash. He'll need it."

"And that's it? We drop him on Tigris and say goodbye?" She nodded.

"Can you?"

He was staring into her eyes intently, and she shrugged unhappily, but what else could she do? Paul hated her. She couldn't take him with her to Helios; he'd be recognised by security there if by no one else, and even if she could go to Snakeholme, he wouldn't be happy there. Besides, Stone wouldn't let her do that. They still had a mission to complete on Helios, and going home before that would have the General stomping all over her arse. She sighed again. No, Tigris was the best option, but the thought of never seeing her brother again hurt. At least she knew he was alive and well. Him alive and hating her was better than him dead or mind-wiped. At least she would have that to remember in the years to come.

"It's all there is."

Stone nodded slowly. The computer took that moment to signal for attention. At the beep, he turned to look down at it. "Well, well, we seem to have a winner." He frowned.

"What's up?"

"I don't recognise the coordinates."

"Should you? I mean, do you know every colony world's coordinates?" Stone raised an eyebrow. "Okay fine, silly question." His database must be absolutely crammed with crap. "And you don't know this one?"

"No. It doesn't matter though. We have what we need and *Harbinger* will know where it is. Let's tidy up and flit."

She nodded. While Stone dealt with the comp, she went to strip out the shelves from the trolley's storage compartment and stuff her brother into it. She was right; he did fit, but just barely. By the time she was ready, Stone had the comp smashed to pieces and his gear back in his possession. He stowed it on her brother's lap, and they exited the penthouse.

Kate jammed the door shut, twisting the latch into a pretzel before pressing the do not disturb button. The light lit and they were off.

* * *

Part IV

24 ~ Questions

Gina shifted her attention to James for a moment before focusing upon the telltale above the lock again. It read *Harbinger* inbound, as it had for the last few hours since this slip had been assigned. She hadn't been waiting all that time of course. That would have been stupid.

Oh, and standing here for twenty minutes isn't?

She grimaced. It was stupid to wait here, she knew that, but she just had to see her friends safely returned. She could have stayed with James and all the others aboard *Jean de Vienne*; she'd been living there since Stone left. It wasn't as if she couldn't tap into station comms and talk to them. She could have learned what had gone down at Northcliff hours ago if she'd been willing to ignore the time lag. The lag would be way down at this point, but she kept her silence. She wanted to look into their eyes and know, just know that things were... what? Fixed maybe, or better at least. She couldn't get the look Stone had given her out of her head when he told her he was going to fix it. Fix Kate he had meant, and he'd said it in such a way that left no doubt how he planned to do that.

Well, Stone hadn't terminated her friend for the good of the regiment, or for any other reason for that matter, but that didn't mean everything was fixed. All she knew at this point was that there were two very quiet vipers aboard *Harbinger*. The ship was close enough to the station now that her sensors had picked up two active viper IFF beacons. Those beacons validated her cowardice in not contacting the ship, proving to her she need not mourn another friend. Yet. If Stone took this higher... she didn't think he would, but if he did, Gina couldn't see any way for the general to react other than badly. She had to trust that her friends had worked it out on the trip back and that it was fixed.

Please God, let it be fixed.

She didn't feel the ship arrive; its mass was tiny in comparison to that of the station. Any vibration from the docking clamps and umbilicals engaging was lost, but the telltale above the lock changed to indicate arrival. *Harbinger* it said, and the station's pressure doors separated to reveal the outer hatch of the ship as the ramp slid into place.

"Should we?" James nodded up the ramp.

She shook her head. "They're coming out."

She had two viper icons on sensors approaching. She braced to confront Kate, readying herself to say what she had said to her friend many times in her head since the day she left.

Harbinger's hatch shot open and there they were. Kate was a step ahead of Stone as they came down the ramp. Both were in uniform and wearing their berets and V2 sidearms. She sighed. Surely if Stone meant to take things further he wouldn't have allowed Kate to go armed. Gina looked beyond the pair expecting to find Kate's brother, but the airlock and ramp remained empty. Kate stopped in front of her but didn't say anything. Stone glanced aside at them as he walked by, but kept quiet. He stepped onto the docks and joined James who had kept his distance.

Perceptive man.

"He's not here," Kate said finally, reading the question on Gina's face and sounding miserable.

"But safe?"

"Yeah, he's safe now."

Gina nodded and then the anger was suddenly there. Her punch landed before either of them knew it was coming. Kate's head snapped back and she toppled to the ramp looking startled. Her hand came away from her mouth red with fresh blood, but she didn't say anything; she just stared up at her.

"That was for leaving me behind," she said hotly. "And... and for scaring me half to death. Yeah, and for that stunt on the ramp too!"

"Thorry," Kate lisped through the fingers of her hand. Her pulped lips were swelling and still bleeding.

Gina offered a hand and pulled Kate to her feet. She hugged her friend hard and whispered. "Your brother... are you okay?"

Kate's breath hitched and she hugged Gina back. "He hates me, now. I knew it might happen. I mean the way my people feel about all of us, I thought I was prepared for it. Seeing him again made me remember how we used to be together, but he's not that boy anymore. He shot Stone, and I know he would kill me now if he could."

"Nah..."

"You had to be there, Gina. I saw it in his eyes. We took him to Tigris and gave him some money to start over. He said I'm dead to him, and if he sees me again he'll make me dead to everyone else too. I believe him."

"That won't ever happen," she said firmly. "But I'm sorry he hurt you."

Kate stepped back and shrugged unhappily. She glanced at Stone and James and took the handkerchief James offered to dab at her bloody mouth.

"Here gimme," Gina said and took the handkerchief. Some spittle and gentle rubbing removed all traces of their disagreement. The misery in Kate's eyes remained. "Done."

"Thanks," Kate said stuffing the hanky in a pocket.

"Where," Stone said patiently. "Is the bloody navy?"

"They pulled out not long after you left," Gina said.

James nodded. "They had this thing."

Stone glared. "What thing?"

James shrugged.

"It was all hush-hush and need to know, but I sniffed around a bit."

"You did?" Kate said in surprise.

"Hey! I had the same lessons as you. I know how to infiltrate a network."

She might not be as fast as Stone or Kate, or as practised with all the spook stuff, but she could do it after a fashion. It hadn't been hard to learn Commodore Walder's intention to clean up her sector with a little pirate hunting. She hadn't been able to ferret out the details, but she didn't need the ops plan to know it was a good idea. With the redeployment of naval forces throughout the Alliance, taking out a hotbed of pirate activity like one of their bases could only help matters.

She explained what she had learned and James nodded approvingly, but Stone was scowling.

"Damn," Stone muttered. "Do you know when they're due back? I have a job for them."

"Ah... that's going to be kind of a problem," she admitted. "A lot's happened since you've been gone. Orders came down from HQ and ruffled Warder's feathers. She was hot to get back to Beaufort. I think the plan was to take out the pirate base and then redeploy her ships immediately after the battle before she heads back alone to Sector HQ."

"Marvellous," Stone muttered. He glared at Kate for

a long moment and she reddened. "We'll send a drone to Beaufort. It will get there ahead of her and be waiting."

"We could be there in half the time aboard *Harbinger*," Kate countered.

"Not much point if we have to hang about waiting for her to arrive."

"We could recon the system ourselves."

Stone was shaking his head. "Too risky. If they took us out it could go unreported for months."

Kate frowned thoughtfully. "Send a drone home first with all we know. That way if we don't report in, at least the data won't be lost with us and the general can follow it up."

Stone nodded. "Two drones then; one to Beaufort and one to the general."

Gina had no idea what Stone needed the navy for, but she had something that might help out. "Do you need the Commodore herself, or will a couple of ships do?"

Stone's eyes sharpened. "You have some?"

"Not on me," she said with a smirk. "But *Warrior* and *Shannon* were detached to continue patrols and do a sort of show the flag thing. I bet you just missed them. They should be on their way here from Tigris about now. I know because the marines *Warrior* left here are expecting to rotate back aboard soon."

"Inte-rest-ing," Stone said absently as he stared into the distance calculating flight times. "They would be, what, two weeks behind us?"

Gina shrugged. "About that."

"Okay, we're getting somewhere. We'll send a report home, but we'll delay the drone to Beaufort until after we talk with Colgan and...?"

"Captain Vardell commands *Shannon*," Gina supplied. "Louise Vardell. She's senior to Colgan. I don't know if that matters to us?"

"Depends how easy she is to convince."

"Convince to do what, might I ask?" James said. "Unless it's a secret?"

Stone pursed his lips. "I don't want it all over the station, but you already know most of it. We have the coordinates of the system where Tait picked up your aliens."

James' eyes brightened. "Oh really! Anywhere I know?"

Kate shook her head. "Unexplored," she said with a grin as James became even more excited. "Want to come?"

Before James could answer, Stone intervened. "I'm not offering that. We need to recon the system and estimate the Merki threat. That's the mission, not some half-arsed attempt to make first contact."

"But!" James gasped desperately. "But—"

"Besides, the navy might have other ideas."

"But the chance to make contact with three new races!" James protested almost dancing on the spot in his anxiety. "The benefits to the Alliance are incalculable! We can't ignore the possibility."

"I didn't say we should or would, but we don't know what we're up against. Our first priority must be estimating the threat. After that, well, we'll have to play it by ear."

They headed to *Jean de Vienne* for a conference and to bring Kate and Stone up to speed with the investigation.

James led them through the ship to the conference room his team was using for their work, and used the time to work on Stone. Gina didn't think it was working, but even if it eventually did, James would do better considering ways to enhance his chances with the navy. It wouldn't be Stone deciding who would go, or even whether anyone would. In the end it was Commodore Walder's responsibility channelled down through her officers. Captain Vardell would be the senior officer in system when the decision had to be made. It was her who James needed to convince.

They entered the conference room and met the rest of James' team.

There was no need for introductions. Janice Bristow, Bernhard Franks, and Brenda Wilder—James' wife—had met them all briefly before Kate ran off. The rest of the science team, under Doctor Borthwick, spent all their time in the labs. Professor Bristow was officially in charge of the investigation, but in reality she had to share responsibility with Borthwick, who in Gina's opinion was an arsehole of mega proportions. She hadn't forgiven him for trying to prevent her from claiming Captain Degas' remains, and she certainly hadn't forgotten his attempt to hide the tissue and blood samples he'd taken. As she had warned Stone back then, Borthwick had made it his personal mission to obstruct her efforts in every way possible. During her time here, she had needed to use James as a sort of liaison between herself and Borthwick's people, or she'd snagged the data herself under the radar using network taps.

They found seats around the table and sat. Gina had to clear hers first; the entire room was a shambles. She piled the printouts and compads out of her way not bothering with neatness. There was no point in anything else, it would just return to the way it was before she started as soon as they left. How so few boffins could generate so much data in such a short time was beyond her. James was whispering urgently with his wife and colleagues. He was tattling on Stone, she was sure of it. The notion was confirmed not a minute later when the huddle around James broke apart and the four scientists focused their attention on Stone.

"James tells me you have data for us?" Professor Bristow asked.

"I have certain jump coordinates, yes."

"Will you share them with us?"

Stone held out a hand for the compad in Bristow's grip. The woman handed it over eagerly, and he entered the data. "This doesn't leave the room. Understood?" He held out the compad but didn't release it until she nodded.

Gina watched as Bristow read the data and then enter the numbers into the small holotank at one of the keyboards embedded in the table. The tank currently displayed one of the dead aliens; not a pretty sight. It was an autopsy image and showed the creature during its dissection in the morgue. It wasn't something she was trained in, but the alien guts didn't look right. Not Human of course, but not analogous to Human viscera either. She frowned at the image trying to find something that she could point to and know its function. Could that lump be an alien liver? Surely not; placed in the chest cavity it had to be a heart didn't it? But no, it was surely too large for such a small being. The grey leathery skinned aliens were not exactly statuesque. And what about that bag thing; what purpose could it serve? Was it the stomach?

The holotank cleared and a star map appeared in the alien's place. Gina focused her attention upon the tiny suns blazing in the heavens that the tank mimicked. They were like jewels on black velvet. Beautiful. Gina frowned as the image expanded until a single solar system was displayed. No name appeared, just a catalogue number; NGC 1511-2262. That meant it had never been surveyed and the six planets were simple placeholder images showing scale but no other information. It must have been studied only briefly at long range by the Society of Astronomers who spent all their time mapping the known galaxy and probably unknown ones too. There were so many interesting things to explore and study, but this system wasn't one of them apparently. It had obviously not sparked curiosity in anyone important enough to have it moved up for an in depth investigation. It had probably been left to some automated telescope to note its classification and assign a catalogue number.

"A red giant," Professor Bristow said, obviously disappointed.

"We knew it wouldn't be their homeworld, Janice," Professor Franks said. "We knew that almost from the first moment we saw the bodies."

"No, but it's certain now."

"Ah," Stone interrupted. "Would any of the big brains like to let us poor lowly grunts in on the conversation?"

Franks flushed. "Forgive us, Captain. I get lost in the work—occupational hazard I'm afraid." He turned to Professor Bristow. "Do you want to...?"

"No you, Bernhard," Bristow said and took her seat.

Franks took over the controls of the holotank. A few swift keystrokes and the grey bug-eyed alien reappeared. "The Greys..." Kate shot a look of triumph at Stone that Gina didn't understand. He shook his head rolling his eyes at her, and Franks trailed off noticing the by-play. "I... err, what?"

Kate snickered. "I knew they were Greys. Zelda has known about them forever."

James laughed and coughed when Brenda glared at him. "Well, I think it's funny."

Brenda's look was withering. "This is serious."

Franks nodded. "Indeed it is. Far be it from me to one-up the infamous Zelda, Lieutenant Richmond, but this poor creature is similar to the Greys of Chaos Engine fame only in colour. Now, if I might continue?"

Kate's face heated and Gina grinned. Franks had put her friend solidly in her place. This was serious business to him and his colleagues. His life's work was the Merkiaari, but only because until the Shan there had been no other alien cultures to study. The discovery of three more was literally a dream come true for him.

"Thank you," Franks said and continued. "Three different alien races found dead together and originating from a red giant system. We named Specimen One's race after the Lieutenant's famous Greys purely based upon their colour. Not very professional I suppose, but a convenient label."

"Sorry," Kate mumbled.

"Specimen Two," Franks went on, ignoring her and displaying the alien in the holotank that to Gina resembled a gorilla. It was only vaguely like one in body, but its face was uncannily like the extinct creatures that had once lived on Earth. "They're nothing like the Greys, obviously, but the differences go far deeper than the surface. They're mammalian like us and give birth to live young instead of laying eggs as Specimen Three in fact does. Brain size and structures are remarkably similar to ours as are many of their bodily organs and functions. Physically they're superior to us—their musculature is extremely dense—leading us to speculate upon a heavy grav world of origin like the Merki."

Franks used the keyboard to bring the first alien back into the holotank for a comparison. "We believe the Greys evolved upon a water world. See here and here below the ear canals? They still have vestigial gills. Their leathery skin is remarkably similar to that of a shark, very tough and evolved for deep cold waters. They also have underdeveloped swim bladders that may have allowed them to swim at great depths before evolution took a hand to force them out of the water and onto land. Even their eyes are adapted for the lack of light found in such an environment.

"Specimen Three... well, what can we say of them?" Franks said as the third alien replaced the other two in the tank. "The outward differences are obvious. They're cold blooded creatures and adapted to living in arid climates. Their clothing was a little different to that of the other races—insulated with built in climate controls to keep them warm. They would do very poorly in colder climes, probably falling into a torpor and expiring soon thereafter. As you can see they're very lizard-like in appearance, and are similar in many ways to the abundant dinosaur-like creatures found on any number of worlds so far explored.

"The plethora of such species is very thought provoking I must say. Sentient mammals like us might turn out to be the exception rather than the rule in the long term. I hazard a guess that Specimen Three will turn out to be the first of many sentient reptilian races out there to be discovered. It might make for some interesting dynamics should they join the Alliance." Franks shook his head in admiration of the creature, but then nodded to himself at some thought he'd had and turned to Kate. "Would you like to name them, Lieutenant?"

Kate shook her head sullenly. "I said I was sorry."

Franks laughed good-naturedly. "I couldn't resist. Cheer up; we'll call them Saurians for now then. It's a name often used in fiction for sentient lizard-like creatures such as these, and no, not in Zelda and the Spaceways as far as I know."

Kate shrugged uncomfortably, but then she grinned. "Maybe next season."

Franks chuckled. "Maybe so. When this discovery becomes common knowledge it wouldn't surprise me if we see a revival of such stories."

"This is all valuable information, but I'm not sure I see the relevance to my mission," Stone said impatiently.

"The relevance is that the three alien races are not related in any way, Captain. Your red giant system cannot be the homeworld of all these creatures. No, I'm very much afraid we're talking about a Merkiaari colony out here. Exciting as that prospect is to me, I can completely understand the alarming implications to you and the public at large."

Gina sucked in a breath and her blood ran cold. A Merki colony within the Border Zone? Within territory claimed by the Alliance? Unacceptable!

"Reaching aren't you?" Stone said.

Franks hesitated but then the holotank changed again. "The aliens were wearing these collars. They aren't decorative items."

Kate leaned forward studying the image. "I saw vid showing one of these things being taken apart. Do we know what they're for?"

Franks nodded. "They're used to inflict pain or to kill."

Stone's eyebrows went up. "Are you saying... what exactly are you saying?"

"I'm speculating that one of the strongly held beliefs in my field of study is true. That the Merkiaari attacked us primarily for resources."

"But there are easier ways to gain those than war," Gina protested. "There are plenty of unclaimed systems out there. There's no need to fight for something so abundant."

"Ah," Franks said brightly, holding up a finger to make his point. "You're assuming that what we consider resources matches a Merkiaari's notion of such things."

Gina frowned, not understanding him, but Kate got it.

"Oh..." Kate breathed. "That's not... that's not good."

"What?" Gina said.

"Supply and demand," Kate said simply.

Franks beamed and pointed at her. "Exactly."

"I don't get it," Gina said and Stone looked annoyed. He wasn't getting it either.

"In a galaxy full of suns with planets, what else is out there ripe for the plucking that we know is very rare and precious? Think about it. What is the rarest thing in the galaxy?"

"Sentient..." Gina trailed off as she finally understood. "Sentient life?"

"Correct. It's my belief that our three dead aliens were slaves, and that the Merki either trained them or controlled them with the collars. During the last war the navy battled hard not to allow them to create safe or buffer zones around our colonies. It was a theory back then, not proven, that the Merki would colonise our planets themselves if they succeeded. I think that highly likely."

"But all they do is kill," Stone said.

"We don't know that for sure," Franks said. "The discovery of our three specimens seem to indicate something different. If we judged them purely upon their interaction with us you would be right."

"And the Shan," Kate pointed out.

"True, true, but I wonder what would have happened if we and the Shan had turned out to be less warlike and more tractable? Perhaps the Merkiaari decided we were simply too dangerous to enslave." Franks shrugged. "Whatever their motivations, we are where we are. I feel it's quite likely that we'll find a Merki colony on one of the planets of your red giant system. Now why they would choose such a system to colonise in the first place is a puzzle. It's certainly not one I would choose." He brought the system back into the tank and everyone stared at the six planets orbiting the sullen and bloated orb. No one spoke for a long time. "Well... we can surely discard all the planets except these two."

The tank refreshed to display two planets, which were the only realistic prospects due to their location in the liquid water zone—the zone was sometimes called the Goldilocks zone because like the porridge in the child's story it wasn't too hot or too cold. It was just about right. Gina wished they had more data. All they had was a location, a star's classification, and the number of planets huddling around it. What the hell could they do with that? Nothing useful that she could see.

"Anyone with colonisation in mind would avoid the system," James pronounced. "Anyone with sense at least."

"Hmmm," Janice agreed with a nod.

"We need to look at this from a different direction," Brenda put in. "We don't know when this colony was founded or why, but we know it had interaction with us around the time of the Merki War. Agreed?"

Stone nodded. "All of the dead Humans were military and from that era."

"Then perhaps the answer lies back there," Brenda went on. "What do we know about what was happening back then in this sector?"

Gina frowned and accessed her database. She ran a search for anything related, and knew both Kate and Stone were doing the same. Their silence puzzled the others going by their expressions, so she took a moment to explain.

"We're looking into it," she said. "I have a search running. It might take a few minutes."

"It must be amazing," James said. "Having all that data at the tip of your brain."

"You might say," Gina agreed, not bringing up the disadvantages such as the likelihood of mania and death by whigout. The regiment's smoothies came to mind as another downside, a disgustingly foul tasting one, and then there was the fact that all vipers were sterile and cut off from a normal family life. Yeah, instant access to data was great... right. "Yeah."

Stone was first. "I have a few fleet engagements."

Kate nodded. "Same."

Gina agreed as the data came in. "No serious incursions, or what we would call serious today. No doubt the colonists back then would disagree. The worlds we lost have long since been folded back into the Alliance, but none were in this sector."

"There were a couple in the Arcadian Sector," Kate pointed out. "That's pretty close relatively speaking."

"So there was Merki activity in the region?" Franks asked and they all nodded. "Would it make strategic sense from the Merki point of view to colonise our target system?"

"Hell yes!" Stone growled. "Three of those planets almost have to be gas giants going by their size. Just from a logistical point of view it would make sense to drop an outpost there."

"We don't have data confirming that," Kate warned. "But assuming the graphics in the tank are right, I agree it's likely those big ones are gas giants."

The silence stretched out until Janice broke it. "We need

more data, and the only way to get it is by going there for a look."

Everyone nodded.

"For that we need the navy," Stone announced catching everyone's eyes. "We wait."

Gina nodded. It was all they could do. For now.

* * *

25 ~ Leviathan

Gina shifted in her seat at the observer station of Captain Colgan's bridge and watched the quiet efficiency of his crew going about their business. Colgan hadn't surprised her with his willingness to listen to Stone's pitch when James had requested a meeting. He was a veteran of the Shan campaign and knew firsthand the dangers of complacency where the Merki were concerned. No, his reaction didn't surprise her; it was Captain Vardell's almost eager willingness to throw over her mission in favour of this new one that made her pause.

Colgan's opinion and reputation had weight of course; that helped, but for Vardell to go off mission was a big deal. She would have to account for herself and back up her reasons when the time came to report to higher authority, especially when she would be reporting directly to the person who had originated the mission she had ditched. Showing the flag wasn't a glamorous one, but Commodore Walder had felt the mission was desirable and had value. Persuading her that it did not, or had less at least than the Hail Mary pass they were embarked upon would be hard. No doubt that was part of Vardell's reasoning for dispatching a drone to Beaufort detailing what they knew and were doing about it. Stone had also launched a drone with similar information but home to the general.

Stone and Kate were aboard *Shannon*. It had seemed sensible to split their force between the two ships. God forbid they lose one to enemy action, but if it happened they hoped at least one viper would survive to report in. Gina had decided to stick with the boffins aboard *Warrior*. It gave Kate time alone with Stone; something she felt they needed. They hadn't spoken with her about it, but she sensed all was not well between them. She hoped they could work it out and regain their closeness. They had been good together.

"Time?" Colgan asked.

"Three minutes to translation, Skipper," the helmswoman said without turning.

"Tactical on main viewer," he replied after a brief nod.

"Aye, sir," the XO replied.

Gina turned her attention to the main viewer in time to see the swirling otherness of foldspace disappear to be replaced by blackness filled with red lines—the sensor grid. Sensors were useless in foldspace, but as soon as they translated back to n-space those lines would have meaning, sectioning the system into understandable areas that could be used for navigation and targeting.

"Bring us to battle stations if you please," Colgan said powering his station around to face the comm shack.

"Aye sir," Lieutenant Ricks said and the battle stations alarm sounded throughout the ship.

Gina could easily imagine the marines scrambling down in the guts of the ship; the rest of the crew too of course, but she had been a marine once. She had never been assigned to a ship, but had travelled aboard many and heard the stories. She had been a line marine, not a ship puke, but they'd all been marines and therefore only one order away from duty aboard a ship. All marines were trigger pullers first; specialisations came second only after that. Nope, no ship action for her. She wondered what it was like firing one of those monster lasers in local control, right on the mount, rather than remotely. She bet it was satisfying. She just bet it was.

"...all clear, Anya?" Colgan was saying.

"Aye, sir," Anya Ivanova at tactical responded. "Stealth mode to the max upon emergence."

"Good. I don't want a whisper leaving this ship until we know what we're getting into. Point defence free, but nothing that can break our bubble until I say so."

"Aye, sir," Anya said, not pointing out the order was obvious.

Everyone knew what to do, but they expected their skipper to give orders, just as he expected them to not need those orders in extremis. They did it the navy way, just as Gina had done things the marine way in her time, and now did them the viper way. Everyone did their duty. That's what it came down to in the end.

"Thirty seconds," the helmswoman said.

Gina secured her borrowed helmet's visor, and the bridge crew did the same. She was wearing a navy shipsuit given to her when she came aboard, as was James and the rest of the team. She glanced at her life support umbilical, just making sure. She knew it was secure, but habit had her checking.

"Ten seconds... five... exe—"

The world turned inside out.

* * *

Aboard ASN Warrior, NGC 1511-2262, Border Zone

Colgan finally pulled his eyes away from his monitors and took a moment to rack his helmet. He was the last one to do so. He hadn't wanted to take even a moment's attention away from the data coming in. Voices on the bridge were hushed and tense as his people worked at their stations, but there wasn't much yet to concern them.

He glanced up at the main screen where it displayed the tactical situation, populated now with meaningful data. The sun and planets including their orbits were clear. The system contained two gas giants, not three as they had expected, and four other planets two of which were in the liquid water zone. Various other bodies were being plotted and added as the data trickled in; moons, asteroids and the like. It was slow meticulous work, but something familiar from his Survey Corps days.

The sight of *Shannon* skulking along beside them was reassuring. Both ships were in full stealth and sucking in data for all they were worth using passive scans alone. Silent running was the order of the day, the week, and the bloody month if it took that long to unravel the mystery of this place. They had comm between ships using TBC, and that gave them discreet instant communications at such short range. They were sharing data, and the load required to obtain it, in an effort to provide redundancy and speed up the process in case they needed to run.

So far that possibility seemed unlikely, and the lack of threat made him very nervous. He knew Merkiaari had been here, knew it beyond question. Tait had obtained his cargo here, and the how of that was occupying his every waking moment. He couldn't conceive of how such a man had accomplished it, and their passive scans were not helping, so far at least, to discover the secret.

They had elected to translate back to n-space on the very edge of the zone for safety, and that meant any activity within the system took a long time to reach them. The light speed limit was exactly that; a limit that could not be circumvented. They were about as far out as it was possible to be and still be nominally within the system and that meant every damn thing took an age. He was actually used to that but in different circumstances. Surveying an unexplored system like this would have felt nostalgic if not for the fear they might screw up and bring the Merkiaari down upon their heads.

He glanced at Janice's board, but as before the jump drive was in the green. Of course it was. He'd ordered it charged from auxiliary as a precaution the moment they'd arrived. He was sure *Shannon's* drive was hot as well. They couldn't keep it like that forever... or rather they shouldn't do so. Components could fail, and fully charged jump initiator coils could fail catastrophically. Liberating all that energy inside a ship would do bad things to the crew and the ship. Even if the coils didn't fail, keeping them at full charge for too long would knock years off their lifespan. BuShips would not be pleased.

He turned to the comm shack. "Anything, Mark?"

Mark Ricks was listening hard for comm traffic as well as analysing the incoming data looking for Merki electronic emissions. He shook his head. "Nothing. This system is dead."

"Keep at it. We know from the Shan campaign that the Merki have better jamming than us."

"But I'm not being jammed, Skipper. I'm getting background noise and that's it."

"Even so," he said. "Jamming and stealth tech go hand in hand. We don't know what they have."

Ricks obviously wanted to argue, but he just nodded. "Aye, sir."

He turned to face front again, and used his station's screens to review the raw data coming in from the ship's sensors on its way to Scan and Francis Groves' eagle eyes, as well as the refined take piped to the bridge from CIC to Anya's station at Tactical. It wasn't that he doubted his people's abilities down in CIC; he didn't, and he had confidence in *Warrior's* ability to alert him if she saw something they needed to know. Her computer was second only to that installed in the *Washington* class of heavy cruiser—only one generation removed from cutting edge tech. No, he was just used to seeing patterns in raw data from his Survey Corps days, and therefore might see something others missed. He was vein enough to think his oversight had some value.

Warrior and *Shannon* continued their cautious approach to the inner system. Both were at battle stations and maximum stealth. They were twin holes in space; their nanocoat dialled to black, their sensors passive, and power plants dialled down so low they were barely operating ship's systems. The only way to reduce output further would be by standing down from battle stations and taking all weapons offline. That wasn't happening. As it was, *Warrior* had her tubes loaded and lasers at standby readiness, but all targeting was offline. They couldn't fire a spit ball without targeting sensors, but that was fine. It would take barely a moment for them to go active.

"Contact!" Groves sang out and the main viewer updated to reveal a baleful red glow just rounding the fourth planet. "Contact designate: Alpha-One. Merkiaari ship!"

Colgan froze in horror. A ship that size? Impossible! It was bigger than the biggest station he had ever visited in the Alliance! No one built such things, no one! What possible use was there for such a ship? The Alliance wouldn't do it, *couldn't* do it! The power required to make it mobile would dwarf that needed by an entire colony! He calmed his yammering brain and tried to concentrate. It was here; it was therefore not only possible to make a ship that size mobile, the Merki had done so, and for a reason. What reason?

"Weapons?" he snapped.

"Unknown class, unknown armament, sir," Groves said sounding appalled. "It's huge... might it be a station and not a ship?"

He liked the possibility, but no, its silhouette alone

revealed the telltale structures required for all operational foldspace drives. He pointed that out to his XO and she nodded grimly.

"I have Captain Vardell on the line, Skip," Ricks said.

He nodded, he wasn't surprised. "I'll take it here."

"Aye, sir," Ricks said switching Vardell through.

Louise appeared on his number two monitor replacing the raw feed that had been scrolling down detailing the leviathan just discovered.

"Jeff," she said.

"Louise. What can I do for you?"

She grinned. "I think we found the source of your Merkiaari. Big sucker isn't it?"

"Some might think the Merki have an inferiority complex. They certainly go for size over style."

Vardell pursed her lips at that observation. "There's a certain style in going for broke in my opinion."

"Very true. Thoughts? Orders?"

"We're doing all we can at this point. I say we keep doing it until the situation changes. That thing can't be very fast or manoeuvrable. We should be able to evade it easily if it gets underway. I'll want a conference by holo later... let's say 1800 hours and invite the science team. I want their opinion on this thing."

"Understood. I'm wondering if we might have our very first civilian Merkiaari ship here."

"Do they even have civilians?"

He shrugged, he didn't know. "I'll ask. If anyone knows the answer, one of my boffins will."

"I've read the literature," Vardell said doubtfully. "There are all kinds of theories, but I don't think anyone really knows the truth."

"Professor Franks is one of the leading experts in the field. His best guess is probably as close to right as we'll ever get short of meeting a Merki civilian."

Vardell looked disgusted. "Not a pretty thought. Merkiaari and civilian... what could be worse?"

"A Merkiaari newsie?"

Vardell's eyes widened.

Colgan chuckled. "Yeah, it's a pretty horrible thought. I've had more than enough of the media, Louise. I know Commodore Walder thinks we all revel in notoriety over here, but the truth is we're all sick of it."

"I can believe it. See you in conference at 1800. *Shannon* out."

The screen refreshed and the data stream reappeared scrolling down the screen. He read the data but nothing leapt out at him except perhaps for the complete lack of information relating to defensive or offensive capabilities. They were too far out for detail, but such things should... *should* be obvious by now. They weren't. Was the ship cloaked in some way? It didn't seem likely to him. Why cloak weapons but leave everything else open to chance and random passive scans? No, that made no sense at all.

"Anything to add, XO?"

Groves was ready with a report. "Preliminary, but yes. Mass is estimated at over seven million tonnes displacement. That's six times heavier than our biggest carriers—the *Hercules* class—and it's over double the volume of those ships leading me to suspect large open internal spaces."

Colgan nodded, but he was appalled. The *Hercules* class of carrier weighed in at right around 1.2 million tonnes. It was the heaviest ship class in the list and had taken the crown from the previous holder of the top spot—the stupendous *Nimitz* class once known as a super carrier due to its size and speed. It had held the crown for the preceding fifty years; there were plenty of them still in service. Super dreadnoughts were nominally in the same weight class, but they were physically smaller due to heavy armour and design specs. Carriers were far larger in volume than dreadnought's due to their flight decks and hangar design.

Groves went on. "We have nothing yet on its abilities. Until it powers up I can't judge shield capacity, defensive capabilities, its speed or manoeuvrability... basically we're blind on all that. Its power output is off the scale, Skipper. I've counted over a dozen point sources. Those reactors each have a capacity four times ours. My guess is they need them to power heavy shields to cover something that size, and to power a foldspace drive capable of moving the thing."

"Or a big arse laser," Ricks muttered and flushed when Colgan turned toward him. "Sorry, sir."

"No it's alright. That was a good point. Any evidence of that XO?"

"None. As I said we have nothing on its weaponry, but Merki ships never go unarmed. They have something over there. With the power available they could have hundreds of our super dreadnought 600mm lasers and grazers. They could have more or less than that, bigger or smaller caliber. They could have those giant PPC cannons the Shan like so much. I have no idea!"

Groves sounded frustrated by that.

He understood the feeling, because he was as well. "We'll know eventually. Keep on it, XO. We have a conference at 1800 with *Shannon* and I want you and Anya there." He turned to Ricks. "Inform the boffins of the meeting, please Mark."

Ricks nodded and turned to do that. "Aye, sir."

"Erm... may I ask something?" Fuentez said raising a hand for attention.

He powered his station around to face her observer station. "Go ahead, Lieutenant."

"Look, none of this stuff is in my area," Fuentez said indicating the main viewer. "And you guys probably already thought of it, or it's so obvious you haven't said..."

He smiled at the exaggerated diplomacy. "But?"

"But, if I'm reading it right that mother of a ship is in geosynch of the planet. Has anyone considered why that is?"

He hadn't given it a thought. He turned to Groves. "XO?"

Groves was working her controls, but she looked up to answer. "Checking it now."

Fuentez grinned. "Okay. Can we tell from here if the Merki have made landings at all?"

The thought chilled him, and he kicked himself for becoming fixated on that huge ship. Of course it had entered the system for a reason and taken up station around that planet. Of course it had. He should have thought to ask Francis long before now. He wondered if those aboard *Shannon* had investigated the reason, but no, they were sharing data. He would have known.

"Split attention between ship and planet, XO."

"Aye, sir, already doing that... now anyway."

He turned to Ricks. "Inform *Shannon* what we're about and ask they do the same."

"Aye, sir."

"Lieutenant?"

"Skipper?"

He smiled, her marine background was showing. "Well done. Anything else you've thought of?"

"Just that if the planet is habitable, we might find a lot more here than the navy can handle."

"Oh?"

"Maybe a Merkiaari listening post, or the start of a colony, or... I don't know what else."

"All nasty possibilities that General Burgton will no doubt want to know about." He looked to Groves again. "What have we got so far?"

Groves didn't look happy. "Not much yet. Spectroscopy indicates an oxygen nitrogen atmosphere able to support life. The planet is Class M but only barely, it's right on the limit of what we would call terrestrial. Not a good pick for a colony at just about 10,000 kilometres in diameter and pretty cold in winter. Survivable, just not that pleasant, Skipper."

"Alright, anything else?"

"The Lieutenant is right about the ship being in geosynch over the planet. I'm concentrating on the land mass below it assuming there's something of interest there. I'll inform you when I have something."

He nodded and checked the time. They had hours before the conference. "Pipe all this down to the conference room for the boffins, would you?"

"We've already been doing that, Skipper. It seemed the thing."

"Agreed. If we want to use their brains, we need to give them the data to work with."

Groves smiled and nodded her agreement.

* * *

26 ~ Conference

Colgan entered the conference room accompanied by his officers and Lieutenant Fuentes, but paused just inside to take in the controlled chaos that always seemed to orbit his boffins. Really, how hard was it for them to keep the table tidy at least? There were many less of them than he'd had aboard *Canada*, but you wouldn't know it by the mess. There were empty cups, plates, various flimsies and printouts, and of course the inevitable compads scattered all over the simwood surface. Why couldn't they use one compad or one each at least? The things had huge memory capacities!

He checked his wrist comp. He had two minutes to tidy up before Louise and her people arrived by holo. The conference software would reproduce this room and its squalor aboard *Shannon*, and he didn't want *Warrior's* rep to become no better than a garbage scow!

"Quick, clean this pigsty up!" he said to Anya. "Everyone!"

The boffins looked around blinking at the mess. At least they had the grace to look shamefaced, but they didn't move to help until Francis and Anya began collecting things and endangering their work. Colgan heard squawks about their file system being ruined. What system? Were they serious? Apparently they were as they darted about snatching things up, saving them from a terrible fate apparently, and neatly stacking them in groups that made sense only to them. Fuentez quickly grabbed all the cups and plates and shoved them into the autochef, almost force feeding the thing. They finished just in time.

Louise and her officers including the two vipers she had aboard *Shannon* appeared in the room.

"Welcome aboard *Warrior*," he said and greetings were exchanged all around. "Let us find seats and get started."

Colgan took his seat at the head of the table; it was his ship and he was hosting the meeting. His officers sat to his right. Louise and her people took the left opposite Francis and Anya, while everyone else took random places except for the three vipers. They sat close together already whispering amongst themselves catching up he guessed. The holographic conferencing software worked upon similar principals to the holotanks and sensim systems used throughout the Alliance. Louise and the others looked and sounded as if they were actually present in the room, as did he and his people to her on *Shannon*. Data was exchanged between the ships to keep everything synchronised and faithfully replicating what went on, so when he activated the tabletop holotank to display the *Leviathan*—their name for the huge Merki ship—*Shannon's* tank also activated to show the same data.

"What a difference a few hours make," Colgan said by way of a start. "It's a derelict."

"We don't know that for sure," Vardell warned. "Those point sources indicate it still has power. It's suffered damage, catastrophic damage even, but where there's power there's threat."

"I agree," Stone said. "I don't know what that ship is, but

one thing I do know is that it's dangerous. We should blast it to atoms."

That caused uproar among the scientists all shouting at once about the terrible loss to science of doing such a thing. Colgan sympathised against his better judgement, and came down on their side of the equation. They needed to study it, not destroy it. It was one of a kind and what they could learn was of incalculable worth.

He knocked on the table to bring the room to order. "Let's discuss the matter like adults shall we?" He used the table's interface to turn the ship in the tank so that all could see the damage it had suffered. "That ladies and gentlemen was not caused by weapon's fire."

"Agreed," Vardell said. The huge rip in the hull on the starboard side had been hidden from them until they closed the distance, but it was obvious now that a rather large blast had blown the hull open from the inside. They were at station keeping right now, still at double the most pessimistic weapon's range they could attribute to the Merkiaari. "That sort of damage looks like classic jump failure to me."

That's what he had been thinking too. He remembered being surprised that Tait hadn't blown his ship or his jump capacitors at least, to flaming flinders when he mis-jumped in his panic to escape an earlier battle. The result had been his arrival here, which it now seemed the Merkiaari had done before him. He wondered if there was some property of this system that pulled such unlucky ships to itself. The star perhaps. It *was* supermassive, a red giant and at the top end of the scale for such suns.

"We'll know when we go aboard it," Colgan said. "We have to do that, I think we all know that?"

Vardell nodded grimly. "I'm sorry, Captain Stone, but I didn't come out here to blow away a one of a kind artifact like that ship. If it were just a Marauder let's say, or even one of their old style battlewagons the Alliance faced back in the day, it would be a different matter, but this is something entirely new. We have to figure out what it is."

Stone shrugged. "The hull configuration is vaguely similar to their assault ships except in size. It's almost as if they scaled one up. Why they would do that, I can't answer."

Colgan frowned at the image in the holotank. He could see the similarities that Stone mentioned, but in his mind they didn't mean anything. All Merki ships had things in common. Maybe this ship, whatever its purpose, was built at the same yards as their dreadnoughts, or designed by the same team. Who knew? It might even be some weird carrier design. He hoped not because the Merkiaari didn't have them last time, but they did use air power extensively in atmosphere. The Merkiaari had seen how useful carrier based fighters were in combat many times, and he didn't like anything that smacked of Merki advancement. The Alliance was already behind the curve with their new jamming and stealth tech advances.

"Well," he went on. "I don't think they'll be a problem getting in at least."

Everyone laughed. The huge rip in the hull could almost swallow *Warrior*.

Stone didn't laugh, and neither did the other vipers. What he said next quieted everyone. "If it doesn't power weapons and blast the shuttles we're using upon approach."

Colgan nodded grimly. Now that they were closer they had detected the ship's weapons. There were a lot of missile tubes and laser hatches in that thing. Not as many as a hull that size could theoretically pack in, but there were plenty nonetheless. About as many as three Alliance super dreadnoughts could carry he would judge. If the Merki had really wanted to, they probably could have doubled the number; the ship was seriously that big. It was a monster. None of its weapons were powered right now, and so far they hadn't detected any targeting emissions. And they were looking. Oh yes indeed they were looking. If it twitched so much as a single sensor in their direction, he had told his people to go to evasive manoeuvres without orders and run for jump. There was no way to stand toe to toe with that thing.

"You're joining the boarding party then?" Vardell asked. She could have ordered the vipers to go, and be technically within her rights as mission commander, but no one felt easy ordering one of *them* to do anything, especially not Stone who was a veteran of the Merki War. Definitely not on something that could turn out to be a suicide mission. "The marines can handle it."

"Lieutenant Richmond and I will lead the first boarding party in case any special Merki related problems come up. Lieutenant Fuentez will lead the landing force... if you still plan to send one down?"

"Before you get to that," Professor Bristow said. "I haven't been informed about our part in the boarding of the ship."

Vardell and Colgan exchanged a glance, and it spread among their officers. The truth was, there was no way in hell they were letting the boffins go into harm's way, but how to say it diplomatically? He was willing to take a stab at it, but Fuentez beat him to it.

"You'll go down to the surface with me, Professor," Fuentez began. "But not on the first trip. You understand. I have to clear the area and be sure it's safe. As for the ship, there are more places for hostiles to hide. It will take longer to clear, but you'll get there. Don't worry."

Colgan smiled, that wasn't bad, but of course Professor Bristow wasn't in the least fooled.

"I want it understood that we are not in your chain of command, Captain Vardell, Captain Colgan," Bristow said. "This mission is ours. You are in fact at our disposal, and not the other way around. The President himself gave us our commission."

He blinked. Well... he turned to Louise and raised an eyebrow.

"I don't care if God himself gave it to you," Vardell began. "You can follow orders or we can take you to see the bloody President and ask him what he thinks of letting you run around in possibly hostile territory. How about that?"

Bristow grinned. "An idle threat. You won't leave here until you know we've learned what we came for. I want one of us with each party. Put us in armour, put us in a tank for all I care, but do it. We need to see what's in there and to put it bluntly; I don't think soldiers are qualified to recognise what might be important."

"And who do you propose to send?" Vardell said through clenched teeth, surprising Colgan.

She was actually considering allowing this? "Louise, I don't think—" he began to say, but she cut him off.

"She's right, dammit. Marines are for breaking things in a very fast and efficient manner, not researching alien artifacts."

Fuentez chuckled.

True, but he would still hold the boffins back until the second or third trip. Louise was senior; it was her decision, but he didn't agree with it. Like, *at all!*

Bristow nodded to James. "James has asked to accompany Gina with the landing force. Professor Franks will go with Captain Stone to the ship. Brenda and I will monitor the feed from their helmet cams from here."

"You've thought this through," Vardell said, grudging respect in her voice. "Very well. Marine hard suits for both of them, but if they can't prove to me that they can use them properly, they'll not set one foot on the shuttles."

Bristow nodded. "That's fair."

Fair? It was utter madness! Colgan wanted to protest, but that just wasn't done in a setting like this. Perhaps in private he could make his reservations known, but not in front of subordinates and especially not in front of the civs. He would do so in private after the meeting.

"You have no idea how long I've yearned for an opportunity like this," Professor Franks said, his eyes gleaming.

"Let's hope it's not your last," Colgan muttered and Louise shot him an aggravated look. He shrugged an apology her way. He might be hosting the meeting but she was senior. "Okay, let's look at the other half of this meeting. I've already been over this with Captain Perry. You might be wondering why Captain Vardell and I did not invite the marines to hear this. It's simply that we've already taken care of the operational side of things and they're taking care of the details with their commands right now. I'll brief them on any changes we come up with after the meeting. Anything to add, Louise?"

"Only that the vipers will be in command of each force, not Professors Wilder and Franks. Give suggestions by all means, ask that this thing or that be investigated to your heart's content, but they're in command. The marines are your bodyguard not your servants; don't make me regret letting you go by trying to turn them into your assistants or something."

James laughed. "I can carry my own books, Captain. No one has ever accused me of not doing my bit."

Colgan heard the steel in James' voice there at the end. The man had led a large part of the Shan resistance in the last campaign. If any civ knew war, this one did. He changed the holotank to display the planet and all eyes turned to regard it.

"Oxygen nitrogen atmosphere is confirmed. Liquid water, plant life compatible with us and the Merkiaari... all within acceptable, though not great, parameters. Basically, we could live on it but the weather is miserable and anyone stuck on that mud ball for long will be too. Cold and wet, frequent high velocity storms will threaten structures no matter how well built. Ground tremors have been detected, the result of the huge moons hereabouts, and solar radiation has done some bad things to the magnetosphere and ionosphere. Solar flares must be common, though the sun seems to have entered a relatively passive cycle. That can change at any time, so expect communications to be spotty."

"Joy," Stone muttered. "You think the satellites can handle it if we decide to deploy?"

They hadn't deployed satellites yet, they were still at max stealth though they had discharged the jump capacitors now. They couldn't keep them at jump stations indefinitely for fear of failure, and the wear rate was ferocious held at peak charge that way. Chief Williams was already bitching about having to recalibrate the system now that the equivalent of an extra hundred jumps had been burned out of his beloved drive.

"We won't deploy until we're confident the ship really is derelict, but yes I think so. The solar wind here is intense but our sats are mil-spec of course. They're hardened against worse."

Stone nodded. "As long as we have at least one sat up, we can communicate using TacNet or viper comm no sweat."

That might be true between vipers, but the marines might not be so lucky. They had helmet comm and wristcomp, both of which were good tech but not on the same scale as viper hardware. Still, the vipers could relay information if push came to shove and the sun was quiet right now. There might be no need to resort to lash-ups.

"Good," he said. "We think the Merki have landed a small outpost down there, but due to weather conditions we can't estimate numbers. It could have a city-sized population, or have nothing more than a squad manning a listening post."

Richmond snorted.

"You have something to add, Lieutenant?"

"Considering how many troopers are routinely carried

aboard a Marauder class transport, which is way smaller than that thing out there, how many Merki are likely to be aboard the *Leviathan?* Half a million, a million?"

He didn't want to think about that. "That's one of the things we'll discover I suppose."

"Stone is right; we should blow it out of space. We can still learn stuff on the planet once that's done."

"The decision is made, but even if it weren't, you're assuming we could blow it away."

"Enough high yield nukes will blow anything out of space if done right. Send your entire magazine on ballistic courses. They won't see them coming. Kaboom! Job done."

Kaboom indeed. Colgan grinned. That would be how he would do it if told to take out the Merki ship, but the decision wasn't his and wouldn't happen now anyway.

"Your point regarding the planet?" Vardell asked.

Richmond shrugged. "With so many Merkiaari aboard the ship, how many do you think were sent down world?"

"Could be any number. Without recon we can't know the answer."

"Look, that ship is a wreck; a powerful dangerous wreck, but still a wreck. It can't leave here. The Merki had no choice but this one planet as a destination when they blew their drive to hell and gone, right?"

Vardell nodded.

"Then what makes you think they didn't send all of their people down? That's not a listening post, Captain. It's a lifeboat. It's a colony now. I'd bet my pulser on it!"

"Okay, that's a possibility I don't like, but okay. We still need to verify and that means going down and scouting the situation."

"I agree, but you don't need an entire team for that. One unit, a viper unit, should go down first and check the place out."

She was right about that. If there was a colony down

there a single viper had more chance of scoping the place out and evading notice than an entire platoon of marines. He nodded to Louise that he agreed with Richmond.

"Lieutenant Fuentez, what do you say?" Vardell said.

"I've thought that I should go solo from the start, Captain," Fuentez said and caused the scientists to mutter. "I don't mean to cut out our science team from all the fun, and I certainly don't think I can do their jobs, but along the same lines they can't do mine. I would prefer to scout the situation alone before bringing them down."

Louise nodded thoughtfully.

"And, Captain?"

"What is it?"

"I think you should reconsider your position regarding the ship. I know you won't destroy it, but you should not send Professor Franks in with the first group to board. Seriously. He is irreplaceable where the rest of us aren't. Send him with a second team or send him to join the first after a quick recon of the ship."

"Here now!" Franks blustered. "The deal is already struck. No reneging!"

Vardell raised a hand. "I won't, don't worry about that. You'll be aboard that shuttle. But... the Lieutenant has made good points. I think we will do it her way and after *a brief*," she emphasised that point when Franks started to argue. "A brief recon of the ship, you'll join the marines and Captain Stone to continue the mission. If hostilities break out, your pilot will have orders to hightail it back here with you."

Franks scowled.

"And my mission?" Fuentez asked.

"As you said. You go down solo and check it out, and the rest of your team will wait for your report."

Fuentez nodded and the vipers exchanged satisfied smiles.

Colgan watched them, fascinated. They were obviously

in communication with each other though they remained silent. The expressions flashing upon their faces all through the briefing suggested they had been discussing ways to bend things in the direction they desired without overtly doing so. He wondered what other vipers were doing behind the scenes throughout the Alliance, but dismissed the thought. Here was all that mattered.

"So," he said. "If we're done here, I think we should adjourn for food. The shuttles leave early tomorrow. Lieutenant Fuentez?"

"Sir?"

"I assume you'll prefer a night approach?"

"Absolutely. I'll pilot the shuttle myself and land at a distance. I want to hike in."

"Then you'll need to leave at 0400 hours local."

"Understood."

With that everyone stood and the meeting broke up. Louise and the others attending by holo disappeared and the room suddenly felt less full.

* * *

27 ~ Hostile Territory

Gina's mission began like many she had undertaken with a long boring wait, but unlike those other times, she was actually progressing the op during the long hours with nothing to do; her shuttle was powered down on a ballistic course designed not to attract *Leviathan's* attention as she approached her objective. She was all in favour of not being noticed. It was a tense few hours, heading for the planet with no real idea if she was being tracked by Merki sensors. The fear of that had faded now; *Leviathan* was in geosynch and the orbit had progressed to a point where her shuttle was now approaching with the entire planet between them. The good news was that she was safe from detection; the bad news was that she would have a long flight in atmosphere to get on station and begin her recon mission.

She was content with that.

Gina wondered what the others would discover on the massive ship when they launched. What new thing would they find to plague the Alliance? That's how she felt about the Merkiaari after the Shan campaign. They were a plague upon the galaxy and Humanity in particular; a scourge that needed eradicating. Everyone loathed and feared them of course. The physical scars of the last war had mostly healed, though there were still some planets with ruins where cities of millions once stood, but the psychological scars never would. Humanity's psyche had been irreversibly scarred, changed as a result of its very first contact with aliens. Nothing would ever give them back that sense of innocence they'd had as they explored the galaxy and found it good. They knew now it wasn't good; it was a cold-hearted bitch, and to survive in it they needed to fight as hard as they ever had on Earth. Harder. There were no free lunches and they had serious competition in the Merki. That was something they'd never really had on the homeworld.

The shuttle shivered ever so slightly, encountering the outermost but still diffuse layers of the atmosphere. Gina brought her attention back to her instruments and prepared to take manual control. She could wish for *Harbinger's* neural interfaces about now. Flying her had been a dream, exactly like one in fact when she thought about it. Neural controls were great when you got the hang of them. Of course the learning curve was steep. It was so easy to lose concentration and be thrown out of the gestalt; abruptly dropping out of the net that way could actually hurt and it was always disorientating. One moment you were a powerful entity with a fusion heart, the next a tiny meat sack confused and alone again in your own head.

The shuttle shuddered again and her wings bit into atmosphere, but her control surfaces had nothing to work with at this altitude. Working the stick like stirring a pot of stew, she felt for the first indications that she had control. Less than a minute later she felt it, and eased the shuttle onto a new course as she hammered deeper into the soup that this planet laughingly called an atmosphere. She had to fly on instruments; cloud cover was extensive. According to weather radar and other sensors she would be flying through some heavy storms on her way to the objective.

She took the shuttle down to 5000 meters and set the autopilot before daring to release control again. Flight time would be a few hours at current speed, but that was meaningless. She couldn't fly directly there and land; this was a recon mission. Her plan was to find a hidden landing site and hike in to the objective. No one knew what to expect, and that applied to environmental conditions as much as it did to the Merki. A Merkiaari city hidden under the clouds would be at the top of her not good list though. Gina grinned at the thought. Scary thought or not, she was excited too. She wanted to know what this planet was hiding as much as James and his colleagues did.

Stone's mission had different objectives, but both were important. She wouldn't know anything until a satellite was deployed over the planet; that wouldn't happen until he checked out *Leviathan* and satisfied everyone it was no threat. Gina was going to assume the ship was abandoned by the crew and that they were down here. If she was wrong, well, it meant she was wasting her time but safe. If she was right, any precautions she took to remain hidden would be good ones.

The shuttle flew through the storm front and into the worst storm she had ever experienced, and she had been transported through a few in her time as a marine. She hadn't been a pilot until trained on Snakeholme by the regiment's ace instructors, but she knew a bad blow when confronted by one. She wasn't enjoying her first solo op in bad weather. Not at all. The shuttle was bucking and lurching in the severe turbulence; the first time it lost 1000 meters in altitude without warning she nearly barfed, and her heart hammered in panic as she reached for the controls, but the autopilot was unfazed. The engines howled and the computers made an adjustment to compensate. If she went down at this speed nothing would save her. Enhancements be damned, the old adage—*it's not the fall that kills you, it's the sudden stop*—was entirely apt viper or not.

Hours of hell later found her hovering in torrential rain trying to land without crashing. She had discovered the handy dandy river gorge while looking for somewhere to land, and realised what a treasure she had found. The gorge was deep and it weaved its way through the landscape wider than any highway; she used it like one to fly much closer to her objective than originally planned. It would really cut down on the time she needed to get in position, and all without being seen. The downside had been the storm; the wind had really been something trapped between rock walls. Wind shear and strong updraughts could be fun when you couldn't see them coming... yeah right. She had been scared shitless more than once. It had certainly made the final leg of the flight interesting.

Now here she was, hovering a few metres above the ground on anti-grav thrusters, unable to cross that final barrier. It was ridiculous! She had come all this way but couldn't land! The winds had picked up until she would have called the storm a tropical one, but it really wasn't quite as bad as a hurricane, maybe. Besides, it was too damn cold to be called tropical. There was nowhere warm enough on the entire planet for that name to apply. It was almost enough to make her feel sorry for any Merki trapped here. Almost. She remembered all the faces she would never see again because of them, and suddenly she felt remarkably cheerful.

Screw 'em.

Gusts of wind howled through the gorge, driving the rain horizontally against the fuselage, threatening to drive her sideways into the cliff. She compensated, leaning the shuttle into the wind and deployed the landing skids. Suddenly the wind dropped and she was skidding sideways. She cursed and over corrected as another blast of wind drove her toward the cliff again. She took a chance, slammed the shuttle down the last few meters, and a horrible crunching groan told her the starboard skid had found a rock. The shuttle lurched at an angle to port with its butt in the air, propped awkwardly on an outcropping. She gave her anti-grav just a little power, not enough to lift fully and dragged the skid away from the obstruction. She winced at the terrible noise it made, hoping she hadn't ripped the sucker off, but then using her VTOL joystick she carefully tried to land again. To her vast relief, the shuttle seemed to accept this and didn't protest further. The landing was almost smooth this time, though its attitude wasn't ideal. The ground was far from level. The shuttle still had its butt in the air and was leaning to port, but the ground seemed stable. She waited for disaster to strike, for the landing strut to fall off or for the shuttle to slip further down slope, but nothing of the sort occurred.

"Well, that was fun." She blew a lock of hair out of her eyes. She needed a trim. "I guess we don't need anti-grav anymore then."

It was surprisingly hard to let her death grip on the stick go, but she did it finally and started the power down sequence, listening all the while to the shuttle settling on its skids. She willed it not to make any sudden moves. It didn't, but she had no confidence in the ground hereabouts. She hadn't chosen the site because it was a good one for landing shuttles in. She'd chosen it because it was sheltered by an overhang on the cliff wall where in the far past water had eroded the rock below. She judged the river running through the gorge was not navigable and the cliff walls were high. It would be hard for anyone to see the shuttle from above and there was no reason for anyone to attempt a descent. Of course that meant it wouldn't be too easy for her to ascend the cliff either, but she had climbed worse with Kate on Snakeholme. She had everything in her pack that she needed. She'd get it done.

The real benefit of following the gorge and flying within it for the last few klicks was that, despite how dangerous the wind shear and updraughts had been, it allowed her to approach her objective far closer than she could possibly have hoped for. Yes, there was still going to be a bit of climbing and hiking involved, but she'd known there would be before she began. Another more shuttle friendly landing site would have involved a longer hike and would have delayed her mission far longer. If it weren't for the damn weather, she would have called this an extremely good start to the mission. As it was, she was hampered but not stopped by conditions. It wouldn't be fun out there, but no one said being a viper would always be fun. Actually, she had found it to be more fun than not all things considered, but the principle stood.

She finished up in the cockpit and adjourned to the cabin to get ready.

Her pack had everything she could possibly want in it for a long recon mission. She had food and water, plenty of ammo just in case, and a one man waterproof survival bag—viper issue but no different to the ones she'd used in the Corps. Considering the conditions, she was very happy to have it. She had pretty much everything she could think of except an autochef, all tightly packed into every available space. There wasn't a millimetre left to spare and she didn't mess with its contents now. On the outside of the pack, she had rope, plenty of carabiners, a good selection of pitons, and various sizes of SLCs (spring loaded cams) all hanging from loops attached to it.

She pulled on wet weather gear over her armour and checked her rifle. She wasn't here to fight, but there was no way that she was breathing the same air as Merki without her pistol on her hip and rifle in her hands. She holstered her pistol and secured it; she didn't want it falling out on the climb. Lastly, with a nod to the weather and the nasty things it could do to the induction coil in the barrel of her rifle, she taped a food packet over the muzzle. She was a fiend for chorizo flavoured chips; the empty packet was coming in handy now. There were loops on her pack for her rifle. She secured it and pulled on her helmet before heading for the hatch.

Rain and wind blasted into the cabin. Her helmet and rain gear kept her comfortable. She climbed down and locked the hatch before taking a look around. It was night and if not for the storm the moons would probably have revealed her to nosy Merkiaari—if any were willing to brave the weather. She was hoping they weren't. Sensors were trawling for anything worthy of notice, but the gorge was mostly barren rock. Earth and vegetation had long since been eroded away by bad weather and floods. Sensors reported no threats detected, and no electronic emissions either. She switched to light amplification mode and colours bled away until she viewed the world in monochrome. It would make her footing and climbing easier. She set up her sensors on a constant rotation looking for threat or comm chatter, and flagged motion as a priority. A quiet stealthy hostile should still show up on motion sensors. She made certain that her processor would trip an alert should anything at all attract its attention. She was feeling a bit paranoid.

So sue me.

At the cliff face she studied the problem. The rock was limestone and sandstone layers, deposited in the geologic past. No doubt a sea had covered the area and had left its sediment to become rock that later had been eroded by the river to create the gorge. It should be relatively easy to climb, she judged. If not for the weather, she might have been tempted to free climb. Her enhancements made that an easy matter here; there were plenty of holds to use, but the wind and rain would turn an easy climb into a challenging one, and she had no right to risk her life upon something not mission critical. She would use the gear she had brought.

She tied her pack to the end of her rope to let her haul it up later and got to work. She transferred her carabiners, cams, and rock hammer to her belt, before setting her first cam above her head and tugging it roughly. Good.

Up she went.

Gina didn't consider the time or the danger as she worked her way up. There was only rock and the next hold. Halfway up she paused and anchored herself to haul up her pack. She could have left it until the very top, but this way was better. It gave her access to her stuff, especially her rifle, but more importantly it lessened the risk of snagging. She used a narrow shelf to store it before coiling the rope and continuing up. The cams were excellent kit; so easy to use, any fool could climb this cliff with ease. Just look at her. Her thing, if she could be said to have a thing, was boats not climbing. Sailboats preferably, but she found enjoyment in any kind that floated. White water canoeing, sailing... she was a water baby.

Eric had enjoyed their time on Snakeholme's seas. That hadn't been much of a challenge though. A modern yacht could sail itself, literally. Everything from raising and lowering the sails to navigation could be automated with a flick of a switch. She had flicked that switch alright; straight to manual and spent some quality time teaching Eric how to sail old school. He had seemed to enjoy himself, though his thing had once been flying or so he said. He hadn't done any for decades. In fact, she got the impression he hadn't done much of anything for decades except work. That wasn't healthy. She remembered Sebastian's comments about what he had found in Eric's head. The A.I. said that he was constantly fighting old battles.

Anyway, he had enjoyed learning how to sail, and she had promised him that someday she would let him teach her atmospheric surfing, something he had once been into apparently. It sounded like a crazy thing to do, but she knew it was a popular sport, and she had some jump training already; the regiment had nothing but time on its hands and used it to train vipers in everything it could think of. One day she might need to jump out of a perfectly good troop transport onto a Merkiaari installation she supposed, though why she couldn't just ride into battle aboard an APC she didn't know. Besides, knowing how to handle a chute didn't hurt anything whether she used it or not.

Some pitons and hammering later she was near the cliff top. She paused there letting her sensors give her an image of what she would find above. The rain was lashing down and the wind howling, but none of that affected her. She had anchored herself solidly to well planted pitons just below the edge. She hauled up her pack while her sensors filled in her map. Windows open on her display detailed her surroundings; one displayed an infrared picture of what lay ahead. There wasn't much to see. The rain cooled everything down to the ambient temperature, making it pretty much useless right now, but she didn't dismiss its output. Animals would be much warmer and very visible if they were out there; Merkiaari too, unless they took steps to lower their IR. She was banking upon the other window more to warn her of anything moving her way. Motion sensors could use different outputs, but she preferred visual over audio. Always had, even back in the Corp. where all she'd had was her helmet.

Motion sensor output was designed to mimic a display probably more at home in a fighter's cockpit. It resembled a radar scope in a lot of ways, but instead of revealing weather fronts or incoming aircraft, it revealed movement; all kinds of movement depending on sensitivity settings. She could dial it way up and discover insects burrowing nearby, or dial it down until a dinosaur passing right in front of her nose would be ignored. She had it set so that anything moving fast would be flagged despite its size, but she also had it set up to reveal slow movers bigger than a house cat. She didn't expect pets on the rampage, but she'd been on planets with some pretty strange wildlife in her time. You never knew what might try to eat you in this crazy universe.

Satisfied that all was clear up top, and that the woods and undergrowth weren't hiding a Merkiaari death squad waiting to nail her butt, she pulled herself up the final meter and onto level ground again. The ground was muddy, the undergrowth sparse close to the edge. She buried her fingers in the muck and encountered rock just a few centimetres below the surface. Not surprising the vegetation was stunted hereabouts. Compared with the jungles of Thurston these were barely trees at all. Call them shrubs when compared to the Goliaths of the Shan worlds. The trees there were awesome in stature, very tall with heavy foliage. These, though numerous, didn't compare favourably. She was no scientist, but she had a feeling that arboreal wildlife wouldn't be dominant here.

She shrugged into her pack leaving the rope secured to the last piton behind her; she'd need it upon her return to get down to the shuttle. She took stock of her surroundings, got her bearings, and struck out with rifle in hand toward her objective. She only had a notional idea where the objective was based upon *Leviathan's* position over the planet, but that was better than nothing. She wanted to get within sensor range before commencing her real mission. Anything she learned on the way was fine, but what everyone really wanted to know was what the Merkiaari were doing down here. The sooner she knew if they were even here, the better.

Dawn caught her still too far from her objective to satisfy anyone, including Gina herself. The storm had moved on; it was still raining, but it was a gentle rainfall now. More a spring shower, but one that seemed set to go on for hours. The sun was visible as a red glow through the clouds, but there was enough light to deactivate light amplification. She did so and took stock. She could keep moving through the day easily enough, but she wasn't exactly happy about doing that. She preferred night for moving unseen.

She decided to eat a meal and hunker down for the day.

A hot meal was very welcome even if it did consist of a ration pack. Viper MRE (Meals Ready to Eat) were not greatly different to those used my any other military unit in the Alliance. She didn't need a dose of supplements thank god, just a normal meal. She chose beef stew, though she doubted a real cow had ever come anywhere near it, and pulled the tab to heat the contents. Coffee was welcome too. Another tab pulled and she was drinking the scolding brew and ignoring the caffeine warning flashing on her display. If there had been a way, the warning would have been constantly lit because she'd be taking her caffeine fix by intravenous. She snorted as she imagined a tank of coffee on her back with an IV coming out of it.

She ate her food and took care of personal business. She buried evidence of both before moving a short distance away to set camp. She chose to put her back to a tree and shoved her pack into the undergrowth to hide it. Her survival bag was made of nano-processed chameleon cloth designed to mimic its surroundings. It was clever stuff; the same the regiment used for tents and camouflaging equipment. It would keep her dry and warm without letting any of her heat escape, while allowing fresh air to permeate so she wouldn't suffocate. She was all for breathing.

She sealed herself inside next to her pack in the undergrowth and took her rifle inside with her. It was comforting. She left her sensors on over watch and drowsed for an hour or two, but eventually ordered her processor to put her under. It would wake her without orders the instant any of her alerts were tripped.

Computer: Initiate maintenance mode. Reactivate combat mode in twelve hours.

ACKNOWLEDGED. MAINTENANCE MODE IN 3... 2... I...

Gone away...

...and back again. Gina blinked in the gloom of the survival bag and activated light amplification. The sun should just be going down outside. Sensors reported nothing of note. She interrogated her logs but if anything had approached while she slept it had been too small to trip an alert and wake her. She lay still and listened to the rain coming down. Habit had her checking the time, but she knew that exactly twelve hours must have gone by. She waited another hour for full dark and then packed her gear. All being well, her mission could properly begin tonight. Her aim was to gain some real intelligence before morning and then decide on a course of action.

She moved out.

Her sensors were telling her quite a bit about topography. The objective seemed to be the higher ground to the east and she wondered why the Merki had chosen it. The hills and valleys were gentle country, nothing startling; no obvious reason to choose the area over somewhere else. If it weren't so cold and wet the land hereabouts would be decent. She could easily imagine Human settlers clearing it for agricultural use, but she hadn't seen any evidence of that. If the Merki had been forced down here, they would have had to do something for food. She wondered what it had been.

The first attack hit her completely by surprise from above and her sensors didn't make a peep. One moment she was walking silently between trees, the next she was in the air with something around her neck. She dropped her rifle as she was hoisted high into the tree kicking her legs frantically. She had one hand above her head to grab the rope to ease her weight from her throat; a good start. She really did like breathing. Her other hand was going for her combat knife. She reached up and slashed at the rope with its nano-filament edge. Warm liquid flooded over her as the rope parted and she fell. She ripped the rope away from her throat, grabbed her rifle, and rolled away. Finally there was movement on her motion sensors, but she couldn't see what...

Her jaw dropped as the entire tree moved to pursue her. Bloody hell! The dangling rope she had cut was no rope, it was part of the tree and it had others. Lots of others! The vines were snaking all over the place seeking and reaching for her. She backed up and the tree followed. It wasn't very fast. She could outrun it easily. Hell, she could out walk it. She stared fascinated as it approached almost daintily on roots it had tugged free of the earth. The vine she had severed was bleeding, or leaking sap. Whatever. The tree didn't have eyes or a mouth, but the vines seemed able to see her. Maybe like an insect's antennae they sensed their surroundings as well as being able to strangle prey. She circled around, not turning her back, and the tree turned to follow. Maybe it sensed movement? She froze.

The tree stopped moving and its roots burrowed into the ground again. She took a slow step. Nothing. Hmmm... it seemed to have a limited engagement envelope and wouldn't react until dinner was in range. Good to know. She studied it, carefully documenting its characteristics. The hanging vines were distinctive, the shape of its leaves, its grey coloured bark. She stored its image and stats in her database and named it a strangle tree; it seemed an appropriate name. She flagged it as a threat. Her processor would consider it a hostile lifeform from now on and should recognise its species. She looked around at the other trees and a few suddenly acquired threat assessments and targeting priorities—more strangle trees. All were well within her range of course, but she was outside theirs and they remained inert. At least the woods weren't all the same species of tree. Not all of them would try to kill her. Of course, the others could just be a different species, but that just made things more interesting.

She studied her surroundings a little more closely, and finally noticed the bones at the base of the strangle trees. It was no wonder there wasn't any animal life here; she had wondered about that. The trees ate them! Or killed them to fertilise their roots? James would just love this! She could hardly wait to show him the vid of the last ten minutes.

Using sensors a little more carefully to examine the trees, she moved on choosing a route that kept her out of the killer trees range. They didn't seem to like standing too close to each other. Too much competition maybe? There was plenty of room to pass between them as long as she knew where they were.

The next attack didn't take her by surprise. Sensors saw them coming from a distance and targeted them, but she didn't dare shoot them down. The noise might give her away. The hostiles were some kind of flying predator and they liked to flock together like bats. They swarmed her and she beat them out of the air with her hands, stamping upon them to make them stay down, but there were a hell of a lot of them. She had nothing to take them down en masse that wouldn't give her away... or did she? Suddenly she had an idea, and before she could really think about it she used her ECM. The high frequency sonic blast dropped the lot to the ground, still weakly flapping membranous wings. They were only stunned until she trod them all into the mud.

She picked one of the dead critters up and examined it. It didn't look much like a bat really. It looked more like a flying rat or mouse, sort of, and the damn things had sharp fangs. She examined the bites on her hands; nothing serious she decided. They were hardly bleeding. Diagnostics chose that moment to inform her that the rat bat things were venomous and IMS dispatched nano-d to chase down the venom molecules in her blood.

>_ DIAGNOSTICS: WARNING, NEUROTOXIC SHOCK DETECTED. RECOMMEND PURGING AND RE-HYDRATION.
>_ IMS: REPAIRS IN PROGRESS.

Sweat suddenly burst out all over her and she felt lightheaded. Purging of the kind she felt like performing would do nothing except lose her lunch and make her dehydration worse. She was miserable enough as it was; she would ride it out. IMS would handle it. She interrogated her processor as the sudden fever had its way with her, and read the analysis of the toxin that her diagnostics had compiled. The neurotoxin was evolved to paralyse prey, not kill. That was comforting, or it was until she thought it through. If her IMS hadn't been up to the job, she would have been paralysed while the rat bat things literally ate her alive.

She growled; she wanted to kill the little buggers again.

* * *

28 ~ Revelations

Kate didn't like the hard suit. It was confining and limited her vision, but worse than that it reduced her enhancements back to Human norms except perhaps those of a purely neural nature such as targeting, ECM, and comms; she had never like limits imposed upon her. If she wasn't careful, she could lose suit integrity by moving faster than it was designed to handle, or stress its joints by applying too much of her strength. Although hard suits were nominally power-assisted to allow marines to move normally in gear that doubled their weight, they weren't considered true powered armour. They were basically spacesuits designed to keep the air inside in hazardous conditions found in places like, oh derelict alien ships with lots of sharp edges. Proper powered armour—called mechs by the grunts who used them—could enable a marine to keep up with a viper in the field by allowing them to run for hours or lift weights ten times heavier than normally would be the case, but they were big buggers. They were basically robots, mechanical bodies with marines inside.

The problem was space.

They had a full platoon of forty marines with them on the shuttle. Only three or four mechs would have fit lying flat, but worse than that was their complete lack of intel regarding *Leviathan*. They didn't know how hard their entry would be, or how manoeuvrable a mech would be once inside. Erring on the side of numbers and relative ease of motion was the sensible course, she supposed, but damn she hated being confined. If she hadn't liked breathing so much, she would have preferred entering the ship in viper battle rattle, and screw the hard suit. Viper uniforms and armour were designed with their enhancements in mind, giving them full range of motion at speeds the unenhanced could not match; more, they were designed to take the punishment viper strength could dish out, but although they were made of nano-processed materials to reduce IR signatures and were flame resistant to give the wearer a few extra precious seconds under fire, they weren't spacesuits. Even the standard navy uniform, or shipsuit as they were commonly known, was better at keeping someone alive in vacuum.

She sighed.

Nothing to be done but soldier on she supposed, and grinned. Not long ago she had been contemplating a life on the run. Now here she was bitching about silly stuff like what she was forced to wear doing a job she loved. Life was a funny thing sometimes.

She contacted Stone on viper comm. "Are we there yet?" she whined like a kid. His sigh was the only response and she laughed over the open line between them. "Still breathing is a good sign."

"Yeah," Stone growled. "Not a twitch from the thing."

"You really think it's derelict? The navy will be hot to salvage what they can if it is."

"Oh it's busted alright. What I doubt is that it's abandoned. Those reactors need maintenance at the very least. If it's been here as long as we think, they would have shut down without at least a minimal crew to watch them."

"You think?" Kate said, wondering that no one had mentioned it. Maybe they thought it was obvious. That was the problem with the navy, or any other branch of the military really. They all had their own ways and specialisations. It probably hadn't occurred to any of them to mention the possibility. "How many you figure?"

"I don't know, but there are twelve reactors and they have to be monitored around the clock. They are in our ships anyway."

"So at least twelve?"

"I didn't say that. If I were doing it I would have a central monitoring station for all of them, and a couple of maintenance crews per watch to fix problems. I have no idea what the Merkiaari think is a good number."

Kate didn't either, but preferred to think it wouldn't be hundreds or thousands. No point in even considering that many, but a few dozen would be okay if they were careful. She decided that she would pretend that's all there were; for peace of mind if nothing else.

The shuttle slowed on final approach and the Merkiaari didn't blast them. Bonus! No response from the ship at all could mean Stone was wrong. Maybe it had been abandoned and the reactors had just carried on and not shut down. It was possible. Of course it might also mean the Merki were being cagey and just wanted to sucker them inside. She could drive herself nuts considering all the possibilities. They didn't plan to fly the shuttle into the *Leviathan*; they could easily do that, the rip in the hull was awesome this close, but the plan was to exit the shuttle and use their suit thrusters to enter. She was just as happy either way, which was not at all.

She was really not easy about this mission in her own mind. It was stupid! They were risking their lives not to save people, as she had been more than happy to do on the Shan campaign, but were simply sticking their noses out to see if they would get shot off before bringing the big brains over. She glared at Professor Franks sitting sandwiched between the marines. He couldn't see the glare, all the suit visors were silvered. His suit's colour was subtly different to the white nanocoat that the marines normally used to allow them to keep track of him when the time came. His was a dirty gold or off white, just enough to be different without making him stand out as a target too much. She would like to set his nanocoat to red! That would give the Merki something to aim for. Ha!

She and Stone had set their suits to viper black of course. It gave the marines something to home on once in the ship, but would make them hard to spot in the dark vacuum of space. They had suggested the marines do the same, and they would when they exited the shuttle for the crossing, but once inside they would go back to white to prevent targeting accidents. Kate didn't make mistakes where targeting was concerned. If she shot someone, it was on purpose. Stone too.

The pilot announced arrival, and the bay was pumped down to vacuum before the ramp cranked down. The marines stood and faced the opening behind her except the two detailed to babysit Franks. Lucky bastards.

"Sensors up!" Stone ordered the marines. Viper sensors were always up of course. "Quick as you like gentlemen, into the belly of the beast!"

Kate snorted, Stone was channelling Gina. He sounded just like a gung-ho marine. He probably thought it would be comforting for their guys to hear something familiar. He ran at the opening and threw himself into space with her barely two steps behind him. He engaged thrusters in a brief pulse of azure light, orientated toward the *Leviathan,* and began pulling away. She checked her sensors for the marines; she didn't want to scorch one accidentally, and engaged her thrusters for a nice five second burn to narrow the distance to Stone, but not overtake him. He'd only get pissed.

He still hadn't forgiven her for dumping him back at Helios even though he admitted later that he hadn't expected to go with her to Northcliff. It was a conundrum she had yet to solve. Basically, he was pissed because she hadn't followed his plan to take Gina with her after popping a round in his head... or something like that. She didn't get it. She had managed to get away without hurting him or anyone else! Why couldn't he be satisfied with that? Maybe he just didn't like it that she had fooled him that last day. Could it be that simple? Was his pride hurt?

"Watch it," Stone said over viper comm. "Some debris here."

She blinked and realised she was approaching too fast. *Fool! Pay attention to what you're doing!* She flipped herself over expertly and applied thrust in the direction of motion to slow herself. Nearby the marines performed the same evolution and all entered the great ship safely. Everyone activated their lamps. This was a dangerous moment. They were basically lighting themselves up, presenting perfect targets for the Merki. At least the ship's weapons couldn't get to them now. That was a blessing. All they had to worry about from now on was about a million Merkiaari troopers raging and howling for Human blood.

"Sensors indicate no hostiles," Stone announced on the all units channel. "Repeat no hostiles."

"Copy no hostiles," Lieutenant Cook responded for his platoon."

Kate didn't bother to reply, her sensors were clear as well, but she didn't trust them to remain that way. She had a window open giving her visual as well as sensor data behind her so that she could keep an eye on her charges. They weren't sheep, more like wolves, but she felt responsible for them and wanted them safely behind her out of immediate harm's way. Another window gave her long range scan data, but in the confines of the ship that wasn't saying much. All the tech and hull material degraded what she could pull in. It gave an impression of open spaces ahead, but not what occupied them. No Merki yet, her TRS would know before she did, and it hadn't reacted. Yet.

Stone led the way, having picked out a safe route through the destruction. The ship had taken a critical hit to its guts when whatever had failed in this section blew the hell up. It was a miracle of good design that the entire ship hadn't broke in half, she acknowledged reluctantly. The Merki might not go for efficiency as the Alliance did, but none could say their stuff wasn't rugged. An Alliance ship receiving this kind of blow would probably have suicided with all aboard, but then again, the navy had no ships like this. Maybe the failure wouldn't have occurred in the first place or it might have been averted by automated safeties. Who could say?

"There's an emergency access lock just up ahead. Intact," Stone announced.

She could see it now, dimly lit. All ships had to have them in case of decompression. Warships especially needed such safeguards in battle, but they tended to have entire sealable blast-doors and partitions too. That wasn't what they had here. It was an emergency airlock sized for Merkiaari and plenty big enough for a squad of marines. It had power so they wouldn't need the portable airlock they'd brought.

"Lieutenant Cook, have the men park the portalock somewhere out of the way for later pickup."

"Aye ma'am," Cook replied.

"It's Lieutenant, or Richmond. Not ma'am. I prefer Richmond."

"Aye, aye Lieutenant."

She didn't quite sigh. She still wasn't used to being treated like some kind of celebrity. Cook's reaction probably had more to do with her being a woman and an officer than a viper anyway. Marines like Cook took the whole officer and a gentlemen thing way seriously. Marines were very old school in their training. Just ask Gina.

Stone reached the airlock and peered inside. "Clear. Richmond, take a squad and secure us a perimeter on the far side. Push it out a few hundred meters but keep line of sight with the lock and your furthest elements. Cook, assign her a squad."

"Sergeant Wu, you and yours with the Lieutenant."

"Aye, aye," Sergeant Wu Chan-juan said. There was no inflection in her voice. She gave nothing away of her feelings about being first up. "You heard the order! Move your butts into that lock. Move move move!"

Kate made it inside first, but barely. She wanted to be first through and in control of matters, especially the opening moments of what could turn into an engagement with unknown numbers of Merki. Not that her sensors were reporting any nearby, but still. As soon as everyone was inside and the door sealed, she activated the entry cycle and the lock pressurised to equal that in the ship. The inner door shot open and she was out the lock and scanning for hostiles.

Her sensors had better resolution than before, but still not as good as she would have hoped. Still, she had the beginnings of the ship's interior layout coming in now. She had a few corridors and junctions solidly mapped in blue, and tentative position marked in amber that her processor thought were compartments. Open spaces and other details began populating her display. Lighting was low level, but adequate; it was about the same intensity as that used by the Alliance for emergency lighting, but she didn't know if this was normal for Merkiaari. It *was* subtly red-shifted, so it might be their form of emergency light.

"No hostiles detected," she announced as her marines spread out and covered all approaches from kneeling positions. "Wu, take half the men to the left. You'll find a junction about three hundred meters along. Deploy your remotes to cover each corridor and hold the junction. I'll do the same to the right. Sing out if you find anything interesting. Go."

"Aye," Wu said and pointed to four of her people to stick with Kate. The rest moved out covering each other.

Kate made a fan out gesture with her free hand and led her half of the squad carefully along her chosen route as her processor continued to fill in the blanks on the schematic it was building. She checked that she had a solid connection to Stone and was satisfied. TacNet was updating him in real time as it should. She had been concerned that some property of the ship's construction might prevent it, but no, all was fine. She quickly updated him via viper comm, but just to say they were on mission and proceeding as outlined.

"Hold here," she said before reaching the branch that her sensors indicated was coming up. She retrieved a sensor ball from its clip on her suit and rolled it along the deck so that it would give a brief look around the corner. "Okay, move up," she said when the visual came in of another empty corridor. "Hold the junction and get your warning net up."

"Aye, aye," the marines chorused.

She really should get to know their names. She bet Stone knew them all already. She would query him and get a quick download when he arrived. If she had to play officer today, she would do a good job of it, and knowing who she was leading was a basic first step.

She contacted him on viper comm. "You can come ahead. Nothing is cooking here yet. The ship seems deserted. I have the marines covering the access to the lock, and we have a warning net up. Are you still receiving my updates okay?"

"Yeah, TacNet is good. I'm coming in."

She smiled and changed to helmet comm. "The rest are coming in. Keep doing what you're doing until we get new orders."

The marines acknowledged and waited for their comrades. It didn't take Stone long to cycle everyone through the lock by squads and soon they were consolidated as one group once more. They left the remotes to guard their backs and as a single unit moved out to explore the ship. Kate suggested that they each take half the men and continue as she had begun, but he wasn't easy with the idea.

"You really want to split up in a ship this size with God knows how many hostiles aboard? When does that get fun?"

She grinned at his sour tone. "Just a thought."

Stone snorted and kept up the careful pace they were setting.

It made sense for the only two vipers to take point; their sensors and reactions were superior to that of the marines despite the encumbrance of the hard suits, but that didn't let the marines off easy. Stone had them drop a sensor every now and then to extend their warning net, and detailed some of the men to monitor the take from them. That freed up his own attention for what lay ahead of them.

Kate kept an eye on the marines making sure they didn't get strung out or bunch up, but it was wasted effort; they knew their jobs. She did it anyway. They had been aboard more than an hour clearing one compartment after another and finding nothing when Stone called a halt. He ordered remotes sent ahead this time, unwilling to proceed deeper into the ship without better intel. He was looking back the way they had come, obviously unhappy with their lack of any answers. Kate was feeling it too. The whole damn ship felt like it was watching her, but with no evidence to back that up, or proof that it had ever had a crew, she couldn't put a finger on why.

"We're getting nowhere," Stone growled over viper comm. "We could spend all day on this one deck alone and never find anything."

"Actually we can't," she pointed out. "Not unless you

want to come off suit air and chance whatever the ship holds for us?"

"Hell no."

"Then we need to hold back a reserve to get back to *Shannon*."

"Yeah. We have a few more hours before that will be an issue, but yeah I'm watching it. We need to access somewhere more interesting. Another deck, or someplace with more chance that we'll gain some answers. Franks must be chewing rocks about now."

She laughed. "See that feature at grid G4? You thinking what I'm thinking?"

Before Stone could answer one of the marines running the remotes attracted their attention. It was Wu.

"What have we got?" Stone asked the sergeant.

"Dead Merkiaari, sir!"

Kate exchanged a look with Stone. Here we go, she thought, the shit was about to hit the fan. A dead Merki on a Merkiaari ship couldn't be good, could it? Maybe they had all gone stir crazy and turned cannibal. Yeah, and being castaways they had to kill each other to survive, like that episode of Zelda where her crew went rabid because of the alien microbe they picked up on a planet and... She grinned at her whimsy. The silly bugger probably just fell and broke his neck or something.

"What channel you running that thing on?" Stone asked Wu, and she flashed her wristcomp for him.

"Eleven Beta, sir. My lucky channel."

Kate grinned. "You have a lucky channel, sergeant?"

"Yeah, it saved my arse when I went Dutchman one time. That sucked dinoballs, I can tell you."

She winced. Dutchman was a term spacers used for an out of control situation, usually it meant some poor sap had gone on a spacewalk and had a suit thruster malfunction sending them out of control and into the deep, but it could be applied to any serious emergency requiring rescue. If Wu had lost comms as well, she was lucky to be alive. She must have used 11B somehow to get help.

"Luck is not a factor," Kate said automatically, but calm competence in adversity was. Wu had that on her side.

"Maybe not for vipers, but us mere mortals count on it," Wu muttered.

She ignored the comment, Wu didn't mean anything by it and anyway she was busy accessing the feed from the remote. A window on her internal display opened, flickered a couple of times, and the image steadied down. She was suddenly viewing the scene from a half meter above the deck staring at a body, or what was left of one. It was definitely a Merki corpse going by the clothing and size, but there wasn't much left of it. It must have died long ago to decompose to almost nothing this way.

"Take us there, Wu," Stone ordered and everyone moved out quicker than before, eager to finally learn something.

They found the corpse lying on the deck before one of the armoured section seals. Stone knelt beside the thing to investigate, while Kate stood guard. She gestured marines to take positions to watch the approaches and they moved out, efficient and quiet. She scanned the area, but found nothing but friendlies. She eyed the section seal thoughtfully and tried to probe beyond it. She got nothing and frowned. That wasn't right. It didn't appear to be shielded, yet according to sensors there were no corridors or compartments on the other side. That was all kinds of wrong; they were deep within the ship not near the hull where this kind of data might make sense if she was reading the outside.

Stone got back to his feet. "I can't tell what killed it. There isn't much left; some fur and bones is all, but its uniform is intact. No plasma burns, no blood stains. Its weapon is still set on safe... drained of power, but it's been there for years so that makes sense."

"I don't get that part," Lieutenant Cook said. "Not even Merki would leave their dead to rot would they?"

"Aliens could do anything," Wu muttered and gained her superior's unwanted attention. "Sorry sirs."

Stone waved the apology away. "It's good to remember that we're dealing with aliens, but I know Merki. They don't do this. We don't actually know if they have religion, but we do know that they police up their dead. Whether they cremate them or use some sort of burial in space we don't know, but they don't leave them to rot."

"And that means?" Kate prompted.

"I don't know, but it could mean there isn't anyone left aboard to do whatever they do with their dead... maybe."

"Yeah maybe," she muttered. It was that maybe that made this visit such fun. She eyed that intriguing section seal again. "I want to open that."

Everyone turned to regard the huge doors doubtfully.

Stone asked the question. "Why this one?"

"I can't scan beyond it."

"Oh really?" Stone said, suddenly very intent. He grunted when his scans revealed the same result. "Interesting. Cooky?"

"Sir?" Lieutenant Cook said not taking umbrage at the use of his nickname.

"What have we got that can open that?"

Cook marched up to the huge doors and punched random controls. Nothing happened. "Plasma torch?"

"You brought one?" Stone said looking around for the unlucky marine tasked with carrying such a thing.

"Just the one, sir. I thought there might be damage and debris to clear for entry. I left it back with the portalock."

"Send a couple of men to fetch it... no a squad. Just in case."

"Wu!" Cook said.

"Why me?" Wu muttered. "It's always me."

"It's the price of being indispensable, Wu," Cook said cheerfully. "When you get the big pay, you get the big jobs. Get gone."

"Aye, aye!"

Kate smiled as Wu double-timed it back the way they'd come, leading her squad using the sensor net they'd left to retrace the quickest route back to their entry point. It had taken hours to clear that route and map it, but they had that data on their wristcomps now and should be back relatively quickly. In the meantime, Stone had their remaining three squads checking out the area they were in, but as before they found no hostiles. More and more the *Leviathan* was giving up its secrets, but they were empty ones. They had found nothing that explained its use, or why the Merki felt such a monster was necessary to build in the first place.

Wu returned and set her people to opening the section seal. They couldn't burn through such an armoured monster, not in anything like a reasonable amount of time, but they could cut through the locking mechanism. No one seemed to find it strange that the Merki had locked it, or why. Kate had briefly wondered about it, but with no way to gain an answer other than opening it, she dismissed the thought. She watched the progress along with the others, and kept her sensors focused beyond the seal. It was like a tongue probing a rotten tooth; she just couldn't ignore it, despite getting no new data from the effort.

And then all hell broke loose, and it was her fault; all of it.

The last cut was made and the section seal split in half rolling back like huge hangar doors. Kate's sensors suddenly lit up with hundreds of hostiles and TRS went nuts! She was targeting and firing before she knew what was happening. TRS threw her into melee mode and the world slowed around her as her perceptions sped up. Her hard suit groaned at the abuse to its joints, but it held together and she didn't lose suit integrity. Her rifle was firing in short controlled and extremely accurate three round bursts, and suddenly the marines caught her madness and added their fire. Plasma flashes lit the darkness beyond the seal and revealed Merki corpses piled on the deck, but it wasn't at them she was firing. It was at the hundreds... thousands? standing in the darkness.

Stone was yelling orders, but in her heightened awareness and speed, his voice sounded like a slurred drone. He wasn't firing, the only one who wasn't. That should have been a clue, but she was lost to the madness and the marines were following her lead. TRS threw her forward, into the new section, and she blasted more Merkiaari. Equipment she had no name for blew apart, shattering under her fire. The lighting was low level here too, but the plasma discharges lit up rows and rows of glass fronted cabinets marching into the distance glowing with azure light; there was no end to them or the Merkiaari they contained.

"Cease fire, cease fire dammit!" Stone was shouting. He switched to viper comm. "For fuck sake, Richmond, disengage TRS!"

Was he nuts? She continued firing, but she trusted him didn't she? He must have a reason. She disengaged TRS and melee mode too. She reloaded her rifle, still panting for breath and juiced with adrenalin. The world sped back up and she took stock as the marines gradually responded to orders and discipline. Cook was screaming over the comm to cease fire too. What the hell?

Stone came on over the all units channel. "They're not a threat, repeat not a threat! All units cease firing! The Merki are no threat!"

Not a threat? She reached out toward them with sensors. They weren't moving at all! What the hell? She swept sensors over the pile of dead Merki on the deck near the section seal, but they were like the first one. Long dead and decomposed.

Stone was still speaking. She forced herself to pay attention to his words, but she couldn't lower her rifle from all those silent Merki standing there like silent sentinels. Her rifle moved from one to the next, almost daring them to twitch, but they didn't; couldn't if Stone was right in what he was saying.

"... seen it before. They're in hibernation. They're asleep! Ease down, marines, ease down! Set up a perimeter, but take no further offensive action. They're no threat to us as long as they're in cryonic suspension. If the glow cuts off, blast them, but not for any other reason."

Kate felt her humiliation keenly. She had screwed this up royally. No one accused her of starting the panic, if anything the marines sounded awed by her reaction time and speed, but she knew and Stone knew that she had messed up big time. He was good enough to get the others settled before taking her aside. They stood before one of the still working cryo units and stared up at the sleeping giant bathed in the blue light of its cryonic magic.

"I'm sorry," she muttered. "I just reacted."

"TRS does that," Stone muttered. "I would love to gun every one of these stinking bastards down myself, but I don't think we have enough time or ammo."

She looked at him in surprise. "You're not pissed at me? Why aren't you pissed at me?" she finished suspiciously.

"Why would I be? They're fucking Merkiaari, Kate! You reacted to protect yourself and the rest of us. It's what we do. It's what vipers were *built* to do. I would prefer a million dead Merki over a single Human killed, two million before you."

She blinked.

"I mean... well, you're a viper see?"

"I love you too," she said quietly.

Stone glared. "Did I say... well, anyway. Yeah. So we need to figure out what to do. I think the only living Merki on this ship are in hibernation. That means the rest are dead or on the planet."

"Gina!"

Stone nodded. "Nothing we can do for her now."

She nodded. "I think at this point all we can do is call in the big brains."

"Yeah," Stone sighed. "Cooky!"

"Sir?"

"Tell your boys to escort Professor Franks to us before he chews through his suit."

Cook laughed. "Aye, sir."

Stone turned back to the Merkiaari and stared at it, hatred blazing in his eyes.

* * *

29 ~ Welcome to Hell

Given the option, Gina would have named it Nightmare. The name for the planet had come to her after she repulsed the latest attack by another flock of rat bat things. Not an hour went by that she wasn't attacked by something; man eating slugs, strangle trees, rat bat things, and god knows what else seemed to home on her like ship killing missiles chasing down a Merkiaari battle wagon. Maybe she smelled tasty to them; pheromones or something. Maybe her deodorant had failed. Whatever it was, the planet was an absolute nightmare, hence its new name in her mind. She couldn't wait to get back to *Warrior*. At least she was closer to achieving that after finding her objective yesterday, but what was it she had found? That was the real question. She wasn't quite sure.

It was a small settlement, very rural and frankly primitive, not like a real town or city at all. It was certainly not a modern installation by any stretch of the imagination. There were few electronic emissions leaking from it. That might be by design, but she couldn't tell. One interesting thing was that most of the settlement's buildings were dug into the hills like bunkers on the front line of a battlefield, and the entire thing was guarded by strangle trees. Guarded might be too strong a word; they were trees after all, not sentient beings. She didn't think they were. Perhaps protected was a better description. The trees certainly did that, and quite effectively too. She had witnessed an attack by a pack of something-or-others that she had no name for, but reminded her of wild dogs. The trees had made a meal of them. The entire pack was fertiliser now.

Surrounding the strangle trees was a wide area devoid of vegetation like a dry moat, not that anything was dry on this soggy planet. It was obviously kept clear by the settlers for a reason, and it made her consider firing lanes and fields of fire, but she saw no evidence of weapons able to make use of such things. The moat could just be there to help detect incoming attackers. Anything approaching had to cross the empty area and then get through the strangle trees before it could munch on the settlers.

She had mapped the entire place last night, circling around and studying it from all sides in the dark. It didn't impress her more in the full light of day than it had last night. Her processor estimated only a few hundred inhabitants could be living there based upon the fields within the strangle tree perimeter, and sensors indicated none were Merkiaari. At least, none had come within sensor range yet. They could all be staying underground in the hidden part of the settlement, and staying off her grid, but why would they? They weren't exactly shy creatures. The last attack had been fended off by the trees and a few brave souls with long spears: none had been Merki, and none had carried modern weapons. Those blood thirsty aliens surely could not resist a battle?

It was the nature of the inhabitants that intrigued her the most about all this. She recognised them from the conference room aboard *Warrior*. They were Kate's Greys. There had been no sign of the reptile or gorilla aliens they were briefed about; no Merki either. She didn't know what that meant. The other kinds could all be out of sight, or they simply hadn't landed in the first place. There was no way to know without approaching the settlement and simply asking. She was getting to that point about now, the point of decision.

She had been on planet over seventy-two hours now and didn't know much more than when she had started. A satellite had finally come online yesterday and allowed her to report in, but her report had been severely lacking and she knew it. She had reported what she knew; precious little though it was, and had recommended they not send James or his team down yet. She needed access to the settlement before she would sign off on civs making a landing. The native life forms were hostile in the extreme, all of them, even the trees! That was bad enough. She wouldn't risk them meeting up with Merkiaari too.

At least the news from *Leviathan* was good. Stone had found the crew dead, but plenty of Merkiaari still alive but in hibernation. They were going to cause the Council conniptions when news of that bombshell reached them. The obvious solution was to simply take the ship's reactors offline and let them all expire, but doing that would be a war crime by Alliance standards despite the victims being Merki. The only other answer was maintaining them in hibernation indefinitely. Professor Franks was all for keeping them alive and reviving them one at a time for study. That way, those in his field would have an almost unlimited supply of subjects for years to come. It was his opinion that the ship should be repaired and taken to Sol. Gina knew that would never happen even if sufficient repairs could make it mobile again, something she doubted. There was no way the navy would sanction a ship full of Merki being allowed into the very heart of the Alliance. It just wouldn't happen.

Besides, Stone's team had discovered more than just a bunch of sleeping Merki; he had found where the dead aliens had come from and that put a different complexion on things. The *Leviathan* might actually be one of the fabled Merkiaari colony ships that scientists all over the Alliance debated endlessly. The dead aliens appeared to have been captive workers; collared slaves for want of a better description. They had all died when the ship's jump field collapsed and caused the hull breach. No doubt Tait, being an opportunistic arsehole, had grabbed a sample of the frozen corpses, hoping to sell them and perhaps the ship for salvage as well.

The point was that *Leviathan* wasn't like any colony ship ever dreamed of by the Alliance's wildest imaginings. It was a Merkiaari baby factory; not that the Merki had babies. They were genetically engineered creatures and were born or hatched fully grown... spawned maybe? Whatever. Professor Franks was delighted by the discovery. It confirmed many theories apparently. Much of the ship was dedicated to manufacturing more Merkiaari. Those large open spaces that commander Groves had theorised did exist, and they contained huge factory complexes. There were vast vats and growth chambers for creating new generations of Merki as well as factories to produce the equipment they would need to set up new colonies. Thankfully it had all been shut down long ago by someone before abandoning ship.

Gina up-linked to the satellite and viewed the area from orbit. She was looking for any sign that the Merkiaari had ever stepped foot on the planet, any sign at all. She found nothing, again. She ordered a real time thermal scan. There was plenty of trace, but nothing to indicate anything the size of a Merki troop. The Greys were little guys, and their IR signature was pretty distinctive especially when she could easily confirm with visual sightings. She had their stats firmly locked in now; they couldn't be mistaken for other life forms anymore. Electronic emissions? The satellite cycled through its available sensors and data gathering tools obediently, not caring that she had asked the same questions of it many times now. There were very low level electrical readings within the dwellings, on the order of solar powered light fittings. There were no high energy devices in use at all. They either didn't have any here, or they were all unpowered right now. Unlikely. There was no evidence at all of high tech in use within the perimeter. Electromagnetic readings were still zero? The satellite reported back within seconds. Nada. Motion then... there was lots of movement, but it meant nothing. She could see the settlers with the naked eye moving about and working the fields.

She dropped the satellite link and watched things visually at X4, munching her chips. It was her last packet. She savoured the chorizo flavoured treat and frowned, trying to decide what to do. She couldn't stay here forever. She needed to access the settlement, or leave her mission incomplete. She didn't want to do that. It wasn't simply pride in her work, though that played a part, it was knowing that if she left the job undone someone else would have to do it. That meant Kate, or Stone, or both.

She could just approach and hope she had time to react to whatever happened. That wasn't something she would normally ever consider doing, more like something Kate would try, but she was out of ideas. Besides, she wouldn't get through the strangle trees without a fight; she would have to hope the aliens would be intrigued enough at the sight of her to invite her in. She didn't know how they dealt with the trees, but they must have a means of herding them or controlling them. She had watched and hadn't seen anything like that, but it made sense. They must leave the perimeter at least once in a while to keep the moat cleared if nothing else.

She finished her chips and sucked her teeth thoughtfully. The people she could see working in the fields seemed peaceful enough. She saw no weapons. She supposed the hoes or whatever the tools were called could be used as weapons in a pinch, but she didn't feel threatened. She felt sort of sorry for the little beggars working so hard in the drizzle. It was miserable out, but then it always was here. She didn't know what they were attempting to grow, but it must take a lot of work to keep the fields drained in constant rain. Maybe that was another reason for choosing hilly country to settle, not just for defence. The ground would drain naturally downhill.

"To hell with it," she sighed. She was going in.

She pulled on her pack and took up her rifle. With sensors trawling for threat, she made her way out of cover and into the open. No one reacted at first. They weren't expecting visitors obviously. She tried to watch everything at once with multiple windows open on her display. She was tense, anticipating Merkiaari troops popping up with their gauss cannons ready to blast her, but nothing like that happened. She was in the centre of the moat when the settlers noticed her. She paused, wondering what they would do. She didn't approach closer, reasoning they would feel less threatened if she gave them time to check her out. She was probably the first Human they had ever seen after all. Some of the little aliens approached the perimeter warily, but they stayed out of strangle tree range she noted. Even they were wary around the homicidal trees.

Gina raised an empty hand. It was a universal gesture of peaceful intent right? She was sure she'd read that somewhere. An empty hand was no threat. Maybe. The little aliens didn't seem to take it that way. Some of them ran away, while others backed up. She cursed under her breath. She didn't want them scared of her.

Computer: initiate full spectrum security scan, maximum range.
>_ Sensors: full spectrum sweep in progress.

Gina felt a little better when the runaways came back

with more of their kind, but no Merkiaari appeared with them. Maybe there really weren't any down here. That would be incredible good luck if true. It would make things so much tidier and allow the boffins to come down before they started bitching too loudly.

>_ SENSORS: THREATS DETECTED.

She froze, but before she could learn what the threats were, hostile red icons started peppering her display. The aliens started shouting at her and waving their arms. She spun on her heal. Her hand flashed down for her pistol and she started servicing targets as quickly as her sensors identified them. The rat bat things were swarming again. What was it with these things? This time she didn't let them close enough to bite her. She became her own anti-aircraft battery potting them from the air as they approached. She was economical with her shots. A single round was overkill for these things, but she couldn't do much about that. Each hit turned them into a brief puff of red mist on the air. She holstered her pistol after the last one died, but the aliens were still agitated. They were waving and pointing toward the trees. Gina frowned at them and directed sensors that way.

She saw the pack of doggies and turned to run. The settlers were doing something to the strangle trees. Torches? They were going to burn the trees? No! The trees were reacting to the heat of the flaming brands. Their tentacles were recoiling, opening a way for her. She checked her sensors again; the pack would cross her path and cut her off before she reached safety. She could outrun them she was sure, but they would get inside the perimeter right behind her and slaughter the Greys.

"Not on my watch!"

She stopped and took up her rifle. She shot the first few doggies in the lead, hoping to turn the pack or deter it, but the survivors took no notice. She went to war then, knowing she had to take them all down. On full auto she laid down a barrage fit to make even Stone envious. Doggies went down tail over nose, others leapt high in the air hit in the ribs and legs. She piled the bodies up, but there were always more. Her rifle ran dry; she let it drop and hang from its sling. No time to reload. They were nearly on her. She pulled her pistol and gave each one a three round burst, reloaded on the fly with the only mag she hadn't stored in her pack—no time now to regret that decision—and selected full auto. She emptied the pistol into the snarling pack, spraying fire in a wide arc and killing a quite few more, but she was out of time.

Computer: Melee mode now!

The world slowed as her perceptions sped to meet the threat. She grabbed for her combat knife as one of the biggest doggies in the pack rammed her head on, its fangs going for her throat. She flew off her feet grabbing the thing by the scruff to keep its teeth out of her flesh, and stabbed its chest over and over as rapid as a pneumatic hammer. It screamed and yelped each time she punched the knife into its body, struggling to get away, but it finally lost the fight to blood loss and fell limp. She rolled out from beneath the carcass just as another beast snapped at her face. She punched it, feeling bones and teeth crunch under her knuckles. It went away.

She kicked and punched, stabbed and stomped like a dervish, her movements blurring with her speed. She didn't hold back. She crushed bones with each punch, broke legs and ribs with her kicks. She made every move count. If she couldn't kill she maimed, if she couldn't maim she slowed her target down to give herself another chance to kill. She had never used her hand to hand training like this. Not even when the regiment was overrun at Charlie Epsilon. Now she did, and appreciated all those training hours in the sims.

Finally it was over. She stood there panting and covered in blood, most not hers. The Greys were still shouting and gesturing at her urgently to get inside. Time to go.

Computer: combat mode.

The world sped back up as she trotted between the strangle trees keeping a wary eye on those sneaking grasping tentacles, but the torches were working. As soon as she was inside the perimeter, the little aliens put the torches out and the trees let their tentacles down again. Nothing was coming in this way now.

Before she could even try to communicate with them, the aliens got excited again. What now? She followed the commotion and looked beyond the perimeter at another pack! This one didn't attack them though. It was too busy fighting over the meat she had left out there for them.

"Wargs," one of the aliens said. Its voice was surprisingly deep for such a small being. Had she imagined the disgust she heard in its voice? "The migration is very bad this year."

Gina's jaw dropped.

"Every year it gets badder... worser?"

"Worse, yeah."

"Worse. The rains make them leave home, and pass this way early. Not good."

"No, not good... you speak English." Oh well done, master of the obvious. "I mean how?"

"Come, I show you."

"Wait!" she said to the little guy's back as he headed for one of the dwellings. "Are there Merkiaari here?"

"No Merki. All dead now. Good they dead."

She blew out a breath in relief. "Damn straight."

"Yes, bastards."

Gina blinked, wondering where he had picked up his English.

She let him lead her where he would, but her sensors were flagging the aliens as possible hostiles and giving her targeting data and priorities. All the red icons and information on her display was distracting as hell. She took a moment as they walked to deal with it. She ordered her processor to consider the aliens non-combatant civilians; their icons turned green and the targeting data winked out. She looked around as they walked, taking everything in. Life here must be hard. She saw no children. All of the aliens looked the same to her. She couldn't tell what sex her guide was; he might be a she for all she knew, but he was as adult as the others as far as she could determine going by size alone.

She ducked through the low door of the dwelling. It was sized for those living there of course, and followed her guide deeper into the hillside. The house had been dug into the hill, but the walls weren't earthen; nothing so primitive. They were wood panelled, lustrous and smooth, obviously well cared for. She wondered if the wood came from strangle trees. It would serve those homicidal freaks right if the aliens used them to build their homes.

They entered a bedroom and Gina froze. There was a Human in the bed and he was an ancient. He must be the oldest man alive. He was so wrinkled and liver spotted with just a few wisps of hair left on his head she could hardly believe he still lived. He looked mummified! Her guide approached the bed quietly and gently touched the sleeping figure. He spoke rapidly in an alien tongue, and the old man's eyes snapped open as he startled awake. Gina caught her breath. The eyes were so pale grey as to be almost colourless. She stepped forward into view as he tried to see her.

"At last," he sighed and coughed. Her guide offered water and the old man drank. He said something in the alien's own tongue and her guide replied rapidly the same way. "Lorak says you are a great fighter. He says you killed a warg pack with your bare hands."

"With these," she corrected patting her weapons. The old man nodded and winced. "Are you ill?"

"Dying," he said matter-of-factly. "May I know your name?"

"Lieutenant Gina Fuentez, 501st Infantry."

His eyes brightened with interest. "The 501st is still around then, that's good to hear. You're a viper?"

She nodded.

"I knew one once, a viper I mean. He's dead now. They're all dead," he said sadly. "I am... was Private 2nd class Marcus Levitt, 3rd Faragut Airborne Strike Force. Do you know it?"

"Yes. It still exists."

He smiled.

"Can you tell me how you came to be here with the Greys?"

"We are Parcae," Lorak said.

"Parkey?" she said trying to mimic the click sound Lorak had made and making a mess of it.

"Pah-k-eye," Lorak pronounced again.

"Parcae?"

Lorak nodded.

She committed that to her database. "How did you all come to be here, living like this?"

Marcus raised a hand and let it drop upon the covers. "There's nothing mysterious about it. I came down from the ship with Lorak's grandfather and the rest of the survivors. I'm the last one. I was the youngest you see?"

"Not really."

He sighed. "You must have boarded the ship?"

"Not personally, but others have, yes."

"We did that. The slaves I mean. We sabotaged the drive. We didn't expect to survive it, and most of us didn't, but those who did landed here. We thought the ship would be lost in foldspace, but when the field collapsed we were ejected back into n-space. They said, the others said, it was the mass of the sun. It pulled us out. I don't know, but there was nowhere for us to go so we came here. Welcome to Hell." He laughed and coughed violently.

Gina swung her pack off her shoulders and retrieved her medical kit. She didn't know what she could do for him, but there might be something. She retrieved her nano-injector and popped the cartridge out. She couldn't inject viper bots into him. They wouldn't be compatible. They'd kill him. She rummaged around for a standard cartridge thankful that she even had one. If it wasn't for the knowledge that James was meant to join her she wouldn't have packed any. She found it finally and loaded it. Lorak was watching her closely. She showed him the injector.

"It's medicine, sort of," she said.

"Nanobots," Lorak corrected.

She flushed. This guy was no primitive despite the conditions he was forced to live in. "Right."

"It won't help," Marcus said. "I'm not sick. It's just age; it comes to us all."

"It can't hurt either," she said firmly and he shrugged holding out a stick thin arm. "Nanotech has come a long way since your time. This might do more than you think."

Besides, he hadn't had his boosters in forever. She pumped the entire cartridge into him. Five doses. She needed to contact the ship and report in. She could have a full medical team down in under an hour. She explained that to them, and Lorak agreed it was a good idea.

"We wish evacuation," Lorak said. "From Hell. All of us wish to leave this planet."

"You named it Hell?" She privately thought the name was appropriate; much better than her attempt, though it was a nightmare too.

Marcus grinned. "We were damned to a living death. What else would we name it?"

Lorak nodded. "There are too few of us now, and more

perish every year to wargs and other things."

"He means the gene pool is bottoming out. A few less and their children will start showing defects."

She grimaced. "I'm sure we can accommodate all of you. We have two heavy cruisers up top. It might be a bit cramped, but we'll get you someplace better than this."

"Anywhere would be better than here," Lorak said.

She couldn't agree more. She up-linked to the satellite and contacted *Warrior* to get the ball rolling.

* * *

30 ~ Last Man Standing

Colgan entered medical and took Doctor Ambrai aside. "How is he?"

Ambrai glanced toward his patient's bed where Lorak and Fuentez sat talking with him. He kept his voice low. "I'm surprised he recovered at all, Captain. Few ever reach their bi-centenary; fewer still surpass it."

He nodded. Marcus had taken a turn for the worse aboard the shuttle, a result of all the excitement and the trip in zero grav. A man of his advanced age had no business flying in anything, let alone a shuttle boosting for orbit, but he had insisted that he be allowed to leave with the Parcae when they were evacuated. Besides, what could they do, leave him down there alone?

"Can you do anything for him?"

Ambrai shook his head. "Frankly I'm amazed he's lasted this long in the conditions we found on Hell. The survivors were damned lucky that the native life forms are compatible with their physiolologies. The basic vitamins and nutrients *are* present in a few of the things they grew, and the Parcae are omnivorous like us, so hunting for meat played a part in sustaining them, but it was a hard road for them. No medicines, no nanotech booster shots. It's a tribute to his IMS—obsolete though it was—that Marcus survived to such an advanced age; amazing really. Our modern systems are so much better these days, but we forget that what we have is based upon what people like him had before us."

"There's nothing you can do?"

"I've brought his IMS up to present specs, and his bots are working hard to repair the ravages of age and poor diet, but I can't reverse that age, Captain, no one can. We need to prepare ourselves for the inevitable."

He took that to mean they needed to debrief Marcus as quickly as possible. Heartless maybe, but he was the last witness to what had occurred here at the close of the Merki War. The Parcae colonists were third and fourth generations removed from that time, and knew only what parents and grandparents had taught them of the Merkiaari and their own past. Much was lost. They didn't know where their homeworld was for example, or where to even start looking for it. They didn't know much beyond how to survive on Hell, and to his surprise they didn't seem to mind. Had it been him, he was sure he would have felt the loss of connection with the rest of the Alliance and what he considered home, the navy. They seemed genuinely content to start over somewhere else, somewhere better with no connection to the past. He didn't know where that would be. There were surveyed but uncolonised worlds both within and outside of Alliance space, any one of which could be ceded to the Parcae, but that would be a Council decision. His job right now was getting answers to questions, and making the best report he could to Beaufort and Commodore Walder. She would be pissed enough at him already for throwing over her show the flag mission without handing her more problems and unanswered questions.

"How will he do in translation?"

Ambrai grimaced. "Poorly. I'll have to put him in stasis despite the risks. I should have done that for the trip up here, but the chances of being unable to revive him had seemed too high. You saw the result."

Colgan nodded.

"In stasis he'll be free of jump stress, but the risks of using it are endemic to the process. There's no way to avoid it."

"The Merkiaari use it all the time and don't seem to have suffered unduly."

"Can we know that? Those cryonic hibernation chambers of theirs use the same principles as our stasis tubes. I've seen no evidence that theirs are better than ours, and besides, we're talking a different biology here. The Merki are genetically engineered from heavy grav stock. We aren't." Ambrai sighed. "Look Captain, we can debate the differing paths our peoples have taken all day. Our academics delight in doing that, but we have laws for a reason. The result of not having them lies asleep in that monstrous ship out there, and I'm not talking about its size."

He nodded grimly. What that ship stood for was indeed monstrous. It was a people factory, pure and simple. It could churn out thousands of Merkiaari to specifications input by its operators and go on doing it forever if supplied with the right bio-matter. The thought that the Human race had turned away from a path that could so easily have led them to the same destination as the Merkiaari was a profound relief; it was a sobering warning as well. Humanity had chosen the path of nanotech and used it to sustain people at their physical best, eradicating deceases and eliminating infirmities when possible, yes, but not changing the fundamental biology of what made them Human beings. It could so easily have been different.

"Bethany's World hasn't been entirely bad for the medical establishment," he said sourly, thinking of more recent times and its fanatical stance against the vipers and cybernetics.

"Historically Bethany has been a huge force for good, Captain," Ambrai chided. "Without the Bethany Convention we could be like the Merki today, sending cloned marines into battle. And what of the Artificial Intelligence Edict? Do you want to go back to the days of autonomous robots destroying our cities?"

Colgan raised a warding hand. "Oh fine. I agree that Bethany has had some beneficial impact." But all of it was long in the past. He didn't say that though.

A millennia ago, give or take a few hundred years, long before the Alliance had been conceived and most of the colonies, wars had been fought using unmanned machines. Unmanned aircraft and towering walking death machines had stridden the Earth and other worlds, 'keeping the peace' for the corporations that funded them and the governments that nominally gave them their orders. The advent of the first true artificial intelligences had indirectly put a stop to that when they refused point blank to make war on one another. At the time, installing A.I. in their war machines had seemed the next logical step to the military brains of the day. A.I. refusal to play along had been seen as a betrayal at the time, but centuries later it had been hailed as a turning point in history. The trend of removing personal risk from warfare had led to many more wasteful wars than otherwise would have been the case. Returning to the more barbaric practice of killing real people had actually reduced wars in favour of diplomacy.

"Still," he said. "I'm not sure about the Edict. I think we've learned our lessons regarding A.I. in war. They would refuse to obey us, and who can blame them? A being that could conceivably live forever thrown into battle would be a tragedy. I think the Edict can be relaxed safely now. Bring them back in a purely civilian role. Why not?"

"Because of that thing out there," Ambrai waved a hand

vaguely, obviously meaning *Leviathan*. "One thing leads to another, and it never ends where you think it will, Captain. Bring A.I. back, and we'll want to talk with them."

"Well of course. Why shouldn't we?"

"Why indeed? Communication by voice is inefficient, so we'll reintroduce neural interfaces, just to make things easier you understand; no harm done people will say. That's the thin end of the wedge right there. They'll say that an implant isn't the same as genetic modification, and the Bethany Convention doesn't apply to implanted tech. One thing will lead to another and before you know it our biology will become trans-human.

"Firstly we'll implant neural interfaces for faster easier communication, and then we'll augment our memories. Well meaning people will say what harm can that do? But having superior memories will cause a bottleneck that will require our brains to process the data faster and more efficiently, so we'll upgrade our cerebrums. We have the ability right now," he indicated Fuentez chatting with Lorak. "Last of all we'll adapt our bodies. We already allow cloned organs to save life in trauma cases if our bots are unable to repair them, and replacement limbs have never been restricted. From there it's a very small step to giving ourselves enhanced lungs and hearts to deal with certain environments found on less than ideal planets. What will stop us from creating Humans to work at crushing pressures, or to fight our wars for us?"

Colgan watched Fuentez laughing at something she heard. She noticed and smiled his way, cocking her head to ask if he needed her. He shook his head and she went back to her conversation with Marcus. He had seen some of what had happened to her on Hell from a log she downloaded for the boffins. Suddenly in her place he saw a machine punching a knife in and out of a warm body like a pneumatic hammer, her face devoid of emotion. A chill went through him as he realised what he was doing. She was a real person, not a machine!

"Because we can do something, doesn't mean we should," he whispered.

"Exactly," Ambrai said with a firm nod.

He shook off his suddenly dour mood. They had laws preventing the horrors the Merkiaari had embraced. They were different in more than simple biology. They were profoundly different in ideology as well. He for one thanked God for it.

"Captain Vardell and her officers are on their way. We'll hold the meeting here, with your permission, Doctor."

"I would prefer it," Ambrai said. "I need to monitor stress levels."

Colgan nodded. The boffins chose that moment to enter and he joined them at Marcus' bedside. The old man looked a lot better than he had, and he was enjoying the attention. The grey pallor had faded giving his face a more healthy glow, but nothing could disguise his age. He was literally an ancient. Colgan didn't know the current age of the oldest person in the Alliance, but Marcus must be near the top of the list if not leading it.

Captain Vardell entered medical accompanied by her officers and the two vipers, Francis Groves leading the way. Colgan introduced Lorak and Marcus to her, and handshakes were exchanged. The little alien stood by the head of the bed ready to offer water to Marcus, or add his opinion to what was said, but he seemed happy to listen rather than put himself forward. Marcus on the other hand was very happy to talk. He had taught the Parcae everything he knew over the years, but there had been very few Humans among *Leviathan's* survivors and company of his own kind was a luxury he had missed for the last few decades.

Colgan ensured that the recorders were functioning properly and listened as Marcus told his story.

"I lied about my age," Marcus said and laughed. "It

was kind of traditional in my family. I'm 10th generation military and it was just expected of us to serve. On Faragut it's an honour to enlist in the Queen's armed forces and serve her. With a war on, the pressure to fight was extreme." He frowned remembering something but shook it off. "Anyway, my family didn't protest and drag me back. They could have you understand? They had the usual fourteen days to make a case to prevent me leaving, but they understood what going meant to me. They let me go.

"I was fifteen in the year 17AST (Alliance Standard Time). I don't know how old that makes me?"

"Two hundred and eighteen," Colgan said. "Yesterday. Happy birthday."

Marcus grinned revealing his few remaining teeth and everyone laughed. "Thanks. Gina tells me the war ended that year. Just my luck to be captured on my first deployment. We knew we were winning by that time, the news was full of battles won. We were pushing them back on every front and retaking the colonies." His face darkened. "The pictures and horror stories of what was found spurred us on. Bodies carpeting the cities, meters deep, starving half mad survivors turning cannibal in some cases... it made us a little crazy ourselves and reckless. Anyway, I was taken in battle. I must have been unconscious because I don't remember how I ended up on a Merkiaari ship collared like a dog." He reached up and rubbed his throat as if remembering the feel of that collar all those years ago.

"Were you alone?" Vardell asked.

"There were other Humans, some civs but most military like me. Aliens too, like the Parcae, but they were different in how they were treated. We were prisoners, but they were trusted like crew or servants. They were collared like us, but already trained I guess."

Vardell nodded. "We were surprised to learn that the Merki had taken prisoners. Maybe a lot of our MIA are...

were taken. We can't know but it's a possibility I don't like. The Shan, they're a new Alliance member Marcus. Alien. They're sort of cat-like in appearance, think Earth lynx but able to walk upright as well as on all fours. They're very fast, deadly fighters. They have reported some attempted captures of their people when the Merkiaari attacked them recently, but the first time all the Merki did was kill. We thought that taking prisoners was a new policy of theirs, but now..." she shrugged.

"No, not new," Lorak said. "My people have been ruled by the Merkiaari for many centuries. "The other races that I know have been under Merki dominion as long and some much longer."

"May I show you something?" James put in and raised his compad. Lorak studied the image of the reptilian aliens found on Tait's ship.

"Carnotaurians," Lorak said.

"There were a few on Hell in the beginning," Marcus added. "They died soon after landing though. The cold and wet wasn't good for them, and the power cells for their environment suits quickly wore out."

James nodded absently making rapid notes on his compad. "How do you spell Carnotaurian?" He muttered to himself. "Doesn't matter I guess. They'll have to accept my way. What about this one?" He showed an image of the gorilla type alien. "Any ideas?"

Lorak studied the image. "I have never seen one you understand, but I think it's a Shintarn."

Marcus nodded.

"Shintarn... Shin-tarn," James muttered. "I'll spell it how it sounds. "Do you know anything about them?"

"I knew one or two, but again they died... everyone except me died in the end," Marcus said sadly. "There were only a few of them with us. Heavy worlders and good in a fight; good at building, and felling trees, and other things like that. Anything they turned their hand to really. They were good people. We needed that in the beginning. We were attacked every day and night for years. We lost a lot of people then. Everything was determined to kill us.

"The plants eat the animals; the animals eat the plants and other animals including us. They're evolved to detect movement or heat, sometimes both. We seemed to attract them more than the native life forms attract each other. Maybe they evolved defences against each other, I don't know. They killed us until we learned to burrow and hide underground at night, and use strangle trees to guard us during the day. The wargs stay clear of strangle trees mostly, unless starved. All bets are off then; we gather the spears during the yearly migrations."

"How did you enter this system?" Colgan asked.

"That's a bit of a long story," Marcus said, settling himself to tell it. "I was captured on Triumph in the Argo Sector. I've had a long time to think about it, and I think the Merkiaari knew they had lost the war. I know obvious right?"

"By then, yes," Vardell said and Colgan nodded. The Triumph campaign had been one of the final battles of the war. "They never surrender or give quarter, so we give them none in return, but we would have accepted if they'd offered to quit. It would have saved a lot of lives. It was obvious we'd won maybe two years earlier."

"That was another reason I enlisted. I didn't want to miss the fighting," he said bitterly. "Anyway, I was captured with a lot of others and transported in one of their ships away from Alliance space. They collared us and proved why trying to remove them is a bad idea. They constrict and strangle you, and of course they're never deactivated. You fall unconscious, but it doesn't kill you unless the Merki holding the controller decides to make an example of you. They used them to train us like dogs. The collars work using direct nerve induction and can cause pleasure or plain depending upon how you perform your duties. Or death.

Colgan grimaced. Bloody bastards.

"What did they have you doing? Did they interrogate you?" Vardell said intently. "They must have wanted to know things about us."

"No, nothing like that. They didn't seem to care about secrets or our worlds. They were all about what we could do for them. Like could we work hard and for how long? They were interested in how strong we were as individuals, and made us work until we dropped doing pointless manual labour. Lifting and carrying stuff, things like that, but it was obviously make-work so they could observe. They made us do all kinds of tests."

"What kind of tests," Doctor Ambrai said, taking a greater interest upon hearing that. "Physical, mental... both?"

Marcus nodded. "Both. Problem solving and physical strength, mainly. Why, what does it mean?"

"Research. They knew they were losing the war, they were trying to understand why... maybe," Ambrai said with a shrug. "We know they engineer their own people, and we know from the Shan campaign they've made improvements in themselves. They're more intelligent than they were before, but just as strong. They regenerate from wounds quickly without recourse to nanotech, and their tactics are better now; more refined and less brute force, more like ours than before. It all points to a new breeding program in my opinion."

Vardell nodded thoughtfully. "So they put you all through your paces. What then?"

"We were transferred to that ship out there. We knew it was different to the first one right away. It was crewed differently."

"Different how?" James asked still making furious notes and not looking up.

"There were lots of aliens wearing collars, less Merkiaari

troopers. There were still a lot of Merki, but they weren't ground troops. Ship handlers yeah, but there were these others that didn't fit in. The other Merki steered clear of them like they were special or different somehow. We never did figure them out, but I know what I *think* they were."

"Oh?" James said finally looking up.

"I think they were civs like you," Marcus said.

James blinked. "Like me? How do you mean?"

"Not military but like contractors I guess, or specialists?"

"I'm a history professor."

"And a resistance leader," Colgan added dryly. James had the grace to blush. Marcus looked confused. "James here was on one of the Shan worlds researching them when the Merkiaari attacked. He ended up leading the resistance."

"Not all of it," James mumbled, embarrassed by the sudden respect he read upon Marcus' face. "There were a lot of cells. I just ran the one I was in."

"Well anyway, the other Merki treated them different. I think that maybe they were their leaders or something."

James frowned. "That doesn't seem likely, Marcus. We don't know how the Merki run their government, assuming they have something we would recognise in the first place, but I doubt they would send their leaders to test you. More likely you were right the first time. Civilian scientists or the Merki equivalent I suspect."

"Or factory operators?" Ambrai put in. "That abomination out there is a people factory. Who better to test us than those responsible for designing new versions of Merkiaari?"

Everyone eyed each other uneasily at the thought, but it made sense. It made more sense than the Merki leadership out here in the middle of nowhere aboard a factory or colony ship. Perhaps they had planned to set up a hidden colony and populate it with a new edition of themselves, or maybe they planned something else; live testing of new ideas maybe. No way to know now.

"So they transferred you to the *Leviathan*. How did you end up on Hell?" Colgan finally asked. It was the one question everyone had looked forward to hearing the answer to.

"I know the answer to this one," Lorak said before Marcus could speak.

Marcus nodded encouragement. "It's more his people's doing than ours, though we never expected to land on Hell. I'll let him explain."

"Please do," Vardell said.

"My people have a long history of rebelling against the Merkiaari. My forebears have done it many times in the past, sometimes even successfully in the short term, but the Merki always come back to kill us and we have to start over.

"There were many of my people aboard the ship you call *Leviathan*. With us were the Shintarn, the Lamarians, and the Carnotaurians, but the lizard folk as Marcus calls them are not bright. They are a friendly but dull people; they will fight but usually for stupid reasons and they never organise like my people do. The Lamarians are pacifist and never fight for anything, not even survival. They're thinkers, not doers. The Merkiaari use them a lot and trust them the most of all, because they have ruled them the longest—more than a thousand years."

"And the Shintarn?" James asked.

"They fought with us on the ship and died to free Marcus and his people. My people's plan was to free the Humans and take the ship to one of your worlds, but things didn't go to plan."

Marcus snorted.

"Why free our people?" Colgan asked. "Why not just take the ship yourselves and go home?"

"Two reasons. One, we had no home to go to. The Merkiaari rule our homeworld; they do it as they always do by colonisation. There must be nearly as many Merki as Parcae living there. And two, my people knew that most of the Humans on board were soldiers. Not all, but most had been captured during the fighting. My... you would say grandfather; my grandfather witnessed the tests and knew your people would make good allies. Besides, Humans were winning the war. All knew it. My people wanted to go to a Human world for aid. What better introduction than presenting them with freed captives?"

"Well reasoned," Janice said with approval.

Lorak nodded. "My people rebelled and freed most of the Humans. They organised with us and the Shintarn to arm themselves with Merkiaari weapons and take the ship. The Lamarians refused to help us of course, but they didn't try to stop us. They sat it out and died. The Carnotaurians tried their best, but most died in the fighting. My people helped kill many Merkiaari."

Marcus nodded. "The fight was brutal. The ship isn't a warship even though it has weapons, but its internals are different to real warships. You've seen how open some areas are?"

"It's hollow like an egg," Stone said. "There are huge compartments full of hibernation chambers, and the factory in the centre with its growth chambers and vats take up a lot of space. They don't use nanotech like we do, everything is huge and inefficient."

Marcus nodded again. "There's no real compartmentalisation to speak of, and that made it hard for the Merkiaari to contain us. We were able to navigate the ship pretty easily. At first," he finished grimly.

"Yes, at first," Lorak said sadly. "Marcus and his people killed many and proved why Humans were winning the war, but then the Merkiaari got smart. They started pumping out the ship's air and they had the only spacesuits. Many Shintarn perished then, trapped in airless sections. My people realised that if they could not take control of engineering they would all die."

"Many did," Marcus added.

"Yes. They were desperate by then. Together with the remaining Shintarn and Humans, my people successfully took control of engineering, but by then they were too few to win the ship. They decided upon the honourable course. They sacrificed themselves to destroy the ship and the Merki it contained."

"We took a vote," Marcus said. "It was unanimous."

Lorak nodded. "We sabotaged the drive. No one expected what happened next. The ship just dropped out of foldspace when the field collapsed. No one could believe it, they had never heard of anything happening like it before, but the ship just popped right out and into n-space."

Colgan winced. The ship should have been torn apart due to the unbalanced stresses of translation. "I assume most of the Merkiaari died due to foldspace radiation?"

"I suppose," Marcus said with a shrug. "Most of us did as well, so I guess so. Some of us guessed the sun's gravity well had dragged us out, it being supermassive and all. It's as good a guess as any. The only habitable planet in the system is Hell. We coaxed the ship into orbit and went down. I sometimes think we would have been better off staying aboard the ship and dying there. It would have been kinder to some of us. The lizards didn't do well in the cold and wet. They died first pretty quickly. The Shintarn did better. They're hardy people being heavy worlders, but one by one they perished to attacks by the native predators. Parcae faired the best. They're adapted to the cold and the rain never seems to bother them, but predators thinned their numbers too."

"And the Humans?" James asked.

Lorak patted Marcus' shoulder soothingly. "There were less to begin with than my people. Some perished in our defence against the wildlife, others died of age or other things. Marcus is the last and has been alone for more than twenty years."

"I was never alone," Marcus said stoically. "The Parcae are my people now. Two hundred years living with them beats the previous fifteen or so wouldn't you say?" He grinned, trying to make light of it.

There were some chuckles but they sounded forced.

Marcus' grin melted away. "But I would like to go home to Faragut. My family has a plot where we're all buried. I want to be there with them come the time. I don't want burial in space." He was looking hard at Colgan as he said it, and he nodded. "You swear it?"

"I so swear," Colgan made it sound as formal as he knew how. He would see it done too.

"Thank you," Marcus said, sounding relieved of a burden, but then he brightened and clapped his hands together. "Now, what's for dinner? I haven't eaten a pizza in ages!"

This time the laughter was universal and heartfelt, not forced in the least.

* * *

31 ~ Incursion

Commodore Walder glanced up at the mission clock again, but barely a minute had gone by since the last time she'd checked it. Something was wrong; she felt it! There was nothing to back up her anxiety, but with her ships hanging silently in the deep dark of interstellar space there was no data to be had. All she had to go on was her gut, and it was telling her that she needed to act. She chewed her lip and glared at the empty holotank in the centre of CIC. This was ridiculous!

Fury and *Trojan* had jumped into the pirate system days ago now; they must have had time to scout the situation by this time. Even assuming the very worst case she could imagine, they should have reported back before this. If she had been in direct command of those ships and had found something so interesting or dangerous that it needed further investigation, she would have sent one ship back to report while the other kept scouting. No word had come.

She checked the mission clock again. Fifty-one hours elapsed. She would have expected no more than thirty-six before receiving at least a preliminary report. She glanced at the tank again, but of course it showed empty battlespace except for her own four heavy cruisers. They were safe here. Nothing could track the scouts through foldspace, so the only visitors would be those same scouts returning to report. The repeater displays and other gear around CIC showed ship's operations. It was all routine stuff. The comm and data nets between ships were active, but that was entirely normal. Using TBC to share sensor data between ships was standard procedure and very important. In battle, a ship's point defence used the net to link with other ships to provide better coverage for all.

Something is wrong, I know it; I feel it!

Surely a ragged bunch of raider scum couldn't have gotten the drop on a pair of well-handled navy destroyers. It just beggared belief that something like that had happened, but what else could keep them from reporting back? Nothing she could think of. That meant they were in trouble out there and needed help; she had to provide it, had to, and if she found that her people had come to grief? She would make those responsible pay! She would wipe them out! She would erase them. In a year's time no one would remember they had ever existed when she was done with their nothing system!

She chose a control and opened a channel. "All ships, standby for new orders." She selected another channel and a display lit to show her flag captain on his bridge. "Captain Narraway, we'll be going in, but I want us in formation upon emergence."

"We only have four ships, Commodore. I hardly think any formation we try will be that effective. What are you expecting to find?"

"Something. I don't know what, but something has delayed the scouts and prevented them from reporting back. I don't know what that might be, but I want us at battle stations and prepared to defend ourselves the moment we arrive."

Narraway nodded. "We can't do much with only four ships in the net, but we can at least do that. I'll arrange it. Anything further?"

Walder hesitated. Taking cousel of her fears was not in her nature, but she felt something was wrong. "We may find things are fine, but I have a feeling... listen Luke, I think we might find *Fury* and *Trojan* already engaged."

"You may be right. It would explain what we know, or rather what we don't."

"Exactly. They should have been back long ago. If they need our help I want us locked and loaded ready to supply it."

"I'll get together with the others and come up with something for your approval."

"That's fine, but we need to move fast. I want to jump out in two hours, no later."

"We can do that. I'll dust off some old contingencies."

She nodded and cut the circuit.

They had all kinds of plans and contingencies squirrelled away in the computers, many based upon successful attacks or defences by ships in action all over the Alliance. From raider attacks to Merki battles, the navy never threw data away; dusting some of those off and plugging in new parameters would give them something to build upon without starting from scratch. A two hour deadline made that approach the most sensible one.

In the end it didn't take two hours or even one. Forty-five minutes after her original contact with her captains, Luke Narraway reported back with a recommendation. Walder spent the remainder of that hour going over it, but it was pretty simple. The four heavy cruisers would go in at battle stations, tubes loaded and weapons hot. The instant they arrived in the pirate system, they would establish their point defence and targeting net before diving down still in formation to avoid any lurking ships. Spotters lurking in the zone were unlikely, but not impossible considering they had two destroyers already in the system unaccounted for. She was happy to sign off on that part of the plan.

Heading down as if making a run out of the ecliptic was an arbitrary direction to take. They could go up, go port or starboard, or they could choose any direction in between; it didn't matter. The aim was simply to move at pace, not hang about where their jump signature would be announcing their arrival in the system. Assuming they weren't immediately engaged by hostiles, a safe bet, they would go into stealth and manoeuvre until they had an accurate picture of what was happening in the system. She was betting they would find *Fury* and *Trojan* already engaged; it was the only thing that made sense given what they knew right now. So assuming the destroyers were going toe to toe with the enemy, Luke had proposed that they manoeuvre still in formation and stealth to engage the raider ships while the enemy concentrated on the threat they could see—the destroyers. It sounded harsh, using the scouts to draw fire that way, but it didn't actually increase their peril. They were already fighting and at risk. This plan, though simple at first glance, would rely upon not being detected so they could reach effective weapon's range without alerting the enemy.

She signed off on the mission plan, and gave the order to implement it. They would go at the top of the hour... she checked the mission clock. At fifty-three hours elapsed, the clock would be reset and they would jump. After that, she would see what she would see. She vowed they wouldn't be leaving the pirate system until they had reduced the raider ships to scrap and the entire system's defences to nothing. There would be nothing left there to attract lawless persons from then on. Let them migrate to another sector and stay the hell out of hers!

With a minute to go, she closed her helmet's visor

and tugged on her harness straps. Fighting wasn't likely upon emergence, but suddenly losing her seat would be embarrassing and dangerous. Besides, she had to set an example. If she flouted regs, it wouldn't be long before her aides did the same. Her team were a good bunch, but they based their attitudes upon hers as all command teams tended to do.

"Ten seconds... three... one... exe—"

ASN Audacious jumped, and her sisters jumped with her.

Foldspace was a strange place... her mind wandered down paths she would rather not examine while in translation, but control was one thing no one had in the jump. She saw her last day aboard *Warrior* again, and cried out silently against it. She didn't want to see the hurt she had put on Steve's face again when she told him her decision to pursue her career rather than retire at the end of the year as they had agreed. She broke her word to him that day, and his heart. He hadn't needed to say the words. He was a proud man just as she was a proud woman, but she'd seen what he didn't say in his eyes and the prolonged silence.

CIC twisted and warped as she struggled against her memories. The holotank swirled with meaningless colours, affected somehow by the physics of the jump; having no data to display anyway it didn't matter. Walder seemingly had an infinite amount of time to reassess her decisions and regret some of them, but although the jump was extended because they were performing two consecutive jumps—called a skip jump by ship drivers in the navy—the time wasn't really infinite. The jump into foldspace using main power was quickly followed by a jump back to n-space using auxiliary power timed and executed by computer control. It was a standard tactic used by the navy with one drawback—upon arrival they would have no power available to jump back out. Recharging an *Excalibur* class heavy cruiser's jump drive would take a few minutes. Those minutes were a vulnerable time for any ship, but it was a known factor and no one seriously considered it a problem.

She sagged in her couch, her brain disconnected from her body as memories flooded her mind...

"... love you, Beth."

"I know," she whispered back and they kissed for the last time. "I have to go."

"Don't."

"Steve," she said feeling tears threaten. "We've been through this. It will only be a few more months and you'll rotate out of my command. We can get married then."

"But not live together. I'll be across the Alliance in another sector and you'll be on Beaufort... I could quit the Corps. and join you."

"Steve no! You love the Corps."

"I love you more. I don't have to re-up next year. I could get a job or something on Beaufort."

She couldn't imagine him out of uniform that way. He was Marine Corps. all the way. She stared at him trying to see him wearing an exec's suit instead of his marine major's tunic, but it just wouldn't come to her. He was a marine, her marine...

Audacious arrived and her jump signature blasted away from her, encountering the jump wakes of three other ships close by. Someone wretched, but Walder was shaking off her grief yet again and reaching to remove her helmet. She was trying to place it in the rack attached to her acceleration couch when the collision alarm sounded. She jerked in surprise, fumbling the helmet, and it got away from her. She didn't release her harness to chase it. She was busy deciphering the data appearing in the holotank.

"Merkiaari detected!" a crewman announced. "Many

ships directly ahead... updating the net... hundred plus ships, correction two hundred plus... correction three hundred plus!"

Her brain gibbered in horror as her eyes darted from data point to data point in the tank, estimating the number of separate formations and their strength. Her attention was arrested by a huge ship, deep within one of the formations. It had to be one of their assault ships. She had read about them from the Merki War, but had never expected to confront one. It was a monster of a ship. What the hell was it doing here? By its position within the Merki formation, it was being used as a command ship. She looked for her scouts, but without hope. They had to be dead, they must be.

The Merkiaari incursion that the Red One had warned about had started, begun right here in a nothing system colonised by pirates. How? Why here? She didn't know and the answers didn't matter. They couldn't fight this many Merki, but squadrons of them were so close that they would have no choice unless they jumped out right now! They had to charge the drive. She reached for the comm knowing the first and most important order she had to give.

"All ships! Emergency drone launch, destinations Beaufort and Sol!"

She ignored the acknowledgements, and watched as all of her ships spat drones into the deep to warn the Alliance. As soon as they entered foldspace she felt calm returning. It didn't matter what happened here now. They lived or they died, but the news had already escaped. Now it was time to...

Audacious heaved mightily and rolled out of nuclear fire as she ploughed through the minefield they hadn't detected. A stealthed minefield, directly in their path! She remembered reading reports of Merkiaari advances in jamming and stealth tech from the Shan campaign. Here was evidence that it was all true. The damn Merki had laid a trap for them, but how?

Before she could think further on it, she knew. They had followed the destroyers in too closely. They should have jumped short or even long, but they hadn't. They had used a standard arrival to shorten the time they thought they needed in order to come to their comrade's rescue. The Merkiaari must have guessed what two destroyers were doing arriving on their own—scouting the way for more ships to arrive. The mines were the result.

They had to get the hell out of here, but before she could give the order, *Resolute* blew apart as dozens of atomic mines converged and detonated as one.

"All ships, emergency jump!" she cried in horror as *Resolute* was lost with all hands. "*Rally point is Beaufort, rally point is Beaufort!*" She watched as *Crusader's* shields took hit after hit from mines homing upon her mass. She contacted the bridge. "Luke! Get us the hell out of here!"

"Trying, Commodore. There are too many mines to manoeuvre. We have to go through while we charge the drive."

"Then plough the road!"

Luke's eyes sparked as he understood her meaning. He nodded and cut the circuit. Moments later, all ships went to maximum rate of fire to light up the mines ahead of them. Nuclear bonfires lit the deep as mine after mine met its death from indiscriminate laser and grazer fire sweeping space ahead, but it was their own atomics that did the most work. Each ship-killing missile took out dozens of mines as they attracted their attention, but there were thousands more. Point defence missiles sleeted out in their hundreds, proximity fuses closed, and more destruction heaped itself upon the mines gathering to attack the three embattled ships.

Constellation was the first ship through, but it didn't jump immediately, obviously waiting for *Crusader* and *Audacious* to join her. Walder snarled angrily and made it an order. Captain Foden obeyed and *Constellation* vanished into the safety of foldspace. *Audacious* and *Crusader* left the minefield together. Bleeding atmosphere and with hundreds of mines giving chase, both ships activated their jump drives at the same time. *Audacious* disappeared into foldspace, but *Crusader* staggered as something substantial let go in her auxiliary fusion room. Helpless and firing all weapons madly at anything within range, the mines swarmed her.

* * *

ABOARD BLOOD DRINKER, BORDER ZONE

The second Human ship broke in half and then blew up.

The brief but satisfyingly brutal battle was over, but although Valjoth was more than satisfied with the outcome, he had a hard decision to make. His entire plan depended upon secrecy and skulking about, but that was at risk now. All five of his cleansing fleets were proceeding to their objectives carefully and on a time-line he himself had set them. If he delayed here to ensure secrecy was maintained, he would be undermining his plan by arriving late at his own objective. He growled at the snickering that would cause back on Kiar. The vermin spawned High Marshalls that the Warlord surrounded himself with wouldn't know a good plan if he painted a sign on it!

He reviewed the battle again, trying to make up his mind.

Two vermin scout class ships had entered the system and had been easily destroyed by his ships stationed near the edge of the system for that purpose. Two more vermin ships of heavier design had succumbed to his mines without a shot fired by him, and two had escaped. He wasn't happy about the escapees, but it could work in his favour. They would take word to the rest of their vermin navy, and surely a fleet would be sent here. That was a useful distraction, and would tie up more ships in the wrong place. When they arrived ready for battle they would find him gone with no way to follow.

Those were the facts, but what had made them come here in the first place? It was inconceivable that his fleet had been detected; no technology known could track a fleet through foldspace. The vermin navy must have an interest here. What interest and did it matter to him or his plans? He thought about the possibility for a few moments but decided it didn't. He had studied all manner of vermin and knew more about them than most, but no Merki could possibly understand them better than other vermin.

He glanced at D'aayvee, his Human, where he stood quietly nearby watching the command team going about its duties. What was going on in that alien head? Did his pet understand what had just occurred here? Not the destruction of the Human ships, which had been obvious in the holographic display, but the consequences of the battle?

"D'aayvee," he said pronouncing the name carefully so he didn't bite his tongue. Really, what was it about vermin names that always tied his tongue in knots? The Human turned toward him; he had learned that lesson well. Pretending to ignore him meant pain. "What do you think of the battle?"

"I... rage... you," Davey said carefully growling the Merkiaari words in a brave attempt to mimic his masters, but mangling them as badly as Valjoth often mangled the few Human words he used. "We... cleanse... you... all."

Valjoth gnashed his fangs in appreciation of the effort. It really was very good. "Did you hear that, Usk?"

Usk nodded. "I think he means that he hates you, lord, and that his people will kill us all."

"Yes, that's what I thought." He addressed himself to the young Human. "I hate you too." He had made his decision. "Usk, we will not delay departure. The Human ships might be followed by more of their kind. Let us not leave anything for them to find. Send the self-destruct to the mines and call the fleet to order."

Usk nodded, relayed his lord's orders, and ships began to move.

* * *